The Acolyte's Passion

The Knight and the Acolyte Book 1

The Acolyte's Passion

The Knight and the Acolyte Book 1

(A Fantasy Erotic Novel)

by

Reed James

Naughty Ladies Publications

Cover art: Consuelo Parra

Model: Lisajen- stock

Cover Layout: Oliviabydesign

Naughty Ladies Publications

www.NaughtyLadiesPublications.com

ISBN-13: 978-1981162727

Table of Contents

Prologue: The Oracle's Words

King Edward IV – Shesax, the Kingdom of Secare

The scented, anointing oils still glistened on my forehead, drying slowly as I stared up at the winding stairs climbing the Lone Mountain. Behind me, the city's bells rang in celebration of my coronation. It was tragic that my father had died young, but it meant my reign would be spectacular.

I was twenty-five, in the prime of life. I had forty or more years as King of Secare ahead of me.

Visions of glory and greatness danced through my mind as I took the first step up the Maiden's Stairs. They were carved out of the dark stone of the Lone Mountain, set with statues of frolicking maidens every tenth step, their small breasts and nubile bodies perfectly captured in pure marble.

I stared up at the stairs, excitement trembling in my chest. My reign now truly began.

Shesax, the capital of my great Kingdom, was built on the eastern slope of the Lone Mountain, sprawling out from the upthrust of stone rising out of the surrounding farmlands. Every king of Secare since my great ancestor General Sekar carved our great kingdom out of the corpse of the High King's failed empire, had climbed these stairs. Once on their coronation, and then every five years thence to seek the Sekar Oracle's advice.

My family had long credited the Oracle's prophecies and advice for keeping our Kingdom strong.

The other nations that rose out of the High King's empire had suffered turmoil and civil wars. The High Kingdom of Hamilten had fractured into dozens of petty Kingdoms and Princedoms. Many had fallen, been conquered, splintered into lesser nations, or fallen to lesser men, like the mages who ruled Thosi.

But Secare remained strong.

The spring sun warmed my rich, red cape trimmed in ermine, and my velvet doublet and hose seemed to trap the heat. It was the height of fashion, right down to the codpiece that demonstrated my virility. But it was damned hot. The golden crown weighed on my forehead. It was heavier than it looked, made of gold and amethyst.

Halfway up, I paused to admire my city laid out before me. It wasn't to take a rest and had nothing to do with catching my breath.

My city looked grand. The palace was a breathtaking construction of blue-swirled marble and the great Chapterhouse of the Knights Deute stood resolute before my palace. The city spread out for miles, a thriving metropolis. The land fell away into haze. I could just make out the green blur that must be Blath Forest. The view from the heights was spectacular.

Rested, I turned and continued my climb.

My legs were sore when I reached the mouth of the Oracle's cave. I trembled as the heady perfume wafted out of the cave's opening. I strode into the incense and entered the cave, my body shaking with excitement.

Maidens moved inside, young and budding, just past the cusp of womanhood, dressed in sheer robes as they attended their mistress – the Oracle.

I trembled in the presence of a demigoddess. She was the daughter of the wise God Cnawen and the Goddess of Art, Rithi.

"Welcome, King," the Maiden of the Voice smiled as she strode forward. She was nubile, her breasts small cones, her blue robes revealing her small, hard nipples and the tight lips of her shaved pussy. She spoke for the Oracle.

The Oracle herself was a stunning creature, dressed in a wispy robe of lilac that contrasted with her burning hair. Her eyes were a green deeper than any human's, shining like emeralds, and her skin was as white as alabaster instead of the light-beige of a Secaran. She was almost pure white. Her face was beautiful and alien, wholly inhuman in the most subtle ways: the shapes of her eyebrows, the curves of her cheeks.

She whispered in a musical language.

"My Mistress is ready to gaze into the future," the Maiden of the Voice purred.

I nodded. "By ancient treaties, I, King Edward the fourth of my name, have come to have my future uttered so I may rule my kingdom with wisdom."

The Maiden of the Oils stepped forward. She was the tallest of the three young maids that served the Oracle. All were eighteen, chosen from among the most beautiful maids of the city to serve for a year caring for the Oracle. She wore a red robe so thin I could see every line of her lovely beauty.

Her smile was sultry as she untied the golden tassels of my ermine cape. She carefully folded my robes and set them in a wicker basket. My cock throbbed as the Maiden of the Tongue– wearing green robes that showed off a pair of small, ripe breasts– added more incense to the smoking braziers.

Purple haze filled the cave.

The Maiden of the Oils disrobed me, her hands rubbing across my muscular chest as the Maiden of the Tongue did the same to her Mistress. My cock ached as I watched the young maiden's tongue roam the Oracle's body, bathing her. The Oracle moaned as her maiden's tongue swirled about her nipples before the maiden moved down the Oracle's body.

"She is preparing the Oracle for your cock," purred the Maiden of the Voice who watched with rosy cheeks.

11

The Maiden of the Oils finished undressing me and then undressed herself. She was lovely and flawless, her pussy shaved and just the hint of her labia peaked out of her tight slit. My cock thrust hard before me as she lifted a clay jug and poured scented oils across her nubile body.

She glistened as she approached and pressed against me. I groaned as her arms wrapped around my neck, her lips gluing to mine. Her body undulated, rubbing the oils into my muscular chest and stomach.

I moaned into her kiss, my hard cock throbbing against her stomach. I held her, my hands sliding down to grip her firm ass. I caressed the swell of her boyish hips, and she was lovely and slim in my arms. She moaned into my lips as I pulled her against my cock.

"Remember, King, she must remain a maiden," purred the Voice. "Your cock will find all the satisfaction in my Mistress."

The Oracle let out a purring moan.

I broke the kiss with the Maiden of the Oils. The nubile girl worked about my body, rubbing her hard nipples and hot pussy against my side and back as she continued anointing me. My eyes were locked on the sight of the Oracle, who appeared no more than eighteen despite being an immortal being, writhing upon the tongue of her maiden.

The Maiden of the Tongue had her mouth buried in the Oracle's pussy. Her enthusiastic licks echoed through the cave. The Maiden of the Voice began singing a wordless melody that brimmed with lust. The Oracle writhed to the music, adding her own passion to the song.

The Oracle's beauty was flawless. Her breasts small and ripe, perky with youth and bouncing as she undulated. Her nipples were mauve and hard. Her fiery curls fell around her breasts, swaying and briefly hiding her delights.

I licked my lips at the breathtaking sight.

The Oracle's hand seized her maiden's short, black hair, pulling the girl's mouth tight against her pussy. Her hips undulated faster and the Voice's song grew louder and more urgent, the beat increasing, building to a crescendo.

My cock ached. I burned to know the Oracle's flesh. I didn't care about the prophecy. I have had scores of lovers, but none, not even my beautiful wife, had ever inflamed me like the Oracle. She was divine. Otherworldly. Ethereal.

My head swam with the incense.

The song grew louder. The Oracle's emerald eyes fluttered as she threw back her head. Her maiden's hands gripped the Oracle's ass, holding on tight as she feasted. She seemed to devour her Mistress, her pink tongue sliding through perfect lips.

Energy rippled through the pink haze when the Oracle came. Awe overcame me. The Oracle cried out in an ancient tongue. The power rippled through me. Her body heaved one last time and then her eyes opened and stared at me.

I shuddered at the alien presence dwelling in those green eyes. She was so ancient I felt like an ant before a man. She had watched the eons pass in the way I might watch the hours. She strolled to me, her hips rolling.

"It is time, Your Majesty," the Maiden of the Voice purred.

The Maiden of the Oils pulled me down onto a bower of silken pillows, my cock thrusting hard before me. She grasped my dick, stroking it as she pressed her nubile body against my left side. The Maiden of the Voice slipped out of her blue robes and pressed against my right, her lips nuzzling at my ear.

The Oracle straddled me. A line of fiery pubic hair ran to the tight slit of her glistening pussy. Her emerald eyes burned with lust as she lowered herself. The Maiden of the Oils held my cock erect, aiming it perfectly so her mistress sank down on my cock.

"Yes!" I groaned as the Oracle's divine pussy engulfed my cock. She was so tight, like a virgin, and her pussy rippled as she settled upon me. A low moan escaped her lips.

"You have a nice cock, King," the Voice moaned. "She approves."

I grinned as the Oracle rose, her hips undulating and swirling about the tip. The pleasure was intense, shooting to my balls. She

13

slid back down then worked her hips slowly back up my shaft. She knew how to tease and please, her pussy gripping me.

The final maiden pressed her body against the Oracle's back, her tongue nuzzling at the Oracle's neck. Her arms wrapped around the Oracle's body and cupped her ripe breasts. The Oracle moaned in delight, her hips undulating faster.

"She is eager for your cum," moaned the Voice, her hot pussy rubbing on my side. "She burns to witness your future. There is such power in cum. Give it to Her."

"Yes!" I groaned.

"Give it to Her!" moaned the other two maidens.

The Oracle purred in delight, her green eyes fluttering as her hips undulated faster. Her ripe breasts jiggled in the grip of her maiden's delicate fingers. Her alabaster skin seemed to shimmer in the pink haze.

My hands gripped her thighs, her muscles rippling as she rode me. My cock throbbed as pussy engulfed it– Slata's heavenly realm manifested. My hands squeezed her thighs as the pleasure built within me. I stroked my hands up to her stomach, my palms sliding across her silky skin.

"Yes, She loves it! She loves your cock, King. Give Her your cum!" The Voice's dulcet moanings were honeyed with excitement. Her hot pussy rubbed harder on my side. "Mmm, yes. Your cock fills Her up. The pleasure ripples through Her. Cum in Her."

"Please, cum in Her!" the Maiden of the Oils gasped, her hot cunt pressing hard into my side.

"Fill Her up with your cum!" the Maiden of the Tongue moaned as she nuzzled the Oracle's neck.

The Oracle gasped in her foreign tongue. She leaned over me, slamming down upon me. She rubbed her hard clit into my pubic bone. My balls tensed. Pleasure radiated out of me from the tip of my cock. I couldn't last any longer.

"Slata's cunt, yes!" I groaned as my orgasm built. "Work that pussy, Oracle. I'm gonna cum so hard."

"Yes!" moaned the Voice. She shuddered against me. "Yes, yes,

yes." Hot juices warmed my thigh as the nubile maiden came.

My cock boiled. My cum erupted.

The Oracle slammed down upon me. Her pussy rippled about my cock, drinking in my cum. Her skin glowed and her hair seemed to become fire. Emerald light shone from her eyes and mouth as she screamed her pleasure.

And then the Oracle spoke in her ancient music and the Voice translated:

"You shall die, Mighty King, upon the Hero's Blade
The High King's Empire shall rise once more
The Hero of the Lilies departs on perilous quest
Duty shall compel her darkness,
But vengeance shall compel your death
You shall die, Mighty King, upon the Hero's Blade"

The pleasure of my orgasm left me. "What?" I growled.

The Maiden of the Voice trembled as she backed away. "I'm sorry, your Majesty. That is the future the Oracle saw."

"The Hero?" My stomach twisted. "She doesn't mean the mythical High King's heir?"

The Maiden shook her head. "I only spoke Her words."

The Oracle rose and turned, my cum leaking out of her pussy down her thighs. The Maiden of the Tongue licked up the line of white jizz to her pussy and feasted once more. The Oracle looked at me, her emerald eyes cold. She spoke.

"You must leave now, your Majesty," the Voice said as she bowed. "The ancient treaty has been honored. You have received your prophecy. May you interpret it with wisdom and humility."

My stomach twisted. I would die? Pater's cock, there was no way that was happening.

Part One

~~~

The Quest

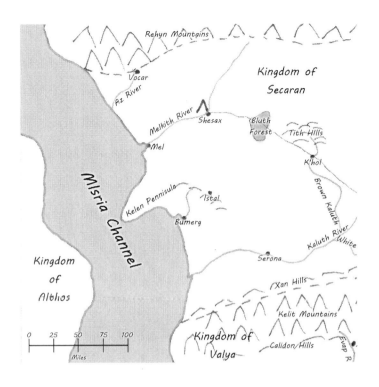

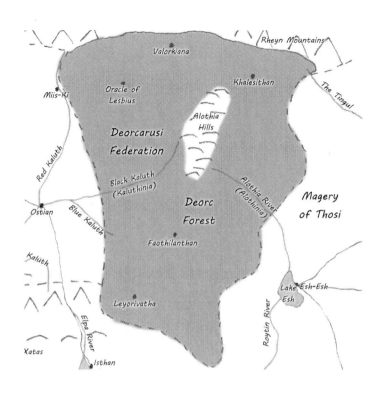

Chapter One: The Descendant of the Lilies

Squire Angela – Shesax, the Kingdom of Secare

My metal armor clinked as I circled Kevin on the training sands at the center of the Chapterhouse of the Knights Deute. The sun was warm, glinting off Kevin's armor. He wore a man's armor, a full breastplate instead of the half-plate I wore that left my midriff bare and revealed a large swath of my cleavage. His torso was covered by a skirt of banded mail. He did not wear his helmet, and his gorgeous face twisted with focus.

I tried not to pay attention as I stepped forward, swinging my blunted training sword at his face. Metal clanged as we traded blows. I was quicker. There was one advantage of the lighter armor women wore. We were nimbler, in addition to being distracting by displaying so much of our flesh. I could see Kevin's appreciative eyes.

He had just returned from his Quest, slaying an ogre, and now he was a full knight.

"That was a sloppy attack," Kevin said, his kissable lips curling in a smile.

"Was it?" I asked, cocking my head. I took another clumsy swing, his sword knocking mine aside with ease.

"Yes. Did you even practice one bit with your sword while I was gone?" he asked, arching his eyebrows.

"I learned a few tricks," I grinned and feinted with another clumsy attack.

He fell for it, his blade slapping down. I changed my stance, pulling my weapon back so he missed my blade before lunging forward and almost landing a blow. He lifted his round shield, deflecting my attack.

I pressed in, using my shield to deflect his blow as my long sword swung hard three times, driving him back. His eyebrows furrowed, and I grinned. He recovered from my attack, taking a hard swing.

His blade crunched into the wood of my shield. My right foot lashed out. I didn't have a skirt of metal bands, only a loincloth of chainmail, and my leg could kick out high. I caught him on the chest. He stumbled back, his shield knocked wide.

I charged in and struck my sword on his breastplate. It did no damage. In a real battle, a longsword was all but useless against full plate. I would need to use a mace or a warhammer to crush and dent his armor. But for training, he pretended it was lethal and fell to the ground.

"Well played," he laughed as I stood over him.

My pussy was hot, my blood pumping. I always loved sparring with him. We had been lovers for three years and I had missed him these last months as he hunted the ogre in the Kelit Mountains to the south.

"I told you I knew a trick or two," I grinned, my hands sliding up the crease on his left side. He wore a cuirass, and it hinged on the right. I found the three straps that held his armor close, two on the breastplate and one on the skirt, and undid them, his armor swinging open to reveal his muscular chest.

"Mmm, I have missed this chest," I purred, my fingers sliding across his pecs, my pussy growing hotter as I touched him.

He pulled off his gauntlets, his calloused fingers grasping my side, sliding up and reaching behind me to the straps that held my half-breastplate closed. I ground my pussy on his cock, the shaft hard beneath his britches. The straps came undone and my large, round breasts spilled out, my nipples hard with battle lust.

Fighting always made me wet, and fighting Kevin made me burn.

"Yes," I hissed as he groped one of my breasts, fingering my hard, pink nipple. His other hand slid up to cup my face, brushing back my flaming curls. I had my mother's fiery hair, but my father's blue eyes.

"I missed you every day in the mountains," he groaned, pulling me down, my red hair spilling about my face.

"I bet you found more than a few peasant girls willing to provide comfort to a Knight on a Quest," I grinned.

"But none were you," he grinned and pulled me down for a hot kiss

My breasts rubbed against his muscular chest. His hand slid down my back and over my heavy, leather belt that my chainmail loincloth hung from. He squeezed the cheeks of my ass, left mostly exposed by the two-inch wide band of mail. His fingers dipped beneath the mail as he kneaded my ass.

I groaned and ground on him, working my clit against the cold metal of my mail. His cock was hard beneath, throbbing with his desire. I kissed him hard, my hands roaming his muscular sides and chest. My Kevin was a strong man.

And it was time for him to eat my pussy.

I broke the kiss, sliding my hips up his body. "Time for you to pay the forfeit," I smiled, grasping his brown, flowing locks. My hot pussy pressed into my mail as I slid higher up his body. Pleasure shuddered through me. "You're going to devour my pussy. I want to cum and cum."

"Of course, my Lady," Kevin grinned, licking his strong lips.

My breasts heaved as I straddled his face, still holding onto his brown hair. I loved it when I won our duels. I pulled his head up, smearing his face against my hot pussy. I shuddered as his thick tongue slid through my pussy. My back arched. I gasped as the pleasure washed through me.

I guided his lips with his hair, my hips undulating. His hands kept kneading my asscheeks, his fingers tightening as his tongue worked through my pussy. He sucked and nibbled on my folds and he nuzzled at my clit.

"That's it," I groaned. "You lost, and now you have to pay. Devour my pussy. Don't miss a single spot. Come on, you can do better. Work that pretty mouth through my hot pussy."

My free hand grabbed my right breast, pinching my nipple as I undulated faster. Kevin moaned, his tongue working faster. He shoved it deep into my pussy, swirling it around. My eyes fluttered in delight, my moans echoing across the training sands.

Metal rang nearby. A pair of male knights dueled. Others watched. I savored their eyes.

"Show everyone how you are my little pussy slave!" I groaned. "Mmm, yes. Devour me! I'm gonna drown you!"

His tongue fluttered through my folds. My insides squirmed. I shifted my hips, smearing my clit across his strong face until his tongue found it. I gasped as he fluttered his tongue against my nub, batting it over and over.

"That's it! Oh, fuck! Work that tongue! Yes, Kevin! My little, pussy-hungry stud! Fuck! Fuck!"

My orgasm crashed through me. I screamed out my delight. My pussy clenched. My juices spilled out into Kevin's hungry mouth. My eyes met Donna, Victoria, and Christina, the squires' eyes envious of my lover's cunnilingus prowess.

"Keep eating me! Keep making me cum!" I screamed, my hips jerking.

Kevin kept assaulting my clit. His tongue must be a blur. My pussy clenched again as more ripples of pleasure washed through me. My clit ached, becoming even more sensitive as my climaxes washed through me.

I gripped Kevin's hair harder, holding his tongue against my clit for as long as I could stand it. My nerves burned with pleasure. My body spasmed and shuddered. My eyes squeezed shut as a mighty surge of pleasure rippled through me.

My clit almost hurt with the agony of my ecstasy.

I pulled away, letting go of Kevin, "Mmm, you were a stud, pussy slave," I grinned.

"I'm so glad I could service you, Mistress," he grinned.

We loved this game. When he won, I was his little cock slave. Dominating him was almost as much fun as when he held my red curls and fucked my mouth. But I never tried to lose, even if it was more fun to.

"I think you need a reward," I grinned, sliding down his body again. I reached his hard cock, grinding on him for a moment.

"Eating your pussy was reward enough," he grinned, licking his lips. "But if it is your will to reward your humble servant, then you have my eternal thanks."

I laughed, shaking my head even as my fingers unlaced his britches so I could pull his thick cock out. He was hard and throbbing, his tip shiny with precum. I smeared my thumb across his tip. He shuddered, his hips bucking.

"Mmm, I missed this cock," I grinned. "You may have the biggest cock in the Chapterhouse."

"I *may* have the biggest cock?" he asked as I rose on my knees and guided his cock to my hot pussy.

"I didn't fuck every cock while you were gone," I groaned as I sank down, his girth stretching my pussy open. "But I did try."

Kevin laughed and groaned. He seized my arms and pulled me down for another kiss. My tangy juices adorned his lips. I loved the taste of my pussy on his mouth. My hips undulated as I rocked on him, my breasts and my hard nipples pressed against his chest. I shuddered as my pussy gripped his cock.

"I did miss you," I moaned when we broke the kiss. "I love you, Kevin."

His arms wrapped around me and then he rolled us over. "I love you, too, Angela."

I shuddered as he kissed me again. My legs wrapped around his waist. I loved his weight atop me. I worked my hips as he fucked me, his cock jabbing deep into my pussy. My aching clit ground into his pubic bone with every thrust.

I clung to his broad back, my fingers digging into his muscles as his strokes grew harder and harder. Kevin was the handsomest Knight Deute, and he was all mine. I shuddered beneath him, savoring the envy of all the women watching us.

"Yes!" I groaned. "Yes, yes! Take me, Kevin! Fuck me! You're driving me wild!"

I stared at the flushed cheeks of the watching women, their hips shifting, their hands between their thighs, fingering their pussies, envying my position. I knew Kevin had fucked them all, but it was me he came back to.

"Work those hips, Angela!" groaned Kevin. "Damn, I missed your pussy! Oh, yes! Keep doing that! I'm gonna cum so deep in you!"

I welcomed that moment. I was enchanted by a red-robed Thosian mage. No child would quicken in my womb this year. I had ten months before I needed another spell cast on me. I would have completed my Quest by then. Kevin would marry me on my return.

I might not need the spell again.

"Cum in me!" I gasped. "Give it to me!"

"Yes!" he groaned, his thrusts hammering into me.

A new woman appeared to watch us. Lady Delilah. Her dark eyes locked on mine. She was so beautiful. Her lips smiled. I shuddered and gasped, cumming hard beneath my lover. My pussy massaged his cock as I stared into Lady Delilah's eyes.

"Angela!" Kevin groaned as he slammed his cock into my depths. "Oh, yes! Oh, fucking yes!"

His cock erupted in me. His hot cum flooded me. My body kept cumming. I shuddered and writhed, moaning as I drowned in Lady Delilah's dark depths. She was such an elegant and beautiful woman.

"Yes!" I screamed.

My pussy clenched harder as Lady Delilah's smile grew. My orgasm reached its peak. My fingers clawed into Kevin's back as my sheath milked every drop of his cum into my pussy. My pleasure grew to a crescendo and then crashed.

I shuddered and panted, my eyes fluttering. Lady Delilah was gone.

"Damn, I missed you," Kevin said, turning my face so he could kiss me.

I savored his kiss, thrusting my tongue deep into him. But I thought of Lady Delilah.

I had known her since I was young. She had often come to my family's estates performing her knightly duties. I was young when I first saw her riding up on her charger, her flaming hair flying behind her, gleaming in her armor. She was sensual and beautiful. My body awakened to desires for the first time. That night, I enjoyed my first, fumbling masturbation, thinking of Lady Delilah as I reached my pleasure.

I had such a crush on her as I blossomed into womanhood. She was my first love, but nothing ever came of it. I was only a child to Lady Delilah. I nurtured my crush, and she was the reason I joined the Knighthood. My mother was against it, but I wanted to be just like Lady Delilah.

I would be like Lady Delilah.

Kevin rolled off of me. I stood up, smiling in delight as I brushed the sand from my ass and back. I fetched my blunted training sword and discarded breastplate. I didn't put it on, letting my naked tits hang out.

"Thank you for the energetic training session, Sir Knight," I grinned as he put on his armor.

"You were always a spirited sparring partner, Squire," Kevin nodded back. We kissed one last time, my hard nipples pressing on his cold breastplate. That was nice. "I must meet with Lord-Commander William for lunch."

I nodded. "I'll be joining you at that table soon." Tomorrow, I would head to the Temple of the Pure, the grand temple to the Goddess Saphique, and receive my Quest from the High Virgin Vivian herself.

"I know you will." He gave me another kiss. "Love you."

I smiled and walked away. My training was complete. I was left to my own amusements. I strolled past the envious women, their fingers sticky, and nodded to them. "Ladies."

They glowered at me. That made me feel even better.

I walked deeper into the Chapterhouse, heading to my small cell. Kevin's cum trickled down my thighs. I loved that feeling. The musk of sex clung to me, that salty mix of cum, sweat, and pussy. It made me feel so alive.

I rounded a corner and there stood Lady Delilah. I gasped in shock.

"What an impressive display, Squire," Lady Delilah purred.

I swallowed, a wave of heat washing through me as she stepped forward. I trembled before her. She was so beautiful. Her hand touched my thigh, her fingers burning against my flesh. I moaned as her fingers slid up, pressing beneath my chainmail loincloth and brushing the shaved, messy lips of my pussy.

"My lady!" I gasped as her fingers penetrated my pussy. Her touch was fire and lust. I moaned as a small orgasm rippled through me. My heart beat faster. I wanted to kiss her. I wanted to touch her but fear clutched me. She was so imposing. So sexy.

I was helpless before her.

Lady Delilah's smile grew hungrier as she withdrew her fingers. She held them up, glistening with a mix of my juices and Kevin's cum. She brought it to her lips, her black eyelashes fluttering as she cleaned her fingers. "Mmm, the taste of youth. You have blossomed into a beautiful flower. A fire lily."

"Th-thank you, my Lady."

"I expect great things from you."

I still trembled as she walked away and disappeared down a side-corridor, her boots echoing. My breath exploded out of me and I leaned against the wall, a big smile on my face. Lady Delilah had noticed me. I would win great honors on my Quest and make her proud.

I gathered myself and kept walking to my room.

Chapter Two: The King's Fear

King Edward IV

I shuddered as John, my High Chamberlain, read the prophecy again with his reedy voice. He was an old man. He had long served my kingdom, first as a scholar for my grandfather George and then as High Chamberlain to my father Reginald. Now he was my chief advisor, and none in the realm were gifted with more of the God Cnawen's intelligence than he was.

> *"You shall die, Mighty King, upon the Hero's Blade*
> *The High King's Empire shall rise once more*
> *The Hero of the Lilies departs on perilous quest*
> *Duty shall compel her darkness,*
> *But vengeance shall compel your death*
> *You shall die, Mighty King, upon the Hero's Blade"*

"I don't need to hear the words again!" I snapped. "They've echoed in my head for the last three days. What do they mean? Who is this hero and why shall she kill me?"

"Yes, *she* is right," John nodded, the candlelight reflecting off his bald pate like sun glinting off the corner of a shield. "Very surprising. Scholars had long thought the Hero would be male, and yet the Oracle's words refute that theory."

"What are you talking about?"

"This prophecy is one of the simplest ever given down by the Oracle." A smile crossed John's aged face. "So simple."

"Then speak plain and explain how I may thwart the future."

"Have you forgotten the studies of your youth, Your Majesty? Did your father waste all his money on those tutors?"

I grinned. "Not all the tutors." Magdalena had a spectacular bosom, and she made the most spectacular moans when she came beneath me.

John's eyes flickered to my wife embroidering in the corner, her impressive bosom, enhanced by her pregnancy, displayed by her plunging, square-cut bodice lined by lacy ruffles. She had the blonde hair of a Princess of Zeutch, the shattered lands to the east.

"Yes, I imagine the sort of lessons you endeavored at," John laughed. "I hope you know of the High King."

I arched an eyebrow. "I mean to recreate his empire and not let some woman do it." I sneered. "How can a woman even hope to rule?" All men knew that a king was the embodiment of Holy Pater, father of the Gods. Only a man could be a father, so only a man could rule a land.

"The Hero was prophesied as High King Peter lay dying. His final words were a promise that his descendant would claim his sword and restore his empire. For Peter knew that he died without heir and his empire was doomed to shatter. Once dead, his words were so feared, his sword, forged by the God Krab himself, was shattered and hidden throughout the Empire."

"If he died without heir, how could he have a descendant to reclaim his throne?"

"He had descendants. Only none were male. Lily, his third child by his second wife. All his sons died, but his daughter survived and had children."

I frowned. "That sounds familiar. Wasn't there a curse?"

"Holy Slata was angered at her husband Pater's devotion to his bastard son Peter. She cursed Peter and ensured all his sons died, and that his daughter Lily and all her descendants would only birth women. As I said, the prophecy is simple. One of Lily's descendants shall kill you."

I glowered. "And how many of those are there? It's been a thousand years. Do we even know her bloodline after so long?"

"Of course." John reached over to a pile of books.

A draft rustled through the room. Queen Lavinia gasped, looking up from her embroidery. A sly smile crossed her lips, and she returned to stitching. I frowned and looked around the room. The door to my balcony was open, a breeze stirring through the room.

And there stood Lady Delilah.

My breath caught. She was an enchanting creature, forever promising me the delights of her lush body while always denying me a taste. No woman had ever denied me but her. My cock hardened as she strode forward, her hips swaying. Her hair caught the candlelight, almost shimmering like fire. It was hard to place her age. She wasn't a maid, but she also wasn't a mother. Her beauty ripe and perfect. Her armor clinked as she walked. She was a Knight Deute, and she had strapped shining greaves over her black, thigh-high boots. A loincloth chain draped from her heavy sword belt, leaving her upper thighs wonderfully bare. Her stomach was flat, and steel cupped her pillowy breasts, her cleavage impressive. A pair of slim pauldrons covered her shoulders, and bracers clad her slim wrists.

"When did you return, Lady Delilah?" I gasped.

"Oh, I have been back for a few days," she smiled, her boots clicking as she walked across the room. She nodded to my wife. I had watched them together. Delilah may have denied me her charms, but she had let my wife sample freely.

"Have you solved your little prophecy yet?" she asked, sitting gracefully beside me, crossing her legs. Those delicious thighs begged to be touched.

"I have," John said, fixing Lady Delilah with a hard gaze. "How have you heard of it?"

Lady Delilah smiled back, her lips ruby and so kissable. My heart throbbed. "I would love to know who you think the Hero of Lilies is? Which of the High King's descendants shall kill our noble king?"

"As I was about to explain before your...umm...timely arrival, the answer lies in this book." He tapped the tome. It had a stuffy title: <u>The Complete Genealogy of Lily of Hamilten, Princess of the Realm, Twenty-Third Revision.</u> "The College of Allenoth has kept meticulous track of Lily and her descendants. Currently, there are eighteen living descendants scattered across the Old Empire's lands. Including five living in our kingdom."

"And which is the one that will kill me?" I demanded, growing exasperated.

"Yes. The telling line is 'The Hero of Lilies departs on a perilous quest.' It really was quite easy to deduce. Only one of Lily's descendants is a Knight. Her name is Angela, and according to Lord-Commander William, she will shortly finish her squireship and embark upon her Quest to earn her spurs and become a full Knight Deute. She is the daughter of Count Francis of Xarin and his second wife, Countess Agnes, who herself can trace her lineage back to Lily in an unbroken line of mothers and daughters."

"Then she must die," Queen Lavinia said, her hand sliding down to rub at her round belly. My son grew in her belly after several years of trying to conceive. A Mage of Thosi had cast a spell to ensure that her first child would be male.

The succession had to be maintained.

"Yes," I nodded, glancing at Lady Delilah. Would she balk at killing a fellow knight?

"She must surely die to protect your kingdom," Delilah answered, her lips curling in a smile.

"This must be delicately done, Your Majesty," John said. "The Knights Deute protect our realm. But they are neutral in matters of politics. If we are found to interfere, there could be...repercussions."

Lady Delilah laughed.

John glared at her. "Do you have something to add, madam?"

"Killing her will be no great chore. She is about to embark on her Quest!"

"And?" I asked Delilah. "It is rare for a Knight to die on a Quest."

Lady Delilah leaned forward, her hand resting on my upper thigh. Her touch burned through my hose; my cock throbbed hard. Her lips were so close, her bosom within reach. I wanted to claim her. But there was such fire in Lady Delilah. She would burn even me for daring. "Not all Quests are equal. There is one that has been attempted many times and not been completed."

I scowled. "But the Quests are drawn by lots. That is one Quest in a hundred. I cannot gamble the future of my kingdom on such low odds." Nor my life.

"Then rig it."

Chapter Three: The Acolyte's Game

Acolyte Sophia

I strode through the Temple of the Pure, my heart beating with excitement. A new pair of novices had arrived. Fresh beauties. Lust burned through my body. I should be praying in the main chapel to the Holy Virgin Saphique, Goddess of Maidens, but that wasn't nearly as much fun as breaking in a pair of eighteen-year-old novices.

My pussy burned between my thighs.

My light-brown curls bounced around my shoulders as I strode through the temple. My small, left breast, not covered by the winding cloth of diaphanous white I wore, bounced, my pink nipples hard. The cloth covered my right breast as it wrapped about my left shoulder and diagonally crossed my body to my waist, leaving my belly button exposed. There it wound about my waist and draped down to cover my ass and legs, leaving a small gap that exposed the tight slit of my pussy.

It was the priestly vestments of Saphique.

My belly piercing glinted in the soft candlelight, adorned by a flashing ruby. I clicked my tongue piercing against the back of my teeth as I walked, my excitement growing. I reached the novitiate cells. The young maidens, just blossoming into womanhood, all smiled at me. They knew why I was here.

I loved young maidens. I had each of them in my bed. I may not be the most proficient Acolyte– at twenty-two I should have already been a priestess for the last year– but I was the most diligent at teaching the novices the joys of lesbian delight. Like our Goddess, none in the Temple of the Pure had ever lain with a man. We were all virgins– only the fingers, tongues, and dildos of women had been in our pussies.

I found the two acolytes in the main room, looking uncomfortable. They wore the same vestments I did, their bellybuttons newly pierced and glinting with gold. Their piercings were unadorned. They would earn their gems. Acolytes, like me, had their tongues pierced with silver barbells and priestesses had their left nipples pierced.

They were gorgeous, their breasts topped by pale-pink nipples as small as buttons. So cute. Curly, dark-brown hair framed their lovely faces and lush lips; their hazel eyes were wide. They had a similar look, both daughters of the nobility, though one stood a few inches taller than the other, who had, perhaps, the more developed bust.

"Novices," I said as I stopped before them, my pussy clenching in delight. "What are your names?"

"Daisy, Priestess," one answered. "And this is my friend Rose."

Such delicious names. And they thought I was a priestess. Perfect.

"Come with me," I ordered.

They gave each other nervous glances.

I smiled. "Don't be afraid. You will find your first lesson very enjoyable."

"Uh-huh," giggled another novice. "Acolyte Sophia will show you a few things."

"And when you get back, we expect you to demonstrate," giggled a blossoming beauty, her breasts swelling into a pair of lovely, round orbs.

"Follow," I commanded. Technically, I could only command a novice when I was teaching them. And this wasn't a sanctioned lesson. But they didn't know that. And as long as I kept up my authoritative tone, these two were so nervous they would do anything.

I loved novices.

They trailed after me, their bare feet slapping on the stone of the temple. I hoped we didn't run into a priestess. But they should all be busy. Besides, I wouldn't get in too much trouble. My mother was a powerful patron of the church, and they wouldn't want to offend a Duchess.

We reached my small room, the floors covered by a delicious carpet and my mattress stuffed with soft goose feathers. Scented candles burned, filling the air with a heady musk. I breathed it in as I pulled in the two cute novices, holding them against my side.

"Mmm, you two are just delicious," I purred and leaned down to kiss Daisy. My pierced tongue swirled through her mouth as she stood there, her lips frozen. I broke the kiss and shook my head. "You can do better than that. Surely you've kissed before."

Daisy gave a shy nod of her head.

"And I bet you practiced on your sexy friend," I grinned.

Her cheeks reddened as she nodded again. Rose squirmed on my other side.

"Of course you did. She's so sexy." I leaned in, my lips just inches away. "Let's try again."

I kissed her sweet lips. This time she didn't resist but kissed me back. My tongue swept through her delicious mouth. I shuddered as her tongue caressed mine, playing with my tongue piercing as she moaned softly.

"There, that was nice," I grinned. Her exposed nipple was hard.

"Yes, Sophia," she whispered.

I turned to Rose. Her hips shifted against me, her bare, bald pussy growing damp on my thigh. "Someone's getting excited."

She nodded, a little more eager than her friend. Rose licked her lips and closed her eyes as she tilted her chin. I leaned down and planted a hot kiss on her lips. My tongue thrust deep into her mouth as my hand slipped down her waist to grope her tight ass. I gave a hard squeeze, pulling her tight against me. She shuddered, her hips undulating, smearing that hot pussy on my thigh. I squeezed her ass through the thin silk of her vestments.

"Wow," Rose whispered when I broke the kiss.

"Indeed," I grinned, licking my lips.

I led the two girls to my bed. "Let's get naked."

I grabbed Rose's cloth, unwinding it from her youthful body. She turned, her boyish hips shaking, her firm breasts jiggling. Eighteen and delicious.

"Perfect," I moaned as she stood naked. Her slit was so tight and delicious. I licked my lips. "Isn't your friend gorgeous, Daisy?"

"Yes, Sophia."

I glanced at the shy girl, her hands folded before her pussy, hiding her charms. "Now let's strip Daisy naked."

Rose grinned and grabbed her friend's cloth, unwrapping her. Daisy turned, her cheeks growing redder as her body was exposed. She stood naked and trembling, her cute, little nipples hard. My pussy burned and I clenched my thighs.

"But you're not naked, Sophia," Rose said, eyeing me.

"Maybe we should change that," I winked at the girls.

Rose boldly grabbed my cloth. I turned, my small breasts jiggling. They were perky and perfect mounds, barely larger than apples. My hips had nice curves, and my pussy was bare. I could control whether I had pubic hair– one of the first things a novice learned.

"Let's have a lesson," I grinned, leading my two charges to the bed. I spread Daisy out on my goose feather stuffed mattress and snuggled on her right side while Rose took the left. "When you have your lover in bed, you want to caress and kiss her everywhere," I said, leaning in to kiss Daisy on the lips.

Rose followed while I nibbled down to her ear, the two novices sighing as their lips met. My clit ached to be touched.

"It's important that you worship her. Every woman has been

blessed by Saphique with pleasure that only we can give each other. Most women prefer brutish men, but we know the truth." My finger traced down Daisy's budding tit to her hard nipple. I circled her nub. "Women will always give you more pleasure than a man. Men take, but we give."

Daisy nodded her head, sighing as her friend copied me, circling Daisy's other nipple.

I smiled, my lips kissing down her shoulder, tasting the salt of her skin as I reached her puffy tit. Daisy gasped as I sucked her little nipple into my lips, my tongue and piercing playing with the hard nub.

Rose engulfed the other, sucking with a frenetic desire. Daisy gasped and shuddered.

"Not so hard," I told Rose. "Let Daisy tell you how she wants to be pleased. Some women like it hard and fast, others like a more gentle touch. And it will change. Sometimes her mood will be different."

"Did I suck too hard?" Rose asked, her face paling.

"A little," Daisy smiled. "But it was kinda nice."

I teased Daisy's nipple and Rose did the same, her lips sucking softer, her tongue swirling around Daisy's nipple. The young woman moaned and shuddered, her hips arching and her legs spasming. She gasped so sweetly.

A sweet scent tickled my nose. Daisy grew wet.

I let my hands roam her body. I caressed and teased her, touching every inch of her smooth skin save one special spot– her virgin pussy. Sometimes my hand brushed Rose's and she would giggle around Daisy's nipple. Daisy squirmed harder, the mattress shifting.

"Sophia," she groaned. "I need...more...down there."

I had avoided her little pussy. I pushed my hand between her thighs, sliding up, drawing every so close to her sweet snatch. "Is your pussy on fire?"

She nodded.

"Say it, Daisy."

"My...pussy is on...fire. I need to be touched."

I smiled at her and kissed down her body. I loved the salty taste of her skin. Her sweet scent grew stronger. Rose followed me, her smooches loud smacks. She even played with her friend's bellybutton, bringing a loud squeal from Daisy.

Rose and I settled between Daisy's spread thighs, her tight slit flushed red and spread open, revealing her pink depths. Juices beaded on her delicate folds. Rose sucked in her breath as she gazed at Daisy's pussy.

My finger traced her parts as I whispered to Rose, naming all the parts of a pussy and how they needed to be caressed. Licking my lips, my tongue lapping through Daisy's snatch. I savored the taste of her pussy, so sweet and fresh. My tongue swirled around her little clit as she gasped and moaned.

"Wow!" Rose gasped.

"Did you see how my tongue licked through her folds from the bottom to the top?"

She nodded.

"Do it."

Rose licked her lips before she lowered her head between Daisy's thighs. Both novices trembled. "Oh, yes, Rose!" Daisy moaned as Rose took her first swipe of pussy. "That was nice."

"How was your first taste of her pussy?" I asked.

"Delicious?" Rose moaned and dived back in.

Her tongue was aggressive but unskilled, swirling around with no clue what she was doing. I nuzzled her ear, whispering instructions while Daisy's moans grew louder and louder. Rose pressed her face deep into her friend's pussy, teasing her hymen and nuzzling at her clit.

"Perfect," I grinned, moving down Rose's body. She was kneeling, her ass so cute.

I had to taste.

I spread her asscheeks apart, my tongue swirling up through her crack to rim her tight, sour asshole. "Sophia!" she gasped as I rimmed her, my tongue and piercing dipping into her bowels.

"That's dirty."

"Nothing about you is dirty," I purred. "Just concentrate on loving your friend while I make you explode."

Rose nodded and moaned before she returned to eating Daisy. "Oh, yes!" purred Daisy. "I love it, Rose!"

My tongue moved lower. Her ass was tasty, but I wanted to devour her pussy. The ruby glinting on my belly piercing meant I had mastered the art of cunnilingus. There were many arts for a priestess of Saphique to master, but this was my favorite.

I spread apart Rose's tight pussy, inhaling her sweet flavor. She had a stronger flavor than Daisy, spicier, a wonderful flavor that coated my tongue. I loved the taste of pussy. They all were delicious in all their myriad flavors.

Rose moaned as my tongue swirled through her pussy, nudging against her hymen. I pressed on her little membrane before I moved up through her folds. I sucked on her little labia and rubbed my tongue stud against her hard clit.

She gasped and moaned. Her hips shifting. I squeezed my thighs together as my own pussy burned. But I had patience. When I was through with these two, they would be begging to eat my pussy.

I sucked Rose's dainty clit into my mouth, brushing my tongue around her nub. She moaned, her hips bucking. I kept up the pressure. Her moans were muffled. She ate Daisy harder as her ass clenched. Her orgasm built.

"Oh, Rose!" Daisy gasped. "Oh, yes! Oh, wow! I'm gonna...gonna explode!"

"Cum, dear Daisy!" Rose moaned. "Let's cum together! Oh, wow! Oh, Sophia! You're driving me wild!"

Rose's juices flooded my hungry mouth as both her and her friend sang out their pleasure. They both shivered and writhed. I kept flicking at Rose's clit, prolonging her orgasm as I drank down all her sweet juices.

"Wow, Sophia," Rose gasped. "I never knew. I've masturbated, but wow."

"Uh-huh," Daisy grinned.

I smiled. "Well, Rose, would you like to teach Daisy how to eat my pussy."

"Oh, yes!" Rose exclaimed, rolling over.

"I would like that," Daisy blushed.

I settled on the bed, spreading my legs wide and pinched my nipples. "Devour me, girls. I'm so hot. You two are so sexy."

Their cheeks pressed together as they both pressed their faces between my legs, their tongues wildly licking around my pussy. I shuddered as their fluttering, inexperienced tongues worked around my vulva and dove into my pussy.

"Lick my clit! Make me cum!" I groaned, pulling harder on my nipples, savoring the hard pleasure.

They did, nuzzling and licking. I moaned, my eyes fluttering in delight. I was so hot. Playing with their nubile bodies had kept me on the edge. Their tongues met in my pussy, both almost kissing each other as they nuzzled at my clit.

I came. My juices squirted their faces. I didn't always squirt. I still hadn't mastered that, yet, but I shuddered and moaned. I drenched their innocent faces with my juices. My hips heaved and bucked. I gasped and moaned.

"Oh, Saphique!" I moaned to the heavens. "Thank you for these sweet girls!"

The door to my room slammed open.

"Acolyte Sophia!" Priestess Georgina snapped.

Chapter Four: A Solution

Acolyte Sophia

"Yes!" I screamed as my orgasm still burned through me, bolting up from the bed as I stared at the angry priestess.

"You little slut! You were supposed to be at prayer!"

"I was praying," I panted as the two novices trembled beside me. "The three of us made sweet worship to Saphique."

Priestess Georgina glared at me, her large breasts heaving. Glittering gems of different hues adorned her nipple piercing and belly ring. She had almost achieved the rank of Virgin, mastering all the lesbian disciplines and would then receive her labia piercing.

"Are those the two new novices?" she gasped.

"Their hymens are intact," I smiled. "I was just giving them a lesson on cunnilingus."

Both novices trembled, their faces smeared with my juices.

"Get dressed and return to your cells!" the Priestess snapped. "Acolyte Sophia had no right to bring you here."

"Yes, Priestess," Daisy squeaked.

Priestess Georgina glared at me. Her jaw clenched. "The High Virgin will see you when she returns from the Palace," Georgina spat. "Maybe she can get you to obey."

"Maybe," I smiled as I stood and slowly dressed. The novices were out the door in a flash, fleeing in fear. "Though I'm sure my mother will happily give another donation to the temple to smooth this over. And it's not like I popped their cherries."

I had done that once. It had caused the poor novice to be kicked out of the temple. She couldn't be properly sanctified and thus couldn't be a priestess. I felt really bad about that. I didn't mean to deflower her. I got carried away.

Priestess Georgina let out a shrill shriek.

"You really must remain calm, Priestess," I smiled as I walked to her. "You should carry yourself with the decorum of our Goddess."

I tried not to laugh as she screeched again.

~ * ~

High Virgin Vivian

"What you are asking is...improper, King Edward," I said carefully as I sat in his study, his pregnant queen embroidering on a nearby chair while the High Chamberlain, John, sat across from me at the table.

"Do you want to see Secare and the world consumed by chaos of the High King's Empire restored?" the King pointed out.

He was a young, virile man. I was sure if I wasn't a lesbian, I might even find him handsome and dashing. As it was, I hated the way he leered at both my bared breasts and the nipples rings adorning my flesh. I led the entire faith of Saphique. I had mastered every lesbian technique. I was sixty-three and yet possessed the body of a twenty-five year old.

And this boy ogled me.

"I do not," I conceded after a moment. "But the Knights Deute have always entrusted the Temple of the Pure to choose their Quests fairly for their female knights. Why should we betray that trust?"

"For the future," he insisted.

"Your future," I countered.

Virgin-Superior Elizabeth, the woman who administered the Temple of the Pure itself while I dealt with the entire faith, snorted in laughter. We had been friends and lovers for decades, rising together through the ranks of Saphique's church. I trusted her.

"Angela must die, but it must look accidental," King Edward insisted, lifting his eyes from my breasts. "The good of all the Kingdoms is at stake. It will be war if Angela somehow tries to press the High King's claim. Haz, Valya, Thlin, Athlos, and the Principalities will rise against her. Even the Magery of Thosi will become involved. This could plunge the continent into decades of suffering."

I glanced at Elizabeth. She arched an eyebrow. She thought there was merit to the plan. I licked my lips. "But such a betrayal of trust is monumental. It might even offend our holy Goddess."

"An offering could be arranged," the King said.

"A bribe?" Elizabeth asked. "Something the Knights Deute could point at and cry foul."

John gave Elizabeth a shrewd look, pursing his lips. "A concession, then."

Elizabeth nodded. "Your father granted our temples exemption from tax collection for five years. That ends next spring."

King Edward's face blanched. "My father was senile when he made that decision. The coffers need that income of the lands– "

"They do not," John interrupted. "And even if they did, the price can be borne. Right, Your Majesty?"

King Edward froze and looked at his advisor. "Right. Perspective. Fine. I will have it extended for another year."

"Twenty." Elizabeth countered.

"Five," King Edward said. "Be reasonable."

"Fifteen," I suggested.

The King's jaw clenched. "Seven."

I glanced at Elizabeth and she gave a slight nod. What a wonderful idea Elizabeth had. I would have to reward her. "Agreed. Angela will draw the quest to slay the dragon Dominari."

My stomach still churned when I returned to the temple. It was monstrous what we were doing, but seven years without having to pay the taxes would bring a bounty. Already our coffers were growing. We could build such monuments to Saphique with this money. And after seven years, King Edward may have a hard time repealing such an act. We could stir sympathy. After all, wise, beloved, and dead King Reginald gave us the tax relief in the first place.

My good mood evaporated when I found Sophia sitting in my office's antechamber, Priestess Georgina glowering beside her. The young acolyte tested my patience in ways few others had. But her mother was wealthy, and her donations kept her haughty daughter enrolled.

"I will deal with you in a moment," I glowered at her. She didn't appear that intimidated. The damn girl knew how much wealth her mother donated.

Elizabeth followed me into my office. "There is one thing, Vivian," she said. "We have to sacrifice an acolyte along with Angela."

I froze. I had forgotten that. It was customary to send one of our acolytes with a female Knight Deute on her Quest to assist with divine magic. And then a smile crossed my lips. "I know just whom to send."

Elizabeth gave me a curious look.

"Sophia."

"Her mother will object."

"Why? It is a great honor to be chosen. I have three letters from her mother demanding to know why her daughter has never been chosen for a Quest."

"Because she's useless," Elizabeth muttered. "I'm not sure she has ever paid attention during lectures on divine magic."

"Exactly. We can be rid of the little bitch and appease her mother all at the same time. Send her in so we can give her the great news."

Chapter Five: Sophia's Punishment

Acolyte Sophia

I was bored as I waited in the antechamber to the High Virgin Vivian. I wasn't afraid of the trouble I was in. So I blew off prayers to play with a pair of novices? I didn't break their cherries. They were still pure enough to be inducted into the priesthood.

I really didn't see what the fuss was. My mother would have to give another donation, and that would be that. Then I could go back to relaxing in the arms of a pretty acolyte or novice. Serving in the Temple of the Pure, the chief temple to Saphique, had its perks. Maybe I would find those two acolytes again. They were a sexy pair.

I squeezed my thighs together as I remembered Daisy and Rose.

I clicked my tongue stud against the back of my teeth. I knew the lecture I would receive. I was the oldest acolyte in the temple. I should be a priestess by now, but I had only earned a single jewel. The ruby glinting on my belly piercing represented the only sexual technique I had mastered— cunnilingus.

Well, I loved licking pussy.

I would have to master another three sexual techniques before I would earn my left nipple piercing and become a priestess. I was close with fingering, and with a little more practice I'm sure I would get analingus. I should apply myself, but it was so easy to get distracted.

I was diligent in my worship of Saphique.

Priestess Georgina glowered beside me, her heavy breasts, the left exposed by her vestments to show off her nipple piercing studded with an emerald and an amethyst, rose and fell. The blonde woman wasn't happy with me.

Maybe I should apply myself and finally become a priestess. Then I could minister to our worshipers. Women of all walks of life came to our temple to worship Saphique in the arms of a priestess for a small donation. That might be fun. Certainly better than some of the tasks they made me do.

I toyed with my light-brown hair as I waited, my thoughts drifting back to Daisy and Rose. They were so sexy. I could still taste their pussies on my lips and feel their soft hands and nuzzling mouths on my flesh.

My nipples hardened and my pussy grew wet. I shuddered, my hand sliding down my stomach to rub at my thighs. My pussy clenched. My tart excitement scented the air. I licked my lips, closing my eyes and pushing my hand between my thighs. I shuddered as I teased the hot lips of my pussy. I slid up to my clit, circling the little bud and–

"Stop that, you little slattern!" hissed Priestess Georgina, smacking my hand. "You are here to be punished, not so you can play with your filthy cunt."

"Sorry, Priestess," I muttered, rubbing at my wrist. I took a deep breath, my small breasts rising, and sighed in irritation.

"You must learn self-control. If you truly aspire to be a priestess, then you must control when you are aroused and when you are not. A priestess has perfect control of all her body's functions."

"Yes, Priestess," I sighed, rolling my eyes.

"I know you love the female form, but it requires more than love to be a priestess. It requires dedication to the lesbian sexual arts. You must rigorously study. Learn all your body's secrets and then discover where those secrets lie on a thousand other women. It takes discipline."

"Yes, Priestess."

Rose and Daisy appeared in my mind, smiling as their nubile bodies pressed together. Priestess Georgina kept droning on and on, but I was lost to my daydream. I didn't rub my fingers against my pussy, but I worked my thighs together. There were many ways to masturbate, and I had mastered all of them as a novice.

I bit my lip as I worked my thighs against my clit. The pleasure built and swelled as I massaged the little bud. My thighs clenched and relaxed. I savored the rise of my pleasure. I embraced it, pulling it into my body as I imagined Rose and Daisy making love, their youthful bodies writhing in newly discovered passion.

What a beautiful sight.

My orgasm shuddered through me. Soft waves rippled against the shores of my mind. I savored the gentle pleasure. I controlled my moans, but a large smile appeared across my lips as the scent of my cunt grew stronger, my thighs sticky with my excitement.

"Oh, you little slattern!" Priestess Georgina's outburst snapped me out of my reverie. "You just masturbated!"

"Yes, Priestess," I smiled, leaning back in my chair. "I needed that."

"Aren't you worried about your punishment?"

I shook my head. I had never been punished directly in my life. I had a whipping girl for that as a child. I had to watch every time she was whipped. But I had never felt the whip or the paddle, and the High Virgin wasn't about to anger my mother by really punishing me for such a small trespass.

The door opened and High Virgin Vivian and Virgin-Superior Elizabeth walked in, both glancing at me, their faces scowling. They were both beautiful women. Like all priestesses, they preserved their youth and appeared to be about twenty-five, though I knew both were far older. The High Virgin's face was predatory, framed by her lustrous, dark-brown hair.

She swept by me, her body almost fully on display, her piercings glinting. She had both nipples pierced, her labia, and her clit, along with her belly button. Gems adorned her piercings, proclaiming her mastery of every sexual art.

"I will deal with you in a moment," the High Virgin said, her dark eyes focused on me.

I smiled back at her, unafraid of her gaze.

The High Virgin's jaw tightened, and she swept into the room followed by the Virgin-Superior. Elizabeth ran the temple. In any other temple, she would be the highest-ranked priestess, elected to be the administrator, but here she answered to the leader of our faith. She was a hard woman despite her willowy curves and delicious, pillowy tits.

"The High Virgin does not look pleased," smirked Georgina. All the priestesses and virgins hated me. They were jealous of my mother's power.

I didn't answer. I glanced at the door and sighed, my feet kicking. I really wanted to get this over with. It was so boring having to wait. I leaned back my head and closed my eyes, drifting to other fantasies, trying to escape this tedium.

The door opened. "Acolyte Sophia," Virgin-Superior Elizabeth called. "Come in."

"Yes, Virgin Superior," I said, standing up and striding into the office.

It was richly appointed, the shelves covered in boring, leather-bound tomes. They were probably on the most stuffy of topics. A comfortable couch sat to the right of her desk, and I knew it had seen much passionate use. The High Virgin sat at her desk and Elizabeth moved behind her, leaning against the wall, her arms crossed beneath both her bared breasts.

I sat down on a stiff chair. "High Virgin," I smiled. "Virgin-Superior."

"Acolyte Sophia," the High Virgin smiled, leaning forward, her hands crossed. I frowned. Why was she so happy? Every other time I had been in here she reeked of disapproval. "I have good news."

"Good news?" My eyebrows furrowed. What was going on?

"The very best," the High Virgin nodded. "You've been selected for the greatest of honors."

Suspicion tightened in my mind. "I'm not being punished?"

"For what?" laughed the High Virgin. "Sleeping with a pair of novices? Skipping a prayer? Hardly the worst thing an acolyte has ever done. I even did it once or twice myself."

I blinked. What had happened? Had someone cast a spell on the High Virgin? Had a Thosian mage enchanted her? Or maybe a changeling had taken her place? But changelings only appeared as men, right?

Maybe I should have paid more attention to my studies.

"What is this honor, High Virgin?" I swallowed.

"Tomorrow, Squire Angela of the Knights Deute comes to the temple to be blessed and receive her Quest."

My stomach clenched. Oh, no. This could not be happening.

"And you have been chosen to be her acolyte. You shall guide her and support her on her perilous journey."

My mouth went dry. "But...but...Maria is the most accomplished Acolyte. Or what about Rebecca? I...I..."

"You are the oldest Acolyte? Who is more experienced than you?"

I didn't want to leave the comforts of the temple. I didn't want to be forced to travel the world and help some stupid knight on her quest. "But...but...my mother. She won't be happy."

"Why wouldn't she be happy?" smiled the High Virgin. "It is such an honor to be chosen. Think of the glory to our Goddess you shall win. You shall rise high in the church's hierarchy. Almost no one reaches the rank of Virgin without journeying on a quest."

I shuddered. Virgins were the senior priestesses, ones who had mastered every art and served Saphique with distinction. Only from the Virgins was a Virgin-Superior elected. And only from the Virgin-Superiors was the High Virgin chosen.

"Your mother will be pleased," Virgin-Superior Elizabeth smiled. "She has written us several letters urging us to choose you and exhorting all your...virtues."

The High Virgin nodded. "Yes. You are the perfect candidate

for this Quest."

I swallowed, trembling. My mother would want this. She dreamed of me being the High Virgin someday. My stomach clenched. I saw it in the High Virgin's eyes— she had finally found a way to punish me.

"I...I...am honored," I whispered, fighting my urge to throw a tantrum. I had learned decorum and propriety from my mother. There was no escaping this punishment. I swallowed, tears beading in my eyes. "Is there anything else?"

The High Virgin shook her head. "You are free until the ritual tomorrow. I would pack."

"Thank you, High Virgin." I stood up, my body trembling. I fought the urge to run. I walked calmly to the door, twisted the knob, and stepped out.

Priestess Georgina smirked when she saw my ashen face. "So what is your punishment?"

"I'm...going on a Quest." Months of rough travel, sleeping on the ground, eating stale food, all so some stupid Knight could slay a stupid monster in the far-flung reaches of the world.

Chapter Six: Dream Lover

Squire Angela

My sleep was punctuated with nightmares.

Monsters prowled in my mind, each looking to devour me. Yellow, bloated ogres attacked me with hard cocks, eager to rape and breed their monstrous spawn in me. Snarling werewolves attacked out of the night, eager to tear my flesh to pieces. Ambushing panthopuses leaped from the brush, their tentacles reaching for my flesh. Cruel efreet whipped me with lashes of fire. Trolls grew back severed limbs as their gnarled hands tried to grab my flesh. Nagas wrapped their serpent-like, lower bodies about my body and crushed the life from me. Angry treants tried to wrap their choking branches about my neck.

And then I felt comforting hands on me as morning approached. They were rough and calloused, but I knew them well. Kevin. He held me, driving off my nightmares. I fell into deeper dreams as my lover protected my sleep.

His hands touched me, his voice soothed me. I would be okay. I had trained to fight bogarts and bugbears and kobolds. I didn't need to be afraid of a rakshasa feasting on my flesh or a naglooshi driving me mad with fear.

Lips kissed my flesh. My dreams grew warmer. The lips touched me everywhere. My nipples were sucked on. My breasts were licked. Ticklish delight filled my dreams as the lips nuzzled at my bellybutton. Strong hands rubbed at my thighs, spreading me apart. The heat gathered between my legs.

Enjoy your dreams, Lady Delilah whispered.

She appeared in my dreams, naked and lovely, and it became her lips kissing down my pubic mound to my aching pussy, her flaming hair spread across my thighs.

I savored the dream as her green eyes flashed at me. Lady Delilah was so perfect. So beautiful. She made me ache with desire. Lips nuzzled at my pussy. I shuddered and moaned, the dream fading as the pleasure increased. I struggled to hold onto the dream, fighting off consciousness. I didn't want to give up Lady Delilah licking my pussy.

Her tongue lapped through my folds, thick and strong, swirling through all my silken delights. I shuddered. The dream fading faster. My body writhed and twisted. Light grew brighter behind my eyes, drawing me up from the depths of sleep.

"Yes," I groaned as my eyes fluttered open.

Lady Delilah slipped from my mind. Kevin was between my thighs, his hazel eyes peering into mine. I shuddered. His lips were strong and his cheeks were whiskered, rasping against the sensitive folds of my pussy.

"Mmm, what a lovely way to wake up," I groaned as I arched my hips. Lady Delilah and her sensual beauty was forgotten as my lover tongued me harder.

His strong, right hand slid up my flat belly, reaching for my heavy, round breasts. I shuddered as he squeezed and kneaded my flesh, his lips nipping at my labia. More sighs escaped my mouth as I let the pleasure flow through my body. His fingers wrapped around my nipple.

Kevin rolled my nub. Sparks of excitement shot through my body. My hips undulated, smearing my hot pussy against his hungry mouth. His whiskers scratched harder at my intimate flesh. I loved the feeling. So masculine and strong.

"Kevin, you stud!" I squealed. "Eat my pussy! Make me cum!"

His fingers pinched my nipple hard. I gasped in delight, squeezing my blue eyes shut. I tossed my head, my fiery curls flying about my face. My breasts heaved as my stomach tensed. The pleasure swelled through me, growing in my core.

Kevin's other hand slid beneath my body. He found my firm ass, squeezing my cheek. His fingers worked at my flesh, moving deeper and deeper into the crack of my ass. I knew what he wanted.

"Finger my ass and eat my pussy! Oh, Kevin, you are the best! I love you!"

My heart thudded faster as Kevin's finger teased my backdoor. I squealed as he circled my puckered sphincter. The sensations built in the core of my body. Kevin's tongue wiggled into the depths of my pussy as he jammed his finger into my bowels. He double-fucked me. My hips bucked and my toes curled.

"Yes! What a stud!"

My orgasm surged closer. My hands reached down, grasping his dark, flowing locks while I ground my pussy against his handsome face as he kept devouring me. I bucked and shuddered in delight as my pleasure kept building and building. My tits shook as I gasped and shuddered.

"Kevin!" I screamed as my orgasm rippled through me.

The pleasure washed through me. My pussy clenched and spasmed as I bucked. My fingers dug into his hair, holding his face to my pussy. I humped and gasped, smearing my hot flesh against his lips as I let myself get lost to the passion.

My moans echoed through my small room. My bed creaked and shuddered as I thrashed. Kevin's hungry mouth kept licking and sucking at my pussy. New sparks of pleasure kept flooding through me while his finger pumped faster and faster in my asshole.

"Oh, yes!" I screamed as a second orgasm burst through me. "Damn, Kevin! You are amazing! Slata's cunt, yes!"

His lips moved up my slit. His tongue found my clit. My eyes shot wide open. My stomach tensed and I sat half-up as he assaulted my tingling clit. It was so sensitive after I came. The rapture was so close to agony. I gasped and bucked, spasming as my mind was lost to the pleasure. His tongue flicked and batted my clit. Every stroke sent another gusting wind of bliss through me.

I groaned. I couldn't take it. I was dying of bliss. My breasts heaved. Pleasure burned through every inch of my flesh. My heels drummed on his broad back as I struggled to breathe. My vision darkened. Stars danced before me.

"Slata's cunt!" I screamed. "Pater's cock! Oh, yes! Oh, Kevin! Please! You're killing me! So amazing! So good! Oh, yes!"

Kevin lifted his lips from my pussy. His handsome face, sculpted to masculine perfection, grinned at me.

"You slayed me," I moaned. "Oh, my Knight, you have vanquished my body."

"Good," he grinned, sliding up my body, his hard body pressing against me. He was all ropy muscles. I held him, pulling him in for a kiss. It was soft and gentle, and I savored my tangy musk on his lips.

"Thank you," I gasped. "Oh, gods, that was intense." I struggled to catch my breath, the pleasure still burning through me. "Thank you, thank you," I moaned over and over.

"You're about to embark on your Quest with a nubile acolyte of Saphique. She's going to be eating your pussy day and night, so I needed to make sure you remember what I can give you."

I giggled. "Oh, I will remember this orgasm until the day I die. No little lesbian acolyte can take your place."

"I hear they're very good."

"But they don't have stubble," I told him, rubbing at his cheek. "You need to shave." I kissed him, rubbing my cheeks against his and savoring the rough feel.

"I've seen a few women that have stubble," Kevin grinned. "Maybe you'll get a homely acolyte that has to pluck her upper lip."

"They better not," I stated. "Not after they gave you that doll-faced acolyte of Slata for your quest." All the male squires would go to the Temple of Motherhood, dedicated to the Goddess Slata, for their blessing and Quest. The Temple of the Pure allowed no man to step foot on their holy grounds. "How many times did she suck your cock?"

"Every morning," Kevin grinned. "She woke me up with these amazing blowjobs. She was hungry for cum. I swear, she sucked any cock that was brandished at her. Those Slata priestesses are horny vixens."

Kevin's hard cock rubbed against my hip. I slid my hand down and grasped it. "And how many times did you fuck her?"

"Every night," he grinned. "She could do things with her pussy that I had never felt. She controlled her muscles in there. It was...nice."

I arched an eyebrow. "I hope you're not bored with my untrained pussy."

"Never. I love you." Kevin kissed me as I stroked him.

I groaned, melting into his kiss as I jerked his hard cock. He throbbed in my hand, pulsing with his need. I rubbed the tip, loving his moans. His arms wrapped around me, pulling my body closer to him, my pillowy tits rubbing on his hard chest.

His lips broke our kiss and then he buried his face into my cleavage. I groaned as he pressed my tits against his whiskered cheeks. He growled as he nuzzled me, his lips sucking and nipping at my flesh as he mounted me.

My legs parted. I rubbed his cock against my thigh, smearing precum around my flesh. Kevin groaned around my hard nipple, vibrating my nub. My pussy clenched. Despite my earth-shattering orgasm, another itch formed in my depths.

"Mmm, Kevin, I need you in me," I groaned. "I need all of your cock I can get. I'll be without it for so long. This acolyte won't have a hard cock to fuck me."

Kevin grinned. "I guess I don't need to be worried."

"You never did," I purred, pulling his cock towards my pussy.

He slid up my body, his hard muscles rubbing on my throbbing nipples. I shuddered as I swabbed his cock against my wet pussy. My lips tingled. I gasped as I nudged my clit. Kevin's hands caressed my sides as he kissed me, his hips thrusting, trying to penetrate me.

I moved him lower through my folds. He felt the entrance to my pussy. I shuddered in delight as he filled me. His thick cock stretched me open. He always did. He must have the biggest cock in the Knights Deute. I had fucked plenty of others, but his always made me feel virginal.

"Kevin!" I groaned in delight as he worked atop me. My hands stroked his muscular back and down to his clenching ass.

"Damn, Angela!" he groaned. "I so missed this pussy."

I clenched down on him as he thrust. The pleasure swelled through me. His groin crashed into my clit while his cock struck all the wonderful spots in the depths of my sheath. Our bodies worked and heaved, my breasts crushed by his chest. I loved his weight atop me.

"Keep clenching your pussy," groaned Kevin. "I love it."

"Is that what the Slata acolyte did?" I groaned.

"Yes! Priscilla did just that. But even better."

I groaned, clamping down my pussy on his cock. I liked it. The pleasure increased as I gripped him. I shuddered as he drew back and slammed into my tight depths. Our lips met again as the fire roared inside my depths. My pleasure churned, spilling through me.

My hips bucked harder. I ground my clit into his pubic bone as my thighs wrapped around his waist. I needed him to fuck me harder. I was almost there. My body tensed as my orgasm built inside me.

"Kevin! Pound me! Make me cum!"

"Yes!" Kevin groaned. "Fuck, Angela! Oh, fuck! Take it!"

"That's it! Harder! Oh, damn!"

Kevin pounded me hard. His cock almost hurt as he speared me. My sheath rippled. My orgasm sparked through me. I bucked beneath him as I squealed in delight. I held onto my lover as my climax washed through me.

"Damn, Angela! Work that pussy! Oh, fuck! So hot! Slata's cunt! Yes!"

Kevin slammed into me as my pleasure receded. His thrusts were more frantic. I squeezed down with my pussy and stared into his hazel eyes. His face contorted. His cock throbbed in my depths. And then his hot seed spilled into me.

I held onto Kevin. I savored him atop me. I wanted to spend every last moment in his arms before my Quest.

Chapter Seven: Impending Journey

Acolyte Sophia

I trembled as I gathered with the other acolytes who would be participating in the Blessing. There were eight of us, seven to anoint the knight-to-be and me to be blessed with her. They all shot me puzzled looks.

"I can't believe you were chosen," dusky-skinned Maria hissed. She was half-Hazian, her skin exotic. "What was the High Virgin thinking?"

"I don't know," I muttered. "You're welcome to change her mind."

Maria's face paled.

Heather gave me a smile. "I guess the High Virgin thinks highly of Sophia."

"She's the only one," Rebbecca muttered, toying with her curly brown hair.

"I'm competent," I scowled at her, trying to put a brave face on the Quest. I didn't feel it. I couldn't sleep at all last night. I even snuck out to a novice's bed to try to tire myself out with sex. That didn't work, though the novice had no problems sleeping.

Fears trembled through my body. I would have to help the

knight-to-be fight some disgusting monster like a vampire or a drake. Or a hydra with all its heads dripping with slime in some filthy swamp.

I shuddered in disgust.

The door opened and Novice Agnes stepped into the room. "The Priestesses are ready to purify you."

I took a deep breath. This was it. The ritual would soon begin . I would be tied to this knight, compelled by our Goddess to journey on her Quest. If I balked, I would be kicked out of the temple and no amount of my mother's money would change that.

"I am the daughter of Duchess Catherine," I whispered to myself. "The blood of kings flows in my veins. I can do this."

My stomach clenched in fear.

"Come on," Heather said, taking my hand. "Let's go."

I trembled as I followed her. We walked through the temple, following the Acolyte into the main sanctum. The statue of Saphique, carved out of white marble, rose above the sanctum, buxom and beautiful, wearing the same, gauzy vestments we did. The artisan, trained supposedly by the God Krab himself, had captured the Goddess's sensual beauty. I could almost believe the statue was alive. The room was covered in pillows and tapestries depicting Saphique seducing the various goddesses into lesbian delights. The baptistery had been uncovered, a small pool filled with the creamy breast milk of the priestess.

The High Virgin stepped forward, her hands cupping her round breasts.

"Bless this pool of your sweet milk, Saphique!" she prayed, squeezing her tits. Milk shot from her nipples, squirting into the pool. Every priestess could lactate at will— the source of their divine magic. The creamy scent filled the room. "Let your purity wash clean our acolytes. Let them imbibe your blessings and be vessels for your divinity!"

Energy rippled through the air. The calm surface of the milk suddenly stirred as if some invisible hand had reached in and swirled through the bath. My nipples hardened and my pussy flushed with excitement, banishing some of my fear. I glanced up at the statue. Her eyes seemed to stare at me.

I took a deep breath and stepped froward, unwinding my vestments and handing them to Priestess Georgina. Naked, I stopped before the High Virgin and the bath. I stared down at the milky surface.

"Be cleansed," the High Virgin pronounced.

I closed my eyes. This was it. Once I had been purified, there was no stopping the ritual. There would be no sudden changes. I would have to leave the temple and brave the dangers of the outside world.

I forced myself to step into the warm, creamy bath. I sank down, the breast milk embracing my flesh. It brimmed with the Goddess's energy; warmth poured through me. The Goddess would be with me on this journey. She would help me, guide me, and protect me.

I sank my head beneath the milk.

White surrounded me. I drank in the milk, sweet and creamy. I shuddered, an orgasm rippling through my body as the Goddess washed me clean. I spasmed as the delight crashed through my mind. I was clean.

I stood up, milk dripping down my body, and stepped from the bath. Priestess Michelle wrapped a white towel around my body, wiping me dry of the milk as Heather stepped into the bath to be purified. I glanced back up at the statue.

Was she smiling at me? I smiled back. Maybe I could do this.

~ * ~

Xerathalasia – Khalesithan, The Federation of Deoraciynae

I threw open the doors to my wife's room, my heart thudding. I blinked in surprise. My sister, Nyonthilasara, reclined on a divan near my wife's bed, naked save for a necklace of beads. My wife herself sat on the bed, rubbing at her pregnant belly, her breasts naked and glistening with sarla sap.

"What is it, my wife?" Atharilesia, my wife, asked. "What brings you bursting into my room?"

I frowned at my sister and then looked to my beautiful wife. "A hunt," I answered. "A basilisk has been spotted in the western woods. I lead my hunters out in an hour."

Atharilesia stood up, moving with grace despite her round belly. A smile was on her lips. "Then you must go and protect our people." Her pointed ears quivered. She strode to me, her breasts jiggling. A cock swung from between her thighs. She had just sprouted it. We had three days to enjoy it, and I was looking forward to conceiving another child with her— a daughter I could carry beneath my heart.

But there wasn't time.

Atharilesia grasped my pointed ears. I shuddered in delight, my hips shifting, my toes digging into the moss that carpeted her floor. "Go, Xerathalasia, and protect our forest so our daughter may grow up in safety."

My hand touched her belly, rubbing across the smooth oils. My sister must have adorned her flesh. I was glad my sister would watch over my wife during her pregnancy. I leaned down and kissed my wife's lips, savoring her love.

"Good luck, sweet sister," Nyonthilasara purred, her oily fingers rubbing at her belly, drifting near to her thighs. She was a tall, graceful Elf. As tall as I was. Our faces were almost mirrors, though hers had a more haughty beauty.

I nodded my head to my sister. "I must go. I would love to tarry in your sweet arms, wife."

"As would I," breathed Atharilesia.

Nyonthilasara rose, stretching her body, her firm breasts jiggling. "I will keep your pretty wife company and distract her from worrying about you."

I kissed my wife one last time and left her bower. I moved along the branches of the great Linden tree and descended the stairs that wrapped the outside of her mighty trunk. My hand trailed along the wood, the trees protective thoughts tingling through my fingers.

"Watch over my wife and child," I whispered when I reached the bottom, kissing the bark.

Chapter Eight: Blessed by Saphique

Squire Angela – Shesax, the Kingdom of Secare

I trembled in my armor, my breasts heaving in the half-breastplate that left my midriff and the slopes of my tits bare. I shifted, my chainmail loincloth clinking as it brushed my thighs. My sword was on my hip, and my fiery curls fell about the shining pauldrons protecting my shoulders.

The doors opened.

I took a deep breath and stepped out of the room into the heart of the Chapterhouse of the Knights Deute. The floor was polished marble embossed with the galloping, red charger, the symbol of the order. I knelt upon the red horse, gazing up at the three figures standing before me. In the center was Knight-Commander William resplendent in his armor, a cape of red spilling off his pauldrons, the nobility of his presence only ruined by his balding, dark hair.

"Squire Angela," he nodded.

To his right was King Edward, a regal and handsome man dressed in tight, blue doublet and hose, silver thread adorning his codpiece and drawing the eye. He was fit and strong, an ermine cape draping his shoulders and a golden crown upon his brow. To William's left was Lady Delilah. My breath caught as I gazed at her perfection. Her hair seemed to burn like fire and her gold-filigreed armor cupped her heaving breasts.

Lady Delilah smiled at me and a flush of warmth shot through my body.

"Lord-Commander William, summoned so have I arrived to do my duty," I said, surprised at how confident my voice rang across the room.

"Squire Angela," the Lord-Commander said, his steely eyes fixed on mine. "You have long been an exemplar among our squires. You have shown skill on the practice grounds and courage on the tourney grounds. You have inspired and coached. You have stood your vigil without complaint. You have embodied all the ideals of the Knights Deute. Your fellow Knights have witnessed your deeds and have elected you to join our august body."

I trembled. "Thank you, sir."

"The Knights Deute have always guarded the realms of men from the monsters that seek to overwhelm us. And it is time for you to take up this task. No longer are you a squire. From this day forward, you are a knight-errant, worthy to join us at the completion of your Quest."

A squire approached, holding a massive, silvered greatsword cradled in his arms, the sheath made of finely worked leather glittering with gold. King Edward grasped the hilt and drew the gleaming blade. The Sword of General Sekar himself, forged at the High King's command in the days of antiquity.

The King grasped it, his hard eyes falling on me. He raised the blade, his jaw throbbing. I faced him as he moved the heavy blade towards my neck. With a single swing, he could decapitate me. Why had I thought that? The king would never hurt me.

The king hesitated, his eyes boring into mine. I tried not to flinch from his gaze, but there was something burning in his dark eyes. My heart beat faster. Had I offended his Majesty? Would he swing the sword and take off my head?

I licked my lips, glancing at the Lord-Commander who had a puzzled look on his face.

"Your Majesty," Lady Delilah spoke. "Remember."

"Yes," the King said. "My apologies." His face relaxed, and he set the blade upon my left shoulder and then lifted it over my head and tapped my right shoulder. "I proclaim you to be Sir Angela, Knight-Errant of Deute."

A tear trickled down my cheek. I was one step away from being a full knight.

"Rise, Knight-Errant," the Lord-Commander ordered, "and seek your Quest. Let your deeds blaze across history as you defend the realms of men."

"Yes, sir," I smiled, my heart beating with excitement.

The king turned and stalked away, pushing the sword into the arms of the surprised squire. Lady Delilah moved up beside me.

"Have I given his majesty offense?" I whispered.

"The travails of state weigh heavy on him," Lady Delilah purred and my heart beat faster. I loved Kevin, but I could never quite shake my girlish crush on this stunning woman. "Come. I shall escort you to the temple."

"Thank you," I smiled. "I'm sure my mother will be happy to know you are still looking out for me."

Lady Delilah inclined her head.

We strode in silence, our boots ringing on the stones. We passed other knights and squires, all who nodded their head. Kevin waited at the drawbridge, leaning against the heavy chain that connected the bridge to the massive windlass concealed in the fortifications. I smiled at him, inclining my head.

He inclined his back and mouthed, "I love you."

We stepped into the streets of Shesax. The Lone Mountain thrust up behind us, towering like a sentinel protecting the capital. The city was laid out before us, reaching down to the blue Melkith River snaking through the poorer sections of town in the valley. Stone bridges crisscrossed the river and a mighty jetty thrust into the broad waters docked with the small river craft that plied trade to and from the city and the sea.

All those we passed bowed to us as we walked through the

curving streets to the Temple of the Pure. It was built of white marble, the entrance flanked by columns carved into the Goddess Saphique's nude likeness. A pair of robed acolytes stood out front, guarding the entrance from any man, though what man would dare offend the goddess by trespassing?

"Lady Knights," the acolytes bowed as we passed into the heady corridors.

Incense filled the halls. Nubile women passed, thinly garbed, piercings adorning their flesh and catching the eye. A hungry smile crossed Lady Delilah's lips as her gaze flicked from the budding flesh of a novice to the heaving bosom of a priestess.

I had never been in the temple, but Lady Delilah knew the way to the sanctum. My heart beat faster. What quest would I receive? There were always monsters prowling remote mountains and dark forests. From across the realms of men, the three orders of Knights sent forth their champions to fight and protect.

We stepped into the sanctum. In the center lay a young, naked woman, about my age in her early twenties. She had green eyes and light-brown hair. She trembled, her small breasts jiggling. She licked her lips and gazed upon me.

My acolyte. She looked soft and pampered.

Seven other acolytes knelt around the room beneath tapestries depicting scenes of lesbian sex. My cheeks reddened. I had enjoyed women, my first crush was even with a woman, but I had rarely indulged in the acts displayed on the tapestries.

"I am Knight-Errant Angela of Deute, here to receive my Quest and the Blessing of the Virgin Goddess," I announced, my voice echoing through the halls.

At the far end, beneath the marble statue of Saphique, set a locked strongbox made of iron. The Quests were inside. One would be chosen by the goddess at random. I trembled, my heart beating faster.

My destiny and glory lay in that chest.

Beside the chest stood the High Virgin. She was a beautiful woman, her eyes far older than her youthful flesh. She radiated power as she stepped forward, her naked and pierced tits jiggling, a welcoming smile growing on her face.

"Welcome, Knight-Errant. The Priestesses of Saphique are honored to renew our ancient friendship with the Knights Deute. All who are women shall find Saphique's Blessing."

With Lady Delilah's help, I disrobed my armor. The acolytes around the room all reached between their thighs and rubbed at their pussies. My sex clenched as my arousal grew. Joining the incense was the hot musk of wet pussy.

"You shall do fine," whispered Lady Delilah as her gentle fingers worked at the straps. My breastplate fell away, exposing my breasts and hard nipples. Her finger circled my areola, sending a hot shudder through me. "Your blood will see to it."

"My blood," I whispered.

Lady Delilah nodded. She went to work on my pauldrons, removing the shoulder protections. Around us, the acolytes sighed and moaned, their fingers rubbing at their wet slits. They were all shaved bare, gold piercings glinting on their smooth bellies.

"You have the blood of kings in you."

"You mean a king's daughter," I answered. I knew my lineage. My mother was proud to be a descendant of the High King through his daughter Lily. Lady Delilah removed my bracers from my forearms.

"A king's daughter has the blood of kings." Lady Delilah undid my sword belt from which my metal loincloth hung. She cradled my weapon with care as she set it down.

I took in a deep breath. "I guess so. Either way, I will complete my Quest and win glory for our Order."

"Yes, you will," breathed Lady Delilah. She knelt before me and undid the straps on my greaves, pulling off the metal plating. Last, she pulled off my thigh-high boots. I stood naked, all eyes upon me, even the seven masturbating women. Lady Delilah rose and stepped back.

"I am a woman," I declared. "I stand naked as proof of my sex before the eyes of the Virgin Goddess." A trickle of juices ran down my thighs.

The High Virgin nodded then motioned to the acolyte lying in the middle of the sanctum. "Then mount Acolyte Sophia."

I stepped forward and straddled Acolyte Sophia. I knelt, lowering my pussy to her lips. Her hands reached up, wrapping around my thighs and pulling me down to her mouth while her green eyes stared into mine.

I shuddered as her tongue slid through the hot folds of my pussy, her tongue stud hard and teasing. I moaned. I had never felt such wonderful pussy licking. Her tongue piercing was a hard ball pressing against the soft folds of my pussy, stirring up the pleasure inside me. Around us, the seven masturbating acolytes moved forward. They knelt in a circle around us, presenting their asses as they bent over. Their fingers were buried in their pussies as they worked their digits in their cunts.

I shuddered, my eyes sweeping around. Each one had a different ass, one was even dusky like a Hazian. Their asscheeks clenched as they worked their fingers in and out of their sweet tunnels. Juices glistened, dripping down their thighs. Their mixed scents washed over me, joining the excitement churned by Sophia's tongue.

"Yes," I sighed, swaying atop her. My hands found my breasts, pinching my nipples.

The fingers churning pussies worked faster with a frantic need to cum. The acolytes all sighed and moaned, gasping as their pleasures built. A symphony of wet fingers churning hot cunt and feminine moans of lust serenaded the goddess. Their gorgeous asses shook and writhed. I groaned, biting my lip as my pleasure grew. Sophia devoured my pussy. Her tongue touched me everywhere, licking and tasting.

Kevin's pussy licking this morning had been amazing, but I was astonished by Sophia's skill. She seemed to know where to lick me and touch me to send the most pleasure shuddering through me. My juices poured out of me. I groaned and swayed.

My orgasm crashed through me.

"Yes, yes! Eat me!" I hissed as I writhed upon Sophia's mouth.

The acolyte kept devouring me. She worked her tongue through the depths of my pussy. She stirred me up. I was shuddering in delight. Pleasures exploded through me, crashing and bursting. Rapture and bliss flooded every inch of my body.

"Saphique!" the High Virgin intoned, moving closer. "Holy Virgin! The Realms of Men are threatened. Gird our champion with your favor! Anoint her with your beauty and passion!"

I groaned again. The air came alive. The acolytes around me all gasped and shuddered. "Holy Virgin!" screamed one as she ripped her hands from her pussy. Her twat clenched and then her juices squirted out, splashing upon my stomach and hip, dribbling down upon the acolyte devouring my cunt.

"Anoint her with your protection and love!" Vivian groaned.

Two more acolytes climaxed, gasping and shuddering, their pussies squirting their juices. Pussy cream splashed upon my breasts, the heady scent trickling up to my nose. I savored the heady scent. I swayed back and forth.

"Anoint her with your purity!"

The remaining four acolytes all climaxed. Juices splashed on my ass, hot and silky. More anointed my breasts and sides. I was drenched in the dew of women. My orgasms burned hot through me. My own juices flooded Sophia's hungry mouth.

The High Virgin stood before me. She grabbed my black hair, pulling my face to her pussy. I shuddered in delight as my tongue licked through her spicy folds, her labia ring and clit piercing hard on my lips.

"Anoint her and give her a Quest!" screamed Vivian as her own orgasm triggered through her body, her juices squirting out of her pussy to splash across my face, drenching me.

I trembled, juices dripping from my flesh and energy crackling through my body. Iron groaned and snapped. High Virgin Vivian stood back as the strongbox burst open and a single square of yellowed parchment rose and tumbled through the air, carried by unseen hands. The High Virgin snatched the paper from the air and unfolded it with delicate care.

I trembled, the pleasures of my orgasms forgotten as I awaited to learn my fate. What Quest would I undertake?

"Knight-Errant Angela of Deute, you are charged on a Quest to slay the dragon Dominari prowling the Despair Mountains. May Saphique watch over you on your journey."

My stomach lurched. No Knight-Errant had ever returned from Dominari's desolation.

Chapter Nine: The Hopeless Quest

Acolyte Sophia

I trembled, unable to believe my ears. I had hoped and prayed throughout eating Knight-Errant Angela's pussy that her quest would be easy. Though I loved pleasuring her, and gave her all my skill, my insides twisted as I waited to hear what horrible Quest she received that would drag me away from the temple for weeks or even months.

"Let it be easy, Saphique," I had prayed into Angela's pussy. "And I'll be the most faithful priestess ever. I'll worship you so fervently between the thighs of every woman. Please, please, please, sweet Goddess."

And then the pronouncement– to slay the dragon Dominari. I groaned. That didn't sound easy at all.

"I...I will accept this Quest as a Knight Deute," Angela declared, her voice quavering. "I shall depart on the morn and not return until I have vanquished the foul dragon Dominari even if it costs me my very life."

I groaned again. Why did she have to say that? I thought Knight Quests were supposed to be easy. How often did they fail? They were trained warriors. They knew how to fight all manner of foul monsters that prowled the world. Could I die?

My heart sank.

Knight Angela rose, her naked body anointed with the pussy cream of my fellow acolytes. She turned and strode over to the other female knight. My breath caught– while both knights were redhead, the older knight was a stunning beauty. Her presence captivated my attention. She radiated power and sensuality. My mouth salivated. I would worship gladly between her thighs.

"Lady Delilah," the Knight Angela said to the older knight.

"You will succeed and win such glory for our order," Lady Delilah purred, stroking Angela's face.

I stood up with my other acolytes, the ritual completed. I trembled as I joined them in snuffing out all the candles adorning the shrine. My eyes kept falling on the two knights as they held their whispered conversation.

The beautiful knight was confident. Lady Delilah. What a lovely name. It so matched her beauty. My heart thudded in my chest and my cheeks blushed. I felt the familiar stirrings of a crush. I hadn't had a girlish crush in years.

"I take it back," Maria whispered as she stood beside me. The acolyte's mouth twisted into a vicious smile. "You are perfect for this Quest. I'm glad I wasn't chosen."

"What?" I asked, frowning at her.

Maria shrugged and strode off, disappearing out of the sanctuary. She was just messing with me. Maria was supposed to get the next quest, and she was jealous that I was awarded this honor. But I bit my lip, my stomach tightening. Was this a dangerous quest? Dragons were rare and deadly, but Knights killed them all the time.

Sir Reginald slew the dragon Wrasitharia when it ravaged Thlin centuries ago. He had ridden out and driven a lance right through the beast's green belly and slew it. A tremble went through me. But the dragon had breathed her green fire and roasted Sir Reginald the moment his lance impacted her chest.

The knight had won, but so had the dragon.

"Damn her," I muttered as I walked out of the sanctuary, hating the fear Maria implanted. "Just because one old knight died means nothing. Angela's probably a better warrior. She's trained."

But the terror followed me all the way to my quarters. Images of huge, scaly beasts with wings that spanned across rivers assaulted my mind. Sharp teeth wreathed in flames and slashing tails scything through the air. Dragons could burn towns to cinders in only an hour. They could feast on entire herds of cattle for lunch.

And they loved virgins.

I threw myself on my bed and clutched my pillow, trembling in fear. I could always quit the priesthood. But...what would there be for me. Mother would disown me. She had plans for me. I was to be a High Virgin one day. She had little use for another child back home. I was dedicated to the Virgin Goddess, useless to marry off for alliances. Even if I could stomach the possibility of being with a man, none would ever want to lie with me and risk Saphique's wrath.

I had no choice. I had to hope this Angela was the best Knight Deute that had ever lived.

~ * ~

Knight-Errant Angela

"You will succeed and win such glory for our order," Lady Delilah purred as she stroked my face.

"Will I?" I whispered, my body trembling.

The Dragon Dominari. How many knights from the three orders had accepted the Quest to kill her? For three hundred years she had haunted the Despair Mountains. They said the land for fifty miles before the mountains was a burned, wasted land. What once had been prosperous farms and tidy villages was now a desolation where none dare tread for fear of the dragon's rapacious hunger.

What chance did I have? Maybe I should retire from the

Knights. I could return to my father's estates and marry some baron's son. I didn't have to do this. I didn't have to die for duty.

"You will succeed, Angela," Lady Delilah whispered, her hand moving down my body, running through the sticky beads of pussy juices that anointed my flesh.

My every inhalation was filled with the mixed scent of hot pussy. My red hair was matted with their cream. The Goddess's blessing tingled across my skin. Saphique was with me, but she was a Goddess of Maidens, not a Goddess that knew how to fight.

How good was her blessing?

"You will be magnificent," Lady Delilah continued, her finger reaching my nipple. She stroked it. "The moment I saw you, gangly with youth and blushing the way only a maid of thirteen could, I knew you would have a spectacular destiny before you."

I shuddered beneath the force of her words. "I do not feel equal to this task."

"Why should you? You have never been tested. You have never been put into the fires and tempered. Until you face adversity, only then will you know what your strength is. Accept the quest and win your glory. Accomplish what none has in a thousand years. You are a Knight-Errant. You have embraced the possibility of death. Do not balk at the obstacle before you. Accept the challenge, rise to meet it, and discover your true strength."

Lady Delilah's green eyes swallowed me. I was lost in their depths. Her words rang through my soul. They strengthened my spine. I was a Knight-Errant. This was what I had always wanted. I nodded my head. "Thank you, my Lady."

Her smile grew, and she planted a single kiss on my lips. It burned hot through me. I let it wash over me. I trembled as it whipped through me. I held onto the pleasure of this moment. I clung to her and treasured her kiss. Lady Delilah believed in me. I would accomplish this task.

I would vanquish the dragon.

Lady Delilah had a satisfied gleam in her eye as she nodded at me. "You are ready for this challenge."

"I am," I said. But my insides still roiled. I ignored my fear and stood there as Lady Delilah assisted me in donning my armor. When the last strap had been tightened, and I was once again clad in steel, I strode out of the temple, Lady Delilah marching at my heel.

But I would need more than conviction. I would need a warrior's blessing tonight to strengthen my flesh and harden my bones.

The acolytes and novices crowded the hallways as we marched out of the temple. Their youthful faces shone with awe and girlish delight. They clapped and cheered for me. I drank in their praise and adoration. It was my duty to protect all the humans of the shattered High Kingdom from the darkness that always sought to stain our lands. Though I was of the Kingdom of Secare, I would protect the Magery of Thosi and the Princedoms of Zeutch. I would defend the Kingdoms of Haz, Thlin, Valya, and Athlos.

I stepped out of the temple into the setting twilight, marching with my back straight. There would be no stopping me. I would slay this dragon. I had no idea how. It would take more than my simple sword.

Kevin smiled when I swept out of the temple. As a man, he could not enter Saphique's domain. My lover's handsome face heartened me. He pushed back his flowing, dark-brown locks off his shoulders and marched towards me in his full plate. Unlike my armor, his covered his entire body. Mine showed off my flesh, my upper thighs and hips, my flat stomach, and my impressive cleavage.

"Angela," he grinned, inhaling boldly. "Don't you smell delicious?"

"All those virgin pussies I was anointed with," I grinned.

"What a pity they dedicated themselves to Saphique," he lamented. His hazel eyes danced with excitement and a question hovered on his lips. "All their sweet delights denied half the world, though we would worship them with such fervor."

"Yes, such a cruel jape has been played on your sex," I laughed, my fear dwindling. I put my arm around Kevin's waist, leaning against him. I took a deep breath. Kevin had been the pillar that had supported me through the worst of my training. "I have to kill the dragon Dominari."

The color vanished from his cheeks. "What? Are you playing some cruel jape?"

"No," I said. "That was the Quest drawn. I will have to find a way to defeat her."

"Pater's cock, but you're dead."

I flinched. This was not the support I was looking for. "I...I will defeat her. I will return to you."

"You actually plan on accepting the Quest?"

"Of course I do," I frowned. "I'm a Knight Deute. Like you. Why would I refuse?"

"Because you'll die," he choked, his face twisted. "Be reasonable, Angela."

"I am. You did not flinch from your Quest."

"It was to slay a fucking ogre, not a Las-damned dragon."

"And would you have quit being a knight if you had drawn this Quest?" Fire burned in my voice. I broke away from him.

"No. But I'm..." He swallowed.

"Because you're a man? And I'm just, what? A weak woman?"

"I didn't mean that."

"You implied it!" I grit my teeth.

"I love you. I don't want to lose you, Angela." He reached out and seized my hand. "I want you for my wife. Quit the knights and I will marry you this evening. You don't have to risk your life, ever. Not when I can protect you."

He seized my hand and knelt. I ripped away from him. "Am I now a weak maid that needs your protection, Kevin? No! I am a Knight-Errant. I will do my duty. I will not be a coward and slink away into your arms."

"Angela, you'll die."

"Then I'll die doing my duty!" My voice was shrill. "I thought you understood, Kevin?"

"Please, Angela. I love you. I don't want to lose you."

"If you really loved me, then you would understand why I must do this."

His face hardened. "Fine. Be a stubborn bitch. Go and die. Throw your life away on this foolishness."

"Foolishness? Protecting the realms of men is foolishness?"

"Gods, you have really bought in to all that bullshit. We're not noble knights. We're not the guardians of the realms of men. We're just warriors. The best warriors. That's all. Nothing we do out in the field is noble or glorious. Trust me. When you get in a real fight and you spill your enemy's guts upon the ground, you'll realize how all the pretty words we speak are empty and meaningless. So don't throw your life away for it."

"How did you ever become a knight?" I spat before I turned and stalked off.

"Angela!" he called after me, but he did not follow. My fist clenched and tears burned my eyes.

~ * ~

King Edward IV

"She accepted the quest," a woman said.

I jumped as I sat upon my chair, almost knocking off the papers before me. Being king involved so much paperwork. It never seemed to end. There were always some new proposal from some pissant baron or self-important mayor, and each of my ministers seemed to have nothing better to do than write me the most tedious reports about the minutia of governing the realm.

Stepping through the open doors that led out to the balcony was Lady Delilah, looking ravishing in her armor. The moonlight streamed in behind her, and her red hair seemed to shimmer as it brushed her gleaming pauldrons.

"How do you do that?" I demanded. "It's three stories up with no handholds."

"If I told you my secrets, your Majesty, then I wouldn't be

intriguing," she smiled.

My blood boiled. I so wanted this woman. But she always rejected my advances. My pregnant queen stirred on our bed, the sheets falling away to reveal her naked breasts and round stomach. The pair exchanged smiles.

It galled me that my queen had known Lady Delilah and I had not.

"So that dried-up cunt gave her the right quest?" I demanded.

"The High Virgin performed just as you bribed her." Lady Delilah sat on my bed, her hand idly playing with my wife's nipple. "I did have to speak with a great deal of persuasion to convince Angela to accept the quest. The poor thing was a quivering mess. The fear seemed to just bleed off of her. She has heard the stories. She understands this is a death sentence."

I grinned. "Excellent."

"Thank you," my wife purred, rubbing her belly. My son grew in there. My heir. He would follow me on the throne. I wouldn't let Angela kill me and usurp his heritage, even if that cunt was the heir to the High King and destined to restore his empire.

The High Kingdom would remain shattered.

"I live to serve the realm," Lady Delilah purred. "Tomorrow, she will depart. It may be some time before she faces the dragon. I'm sure she will struggle hard to kill Dominari, but she will fail like they all have."

"Good," I nodded. "You are close to the girl?"

"She thinks we're close." Lady Delilah's voice was pure sex purring around the room. I throbbed to take her.

I clenched my hand, fighting the desire to seize her. It had not gone well for me last time. I do not know why I let the woman bare steel against me and live. She was just...the Lady Delilah.

"You will need to keep tabs on her," Lady Delilah said, producing a broach from a pouch. It was golden and studded with garnets. It flashed through the air as she tossed it to me. I snatched it, staring down at the brooch. "I will give her a matching broach. A token of my esteem."

I stroked the garnets. "You've had a mage enchant it?"

"I have. It will let you keep informed of her progress."

"Wise," I said, inclining my head to Lady Delilah.

A pleased smile crossed her lips before she rose. "I must depart."

"Must you?" my wife moaned, seizing the knight's hand.

"I have tasks to attend to, Queen Lavinia, else I would stay and enjoy the succulent bounty of your ripe flesh."

My wife shuddered. "Then go and be about your tasks."

"Your Majesty." Lady Delilah kissed the back of my wife's hand, and then turned to me, inclining her head. "Your Majesty, with your leave, I shall withdraw."

I wanted to command her to stay and let me enjoy her body. My wife and I could share her, but those green eyes pinned me to my chair. I did not have the strength to rise and refuse her request.

"You may withdraw," I choked out. Why did this one woman have so much power over me?

Lady Delilah walked out onto the balcony. I managed to stand, rushing after her. I wanted to learn her secret. The air whooshed, and a breeze washed through the room. I reached the doors and peered out at the balcony. But she was gone. I rushed to the edge, peering down at the gardens below.

No sign of her remained.

"Come to bed, my husband," purred my wife. "I can feel your frustration. Let me satiate you."

I turned from the balcony. My wife writhed on the bed, her hands rubbing between her thighs. Her excitement brushed my nose, a tart musk. "You mean, you want me to satiate your frustrated desires, dear wife?"

"She left us both in need."

My wife was a royal beauty, a Zeutchian princess. Her blonde hair spilled across the bed, her breasts large and round, brimming with fertile delights. It was often joked that princesses were the most important export of Zeutch. The nation was fractured into a loose alliance of princedoms. While each ruling prince had royal blood and proud lineages, they possessed little power. It was safe to take a bride from among their daughters without fear of hidden strings.

I pulled off my doublet, my cock straining my tight hose. My muscles rippled as I moved to my wife. She was such a radiant flower. Not the most beautiful woman in the palace, but she had a queenly bearing.

She rolled onto her hands and knees, presenting that gorgeous ass and the shaved lips of her pussy.

Chapter Ten: The War God's Blessing

Knight-Errant Angela

My anger only grew hotter with every step. I cursed beneath my breath at Kevin. How had I misunderstood his regard? I thought he understood me. He should have understood me. The Knights Deute had always accepted women as equals in their ranks in both skill and knowledge. So why did he think I was too weak to face this task?

How could I be with a man who thought so little of my abilities?

So many times I thought of marrying him, of the pair of us questing together as we performed our duties. But that's not what he wanted. He wanted me to stay at home while he gallivanted about the lands. That was not the life I wanted.

If I wanted to be a wife and mother, I would never have left home.

My armor clinked with every step. I stalked past the temples to the other gods. The grand temple to Slata, the impressive temple to Pater. The whores of Biaute lounged before their temple, displaying their perfect beauty. The temple of Firmare displayed the Goddess's fruitful bounty, while Luben's temple stood steadfast and eternal as a couple walked out, just married and beaming with their love. I stopped at Gewin's temple. Strong walls reared above me, carved from austere, gray granite. It was almost a fortress. The warrior-priests stood guard, swords belted at their sides over robes of red.

I marched forward, my boots ringing on the steps. "Who approaches the Temple of the Knight's Duty?" a priest challenged in a booming voice.

"Knight-Errant Angela," I answered, stopping before them. "I seek the Blessing of Battle to strengthen me on my perilous quest."

"And what Quest do you undertake, Knight-Errant?"

"I must slay the Dragon Dominari." My insides knotted with fear. Was Kevin right? Was I throwing my life away over the foolish words of our order?

No. Lady Delilah was right. I had the strength to rise to this challenge. I would slay the dragon.

"Great peril awaits you," the priest said. "The noble God Gewin will aid you, as he aides all warriors who seek the toughest foes. Enter. How many priests shall attend your blessing?"

I took a deep breath. I would need as many blessings as possible. "Nine."

"A bold number, even for a woman," the priest said. "But you will need such strength. Know that the ritual fails if you succumb before you have finished with all nine."

"I will succeed," I said, forcing down the wave of heat through me and the itch swelling in my pussy. I would have to be disciplined to achieve their blessing.

The doors opened. I strode into the temple.

~ * ~

Xerathalasia – Deorc Forest

I stood still as tall and willowy Quenyathalee painted my naked body with browns, greens, and blacks, forming a swirling pattern of camouflage. My other huntresses had already painted their bodies, their quivers slung on their belts, their bows gripped in their hands. I had hunted with all of them many times, save for young Xiloniasa. She trembled, her body petite with her youth.

"It will be fine, Xiloniasa," I told her as Quenyathalee painted the patterns across my round breasts.

The elf-maid nodded her head. "I will do my duty," she said, her voice high with fear.

Fear was to be expected. A basilisk was a fearsome beast to hunt. Their gaze could petrify any who glimpsed the beast's red eyes. And even if you avoid that fate, their bite was venomous, slowly consuming your flesh.

"Xerathalasia has never failed in her hunt," Deliasonele praised. "She has never lost a hunter. So relax, Xiloniasa. When we return, every elf-maiden will burn to be your lover. They will throw themselves at you, each begging to be taken as your wife."

Xiloniasa grinned. "Really?"

"Hunters get all the best pussy," Relythionaia laughed, her green braid swinging back and forth as she tossed her head. "I remember how hot they were for me after my first hunt. I was in heat, my cock throbbing hard. They all begged for me to fuck their pussies and marry them, but I only enjoyed their asses. I wasn't about to be tied down in marriage. Not when there were so many vixens throwing themselves at me."

I shuddered and remembered how my blood pumped hot with lust after my first hunt. I had been a maid like Xiloniasa and drunk on the success. All the nubile elves were throwing themselves at me, but it was my future wife, Atharilesia, that had claimed me. She had taken me back to her bower and devoured my pussy over and over.

"You're getting excited," giggled Quenyathalee. "Pity we don't have time to fool around."

"A pity duty has to come first," I rebuked as she finished with my body paint. I grabbed my belt woven of willow bark and strapped it about my waist, my quiver hanging off my right hip bristling with arrows I had personally made. I grabbed my bow and looked at my huntresses. "Another beast has wandered out of the dark. Let us remind the monsters why they do not walk through our forest."

The elves all nodded, their pointed ears twitching. They were all eager for the hunt. Nothing was more thrilling. We slipped out of the hollow of the old willow tree and padded like ghosts through the trees of Khalesithan and out into what the humans called the Deorc Forest. To us elves, it was merely our home.

~ * ~

Knight-Errant Angela

I followed the red-robed priest into the temple. It was austere, the stones of the walls, floors, and ceiling rough and undressed like a border fort. There were murder holes in the ceilings wherever hallways met, allowing defenders to pour boiling oil or burning pitch down on invaders.

Other priests and priestesses passed, each dressed in their red robes. The ones with knives were their novices, just learning all the techniques of battle. The priests wore short swords, and the master of this temple would wield a long sword. I fought my desires. I would need to master them.

I had to fuck nine men without cumming. It would be a chore. But I if I could, I would win Gewin's blessing. Nine priests would give me the strength and fortitude to meet this quest. It would be a start.

I was led to an austere cell, the floor hard stone. No furnishings adorned it. "Undress and await," the priest said. "We shall find you our most fit warriors for you to test your discipline against."

I nodded and began stripping off my armor. Sexual energy was a potent force, and priests could work powerful rituals with it. Even the mages of Thosi used sexual fluids to power the elemental magics they wrought.

Naked, I knelt and waited. I ignored the discomfort of the

stone beneath my legs and the growing itch in my pussy. I had been with two men before. I couldn't help but be excited at the prospect of nine strapping, powerful men ravishing my body at once.

And I couldn't cum. I needed to keep my discipline. I was a Knight.

The minutes seemed to tick by. I counted my heartbeats to keep track of the time. A bead of sweat trickled between my breasts. I fought the urge to wipe the ticklish drop away. I needed my discipline. I needed to ignore the needs of my body.

The door opened. A powerful man entered, his muscular body filling out his red robe. He had a fierce beard of black, a longsword dangling from his waist. He was the master of this temple. His arms folded before him, adorned with scars. He was a hard man, a veteran of many battles. Behind him, eight other priests entered, each strapping and muscular. Their arms were thick and scars adorned their flesh.

My pussy clenched at the sight of them as they disrobed. Their cocks were hard and their muscles gleamed with oil. Their skin ranged from pale Secaran to dusky Hazian. I licked my lips, juices trickling out of my sex.

"A powerful warrior kneels before me," the master declared as he too disrobed, his cock jutting hard before him. "She seeks to test herself against nine. Pride and desperation beat in her breast. The hunger for victory drives her. She beats with Gewin's own heart! Let our God savor her prowess. Let him bless her discipline!"

The master seized my red hair and slammed his cock hard into my mouth.

Chapter Eleven: The Knight's Gangbang

Knight-Errant Angela

The ritual began as the master's cock buried into my mouth. A powerful thrust. A warrior's thrust.

His balls slapped at my chin. I groaned, sucking hard. He took me, dominating me. It was so intoxicating. My tongue swirled around his cock. He tasted of salt and masculine musk. I inhaled his scent. I shuddered; his cock slammed deeper and deeper into my mouth.

Other hands seized my hips, lifting me. I groaned as another hard cock prodded my thighs. My pussy clenched as he grew nearer and nearer. I was so hot and wet. How could I resist cumming? I was already eager to erupt. Why didn't I masturbate while I waited?

How could I have been so stupid?

A cock slammed into my pussy. I groaned around the master's dick. The shaft in my sheath was thick, spreading me open. Pleasure shuddered through me. I bucked my hips into his thrusts as I struggled to maintain my discipline. I clenched and relaxed my pussy. I needed to make him cum as fast as possible before I succumbed.

"What a woman!" growled the man fucking my pussy. "Work

that cunt! You are so wet! She will never make it! She's a whore!"

The master chuckled. "The way she sucks my cock. She's eager for my cum. Mmm, that's it. You're just a slut, not a warrior."

Anger burned in me. They were like Kevin. I would show them.

My hands found the Master's balls. I massaged them. I wanted his cum fast. His hands tightened in my hair. He fucked me harder, his balls slamming against my chin as his cock buried down my throat with every thrust.

I wouldn't cum. I would beat these men.

"That's it, slut! Work that pussy! Oh, damn! What a hot sheath! I don't think she's a fighter. I think she's a fucker. She should be one of Slata or Biaute's whores, spreading her legs for every man that wants her. Damn, she's boiling."

My pussy tightened. I wanted to cum so badly. But I wouldn't. I sucked at the Master's cock and massaged the dick in my pussy. I clamped my sheath down hard, twirling my hips. The dick fucking my pussy slammed deeper and deeper into me.

"Fuck! What a whore!" said the priest fucking my cunt. His hands tightened on my hips.

"Do not let her win!" groaned the Master. "Make the whore cum!"

"Damn it!" The cock in my pussy erupted. That wonderful flood of hot cum poured into me. My pussy rejoiced. I groaned, fighting against my rising orgasm. The pleasure burned through me. My flesh begged for its release.

But I was stronger.

"I failed, my brothers," the man groaned, his cock pulling out of my cunt. His cum dripped out of me, trickling down my thighs.

I could do this.

I massaged harder at the Master's balls. I wanted his cum pumping down my throat. I wanted to devour every drop of his cum. His cock swelled and throbbed in my mouth. His thrusts grew harder, his balls slapping hard into my chin. I felt like such a whore. It was such a turn on despite how degrading it was.

"Drink my cum, whore!" the Master groaned as his cock

erupted salty jizz into my mouth. I groaned, swirling it through my lips and drinking it all down. Another rush of pleasure washed through my body, ending at my pussy.

Let me cum, my hot cunt begged.

"No," I groaned.

"Take the whore! Ravish her!" commanded the Master. "Make her explode with pleasure!"

"You'll be the only one exploding," I laughed. "Come on! Fuck me! Dump your cum in my body! But I won't orgasm. Your cocks aren't good enough for me!"

The Master grinned at me through his bushy, black beard. "What a woman!"

Two more men grabbed me, one with dusky skin and a bald head. He pulled me down on to his body, my tits rubbing across his chiseled chest. "Come ride me, whore! Show me how you work those gorgeous hips." He smacked my ass, the sting shooting to my pussy.

"I'll give you a ride you'll never forget."

"Gewin's cock, but you're a feisty bitch!" he chuckled as I straddled him. "Come on. Ride me! Let me feel that tight cunny cum on my cock."

I laughed. "This little thing?" I wiggled his cock as I guided it to my pussy. "I'm not sure I'll even feel it."

"Oh, you'll feel it." He seized my hips and pulled me down on his cock.

I groaned as he filled me. I leaned back, my breasts bouncing as I savored his cock. The other man pressed up behind me, his dick rubbing on the soft pillows of my ass. He felt wet, lubed with oil. My asscheeks clenched.

"Stick it in," I hissed at him over my shoulder. "I'll make you both cum without breaking a sweat!"

The second man wrapped his arms around my body, gripping both my large breasts. My nipples ached as he pinched them while his cock nudged between my butt-cheeks, only grazing my sphincter and sending shuddering thrills through me.

88

"You can't even find my hole," I laughed. I reached behind me and grasped him, guiding him to my hole. "It's right there."

"Thanks, whore!" he groaned as he buried into me, pushing me down onto the dusky-skinned man's cock. I groaned as my ass clenched down on their hard shafts. They throbbed between my cheeks. I shuddered in delight, milking him.

The other priests jerked their cocks hard. Cum spurted, splashing on my naked tits or on my face. But I hadn't touched their shafts. I hadn't pleased them with my body. I saw the looks in their eyes. They wanted to last longer. They were getting their excitement out of the way. Their hot cum dribbled down my body as I writhed between the two men.

"Look at the whore! She loves it!" laughed a young priest with blond hair and a gorgeous smile.

I rubbed at my naked tits, smearing the cum into my flesh. "Give me more, boys. I want a challenge. I want Gewin to see how disciplined I am!"

"She's a cum slut!" grunted a hairy man with rust-red hair. His cock was thick and throbbing. He jerked it fast just inches from my face. I tried to lean forward and capture his tip as it throbbed purple. If I could reach him and finish him with my mouth, he'd be vanquished.

He stepped back. "Cunning slut!" he groaned and then his cock erupted. Hot jizz burned across my face. I opened my mouth, swallowing the salty treat. My pussy convulsed. I moaned, my body giving in to the lust.

The man fucking my ass sped up his strokes. "She's getting close to cumming. Our sticks are vanquishing her slutty body!"

I was slammed down harder and harder on the dusky man's cock. I straightened up, trying to keep my clit from brushing his pubic bone. I groaned, more cum spurting onto my body. I was dripping with the salty seed. I rubbed it into my skin as I fought my orgasm.

"I think she needs a little help!" grinned the dusky-skinned priest.

"Oh, you bastard!" I gasped as he rubbed at my clit. "Fuck, fuck, fuck."

I pumped my hips, straining against my pleasure. My body ached. My nipples throbbed. My poor clit cried out for relief. He kept rubbing the bud. The sensations shot through me. No. I would not surrender. I was a knight. I would keep my discipline.

"You will cum first!" I growled, working my hips harder. Both cocks buried into me. I shuddered, gripping them with my ass and pussy. I shifted and writhed. I fucked both men with all the passion I could muster. "I will vanquish your throbbing shafts. You can't resist the delights of my holes."

The dusky-skinned priest clenched his jaw. My pleasure began to recede as he fought against his. I moaned. I wanted this more. I would beat him. I slammed down on his cock, swallowing it to the hilt in my pussy.

"Your cock's amazing!" I growled. "My pussy loves it. You have the best cock in the room."

"You saucy siren!" he gasped and then his cock erupted into my pussy.

I savored the hot cum. I clenched down my ass, humping back onto the shaft fucking my bowels. "You're next," I winked at him. "I know you just want to unload into the velvety depths of my asshole. Just let yourself go."

"Fuck!" he snarled. "Your ass is delicious. Dammit! She's won!"

His cum spurted into my asshole. I gasped in delight. And then I clenched my teeth. My orgasm had almost rolled over me. I couldn't weaken. I had to be strong. I had five more cocks to vanquish. They had all jerked themselves to orgasm, their cum dripping from my body. They would be even harder to satisfy.

I was up for the challenge.

Chapter Twelve: A Sapphic Dream

Acolyte Sophia

Somehow, I had fallen asleep. I didn't know how it happened. I was lying in my bed, petrified with fear while images of dragons danced in my head. I knew I had to sleep, but I just couldn't find it. Tomorrow morning, I would ride to my death. I knew it. I was doomed. I had sworn to the Goddess Saphique. I had no choice but to go.

And then I had fallen into sleep. I wasn't haunted by nightmares of fire-breathing dragons roasting me like a chestnut. I didn't dream of the armored beasts landing before me and ripping into my flesh with a teeth-filled maw.

I dreamed I was on an island, sapphire water washing onto the white sands. Women frolicked naked around me. Some were making love while others made sport, splashing in the sparkling waves that lapped gently at the shore.

"The Isle of Women," I whispered. The Paradise which resided in the Astral Plane where the Virgin Goddess dwelt, a sanctuary where no man could ever tread.

"Yes," a beautiful woman whispered, shining with pink light. Saphique.

I shuddered as I gazed at my Goddess. She was petite and comely, a shy maid blushing with her virginity. Her love washed over her and she pulled me to her small breast. My lips engulfed her nipple. I suckled as she caressed my light-brown locks, her creamy milk flooding my mouth.

She tasted divine. Her breast milk was ambrosia. My toes curled as an orgasm rippled through my body. I nursed and suckled. I swallowed every drop I could. She was delicious. I never wanted to stop nursing from my Goddess's breast.

"Do not be afraid, my little acolyte," she purred. "A great wrong has been committed, so I shall aid you."

What wrong? But I couldn't pull my lips away from her nipple to ask.

"I grant you my milk. Let your breasts produce my bounty and let it aid you on your perilous quest."

My nipples burned with heat. Another orgasm rippled through my body, washing through my mind with such bliss.

"You must be strong for Angela. A great destiny is laid before her."

Her breast ran dry. I lifted my lips and stared into her dazzling eyes. "But...how do we defeat the dragon? They are such dangerous beasts."

"I know not." Her smile was soft and sad. "But where do all travel who seek knowledge to important questions?"

"I don't know."

...*Sophia*... a distant voice called. My body shook.

"Our time is over. Know that you are in my thoughts, my little acolyte." The Goddess's lips met mine. I shuddered in delight.

...*Sophia, wake up*...

The new voice drew me from my Goddess. I fought, holding on to my Goddess's slim neck. But my grip wasn't strong enough. My eyes snapped open and I gazed into Rebecca's eyes. My fellow acolyte shook her head. "Come on, Sophia. It's time for you to go."

"Right," I muttered. "But...where do all journey who seek knowledge to important questions?"

Rebecca cocked her head. "What are you talking about?"

"Something important," I said as I stood up.

"Well, get dressed." Rebecca opened my chest of drawers and pulled out my travel vestments. They were a simple, white gown that covered most of my flesh. It was the opposite of temple garb, but the outside world had weather and cold. And men. They did not deserve to see my flesh. There was a tan riding cloak that went over a simple, white robe made of wool.

I dressed as I pondered the Goddess's words. "There are stories about people who search for the answers to important questions, right?"

"Yeah," Rebecca nodded.

"Where do they go?"

"Libraries," she shrugged.

"In the stories?" I asked. "Don't they go to dangerous places? Remote places where spirits or oracles wait."

"Like the oracle the king visits?" Rebecca asked. "Only our king is allowed to see the Oracle of Sekar."

"There are other oracles," I pointed out. "We learned about them in all those boring novitiate classes. There's the Oracle of the Sands in the Halani Desert."

"That's so far away."

"Um, the Oracle of Whispers." I shuddered at that one.

"Who'd want to visit the Dead Isle?" Rebecca's face blanched. "Oh, there's the Lesbius Oracle. She only sees women and she's in the Deorc Forest."

My eyes widened. "That's exactly the oracle our Goddess would choose."

"But the elves?" Rebecca blanched. "They'll fill you full of arrows for violating their woods."

"Oh, those are just tales. Elves are..." I frowned. "Well, I'll have a knight." And my milk. Only full priestesses were given this honor. Having breast milk meant I could channel Saphique's divine magic.

Rebecca pushed a satchel into my arms. "Here. The supplies are already packed in your saddlebags, but this satchel has three Potions of Healing, an Ampoule of Holy Milk, and a dagger anointed with the High Virgin's purity. It'll glow if there's danger around."

I reached in and pulled out the dagger in its sheath. It was almost as long as my forearm. I shivered, then hung it from my belt. I almost felt like a heroine in a story being sent out with magic items.

Well, I was heading out on a quest. "Okay, let's go," I said, still trembling. But the Goddess was with me. I could face this fate.

~ * ~

Knight-Errant Angela

The cock came in my pussy.

"Let Gewin's blessing fall on this mighty warrior!" proclaimed the master.

Red light blazed around me. I shuddered in delight. I had taken on all nine cocks without cumming. I had fucked for hours and hours. The energy poured into me, washing away my exhaustion as it seeped into every muscle and bone, strengthening me.

"The Warrior God shall walk with you," proclaimed the master. "He shall guide your swings and parries. You shall vanquish your enemies and bring glory to your order, Knight-Errant Angela."

I rose, standing proud. "I shall fearlessly face the dreaded dragon. With the mighty Gewin's aid, I shall smite her and bring back her head as proof."

The warrior-priests all roared around me. All their degrading words had been lies. They didn't think I was a whore or a slut, but a warrior. They merely tried to weaken my resolve with their filthy talk. But I had maintained my discipline. I had vanquished them without cumming. I donned my armor and belted on my sword. I marched out of the temple with pride.

At the gates of the chapterhouse of my order, Lady Delilah waited holding the reins of my charger– a tall, ebony horse stallion named Midnight. He snorted when he saw me, biting at his bit. Metal barding clad him. He was a warhorse. As fierce as any who had lived.

"I have a small token of my esteem," Lady Delilah purred, holding up a garnet-encrusted broach. "I wish you to wear it into battle."

I blushed. "I would be honored." I took the broach from her hands and draped it over my neck so it dangled between my breasts. "Thank you, my Lady."

Lady Delilah nodded her head. "Your saddlebags are packed with all you need."

I nodded and then looked around. Part of me hoped Kevin appeared to apologize. My heart beat fast, but my lover did not have the courage to face me. I didn't cry as I mounted my saddle. The acolyte Sophia rode up on a white mare. She sat side-saddle with grace. She had noble blood, holding her reins with delicate hands.

"Knight," she nodded when she reigned up.

I took a deep breath. The sun was lightening the horizon. "Are you ready?"

"Not really." A faint, half-hearted smile crossed Sophia's face and her emerald eyes fell. Then she straightened. "But we must depart."

"Yes."

"Angela, do you have any idea how to kill the dragon?"

"None," I answered. She would be my companion on this journey. She deserved to know.

"Then our first stop should be the Lesbius Oracle for guidance," she declared and flicked her reins. Her mount walked with stately grace. "Let's go, Lady Knight."

I heeled Midnight and caught up to her, my armor rattling. An oracle sounded like the perfect start. Even if it was in the Deorc Forest. We would have to avoid the elves.

Compared to slaying a dragon, that had to be easy.

Chapter Thirteen: Saddled Arrogance

Acolyte Sophia – Shesax, the Kingdom of Secare

My heart beat with excitement as we crossed the Merchant's Bridge over the Melkith River that flowed through the sprawling city of Shesax. Behind us, the Lone Mountain thrust up like a rock spire to pierce the fluffy, white clouds drifting across the sun. Ahead, the sun rose, shining golden light in our eyes.

The Merchant's Bridge connected with the K'holene Highway, the great merchant road that led to the mining city of K'hol. I had ridden this very road from my mother's estates in the Tith Hills the day I came to Shesax to serve in the Temple of the Pure. Beyond K'hol, the road led to Ostian and down south to the Kingdom of Valya.

I sat sidesaddle on my white mare Purity, a gift from the Temple of the Pure. Knight-Errant Angela rode beside me on her monstrously large, black stallion Midnight. He was the meanest horse I had ever seen, his hooves stamping hard, his eyes vicious, and his neighs wild. He was a warhorse, trained to kick and bite in battle, and he was nothing like my sweet, gentle mare.

Angela sat stiffly upon her saddle, her face drawn. I knew nothing about her. We had only met last night for her Blessing, and then I was concerned mostly with eating out her pussy. And what a delicious pussy she had.

I couldn't help staring to the east where the dragon Dominari lay. We had to slay her. Well, okay, Angela had to slay her. I was just along to provide support. I did not understand why I was needed. It was some ancient tradition that Acolytes of the Goddess Saphique would journey with the female Knights Deute on their initiation Quests. It was stupid. I wanted to be back in the temple lounging with a nubile novice. I missed those two. They'd been so cute.

The city of Shesax bustled. I was surprised that so many people were awake. The sun had barely risen. Shouldn't they be asleep for hours more? I tried to never be awake so early unless I had some stupid duty to attend at the temple. There were so many of them.

"The city sure is bustling," I said, trying to start a conversation. "Is something going on?"

Angela glanced at me, her blue eyes narrowing. She had fiery-red hair that fell about the shining pauldrons of her armor. Her breasts were impressive, cupped by her half-breastplate, and her midriff, left bare, was flat and toned. She wore knee-high boots, covered in armored greaves, but her upper thighs were bare and delicious. A shield hung from her saddle and a sword from her belt.

"You do not leave the Temple much," Angela said.

"What's that supposed to mean?" I demanded.

"Most in Shesax rise before the sun, at least the common folk do. There is much to do, crafts to perform, shops to set up."

I blinked. "Oh."

Angela muttered beneath her breath.

"I didn't catch that?"

Angela just gave me a sweet, forced smile. I suspected what she muttered wasn't nice. I gave an imperious huff, lifted my chin, and tossed my light brown hair. Did this woman know who I was? How dare she insult me.

The crowds parted for us, calling out, "Good luck, sir Knight." and "May the Gods watch over you on your Quest, sir Knight." Did any of them care I was with her? I kept my head held high. I was the daughter of Duchess Catherine of Tith and an Acolyte of Saphique, the Virgin Goddess.

"Do you plan on riding sidesaddle the entire time?" Angela demanded as we neared the gates of Shesax that opened onto the farmlands that surrounded the city.

"How else would I ride?" I blinked. "I am a noble woman, not some uncouth peasant. It's hardly dignified to ride like a man."

"And what happens if you have to ride at more than a trot?"

I rolled my eyes. "Sir Angela, I rode from K'hol to Shesax sidesaddle. It will be fine. And I would prefer if you addressed me as Acolyte Sophia or my Lady. I am the daughter of a duchess."

Angela actually laughed. "Out here, you're more like my squire. My little acolyte that I'm saddled with. I have my doubts if you'll even be useful."

"I'm plenty useful," I huffed. "I know magics and have healing potions. You will be thankful of my presence. If not, I will just ride back to the temple."

Please, do not be thankful.

I held my breath as she gave me a considering look. Her blue eyes grew considerate. "No. I need you. You are my witness that I have performed my Quest and keeping you alive is part of the task. I must defend not only the realm, but your pampered ass."

I lifted my head and gave another imperious toss. Anger boiled through me. No one had ever talked to me like that. "You are rude and uncouth. How a peasant was ever allowed into the noble Knights Deute, I will not understand."

"I'm the daughter of a count," Angela answered as she heeled her horse through the gate and out of the city.

"I find that hard to believe," I muttered as Purity followed Midnight.

The peasant farmers were already out in their fields. Like the poor commoners of Shesax, they had risen far too early. Dark-brown soil, almost black, was tilled by oxen, donkey, or horses, each pulling a plow while a farmer walked beside, leading the beasts. Children followed in the wake, planting seeds in the fresh furrowed tills. In other fields, peasants pulled weeds and threw them into wheelbarrows.

"Such dirty work," I sighed.

"Most work is," Angela answered.

How did I get stranded with this unpleasant woman?

The sun rose higher and the day grew warmer. The wind blew, but it carried the foul scent of manure from the fields. I grimaced and wished I had a perfumed handkerchief, a scented pomander, or even a fresh orange to hold to my nose. Sweat gathered on my forehead. I slumped my shoulders. My poor butt was growing sorer and sorer. This was as unpleasant as the first journey.

"Why don't we take a break and enjoy a refreshment?" I asked.

Angela glanced at me. "We're only an hour from the city. It's far too early for our midday break."

"Midday? Surely we would take a break before then."

"We're on a quest, my Lady," she sneered. "Not a pleasant ride through the country. And what refreshment do you expect to have here?"

"Perhaps a sweet wine to help wash away the dust of the trail and a light repast?"

"You have a waterskin. It's plenty refreshing." Angela pulled her own skin and drank water.

I grabbed mine and frowned. I had noticed it on my saddlebag, but hadn't realized what it was for. It was a leather bladder with a wooden stopper plugging the opening. I pulled it out and put it to my lips. I frowned. No water came out. I lifted it higher.

"Give it a squeeze, my Lady."

Her tone was so insolent. I squeezed, and warm water flooded my mouth. It was not the refreshment I craved, but it was better than nothing. I lowered the waterskin and capped it. "And what are we eating for our midday meal?"

"Trail rations." Angela grinned at me. "A hardy mix of dried fruit and nuts mashed into beef and turned into jerky."

I shuddered.

The journey became quite monotonous. When I traveled with

my mother to Shesax to start my novitiate, we had singers to serenade us, servants to care for us. When we grew tired of riding, we would slip into the carriage and eat lemon cakes and sip lavender water.

I squirmed. My butt ached. My back was sore. The sun was so hot on my brow. I raised the hood of my robe to shade my eyes. I drained my waterskin before noon and my bladder began to grow full, but Angela showed no sign of stopping.

I decided I wouldn't show her any discomfort. She rode her horse like nothing was the matter, her back as straight as when we left Shesax. The profile of her face was lovely. She had to be nobly born to possess such perfect features, and that hair bespoke of foreign blood. It shimmered in the sunlight as it bounced on her armor.

"What are you looking at?" Angela demanded. "Do I have a speck of dirt on my face?"

"I...what?" I demanded.

"You were staring at my face, my Lady."

My cheeks burned. I looked ahead. "I was doing no such thing. I was watching the...um...interesting sights."

Angela looked to her left. "Right. Because a peasant mucking in the field would interest such a refined lady as yourself."

I wanted to scream. But I wouldn't.

I was grateful for our midday break. We found shade beneath a chestnut tree. Angela sat on the grass as she chewed on her trail rations. I walked around, letting my legs stretch out, and rubbed my poor, abused bottom.

Maybe Angela would kiss it better.

I glanced at her. She took a vicious bite out of her trail ration, almost ripping the poor piece of jerky in half. I glanced at my own. It was brown and beaten thin. And it was hard. I tried to take a small bite. It was salty. I grimaced, but my stomach growled. So I bit harder. I had to work to bite my teeth through the tough food. I may as well be eating leather.

I chewed on it for a whole minute. It was spiced, and there was a faint trace of nuts and fruits mixed into the meat. I swallowed and ripped off a second bite. Angela had already finished and sipped from her waterskin as she stared out at the sky. I paced as I worked the jerky in my mouth. My eyes kept sliding back to her, studying the slopes of her breasts and the sleek lines of her thighs.

I haven't cum once today. I couldn't remember the last time I had gone so long. Certainly not since I joined the Temple of the Pure. An itch flashed through my pussy. I shoved the last of my jerky into my mouth before I leaned against the tree, squeezing my thighs together.

I let out a sigh as I rubbed my clit. I was skilled at masturbation. I was trained. I could get myself off just by pressing my thighs together. I closed my eyes and let out a second sigh. I pictured Angela kneeling before me.

I am so sorry for how I treated you, my Lady, she purred, her hands reaching out to rub at my sleek thighs. *I humbly beg for your forgiveness.*

I understand. You were overwhelmed by my beauty.

A flutter of pleasure went through me. I sighed and squirmed. My palms grew damp. I gripped the hem of my white robes, wanting to lift them up so I could finger myself. But there were men around, working the fields, and I couldn't let them see my naked treasures. I was dedicated to Saphique. No man could ever know my flesh. Only the sweet touch of a woman was permitted.

My nipples ached as I imagined Angela pushing up my robe, her hands sliding up my thighs. Her breath was warm on my pussy as her teasing fingers neared closer and closer. My pleasure swelled inside me. I squeezed harder on my clit, working my thighs to massage my bud.

That's it, I whispered in my imagination. *You can apologize with that delicious tongue of yours.*

I bit my lip as my fantasy-Angela licked her tongue through my pussy. Her tongue was lithe, stirring through my folds as she moaned in delight. My fantasy savored the taste of my pussy before her lips wrapped around my clit. I shuddered again, my hips bucking.

I sucked in my breath.

Mmm, yes, Angela. Eat my pussy. Put that tongue to use. You will be my little, lesbian slave on our journey.

Yes, my Lady! I want to worship your pussy. You taste delicious.

We'll kiss and suck and love each other all the time, I moaned in my imagination. My clit throbbed. My pussy clenched. My orgasm swelled. *Whenever I have an itch, you'll be more than happy to scratch it.*

More than happy, my Lady! I love your pussy! And your sexy body! You're so beautiful. I love your small breasts and cute nipples. I love your wide eyes and gorgeous smile. And your ass is perfect, just plump enough to grab ahold of.

"You're so kind," I whispered.

"What?" the real Angela asked.

"Nothing!" I gasped as my orgasm shuddered through my body. I clenched my teeth as the pleasure burned through me. My juices flooded out, pouring down my thighs. I loved this moment. My fingers balled up my robe as I quivered.

"Are you sure? You seem in pain," Angela said as she stood.

"No, no, I'm fine," I panted, a big smile crossing my lips. "Mmm, I'm more than fine. I'm ready to get back on the trail."

Angela furrowed her eyebrows. "Did you just...?" She shook her head. "But you weren't even touching yourself."

I strode to my mare, my body buzzing with pleasure. "Come along. We need to get going." I climbed up into my saddle and all my good mood evaporated as my poor, sore bottom sat upon the hard leather.

Chapter Fourteen: Bedtime Voyeurism

Knight-Errant Angela – K'holene Highway, The Kingdom of Secare

Sophia was a pampered, spoiled, bratty, annoying, whiny, sexy woman. She aggravated me. All she did was complain. *When I traveled to Secare, I had a thousand servants to wipe my ass and blow my nose,* I imagined her whining. *So I expect the same out of you, Sir Angela.*

"I'm a fucking knight, not her wet nurse."

"Hmm?" Sophia asked. She had her hood up over her pale face. She was beautiful, with wide, green eyes and when she did smile, it lit up her face. She was petite, wrapped up in a white robe that concealed her figure instead of the diaphanous wraps she had worn in the temple that left her body nearly naked.

"Nothing," I answered.

She licked her lips, her silver tongue piercing flashing. That piecing had felt amazing when she ate my pussy last night. A hot flush went through me. I was mostly used to riding on horseback, but sometimes the rub of the leather saddle on my flesh was exciting. My clit tingled and my pussy grew moist. The moans of all the acolytes echoed in my mind as they masturbated around me, their pussies clenching and squirting their juices on me.

My thoughts drifted away from them to Kevin. His naked, sculpted form appeared, covered in muscles, his cock thrusting thick and hard before him. My pussy clenched, aching to be filled by him. He always knew how to love me.

My heart clenched. Pain filled me. How could he doubt my commitment to the Knights Deute? He had called the order's duty bullshit. He wanted me to quit and become his wife just so I wouldn't face death. I had misjudged him. I thought he understood me. That he respected me. He should have been proud that I was committed to perform a Quest no knight of the three orders had completed successfully.

Tears burned at my eyes. I forced down my pain. I had to be strong. I couldn't lament over my boyfriend's insults. And I most certainly couldn't break down and cry before Sophia. I wouldn't give the bratty cunt that satisfaction.

Our shadows grew longer and longer before us as the sun set behind us. "When do we stop for the evening?" moaned Sophia. "Surely we have traveled far enough, Sir Knight."

"When we reach Vrex," I answered. "There's an inn. We should be there by nightfall, okay?"

"Fine," she muttered. "And how long is that?"

I grit my teeth. "A few hours still, my Lady." I put all the derision I could into my words. Why had Vivian, the Holy Virgin of Saphique, chosen this whiny brat to be my acolyte? Sophia clearly resented this task foisted on her. I always thought the best acolyte was chosen, one eager to serve her Goddess in this important Quest.

I gripped the reigns of Midnight. I too was eager to reach Vrex. A day in the saddle was wearing in armor. My lower back ached and my legs were sore. Not as sore as Sophia's butt. She kept squirming in her saddle, trying to relieve the pressure.

The village of Vrex appeared ahead, built on a small rise overlooking the highway. It was a collection of thatched roofs and whitewashed walls. The only slate roof was the Generous Courtesan, the inn that dominated the center of town. It was a well-kept inn, catering to the traveling merchants and nobility that passed through Vrex to and from the capital.

"Thank Saphique's hymen," Sophia muttered as we left the road onto the cobblestone of the village.

I arched an eyebrow. "I wouldn't think an acolyte of Saphique would blaspheme."

A mischievous grin crossed Sophia's lips; she almost seemed like a real person. "You would be surprised the rules I've broken."

We reached the inn and a dirty boy took our horses. "Watch out for Midnight's bite," I warned. "He can be vicious. But feed him some oats, and he becomes as sweet as a puppy."

Sophia dismounted and almost fell over. She groaned as she stretched her back and legs. A loud rumble erupted from her stomach and she blushed. "I do hope they serve proper food here."

"Oh, yes, m'Lady," grinned the stable boy. "Got the finest food 'ere. You'll be burstin' at the seams once you've eat'n the nosh."

"Sounds lovely," muttered Sophia.

The innkeeper was a round-faced man named Hal, and he greeted us with a jolly smile. I paid for a single room with two beds along with a meal and stables for our horses. I led Sophia out to the inn's common room. Her eyes widened. Serving women bustled about as laughing men fondled their breasts and asses, the women giggling back. Men drank tankards of dark beer and ate a rich stew of beef and vegetables. My mouth watered at the smell.

"This is...different," Sophia muttered. "When I stayed here with my mother, we rented a private dining space."

"That costs coin, my Lady," I answered, giving her a mocking smile. "And we will need to be miserly with ours."

"Yes, yes," she sighed, and then smiled as a lass of eighteen sauntered up, her dark hair falling down her back in a thick braid and a shy smile on her lips.

"If it pleases you, m'Lady, I am Delores, and my father, the good innkeeper, has asked me to wait on you this evening."

"Perfect," Sophia purred, licking her lips. "You are just delicious, child."

Delores's cheeks reddened.

"Thank you, m'Lady."

"Do you have a bath?" Sophia asked.

"Of course. I can attend to you."

Sophia nodded. "And do you know how to massage weary flesh?"

"Massage. No, m'Lady."

"I'll show you." Sophia gave a wicked grin. "Now, if you would bring us our meal and two glasses of your finest wine."

"Ale is fine for me," I interrupted.

Sophia wrinkled her nose. "Thank you, sweet child."

I frowned at her. Why was she acting so sweet?

Delores scurried off and returned with a platter: two bowls of the steaming stew, thick slices of brown bread, a heel of butter, and our drinks. She sat it down on our table, then moved behind Sophia's chair, patiently waiting.

Sophia sniffed the stew. "It doesn't actually smell that bad. I guess I'm just so hungry."

"Yes, hunger has a way of spicing food, my Lady," I smiled.

"Are you ever going to stop with the sarcasm?" Sophia asked. "It is most unbecoming."

"I'm sorry to have offended you, my Lady."

Sophia shook her head and dug into her stew with a wooden spoon. After a moment, I joined her. It was delicious. I smeared butter on the bread and dipped into the savory stew. The warm food washed away some of the exhaustion of the road. I savored it, washing it down with the strong ale. The ale had a kick to it.

Sophia sipped at her wine as she devoured her food. I think she was surprised by how fast she finished. She pushed back the bowl and finished her wine. "More than adequate," she nodded to Dolores. "Now I am in desperate need of a bath."

I ordered a second flagon of ale and sat back in my chair. I nursed it, pondering the dangers ahead of us. Somehow, we had to find the Lesbius Oracle in the dark, unmapped Deorc Forest. It was haunted by Elves and monsters. It could be almost as perilous as our quest itself. And I doubt it would help. I took another sip. Lady Delilah was sure I could accomplish this Quest, but I wasn't special. Many knights had died already trying to kill Dominari.

Why should I succeed where they failed?

Fine. Be a stubborn bitch. Go and die. Throw your life away on this foolish folly.

Kevin's words echoed through my mind. The noise of the common room faded. Pain shuddered through me. I took another drink as tears trickled down my cheeks. I had thought I would marry Kevin after my Quest and once we were both knights. I had such romantic ideas about journeying with him, fighting by his side by day and making love to him by night.

Was he right? Was I just being foolish?

No. Lady Delilah believed in me. She was a true knight. She wasn't a coward like Kevin. I slammed down my tankard, spilling some of my ale. "I can do this," I muttered. I stood up, my armor creaking. "I will do this."

"Will do what?" a handsome man at the next table smiled. He looked a little like Kevin. His hand reached out, patting my thigh. "Because I have a few ideas about what you can do."

I grabbed his thumb and twisted, pulling his hand away from my thigh. He groaned in pain. "Sorry, Sir Knight," he gasped.

I could kill the dragon, and getting drunk and crying into my ale wouldn't help. We had many long days of travel ahead of us. I should get my rest while I have a comfortable mattress on which to sleep. I strode out of the common room and headed up the stairs.

I threw open the door to the room. "Like this, m'Lady?" Delores asked.

"Oh, yes, just like that," moaned Sophia.

My cheeks reddened. Sophia was naked on her bed, lying on her belly. Her hair was wet and her skin glistened, fresh from her bath. Delores knelt in a thin shift between Sophia's legs, her hands rubbing at Sophia's plump butt.

"Keep kneading," sighed Sophia. "Massage away all the pain."

I shook my head as I stripped off my armor. Sophia's green eyes found me, a contented smile on her face. My cheeks grew hotter, and an itch formed between my thighs as I undressed, exposing my naked body to her gaze.

"Keep working those fingers," Sophia sighed. "Mmm, you are such a sweet thing."

"Thank you, m'Lady."

"Now work your fingers into my crack. Don't be afraid."

"Okay." Delores swallowed. Her fingers pushed between Sophia's butt-cheeks, spreading the plump mounds apart as she worked. "How's this, m'Lady?"

"Heavenly," purred Sophia. "you are doing great."

I sank down on my bed, slipping beneath the covers. My nipples were hard and a hot itch burned through my pussy. I bit my lip, squirming as my passions heated up. I tried not to glance over at the next bed, but it was so hard.

"And don't be afraid to use your lips," added Sophia. "Kisses are quite relaxing."

"They are?"

"Uh-huh."

Delores glanced at me for a moment, and then she leaned over and planted a kiss right on Sophia's butt-cheek. Sophia sighed and Delores kissed around Sophia's cheeks as the girl's fingers massaged. I squeezed my thighs together as my pussy burned hotter.

"Don't forget to kiss between my butt-cheeks."

Delores gasped. "But...m'Lady, that's..."

"I thought you were here to serve me," Sophia pouted. "I need your sweet lips to kiss my flesh to relax."

"Yes, m'Lady," she sighed.

Delores lowered her face, pressing between Sophia's butt-cheeks. My fingers slid down my body as the young woman nuzzled at Sophia's sphincter. Sophia moaned in delight, shifting on the bed. Her eyes locked on mine, her smile grew as she saw my hand move beneath my sheets.

I flushed in embarrassment, but I was so horny. My fingers brushed my shaved pussy lips, gathering the slippery juices before I

108

moved to my clit. I sighed as I rubbed my aching nub with slow circles.

"Lick lower," purred Sophia as she spread her legs. "My pussy needs to be massaged."

"Yes, m'Lady," sighed Delores, her own hips shifting.

The maiden moved lower and pressed her lips against Sophia's pussy. Sophia gasped in delight, her hips bucking as Delores nuzzled at her pussy. I couldn't see, but I could hear the maiden's wet licks as her tongue slid through Sophia's folds.

"Do I taste delicious?" Sophia asked.

"Oh, yes, m'Lady," purred Delores. "Like the sweetest honey."

Sophia moaned in delight as Delores continued pleasuring her. I rubbed harder at my clit, my breath quickening. The sheets slid down, exposing my heaving tits. Sophia's eyes burned as they locked onto them.

"I can help you out, Angela," she moaned. "I think you remember how sweet my tongue was."

I froze. "I'm fine, my Lady," I answered and rolled onto my side, facing away from them. I closed my eyes, the sweet sounds of Delores's pussy licking and Sophia's sighs filling my ears. I tried to picture a man's fingers on my pussy. I pushed three fingers into my depths, fucking them, picturing the handsome man downstairs.

"Eat my pussy!" gasped Sophia. "That's it. You little slut. Devour me."

I tried to hold onto the fantasy of a man fucking me, of his thick cock slamming into the depths of my pussy, but Sophia's vulgar words filled my mind. I pictured her hot pussy pressing on my mouth, my tongue licking through her folds.

"Oh, yes!" moaned Sophia. "I'm gonna cum on your face!"

My fingers pumped faster, my pussy clenching down on my digits.

"Yes, yes! You fucking slut! I love it! Work that tongue through my folds. Worship me! Mmm, yes! I'm so glad your father gave you to me! Oh, yes!"

The heel of my hand ground on my clit.

"I'm gonna cum on your sweet lips. I want you to drink all my juices."

"Yes, my Lady," I whispered as my orgasm swept over me. I shuddered on the bed. Hot pleasure washed through my body. My pussy spasmed about my fingers. I kept rubbing, sending more waves of bliss crashing through me as I licked my lips, wishing I had Sophia's juices staining them.

"Oh, yes! That's it, slut! I'm cumming! Oh, yes! Saphique's hymen, yes! You have a delicious mouth! Oh, wow! Oh, damn! By Slata's cunt, that was perfect."

"I'm glad I could please you, m'Lady," Delores whispered.

My eyes grew heavy. As Sophia and Delores kissed, I drifted off into sleep. My dreams were passionate. I made love to Sophia while a blood-red dragon watched on. I knew I should fight the dragon, but I just couldn't stop sixty-nining with Sophia. The dragon approached us, snarling and breathing fire.

Her jaws snapped, full of sharp teeth, and her long, dagger-like claws scraped across the ground. Massive wings flapped as the dragon loomed over us. I shuddered and came on Sophia's mouth as I devoured the acolyte's pussy.

Dominari would kill us. Her jaws opened.

I woke up in a sweat. Sophia and Delores were asleep, cuddling on the other bed. I rolled onto my back and stared at the ceiling. I focused on Lady Delilah's words. I could do this. I repeated that over and over as I fell back to sleep.

Chapter Fifteen: Dangers of Riding Sidesaddle

Acolyte Sophia – Blath Forest, The Kingdom of Secare

The second day passed much like the first. My poor bottom grew even sorer and Angela grew ever surlier. The only change to the landscape was the growing shadow on the horizon– Blath Forest. It started out as a green haze around noon, and by the time we reached the town of Mruenz, it loomed before us. I remember the forest as a pleasant diversion on my trip to Shesax, but that was in a train of hundreds of servants and guards.

It would just be the two of us.

I found another compliant innkeeper's daughter to "massage" me. She was plump and delightful, with big, soft tits upon which I slept. While we made love, Angela fingered herself on her side, facing away. I so hoped she would join in on the fun. I just knew if I could make her cum a few times, she would relax.

Early the next morning, we entered the Blath Forest. The road wound through the tall pine trees. Thick ferns grew around the base of the trees, forming a barrier that hid anything more than a dozen feet out of sight.

It was cool, at least. The wind stirred the tall trees. They creaked as they swayed. Pine needles would drift down, spinning through the air before carpeting the road. I let my hood slip off and, for a few minutes, enjoyed myself. Birds chirped above, singing happy songs, almost serenading us like my mother's entertainers.

But soon the pain in my bottom returned. It wasn't as bad today. I was getting used to riding.

I tried to engage Angela in conversation again as we crossed a babbling brook. "That pool looks so refreshing," I said, pointing out where a part of the brook filled a small depression, the dark water swirling about in a slow circle. "I have always enjoyed skinny dipping."

"This is not a pleasure trip, my Lady," Angela snapped, her tone dripping venom.

"I didn't mean we should stop," I huffed. "I was merely sharing my joy of swimming and frolicking with a friend."

"I doubt you'll have one of those on this trip, my Lady."

"Yes, I am realizing that," I said, lifting my chin. "You are far too dour to have even a little bit of fun. You are stiffer than that armor you wear."

"Be quiet!" hissed Angela, her head snapping around.

"I will not be quiet! I have just as much right to speak as you do! So you will listen to– "

Angela's face was livid as she whipped her head back to face me. "Shut your stupid, spoiled mouth. There is something– "

The monster sprang from the brush. It was tawny, snarling like a giant cat while tentacles writhed from its back. It crashed into Angela and her horse. Midnight neighed in pain while Purity whinnied in terror. My mare bolted. I grasped the reins, bouncing on my saddle. My body shifted. I couldn't ride this fast. Not sidesaddle.

"Stop! Purity! Stop!" I yanked back on the reins, but she had clamped her teeth on the bit. She wouldn't obey. "Purity, you will – "

I fell off the back of my mare, landing hard on the road. I groaned as I rolled. I looked up in horror down the road. Midnight lay on his side, his legs kicking, bright blood staining his hide.

Angela was on her feet, facing the beast. It looked like a large cat, bigger than any hunting dog, but there were four tentacles thrusting from the monster's back.

Fear clutched my heart and I ran after my mare.

~ * ~

Knight-Errant Angela

The panthopus snarled at me. My horse kicked on the ground, his rear leg lamed by the beast's claws. Somehow, the panthopus had gotten its claws beneath the barding and ripped Midnight's muscles. I could do nothing for my horse as I backed away.

Panthopuses were dangerous beasts that prowled the Blath Forest. They usually didn't attack, but it must be mating season. The monster's cock dangled hard between its hind legs, red and covered in spiny protrusions. It needed to mate, and would use any female animal it could. Like many monsters, it was a foul creation of the mad Biomancer Vebrin.

The tentacles slithered out towards me. I swung my sword, but my blade passed right through the tentacles like they weren't there. The beast could displace itself, making you think it stood a foot farther to the right or left. Its real tentacles, invisible to my eyes, struck the front of my armor and brushed my stomach, leaving behind a thick slime. I shuddered. My nipples hardened beneath my breastplate and my cunt grew damp.

The slime of a panthopus secreted an aphrodisiac.

"Fuck," I gasped as I jumped back. My breastplate pulled away, gripped by its tentacles. My backplate fell off, exposing my naked breasts bouncing about, both tits covered in the thick, sweet-smelling slime.

I licked my lips as I glimpsed the monster's cock. How wonderful would that feel inside me.

No. I need to focus.

113

The tentacles lashed out. I swung to the right of them, hoping I had guessed correctly. The panthopus tentacles writhed as they dodged out of the way. I had. I grinned, rushing forward. The beast actually stood to the left. Its invisible paws mucked up the ground as it shifted. I stabbed with my sword, hoping to get a killing blow.

A tentacle wrapped around my vambrace. The panthopus jerked my arm to the side and twisted. I gasped in pain and my hand relaxed. My sword fell to the ground. I reached for my belt knife, but another tentacle wrapped around my other arm, growing tight, infecting me with more lusts.

"Fuck!" I gasped, shuddering in delight. "Stop this!"

The panthopus growled as its remaining two tentacles explored my body. They slid up to my naked breasts, the suction cups covering my nipples as the tentacles entwined around my tits. They squeezed and milked, my nipples bursting with excitement.

"Help!" I shouted as I struggled.

The panthopus stopped displacing, the image shifting to the right, and suddenly the real beast appeared. It licked its chops. I tried to kick, but my legs were too weak. Its rough tongue licked up my leg. My pussy clenched. What would that tongue feel like?

The monster purred as its tongue slithered closer to my cunt. Its tentacles worked harder on my tits, covering them in more of the wonderful slime. I shuddered and bucked, spreading my legs apart. Its tongue reached my pussy.

"Yes!" I gasped as it took a lick. Its tongue probed into my hole before flicking up and brushing the tip of my clit. Ecstasy burned through me. I shuddered and bucked in delight. Its tentacles squeezed harder at my breasts, my nipples aching in delight as the suction cups worked on them almost like a pair of sucking mouths. "Eat me!"

The panthopus purred louder as it devoured my pussy. Its tongue swirled through my flesh. Its tongue was so much bigger than a human's, covering huge swaths of my pussy in a single lick. The rough texture excited my flesh. When it brushed my clit, I bucked in delight.

"Gods, yes!" I moaned, my pussy clenching.

I came on the monster's tongue. Pleasure burned through my body. I gasped and bucked in delight as I was consumed by its passion. My back arched as I howled in delight. The monster buried its tongue deep into my pussy, drinking my juices.

My excitement spurred the monster to lick me harder. Its tongue would dip between my asscheeks and lick at my sphincter before swiping across my pussy. Over and over, faster and faster. I bucked against its tentacles as I moaned in delight. I couldn't believe how much pleasure I was getting from a monster.

I should be afraid. If it fucked my pussy, I would bear a litter of the foul things. I didn't want that. I had to fight, but the pleasure was fantastic. I came again. The bliss hammered my mind, washing away that last fear.

"Gods, yes! Eat me! Fuck me!"

I shuddered in its tentacles' grasp when it flipped me over. I knelt on the ground, its tentacles moving from my arms to grab my thighs and pull me beneath its body. Its soft fur rubbed on my back and its spiny cock nudged at my asscheeks.

"Fuck me!" I begged, humping my hips. "Ravish me!"

Chapter Sixteen: Monster's Lusts

Acolyte Sophia

My sides ached. I slowed to a stop and glanced behind me. Was Angela okay? Why had I run? I was supposed to help her. But the thing had been so terrifying. It had dispatched Angela's warhorse with a single attack. Fear twisted my stomach.

I bit my lip, not sure what I should do. I was torn. Part of me wanted to run away. But I was the only one that could help Angela.

But what help could I give her? She was a knight. She had probably killed the monster on her own.

But I did have divine magic.

"But what magic could I perform to stop a monster?" All the magic I knew was for healing. I could heal her horse. Maybe that would help?

I heard a woman's voice on the wind. It sounded like a moan of pain or pleasure. I swallowed. My hands grew dry. What should I do? I chewed on my lip.

I had to help her. It was my duty. I took a step towards the fight. My body trembled. I took a deep breath and forced myself to take a second step. And a third step. It was so hard. My shoes were so heavy, like they were made of lead instead of leather.

"This is like all the stories," I whispered. "The Knights always need their Acolytes to do some clever trick."

I took a fourth step. It didn't grow easier.

~ * ~

Knight-Errant Angela

The monster's spiny cock slid into the crack of my ass. It brushed my sphincter as the beast humped its hips. It was so eager to fuck me, but it couldn't seem to find my hole. I arched my hips, my pussy clenching in delight.

Roaring in frustration, the panthopus thrust its hips. The tip of its spiny cock entered my bowels. I shuddered as hot pleasure shot through me. Purring in triumph, the monster hammered its hips, driving its spiny dick deeper into me.

"Yes!" I moaned.

The monster's cock was covered in these soft, spiny projections. They teased my bowels, adding more pleasure. It sawed in and out, stimulating me. I shuddered beneath him, bucking my hips. Its tentacles roamed my body. I groaned in delight as one brushed my pussy lips.

Hot saliva dripped on my neck as the panthopus's tongue lolled out. It purred as it fucked me. Its soft, furry body covered my back, adding a sensuous massage while its sharp claws scraped on my pauldrons.

"Fuck me!" I gasped. "Fuck my ass! Oh, yes! And shove that tentacle into my pussy! Make me cum, you fucking monster! Oh, yes! I love it!"

I came as the rubbery tentacle wormed into my pussy. The suckers clung to my sensitive flesh as it worked in and out of my convulsing tunnel. Hot passion rippled through my body. I bucked back into its thrusts, my asshole clamping down on its cock.

Its hips fucked me faster. They slammed that cock in and out of my asshole faster than a man. My body was alive with bliss. I gasped and panted. I savored every inch of its wonderful cock spearing my ass while its tentacle violated my pussy.

"Yes! You fucking beast! Make me cum again! Don't ever stop fucking me!"

The panthopus growled. Its thrusts grew harder, more frantic. I shuddered, savoring the build up of my orgasm. It slammed into my asshole. Its spines caressed my velvety flesh, shooting pleasure to the bliss bursting through my pussy.

The monster roared as it came in my ass. Flood after flood of hot, thick spunk filled my ass. I squeezed down on its cock, eager to milk him of every drop. My orgasm exploded through me as its cock withdrew, my ass clenching in delight.

"Yes, yes, that's what I needed."

The beast ripped its tentacle from my pussy. Its cock was still hard. The wet tip slid down my taint and brushed the lips of my pussy. I froze in fear as I remembered what would happen if it came in my pussy.

"No!" I shouted as it slammed in, my pussy bursting with joy as the spines caressed all the wonderful nerves in my sheath. "Stop fucking me!"

~ * ~

Acolyte Sophia

I rounded a corner in the road and gasped in shock. Angela gasped and moaned as she was violated by the monster. The beast had stripped off her armor, and slammed its filthy cock in and out of her pussy.

"Stop fucking me!" she moaned.

I shuddered. I didn't know what to do. I looked around in fear. What should I do? I couldn't stand by while she was being fucked by a monster. It wasn't right. No woman deserved that. I was an acolyte of Saphique, charged with defending women's purity.

But what could I do against a monster?

"Oh, gods, yes! So good! But you have to stop! I don't want to bear a litter of monsters!" moaned Angela! "Oh, Pater's cock! I'm cumming again!"

She writhed in joy.

I had to do something.

Her sword lay fallen nearby. I swallowed and stepped forward. The monster purred and growled. Its tentacles were wrapped around her breasts, squeezing and kneading them. My body trembled. Every step I took, I expected the monster to notice me.

I reached the sword and grasped the hilt. It wasn't as heavy as I expected, though it felt unfamiliar. I moved forward. The beasts hips fucked faster and faster, like it was building to its orgasm. I closed my eyes and stabbed.

~ * ~

Knight-Errant Angela

The panthopus roared in pain and leaped off of me, ripping its cock from my pussy. I shuddered in relief even as the bliss of my orgasm roared through me. I forced myself to stand and face the monster. It swayed, blood pouring from a wound in its side.

What happened?

Sophia stood trembling nearby, holding my sword, the tip stained red. I grabbed the blade from her hands and she squeaked in fear. Then I rushed at the wounded beast, swinging my blade even as its cum poured from my ass.

The monster raised its tentacles. I sliced through two. It howled in more pain. I couldn't let this beast breed with any more women, even if fucking the beast felt fantastic. It turned and lunged at me. I caught the raking claws on my arm vambrace as I slammed the sword into its gullet.

Gurgling, the monster slid dead from my blade.

"That was amazing!" gasped Sophia and then she ran and hugged me.

My body still burned with the monster's aphrodisiac slime, and I put my arm around her and kissed her hard without thought.

Chapter Seventeen: Misunderstood Kiss

Acolyte Sophia – Blath Forest, The Kingdom of Secare

Angela kissed me.

My heart stopped.

Her lips were hot and soft. Her large, naked breasts pressed against my traveling robes. My nipples hardened and a flush of heat washed through me. I closed my eyes and let the strong woman hold me, her tongue claiming my mouth. My head spun.

The fear and excitement of the fight against the monster morphed into pure lust. I moaned into her kiss. I had forgotten about everything. The tentacled, panther-like monster lay dead nearby, Angela's sword impaled into its furry body.

Angela's hands found the soft, leather belt that held my robe closed. It came off, dropping my satchel of potions and enchanted dagger to the forest road. The robe parted, my pale, naked form revealed to Angela's exploring hands.

Her tits pressed on my small breasts. They were covered in something sticky. A hot flush ran through my body. My pussy became molten fire. I forgot about everything but this wonderful woman in my arms.

Angela growled into the kiss, her hands sliding around my

naked hips beneath the robe to squeeze at my ass. She pulled my pussy against the cold chainmail loincloth that covered her sex. I ground my clit on the hard metal rings, shuddering in delight.

"Fuck!" Angela snarled. "Pater's cock, but I need to fuck you."

"Ravish me!" I moaned as she pulled me to the ground. "Do whatever you want to me, sir Knight."

Angela was atop me, her red hair falling into my face as she kissed me again. Her hips ground, rubbing her chainmail loincloth into my pussy as we kissed. My hands slid down her naked back to her ass covered by another thin strip of chainmail. I squeezed her butt, pulling her harder against me. My clit burst in delight.

"That's it!" groaned Angela as she ground on me. Both our clits were rubbing on the chainmail, separated by the thin links of metal. "You're so fucking hot!"

"So are you!" I gasped. "Slata's cunt! I've been wanting this since we left. Why didn't you ever join my bed at the inns? We could have made such sweet love."

"You're such a spoiled brat," she groaned, humping harder. "Oh, yes! Pater's thick cock! Mmm, that's nice! I'm gonna cum!"

"Spoiled?" I gasped in shock, my fingers tightening on her asscheeks. My pussy spasmed. I was so on fire. The sticky substance on her breasts made my skin tingle and burn. My eyes fluttered. I wanted to be mad at her, but I was so damned hot for her.

"Always whining and complaining!" gasped Angela. "But not today! You helped! You saved me from being bred by the monster!"

"I did!" I moaned. "Oh, yes! I did! I saved you!"

"And you're so cute and sexy!" Angela leaned down and gave me another hot kiss.

My heart beat faster. Angela was a beautiful woman, strong and graceful. Her body was perfect, no fat, great curves, bouncing tits, and her face. She could be intimidating and sensual, passionate and powerful. She was a sexy warrior.

My orgasm shuddered through me. I moaned into her kiss. Our hips ground together. I never wanted to let her go. My body quivered and thrashed beneath her. My nipples kissed hers. My body drank in every sensation as my juices flooded out onto her chainmail.

"Gods, yes!" Angela gasped as she broke our kiss. She ground harder against me, grinding the metal into my sensitive clit. Another wave of orgasmic delight shuddered through me. "Oh, yes! Saphique's virgin cunt!"

Angela came. I nibbled on her chin as she groaned and shuddered. Her body squirmed atop mine. The chainmail rasped over my clit. The pleasure was intense, almost painful, on my sensitive nub. I shuddered as bliss kept rolling through me.

"Damn, you are sexy!" Angela groaned, leaning down to kiss me. "But I need more."

"I know just the thing," I purred. "Roll onto your back."

Angela rolled off of me. The sunlight fell on her heaving breasts as she squirmed. What little armor she wore– her shoulder pauldrons, bracers on her wrists, and greaves over her leather boots – glinted and flashed. She seized her breasts, squeezing her nipples as she writhed and moaned.

I slipped out of my robes and cloak, letting my clothes pile on the ground, and padded naked over to my discarded pouch. There were three potions of healing, an ampoule of holy milk, and a virgin's best friend– a dildo carved of fine marble polished to a slick sheen.

"You naughty acolyte!" gasped Angela when she saw the black shaft swirled with white.

"This is no ordinary dildo," I grinned, spreading my thighs and shoving it into my flesh. "Holy Saphique," I chanted, my juices coating the shaft. "Give life to my toy so I may give pleasure to all who love you."

The dildo hummed to life in my pussy, vibrating hard. I shuddered in delight and pulled out the magical shaft. Angela frowned as I moved towards her. The shaft's edges blurred as it hummed back and forth, and droplets of my pussy's juices flew off like drops of rain.

"You'll love it," I grinned as I straddled her face.

Angela pulled me down with eager hands, her lips nuzzling into the folds of my pussy. I shuddered in delight, squirming on her face. Her tongue slid through my folds. She lacked the skill to be an acolyte of Saphique, but her tongue still knew where to touch to excite me.

I leaned down, rubbing my belly against her hard nipples as I spread her thighs. I pulled the chainmail loincloth to the side, exposing the shaved lips of her pussy. Her tangy excitement washed over me. A salty scent mixed with it– cum. The monster had ejaculated in her ass.

"I'm so sorry," I whispered. I knew most women enjoyed a real cock, but I shuddered to think of a real penis inside me. I was still pure, untouched by man.

I kissed at her thigh as I rubbed the vibrating dildo up and down her her vulva, teasing the lips of her labia. Her vulva was flushed with her excitement and dewy with her juices. Her hips undulated as she moaned into my cunt.

"Stop teasing me," Angela moaned. "I need it in me! Fuck me with it! Make me cum!"

"I will," I purred. "Just relax. I'm temple trained to please a woman."

A ruby adorned my belly piercing, proclaiming my mastery of cunnilingus. My lips kissed closer to her vulva as I teased her. Angela's tangy juices flooded out as her excitement grew, puddling down to her asscheeks. The scent was intoxicating. I shuddered, clenching my pussy and releasing a flood of juices for Angela to devour.

Her tongue flailed through my pussy. She was frantic to cum. My lips kissed on one side of her slit while I moved the vibrator closer. Her labia were cute, protruding out of her slit like a pink ridge. I licked with my tongue, my piercing sliding along her flesh, and brought the magical dildo to her labia.

"Yes," she gasped as the humming pleasure teased her.

Angela's fingers squeezed on my ass. She gasped and moaned into my pussy. She devoured me as I ran the vibrating dildo up and

124

down her labia. The black tip grew shiny with her dew. She shuddered beneath me, her stomach clenching and flexing beneath my small breasts, caressing my nipples.

"Fuck me," she begged. "Stop teasing me!"

I smiled, my pink tongue and hard piercing flicking at her clit. She squealed into my pussy as my tongue stud brushed her clit. I loved pleasuring a woman. I was so glad to give Angela this pleasure. I wanted her to remember our first lovemaking.

I pushed the dildo into her pussy. She gasped and spasmed. "Oh, yes! That's so wild! Oh, my Gods! Gewin's mighty cock, that's amazing!"

I groaned in delight. My orgasm built as I pleasured her. I slid the dildo in and out of her pussy, her pink labia clinging to the black shaft. My tongue nuzzled at her clit, swirling around the sensitive bud and gathering up the tangy juices that flowed from her pink depths. I loved rubbing the tip of my tongue stud against her clit and making her moan into my pussy.

"Mmm, you are delicious," I purred. "Do you like my toy, Angela?"

"I love it!" she gasped. "Sophia! I've never! Oh, damn! By the Gods, I'm gonna cum so hard!"

"Good!" I moaned and took another lick at her clit. "I want you to erupt. I want you to cum so hard on my dildo. I want you to feel my love."

"Love?" groaned Angela. "Oh, yes! Slata's hairy cunt! I'm gonna cum! Fuck me faster! Harder!"

I listened to her, moving my hand faster. I sucked my lips onto her clit. She screamed in delight into my pussy. Her tongue shoved deep into my hole, fucking me like I fucked her cunt. My pussy clenched. I shuddered and came, squirting my juices into her mouth while I moaned about her tiny clit.

"Yes! Gods, yes! You wonderful slut! I'm gonna cum, Sophia!"

"Do it!" I moaned. "Give in to your pleasure! Enjoy the gift Saphique gave all women! Cum!"

Angela spasmed beneath me. She groaned and gasped, cursing

as her delight rolled over her. I sucked on her clit and shoved the vibrating dildo deep into her depths. Her thighs squeezed on my face. She bucked hard beneath me. I nibbled and sucked on her nub. I prolonged her orgasm.

"Oh, Gods!" she gasped. "Oh, Gods! I'm still cumming!"

I gave her multiple orgasms. I attacked her clit as she thrashed beneath me. I paid attention, bringing her to the limits of her pleasure, and then backing off and letting her simmer. I lifted my pussy from her and turned around, snuggling against her and kissing her on the face. Our tongues tasted each other's passions. I could stay like this forever, just holding her.

A horse neighed in pain.

Chapter Eighteen: The Knight's Resolve

Acolyte Sophia

Angela gasped and pushed me away, shouting, "No, Midnight!"

We were so caught up in our lust we had forgotten about her wounded charger. He lay on his side, his flank clawed up by the monster beneath his steel barding. Angela rushed to her horse, falling down beside his head.

"I'm so sorry," she moaned. "I can't believe I let myself get so caught up." She kissed his nose as he neighed in pain again. "You were an amazing horse. I'll miss you."

She drew the dagger from her belt.

"What are you doing?" I gasped.

Tears burned in her blue eyes. "Putting him out of his misery. He's lame."

"Don't! I have healing potions." I scrambled for my pouch and pulled out one of the glass bottles, its base round, filled with a milky liquid. I rushed over to her, pulling out the cork stopper with my teeth. "Here, have him drink this."

"Thank you!" Angela gasped, tears spilling down her cheek. She poured the milky contents into Midnight's mouth. "Drink," she whispered as she stroked his neck.

The horse neighed. His legs kicked. The bloody cuts rending his hide glowed with a pink light, sparks dancing in the air, and then the light died. His hide was unmarred, though still matted with the blood he lost. Midnight heaved his body, rolling onto his knees and standing up with a great strain. He shook his mane, his barding clanking.

"Thank you, Sophia!" Angela kissed me again.

I loved kissing her.

~ * ~

Knight-Errant Angela

It was a mistake to kiss Sophia. The first time, I had been consumed with the aphrodisiac of the panthopus's slime. But the second time, I didn't have that excuse. The moment I broke the kiss, I saw the infatuation in Sophia's green eyes.

As we searched for her mare Purity, who had bolted during the fight, she kept brushing against me and trying to hold my hand. It would be sweet, but Kevin still held a place in my heart. Sophia was a sweet girl and, despite us being the same age, she was still a girl. Immature, bratty, and cute all at the same time.

We found her horse after an hour. Purity stood calmly on the edge of the road eating at a patch of grass. Sophia squealed in delight and ran to her mare, hugging the white horse's head and planting a kiss on the horse's snout.

As we rode through the Blath Forest, Sophia kept her mount close to mine. She wasn't riding side-saddle like she had the first three-and-a-half days of our journey. When the panthopus attacked, Sophia had fallen off her mare when she bolted. Straddling her saddle caused the hem of her robe to slide up, baring her naked calves. They were...fetching.

Sophia was beautiful, her playful, green eyes were always darting about, and her petite frame was always moving as a new

128

sight drew her attention. She wasn't whining and her face wasn't twisted into a petulant pout. It was an attractive face, and she glowed when she smiled. Every time she licked her lips and her tongue stud flashed in the sunlight, my pussy clenched– that metal stud had felt amazing on my clit.

By evening we left the woods and reached another village. Sophia was so eager for the bed. She devoured her simple stew without complaint and then dragged me upstairs. I should have stopped her, but I couldn't fight her enthusiasm. She made love to me with a fierce passion. I could see it in her eyes how much her infatuation burned inside her.

I felt guilty afterward as she lay cuddled against me. Her lips moved, and I could almost hear her whisper, "I love you," as she drifted off to sleep.

But I loved Kevin. Even if he made me so angry that I wanted to strangle him. My heart was torn, and sleeping with Sophia wasn't helping. I almost felt like I was cheating on Kevin. We had an open relationship. I never felt like I was cheating when I had other lovers. Maybe it was Sophia's crush. She was cute and beautiful, and my heart raced when I was around her.

I vowed to stay out of her bed tomorrow night. I needed to let her know that I enjoyed fooling around, but I didn't love her. She was just too immature for me. I watched her fall asleep, stroking her face.

"So cute," I sighed, my heart aching. I hated the guilt. Why should I even feel guilty after the way Kevin acted? Why did I have to still love him after he doubted my commitment to the Knights Deute?

I watched Sophia's face relax. She was beautiful as she slept, a precious doll.

Sophia was bubbly the next morning, eager to set off down the road. She didn't seem as sore as she had the first day, growing used to riding all day. The sun was just rising before us as we set off down the road. The farms turned into ranches as we entered the Tith Hills. Herds of cattle grazed the hills around the mines. We passed slower wagons heading east towards the city of K'hol, carrying the ore found in the mines.

After midday, Sophia pointed at a well-maintained road. "That leads to my mother's estates," she smiled.

"A shame we don't have the time to visit her."

Sophia nodded. "Maybe on the way back."

"Yeah." I forced myself to sound cheery and positive. Would we come back? No knight who went after Dominari had returned. While Lady Delilah was confident I could succeed, and Sophia had high hopes the Lesbius Oracle would guide us, I harbored doubts.

Kevin's words returned. My anger flared. I loved and hated him. How could he doubt my commitment to the knights? It was my duty to try to kill the dragon.

"We are coming back, right?" Sophia whispered, her lower lip trembling.

"Yes," I nodded and reached out to take her hand.

She gave me such a happy, love-filled smile. Why did I take her hand? Why did I keep encouraging her crush?

We reached the city of K'hol. A dark reek hung over the town. Smithies and foundries burned across the city, smelting and forging the valuable copper and iron found in the Tith Hills. The commoners all seemed stained with soot. Even the buildings had a thin, grimy veneer from all the foundries.

We found an inn and despite my resolve, I fell into bed with Sophia again.

Chapter Nineteen: Elvish Heat

Xerathalasia – Western Deorc Forest, The Federation of Deoraciynae

We finally found the basilisk's trail on the fifth day of the hunt. We had crossed the Deorc forest, nearing the western edge. The elvish villages we had passed were all scared of the monster's presence. Two elves had been killed and a third petrified. All had been mated by the basilisk first.

"Spoor," Quenyathalee pointed out. She was a tall and willowy elf. Like myself and the rest of my hunters, greens, browns, and blacks painted her naked body.

"What do you think, Xiloniasa?" I asked, motioning for the young, petite elf to come forward.

"Me, Xerathalasia?" she squeaked. She hung in the back, crouching in the brush. She had been at the rear all day.

"Yes," I nodded. "You need to learn." Xiloniasa was a new hunter. She moved with skill and grace, and had a keen eye. She was timid, but experience would help to correct that.

"I...well..." She shifted her shoulders, her eyes narrowing and her long, pointed ears quivering.

"What is wrong?"

"She's in heat," chortled Deliasonele. "First time, Xiloniasa?"

Xiloniasa nodded her head. "I...yes. It's my first time. I...I didn't know it would happen while we were on the trail." She swallowed and stood. A cock had sprouted from her pussy, thrusting hard before her. She grasped it, giving it a stroke. "I'm so hot. It's so hard to think."

Relythionaia tugged on her long braid of green hair. "That's an impressive cock you grew, Xiloniasa."

"Thanks." The younger elf looked down at her dick. "I...I think I need...to be satisfied."

"With a cock that hard, I think you do," Deliasonele grinned. "Start stroking."

"Could I...get some relief from one of you?" She stroked her cock. "It's just begging to be touched by someone else."

I knew that feeling. Once a month, for about three days, an elf would go into heat. Our hermaphroditic nature would assert itself and a cock would sprout. It was easier now I was older, but I remember my first few times. I just had to fuck a woman. I didn't care in what hole or if I would get the elf-maid pregnant. That's how I married Atharilesia. We were both so horny, she let me fuck her pussy. We've been married ever since I came in her pussy's depths. I knew in other races, marriage could be complicated, full of strange rituals, but for elves it was simple– if you fucked her pussy, you were married.

If I was ever to fuck another elf's pussy or let an elf fuck mine, I would commit one of our greatest crimes– adultery. Of course, my mouth and ass were free to be used. I couldn't get pregnant by blowing an elf.

"I'll help you out," I purred. "Relythionaia, care to help."

"Sure," Relythionaia smiled. "Going into heat happens on the hunt, Xiloniasa. Never fear, we'll keep you satisfied, and you'll do the same for us."

My pussy itched as I knelt before Xiloniasa. Her small breasts rose as she shuddered. Relythionaia knelt beside me, an impish smile on her lips. I had fucked Relythionaia's ass and mouth many times on the hunt, and her cock knew my asshole almost better than she knew her wife's pussy.

The life of a hunter often kept us away from our spouses and families.

I was glad my sister Nyonthilasara was there to keep my pregnant wife company while I was away.

Xiloniasa shuddered as I ran my tongue up her shaft to her tip. Relythionaia copied me, her pink tongue flicking along the sensitive tip of the cock. I let my tongue swirl, brushing Relythionaia's. Our lips met, kissing briefly around Xiloniasa's cock.

"Oh, wow," Xiloniasa gasped. "That's so much more intense than having my pussy played with."

"Cumming with a cock is the best," Deliasonele sighed. "I wish I had one every day."

"You'd never get anything done," laughed Quenyathalee.

Xiloniasa's hands gripped my green hair as we teased her cock. She let out another moan, her cock throbbing against my lips. She shifted as I nibbled on her tip. My lips kept brushing Relythionaia. We kissed and played with Xiloniasa's cock.

"Please, I need more! I need to cum," the young elf moaned.

"Mmm, I bet you do. You're so backed up," I purred.

Relythionaia swallowed Xiloniasa's cock. The young elf moaned as I kissed and nibbled down her shaft. I reached the wet folds of her pussy. I licked and nuzzled. She tasted like roses. I savored the flowery nectar as my tongue flicked through her delights.

"Wow! That's so hot! The pleasures are mixing together," panted Xiloniasa.

"Xerathalasia is the best at pussy licking," Deliasonele giggled. "Just let her tongue take you away while Relythionaia sucks all the cum out of your cock."

"Matar's cock, yes!" Xiloniasa groaned.

I fucked my tongue deeper into her pussy as Relythionaia sucked loudly. The wet slurping made my pussy so wet. I shoved a hand between my thighs. I found my aching clit, stroking it with my fingers as I moaned my delight into Xiloniasa's tasty snatch.

Xiloniasa's hips thrust forward, pushing her cock deeper into Relythionaia's mouth. Hot pussy smeared across my face as I struggled to keep my lips licking through the folds. Xiloniasa seized Relythionaia's braid, clutching it hard as she fucked the elf hunter's mouth.

"Swallow her cock all the way!" Deliasonele called out. "Deep-throat the horny slut!"

"Oh, yes!" Xiloniasa shuddered as her cock disappeared all the way into Relythionaia's mouth. "That's so hot."

Relythionaia moaned before sliding her mouth up Xiloniasa's cock. Her lips came off with a wet pop. "Your turn, Xerathalasia. Let me get a taste of her hot pussy."

"Mmm, yes," I purred, licking my lips of the sticky nectar.

Our cheeks brushed as we swapped position. Xiloniasa squealed as Relythionaia buried her lips into the young elf's pussy. I grinned at the pleasure contorting across Xiloniasa's face before I swallowed her cock into my mouth.

"Xerathalasia!" she moaned as I bobbed my mouth. "Matar, yes!"

I bobbed faster, sucking harder. I was eager for her sweet cum. My hands slid up, squeezing her small, firm breasts. I found her nipples and pinched. Xiloniasa thrust her hips forward, slamming her cock deep into my mouth while Relythionaia devoured Xiloniasa's pussy.

"I'm gonna cum!"

"Flood the huntress's mouth!" cheered Deliasonele. "Give her a big blast of your sweet cum!"

Xiloniasa shuddered. She let out a squeak, and then her sweet cum flooded my mouth. I savored the thick, salty-sweet jizz. I swirled it about my mouth before I swallowed it. The warmth filled my belly as a second blast flooded my mouth.

"Oh, wow! That was amazing!" Xiloniasa panted as my mouth slid off her cock.

"She's still hard," Quenyathalee pointed out.

"I told you she was a horny slut," Deliasonele said.

"I need more," Xiloniasa groaned. "A mouth wasn't enough. Can I fuck your pussy, Xerathalasia?"

"I'm married, remember," I grinned as she jerked her cock.

"Oh, right! Deliasonele, you're not married. Let me just stick it in! I won't cum in you!"

"Right," Deliasonele said, rolling her eyes. "You'll probably explode and knock me up. And I don't think you want to be married to me. I'm too wild for you, girl."

"Relythionaia?"

"I have a fiancee," Relythionaia laughed. "As soon as one of us comes in heat when I'm home, we'll be married."

"You can fuck my ass," I told her, flipping onto my hands and knees. "Come on, get your first taste of tight, hot ass!"

"She's got a great one," Deliasonele moaned. "Get in there and pound her before she changes her mind."

"Yes!" groaned Xiloniasa.

The young elf fell to her knees behind me. I shifted beneath the detritus of the forest as her cock nudged at my asshole. She rubbed it up and down, smearing her precum against my sphincter. My pussy clenched. Part of me wanted Xiloniasa to fuck my pussy, but I could never cheat on Atharilesia.

"Sweet Matar, thank you for my cock!" Xiloniasa gasped as she slammed into my asshole.

"Yes," I groaned, throwing my passion-filled prayer to the hermaphroditic goddess that had spawned Elves, Gnomes, Dragons, Sylphs, and Naiads– the five hermaphroditic races. "Thank you for your gifts, Holy Matar!"

Xiloniasa fucked my ass with a frantic need. I shuddered as her cock rammed into my depths over and over. She didn't take her time. She was too horny, too caught up in her first heat to care about anything other than her pleasure.

She would learn to make love.

My pussy clenched as the fiery fervor of her hammering cock radiated out of my bowels. I gasped and moaned, bucking back into her thrusts. My fingers bit into the soil. Her flesh slapped into mine, ringing through the dark woods.

"So good! Oh, wow! I love your ass, Xerathalasia!"

"Just keep fucking me, slut!" I groaned. "Pound me! Make me cum so fucking hard! Sucking your cock made me so horny!"

"Pound her!" groaned Deliasonele. "Work that cock in and out of her tight ass. Make the huntress scream out to Matar!"

"Yes, yes!" I panted, clenching my bowels down on her cock as a wave of heat washed through me. "Just keep fucking me. Make me explode!"

My pleasure swelled. I rocked my body, my breasts swaying beneath me. My back arched, and I threw back my head, my green hair flying about me. My pussy gushed juices. My nectar trickled down my thighs and perfumed the air with the scent of marigolds.

"Xerathalasia! I'm gonna cum! I'm gonna flood your ass! Sweet Matai, yes!"

"Sweet Matar!" I screamed as Xiloniasa slammed her cock into my depths. My orgasm burst through me. My asshole clenched down on her thrusting cock. My pussy erupted, squirting juices as my sex convulsed, wishing it was filled with a thick shaft. Stars burst in front of my eyes.

Xiloniasa's strokes grew more frantic. She gasped and shuddered. Her hands seized my hair, pulling hard as she buried her shaft into my asshole. Her cum squirted hot into my bowels. I shuddered, gripping my asshole down on her cock and milking out all her elf-cum.

"Yes, yes! That was wonderful," Xiloniasa panted. "Thank you."

"You're welcome," I moaned, my orgasm buzzing through me.

Her cock softened in my ass. She pulled out, her dick dangling before her, a drop of cum falling from the tip. She had a big smile on her face, sweat gleaming on her brow. Her camouflage paint had run, streaks of green and black dripping down her body.

"Okay," I said as I stood. I shifted, cum dribbling out of my ass. "I'm going to clean up while Xiloniasa exams the spoor. Tell me how old you think it is."

"Right," Xiloniasa nodded, moving towards it. "A few days," she reported.

"Good," I nodded. "Find the trail. You're taking point."

"What?" Xiloniasa gasped.

She needed to learn. Besides, the rest of us would be watching the trail, too, if she made any mistakes.

Chapter Twenty: The Knight's Hunger

Acolyte Sophia – Ostian, The Kingdom of Secare

We reached the city of Ostian late in the afternoon of the second day after we left K'hol. We crossed a rise, and the city appeared before us. My eyes widened. I had seen rivers before– the Melkith that flowed by Shesax was wide– but I had never realized how big they could get.

"The Kaluth," Angela smiled at the broad expanse that wound wet through the plain towards the sea.

The city was built where two mighty rivers met, merging to form the Kaluth River. Massive bridges crossed the smaller rivers, and the city sprawled around all of them. Small ships docked on harbors cut into the Kaluth.

"It's wider than Shesax," I gaped.

Angela nodded. "They built Ostian where the Red Kaluth flows down south from the Rehyn Mountains along the Deorc Forest before flowing southeast and meeting with the Black Kaluth. We'll be following the Black Kaluth into the Deorc Forest. Its headwaters are found somewhere in those woods."

"It must be the largest river in the world," I gaped as we rode down the hill and joined the throngs of wagons and travelers flowing into the mighty city.

"The Tingul is even larger. They say its mouth is almost two miles wide when it dumps into the Nimborgoth."

"We'll have to cross the Thingul to get to the Despair Mountains, right?" I asked, struggling to remember my geography.

"It forms the border between the Magery of Thosi and the Princedoms of Zeutch."

I nodded, remembering the map. The Despeir Mountains, where the dragon Dominari haunted, formed a barrier between the Princedom and the dreadful Empire of Shizhuth. I had heard foul stories of the naga that ruled that Empire and their cruel treatment of the humans they had enslaved.

"It'll be a long time before we reach there. We still have to find the Oracle," Angela said. "Then we'll learn how to defeat Dominari."

I nodded. Angela was so wonderful. Strong and courageous. I could follow her anywhere. I heeled my mare to a trot, eager to get into the city. Riding with my legs straddling a horse turned out to be more comfortable than side-saddle, even if every rough wagon driver we passed stared at my calves. At the end of the day, I was still sore, but I didn't hurt. My legs were growing toned, and I had lost some of the plumpness from my bottom.

The sun had set by the time we reached the city and crossed into the central ward, the triangular part of the city bordered by the Red Kaluth to the north and the Black Kaluth to the south. This part of the city was much more genteel than the rougher district we passed through on the other shore. If I wasn't with a Knight, I would have been afraid of being molested by some of those rough men.

We took lodging at the Chequered Inn, its sign made of checkered red and black squares. It was a warm inn with a cheery fire burning in the common room. A minstrel played a lyre in the corner while serving maids with low-cut blouses roamed the tables.

"Mmm, there are some fetching women here," I grinned at Angela.

"Hmm?" she asked, staring down at her cup of wine.

"Look at that beauty," I said, pointing at a woman with dusky, Hazian skin and a generous bosom almost spilling out of her blouse. "Wouldn't she be wild to join us in bed tonight?"

"I guess," Angela shrugged.

I frowned. "What's wrong?" I reached out to touch her hand. She was so soft. A warm thrill filled me. "Do you want me all to yourself?"

Angela didn't answer. She took a sip of her wine and let her gaze pass over the room. She froze, and a soft smile spread on her lips. "Well, there are a few nice sights over there," she purred.

I looked in the direction of Angela's gaze. A blonde serving maid laughed as a roguish man fondled her bottom. I frowned at that, but the woman didn't seem to mind. "Yeah, the blonde's scrumptious," I purred.

"Hmm?" she asked, still looking over there. "Yes, the blond." Color appeared in her cheeks. The man was looking back at us. I suppose he was a handsome man, the type that women swooned over in the stories, with straw hair flowing past his chiseled looks. His eyes were bold, ogling Angela in her revealing armor.

I frowned at the man. "He has no right to stare at us."

"What?" Angela blinked, tearing herself away from the appreciation of the blonde serving girl. I couldn't blame her. She was yummy.

"Nothing," I sipped my wine. "Do you want me to invite the blonde to our room?"

"Blonde? Why would you..." Her eyes widening. "Oh, I see. Sorry. Maybe that would be a good idea."

"Ooh, you want to have fun tonight."

Angela squirmed. Her cheeks were red and her eyes dewy. "I do. Why don't you seduce the blonde and take her upstairs after we eat."

I nodded my head in excitement.

The food came, a roast covered in a wonderful sauce and served with fine, white bread and buttered yams. It was the best meal I had since leaving Shesax. I kept my eye on the blonde serving maid as she swayed her fine rear about the serving room.

"Delicious," I purred as I finished my meal and watched that sweet rump.

I wiped my napkin and stood. "Don't take too long, or you'll miss out on all the fun."

Angela nodded her head. "Don't wait for me. Just have fun with her."

I grinned and strolled after the blonde, a sway in my steps.

~ * ~

Knight-Trainee Angela

The handsome man's mouth was hot on mine as he pushed me up against his bedroom door. It wasn't the blonde serving maid that caught my eye. This roguish man's bold stares had lit a fire between my thighs. Sophia was nice, but she wasn't a man. She didn't have everything I needed.

I prayed to Saphique that Sophia wouldn't be too hurt when I didn't show up to the room, but she did have the blonde serving maid to play with. Hopefully, she would be so consumed with her new playmate she would forget about me.

It might even help to get her crush out of her system.

Renard, the ravishingly handsome, blond man opened the door. I stumbled in, my heart thudding. He had eyes like Kevin's, bold and hungry, stripping me naked. I hoped Renard's codpiece's size advertised his cock's girth. My pussy clenched as his hands undid the buckles on my armor.

"I've never ravished a lady knight before," Renard growled. He had the harsh, strong accent of a Zeutchian. My pussy clenched. "I don't have to hold back. You're no delicate maid, but a warrior ready to be fucked."

"Yes!" I moaned. The only cock I've had since leaving Shesax belonged to a monster.

I tore off his shirt, exposing the hard muscles of his chest. He had scars from fighting. I stroked them before he kissed me, crushing my pillowy tits to his strength. His hands slid down and cupped my ass, pulling me against his codpiece. He was hard. And big.

Renard threw me down on the bed as he ripped off the tight hose clinging to his thick legs. His cock sprang out hard and thick. I purred in delight as I rubbed a finger through the dewy lips of my pussy. I was hot and wet, ready to be fucked.

"Come on and fuck me!" I groaned. I was tired of foreplay. That was all making love to Sophia was. Foreplay.

Sweet, wonderful, loving foreplay.

I pushed down my guilt. She was playing with the maid. I doubt she even missed me. She would cum a few times and fall asleep in her lover's arms.

I shoved a pair of fingers into my pussy. "See how wet you've made me, stud!"

"Pater's proud cock!" he growled. "I wish all the women were like you. Bold and ready. You know what you want."

"Your big cock!" I rubbed at my clit. The pleasure trembled through me.

Renard mounted me. My legs parted. His cock slammed into my depths. The headboard slammed into the wall as he drove his thick dick into me. My pussy shuddered in delight, spreading before his girth. I worked my hips, grinding my clit against him as I savored the animalistic passion.

"That's it! Work that cunt on my cock! Slata's cunt, I thought knights were supposed to be noble, but you're just a slut!"

"Fighting's lusty work!" I growled, my fingernails digging into the meat of his ass. "Come on! You can fuck me harder! Make me cum on your cock, stud!"

"Fuck!"

His strokes grew harder. My clit mashed into his pubic bone. My pussy ached. I welcomed the wonderful pain. I gasped and grunted beneath him as I fed my desires. His strong chest crushed my breasts, my nipples throbbing with pleasure.

Our hips bucked together. I squeezed down on his cock. I shuddered. My toes curled. I clawed his back as my passion grew. He fucked me so hard. I boiled inside, the pleasure shooting through my body.

"Sweet Pater's cock!" I screamed as I came. "Oh, fuck! Keep pounding me! Make me cum again, stud! Don't you dare blow your wad yet!"

"I'll keep fucking you all night," he growled.

We changed positions. I knelt like a dog, letting him plow me from behind. I gasped and shuddered as his cock drove so deep into my pussy. I arched my back, cumming again as he hammered my depths. I milked his cock, savoring the pleasure.

His cock erupted into my depths. My orgasm burned through me. Such sweet release. I forgot everything but the pleasure as he spilled in me.

And then we collapsed in a sweaty heap.

The guilt returned. I had cheated on someone. But was it Kevin or Sophia?

Renard slapped my ass. "Ready for another round?"

"Yes," I hissed. I needed to drive away the guilt.

Chapter Twenty-One: The Acolyte's Loss

Acolyte Sophia

I woke up alone. My cheeks were still stained with my tears. Angela had never shown up to our room. I could hear her in the next room, gasping and moaning as a man fucked her. I had been in the throes of passion, the blonde maid's delicate lips nibbling at my pussy when I realized it was Angela in the next room.

My excitement fled. I threw the maid out of my room. I didn't even give her time to dress. She fled the room clutching her clothing. I thought Angela loved me. Things had been so wonderful since the forest. We were in this together. Fighting monsters by day and making love by night.

So what happened? Why did she go to bed with a man? A Las-damned man?

I wiped my eyes with a damp washcloth. I gathered myself. I was the daughter of Duchess Catherine of Tith. I needed to remember that. Angela was just a knight, the daughter of some lowly baron.

I dressed and headed downstairs. She was already waiting for me. "Good morning," she said, forcing a smile.

"Sir Knight," I nodded coolly. I fought my emotions. Why

didn't she love me? Wasn't I good enough for her? What could a man offer that I couldn't? "Let's break our fast and head down the road."

"I'm sorry about last night," Angela said, "it's just..."

"You did not want to spend it with a love-sick girl," I muttered. "I understand now."

"That's not it," Angela sighed. "It's just...we don't really know each other. You don't really love me."

Her words hurt. Of course I loved her. I wouldn't feel so crushed if I didn't. "Don't tell me how to feel!" I snapped at her. I stood. "I'll be in the stables."

"Sophia," she sighed. "I'm sorry. I didn't mean to hurt you. I was hoping you would be happy with the maid."

"Because I have to fall in love with every woman I fuck?" I spat. "You were hardly my first, sir Knight."

I stormed out to the stables. Alone with Purity, I cried.

~ * ~

Knight-Errant Angela – Outskirts of the Deorc Forest, Kingdom of Secare

The last two-and-a-half days had been miserable. Sophia had barely spoken a word to me. And when she did, she called me "sir Knight." We had separate rooms at the last two village inns, at her insistence. I could hear her cry herself to sleep through the thin walls.

Every time I tried to apologize she would grow cold and haughty.

We followed the banks of the Black Kaluth, riding across the pastures on a shepherd's path. The Forest loomed before us. The Kingdom of Secare had long signed treaties with the Elves. Trees could be cut up to a certain line, after that the forest was virgin.

It was a crisp line. The rotten tree stumps covered in vines and spotted with fungus ended at the wall of ancient pines reaching into the sky. There was no trail. I did not understand how we would navigate the woods. And what would happen if we ran across the elves? "We need to be careful," I told Sophia.

"Yes, sir Knight," she said, her chin raised. Her eyes were puffy and red.

"I mean it. You have to stop pouting like a child."

Her face tightened. "I'm sorry for being a silly child and burdening you with my silly crush."

"Dammit, Sophia!" I reached out and grabbed her right shoulder, forcing her to face me. Purity gave a whinny as her rider squirmed. "This is serious. The elves are dangerous and monsters prowl in the woods. You need to act like an adult. I'm sorry that I don't love you. I have a boyfriend. His name is Kevin. Maybe I should have said this earlier, but it was nice sleeping with you. I could forget about him and all our dangers while we were making love. I didn't mean to let you think I cared about you."

Sophia flinched. "I..."

"I didn't handle it well either. I'm sorry. But we need to work together, okay? It's just me and you. No more civilization. It's the wild in there. If you can't handle that, then turn around. I can't coddle you in there."

Color appeared in Sophia's cheeks. She took a deep breath. "Okay. Fine. I'm still mad at you, but I'll stop...pouting."

"Be mad." I sighed. "I deserve that much. I am sorry about what happened in Ostian."

Sophia nodded and then her eyes grew wide. "We're really marching in there?" She stared at the dark woods.

"I'm afraid so." I took her hand. "We'll do it together, okay?"

Sophia nodded and gave my hand a squeeze.

A hot flush shot through me. Together, we rode into the woods.

~ * ~

Xerathalasia – Western Deorc Forest, The Federation of

Deoraciynae

I stood in the brush, my bow ready, an arrow knocked. My heart pounded and my body trembled as I strained to listen. Xiloniasa stood nearby, the young elf tensed and ready to act, blending into the brush. If I hadn't seen her take the position, my eyes would miss her in the dense foliage.

It had been four days since we found the spoor. We had finally tracked down the basilisk. Relythionaia was twenty feet away, crouched beneath a tree, her body painted like bark. I could only see her eyes. My other two hunters, Deliasonele and Quenyathalee, were flushing the basilisk out while we covered the game trail it would run down.

In the distance, my two hunters crashed through the brush. Basilisks were cautions monsters. Such strange behavior from its prey should startle it. Any moment, the monster should scurry down the trail, ready for our arrows to fell it.

My heart beat faster. I took slow, deep breaths to control the shaking in my limbs. My ears strained, listening for any clawed steps or the rustling of scales. My eyes darted, never staring at any one spot, fearing the color yellow— the basilisk's eyes. If our gazes met, I would be petrified, cursed into stone and kept in stasis until a Priestess of Matar could break the enchantment.

Leaves rustled behind us. Was it the wind? I felt no breeze, but we were deep in the forest. I looked up at the limbs above us. They didn't sway. Something was behind us. Was it an animal fleeing the noise my hunters made, or had the basilisk gotten—

A dark-scaled body lunged out of the brush at Xiloniasa. The young elf looked instinctively down as she swung her bow around. The basilisk's gaze met hers as she drew back her bow. My heart froze as the monster's gaze petrified her. Her skin turned dull gray, her cry of panic frozen on her lips. Her body couldn't balance as a statue and crashed into the brush.

I released my arrow and squeezed my eyes shut as the basilisk turned and, crowing like a rooster, rushed at me.

Chapter Twenty-Two: Redheaded Elf

Acolyte Sophia   Western Deorc Forest, The Federation of
Deoraciynae

I patted Purity's neck as the dark trees loomed over us. The elvish
forest was untouched by lumberjacks, the trees growing tall and
proud. The Blath Forest, where the panthopus attacked us, had seen
generations of humans' touch: cutting down trees, trapping,
hunting, and herb gathering. Roads had been blazed through it.
Here, Angela and I led our horses across game trails.

The trees were too thick to allow riding. My feet ached in my
shoes. I had never walked so far. They throbbed with every step.
Angela strode before me in her armor, leading her fierce charger,
Midnight. The horse clanked with every step, his metal barding
rattling. I winced as branches scraped down the metal.

"Can we take a break?" I asked. "I'm not used to walking."

Angela sighed. "Fine."

My emotions were so mixed. I was still angry with Angela, but
she was right. We had to work together in the forest. Somehow, we
had to find the Lesbius Oracle and not get killed by the elves. They
were reputed to be a fierce race, protective of their forest. If we

harmed their trees or the animals that dwelled in harmony with the elves, they would hunt us down.

I trembled as I paused by Angela. I couldn't help glancing at her. She was so beautiful, with red hair that fell about her gleaming pauldrons, and large breasts that gave her an impressive cleavage. Her half-breastplate cupped those wonderful mounds, lifting them up and making my mouth water.

A pendant nestled between her breasts and Angela's fingers stroked it absently.

"Who gave you the amulet?" I asked. My words came out as an accusation and I flushed. I couldn't help it. I did love her, despite Angela's assertion it was just a girlhood crush.

Angela's eyes tightened.

"I'm not trying to start a fight," I said, holding out my hands. "It came out wrong." I swallowed. "Was it Kevin?"

Her fingers clenched about the garnet pendant at the mention of her boyfriend. "No."

"Oh, okay." I swallowed, my head swiveling about to stare off into the brush. The forest all looked the same, dark and green bushes around the trunks of towering trees. I couldn't see more than a few feet before the forest swallowed up everything. Silence hung between us. I wanted to reach out and take her hand.

Why did love have to be so painful?

Birds chirped in the trees. Angela's hands clenched and relaxed on the amulet as she leaned against the tree. I shifted. The silence was too much. I had to say something. "So, um, who did give it to you? Unless it's too personal."

A smile crossed her lips. I was surprised by how girlish it was. "Lady Delilah."

My stomach twisted. She said the woman's name with such a breathless fondness. "So, um, you have a crush on her?"

"A girlhood crush," Angela admitted, her eyes glancing at me.

I flushed. My love for Angela wasn't like a girlhood crush.

"When I was young, around thirteen, Lady Delilah visited my parents' estate." Angela's smile grew, and a flush crossed her cheeks.

Her breasts rose as she quickened the speed of her words. "She rode up on a black charger dressed in her armor. She was a Knight Deute, and she took my breath away. A black cape draped down her back, the contrast making her flaming-red hair almost seem to burn. She was graceful and beautiful. For the first time, I had awakened to sexual desires. I masturbated to Lady Delilah that night. In the quiet of my bower, I discovered the pleasure that existed between my thighs."

A shudder ran through Angela. She closed her eyes and clutched her amulet.

"Was she the knight who was with you during the ceremony?" I asked. I vaguely remembered an older knight with red hair. She had been a mature beauty.

Angela nodded. "Lady Delilah is the reason I am a Knight Deute. I was inspired to follow in her footsteps." She laughed. "I had the foolish notion that when I arrived she would fall in love with me and we would go on adventures."

"But nothing ever happened?"

Angela shook her head. "Lady Delilah was rarely around. She was always out questing. And as I trained, I matured and outgrew my silly crush. I met Kevin and..." Pain clouded her eyes. "Well, anyways, before we left, she presented me the amulet. If it wasn't for her support, I'm not sure I would have had the courage to go on this quest."

I nodded my head. If it hadn't been for the Goddess Saphique appearing in my dreams, I wouldn't have had the courage to continue on the Quest. I would have been thrown out of the priesthood and my mother would have been disappointed. She had such grand dreams of me becoming the High Virgin of Saphique, the highest priestess to the Virgin Goddess.

"Well, are you rested?" Angela asked, letting go of her amulet. It fell down between her breasts and disappeared behind her breastplate.

"I guess," I sighed. "My feet still ache."

"You'll probably form blisters. Can you heal yourself with your magic?"

I had magic. Saphique had given me her blessing, but I wasn't used to casting it. I did have two more healing potion, but using one seemed like such a waste. "Maybe," I answered. I should be able to heal myself.

"Good. I would hate to lose time because you became unable to walk."

"Sorry for being weak," I muttered. "I'm just a spoiled girl, after all."

Angela's eyes hardened. "I thought we agreed no more of that."

"Sorry." My eyes burned. Why couldn't Angela see how much I loved her and return it? I wanted to hold her. "Let's keep going."

Angela grabbed Midnight's reins and led her horse down the game trail. Walking through the woods wouldn't have been too bad if the ground was level. But it wasn't. The trail snaked around any obstacles. Tree roots crossed the path, ripping through the packed dirt. And it turned out walking downhill was as much of a strain as uphill as my thighs burned as I had to step with care to avoid tripping.

My light-brown hair was a tangled mess. Leaves and twigs kept snarling in the strands. The branches all tore at me, snagging on my beige clock and white robes. Angela wore her kite shield strapped to her right arm, pushing back the branches with it and protecting her face.

Strange sounds echoed around us. Animals scampered and growled. Birds chirped. Squirrels darted up and down tree trunks, and other things scurried out of our path through the leaf-strewn ground. I would catch flashes of small, furred bodies and shudder. What sort of rodents darted through the bushes?

Something big lumbered through the brush near us. I squeaked in fear as a large, black-furred body passed through the trees. I had heard bears could attack a person. The creature seemed more than large enough to be a bear. Angela drew her sword and watched the bear. It ambled off, disappearing deeper into the forest.

I sighed in relief.

A few minutes later, Angela froze. I peered around her and gasped. A woman stood on the trail, naked save her red hair. But she wasn't human. Long, pointed ears emerged through her coppery curls and her face was narrow and inhumanly beautiful. The lines of her face were wrong, the angles of her cheekbones slanted down at a steeper angle. She was tall and slim, taller than an average man. Her hips shifted and I blushed– a thick cock dangled between her thighs.

"We mean no harm to the elves of the Federation of Deoraciynae," Angela called out. "We are on a quest for the Lesbius Oracle."

The elf beckoned with her hand before she turned and darted down the trail. Her hair was bright, flashing between the trees as the elf moved with such grace. Angela sheathed her sword, grabbed Midnight's reins, and followed at a jog.

I groaned and forced my weary legs to keep up with Angela.

The trail bent and wound. The elf was ahead of us. Only her red hair flashing through the trees let us know we were still behind her. Angela's armor rattled as she kept up her jog. I stumbled behind her, trying not to trip on the roots as my side began to ache.

We fell farther and farther behind the redheaded elf. "Pater's cock," Angela groaned. "I don't see her anymore."

"No," I heaved. "I...don't...either..." It hurt to speak. Sweat drenched my face and my hand grew slippery as I held Purity's reins. My gentle mare nuzzled my hand as I stopped. "I think we lost her."

A woman shouted and a rooster crowed.

"What was that?" I gasped.

"Not sure," Angela said. "But it's coming from the direction the elf ran. Maybe she's in trouble. Come on."

"Right," I groaned, and forced myself to move.

Chapter Twenty-Three: Monstrous Mating

Xerathalasia

My bow twanged as I released my arrow. I squeezed my eyes shut. Wood scraped along scales. It sounded like I only glanced the basilisk with my arrow. I couldn't open my eyes. If I looked into the basilisk's golden eyes, I would suffer Xiloniasa's fate— petrification.

"Xerathalasia! Move!" Relythionaia, another of my hunters, shouted. An arrow hissed, and a rooster crowed. She must have wounded the basilisk.

I threw myself forward, hoping I didn't crash into a tree trunk. I rolled along the ground and crashed into a brush. Something heavy thudded past me. I risked a glance. The basilisk crashed past me. It had dark, dull-green scales over most of its body, squat and four-legged like a lizard. A fat tail swung behind it. The scales turned into brown feathers at the head. It had the head of a rooster, with a red comb along the crest and a sharp, yellow beak. More brown feathers adorned its taloned, bird-like feet.

The basilisk turned its head. I snapped my eyes shut and drew an arrow from the quiver at my hip. My naked breasts heaved as I drew my bow and fired blindly. The monster didn't cry in pain. I missed. I scrambled back as it crashed towards me.

My ears twitched. Its taloned feet tore at the ground. It crowed and clucked its beak. My flesh crawled. A basilisk's bite was venomous. I strained my ears and judged how close the monster was. I dived to the right and let it barrel past me.

Another arrow hissed. I risked another look. Relythionaia stood a few feet away knocking another arrow. One of hers had already embedded in the thick hide of the beast right above its shoulder. The basilisk turned on her and lunged. Relythionaia closed her eyes in time.

"Dodge!" I shouted.

My hunter dived right. It was the wrong direction. The basilisk's beak snapped out, tearing a viscious wound into her naked thigh. Relythionaia gasped in pain and fell to the ground. She convulsed and then fell unconscious. Basilisk venom didn't kill, instead it rendered its victim unconscious.

Basilisks preferred to mate with their prey before feasting.

I turned around, putting my back to the beast as I plunged into the brush. Everything had gone wrong. Relythionaia, Xiloniasa, and I had waited to ambush the basilisk. We had tracked it down, and my other two hunters, Deliasonele and Quenyathalee, were supposed to drive it into our ambush down a game trail. But the basilisk had somehow gotten behind us and attacked poor Xiloniasa.

I crashed through the brush. "Hunters! To me!"

The basilisk clucked behind me, crashing and scrambling through the brush on its four legs. It was fast. I couldn't risk looking behind me. I couldn't take the chance I would look into the beast's golden eyes.

I wanted to return to my wife. Atharilesia was pregnant with our first daughter. I wanted to hold her in my arms. I couldn't die here in the woods because a hunt went bad. I had been leading hunts for forty years. I was a master in the woods.

My feet avoided roots and rocks as I ran barefoot. The brush didn't scratch my naked flesh. The plants parted for me. I was an elf, born of the element of wood. The foul basilisk was an interloper into my forest, a foul creation of the mad Biomancer Vebrin and loosed upon the world.

I dodged around a tree. I flowed over a mossy log. And still it chased. I turned to the right. I needed to double back and find Deliasonele and Quenyathalee. But the basilisk was persistent. It crowed again. It sounded closer.

Could it run faster than an elf?

My head kept turning. I kept wanting to look behind me and mark my pursuer. I fought my instincts. I vaulted over a mushroom-covered stump and landed amid soft ferns. The feathery fronds parted for me. I burst out on the game trail that would lead back to the ambush spot.

The basilisk crowed. A weight struck my back.

I crashed to the ground. Sharp talons scratched my back. I screamed out in surprise. The trail rushed up at me. I rolled on the hard ground, a rock bruising my side. I ended up on my back. The basilisk was between my legs, his forelimbs grasping my thighs, the sharp talons pricking my skin. Its beak pressed against my pussy, the red comb atop its head flopped as it nuzzled.

A hot, thick tongue licked out. I groaned. It would fuck me before it killed me. I closed my eyes before it looked up at me. I felt around for a weapon. I had to do something. The tongue slithered between my pussy lips and flicked my clit.

A hot rush washed through me. My nipples hardened. I shuddered as my body betrayed me. I fought my desire as the hard beak rubbed at my clit and its tongue probed the depths of my pussy. My cunt throbbed and my juices flowed. The basilisk crowed in delight, fucking its tongue deeper into my depths and swirling around the walls of my pussy.

I groaned. It felt good. I shook my head, fighting the depravity of the moment. "Stop!" I gasped.

The monster didn't listen.

My toes curled as its tongue slithered through my pussy. Its taloned claws squeezed harder on my thighs as I thrashed, pinning me in place. I had to keep my eyes closed as my hands swept across the ground for something to attack the beast with.

I brushed my leather quiver that hung from my side. I had arrows. I could stab the monster. My hand reached the top of the quiver. It was empty. The arrows must have tumbled out when the basilisk tackled me.

I cracked my eye as I peered to the left, looking for the white-gray feathers fletching my arrows. I saw nothing.

The basilisk crowed again. Its tongue swiped up, brushing my clit. I spasmed and gasped in delight. The pleasure rippled through my body. I moaned and squirmed. Part of me wanted to give in and enjoy the monster's molestations.

But I couldn't. I had to keep fighting.

"Matar, help!" I prayed to the hermaphroditic goddess of nature. She had birthed elves along with the four other hermaphroditic races. The basilisk's tongue licked over and over at my sex. It loved my pussy juices. My hips bucked against his tongue and hard beak. "Matar's big cock!" I cursed as the pleasure oared through me.

The basilisk's hard beak pressed into my pussy, rubbing up and down my flesh. My folds burst with pleasure. My fingers clenched into the hard dirt of the path as I climaxed. The pleasure washed through me, drowning out my fears. I was left with only lust. The basilisk's tongue collected my juices as they gushed into its mouth.

"Damn!" I groaned. "Oh, damn! So good! Matar, yes!"

Another orgasm flooded my body. My hands found my breasts. I squeezed them and pinched my nipples. I pulled on them, stretching out my tits as my body quavered beneath the amazing tongue of the basilisk. Every time the monster licked and nuzzled me, I burst with more pleasure. I screamed out for everyone to hear.

"Yes, yes! Eat me! Oh, damn! Matar's big tits and big cock! Oh, yes!"

My pussy convulsed about the basilisk's probing tongue. It was amazing. I screamed out my delight. My passion echoed through the woods. The basilisk crowed in delight. My thighs spasmed, brushing the ticklish feathers adorning its head.

The basilisk lifted its head and crowed loud. It was a possessive

156

crow, declaring to all the world it had claimed elvish pussy. I shuddered and heaved as its heavy, scaly body crawled up mine. My nipples rasped against its dry, hard scales, sending electricity shooting down my body. Its tongue licked my face. I opened my mouth and tasted the marigold passion of my pussy on its tongue as we kissed. Its hard beak rubbed on my soft lips.

A hard cock rubbed at my thigh. The heavy beast shifted. It was so squat it had no trouble nudging the folds of my pussy with its cock. I groaned. I hadn't had a cock in my pussy in months. It always seemed like I was out on a hunt when my wife went into heat and sprouted her dick.

"Matar, yes!" I groaned as its thick, hard cock pressed into my pussy.

It differed from an elf's girl-cock. It was tapered, growing larger and larger as it drove deeper into me. My pussy ached as it stretched around the thick base. I wrapped my arms around the basilisk, lost to the pleasure. I rubbed my face into the soft feathers that adorned his rooster-like head as his rough scales rasped against my breasts, belly, and thighs.

"Fuck me!" I hissed, humping my hips. "Pound me with that cock! Oh, Matar, yes! I needed this! I needed to be fucked in my pussy!"

I had no guilt. The basilisk couldn't impregnate me. It wasn't cheating on my wife. Only letting another hermaphroditic cock fuck my pussy would be cheating. I couldn't get pregnant. I could enjoy the monstrous dick slamming into my depths.

"Oh, yes! Oh, fuck! Keep working your cock in and out of me! Mmm, yes! That's it! Matar, yes! What a wonderful cock!"

I kept moaning and panting as the tapered dick reamed in and out of my pussy. My nipples were on fire as they rasped against its rough scales. The basilisk clucked its beak in delight and crowed as it buried its cock over and over into my hot depths.

Its talons scraped the dirt beside my body as it rammed its cock faster and faster into me. My fingers scraped along its armored back as the pleasure swelled inside me. My clit exploded with bliss every time the monster slammed its dick into my hot depths. I arched my hips, grinding my sensitive clit on its rough scales.

"Yes! Matar, yes!" I screamed as I came.

My pussy writhed about the amazing cock. I bucked and squirmed as the pleasure hammered my mind. I didn't care about anything. Only the pleasure. It filled my mind. I held my basilisk lover tight as his thrusting cock triggered another orgasm.

They followed one after another. My nerves burned with passion. My muscles contracted. My pussy ached and my clit throbbed. Every orgasm made my nub more and more sensitive. The pleasure became the sweetest agony. My toes curled as I humped faster.

"Pound me! Yes! Matar's big tits! Keep fucking me! Never stop!"

The basilisk's thrusts grew rapid fire. Its pelvis hammered faster than any elf could fuck. The cock slid in and out of me so fast, my pussy felt ever-full. The basilisk crowed the loudest, proud of its conquest.

Hot cum squirted into me. The basilisk kept crowing. I screamed as my orgasm burst through me. Thick cum was in my pussy. It overflowed me. So much pumped into my body. It spilled out, running down my ass.

"Matar, yes!" I gasped.

The basilisk thrust one last time. My pussy squeezed out the last of the cum. Its cock shrank out of me. I gasped and heaved, the pleasure still buzzing through my veins. I almost fell into a stupor, exhausted by the amazing fuck.

And then the fear struck through me. It had satiated its lusts. Now it would feed its other hunger. I grasped its neck as its beak snapped at my face.

"Deliasonele!" I screamed. "Quenyathalee!"

The basilisk crowed in frustration as it tried to kill me.

Chapter Twenty-Four: Fighting Blind

Knight-Errant Angela

The woman's shouting grew louder. A sharp beak snapped. The trail took a sharp turn. I slid to a stop. An elf with short, green hair lay beneath a large lizard, her hands fighting to hold back a sharp rooster's beak.

"Basilisk!" I gasped.

"What?" Sophia asked as she stopped beside me.

I squeezed my eyes shut and with my freehand grabbed Sophia. I covered her eyes with my hand and pulled her off the trail. She gasped and struggled against me as I pressed her body against a large tree. Her body was lithe. Memory of the times we made love flashed through me.

But my fear drowned them out. I couldn't let Sophia get hurt. "That's a basilisk. If you look into its eyes, you'll be petrified."

"Saphique watch us," gasped Sophia, "and protect your daughters."

"Yeah," I nodded.

The elf cried out again in her musical tongue. She wasn't the redhead elf we had chased. Where had that one gone? Well, it didn't matter. "Stay here," I whispered.

I raised my shield strapped to my left hand, blocking the basilisk from my sight. I drew my sword and advanced down the trail. I could only see a few feet before me beneath my shield. The basilisk thrashed and crowed as the elf screamed.

The thick, swishing tail of the basilisk appeared at my feet. I closed my eyes, moved my shield, and swung. My sword bit into flesh. Not deeply. The scales were hard. The basilisk crowed in pain. I raised my shield as it scrambled towards me.

The monster crashed into my shield. Metal rasped as its talons and beak scraped against it. I thrust my sword around the shield, hoping to find the basilisk's flesh. The tip scored along its hard scales, not penetrating its side.

"Damn!" I shouted as the monster's ferocious attacks drove me back. I thrust again, angling my blade to hit its feathered head. It had to be more vulnerable there with only feathers and no scales.

"Angela!" Sophia cried out in fear.

"Keep your eyes shut!" I shouted. "Stay in the trees!"

The basilisk swiped beneath my shield, scratching my armored, left greave. Its talons grabbed me and jerked. I stumbled backwards as the monster rushed me. It crashed into my shield again. I gasped as I was thrown to the ground. I kept my shield up as the monster leaped on me. Its weight was heavy. The top of its beak appeared over the rim of my shield, snapping and clucking as the monster sought my flesh.

I closed my eyes and struggled to thrust my sword into its belly. On my back, pinned beneath the creature, I had trouble stabbing. I couldn't draw back my arm to get any momentum or to put my body's weight behind the attack.

"Las's pox-ridden cock!"

The elf shouted something. A bow twanged. The basilisk crowed in pain and scrambled off of me. I risked a peek. The elf dived into the brush as the basilisk charged down the trail after her. I forced myself to stand, heaving in breath. I charged after the monster, ready to raise my shield if it snapped around at me. A pair of arrows had embedded an inch into the beast's scaly hide and my sword had only scratched its flesh.

I slammed my sword down on its back. My blade left a shallow cut into its flesh before bouncing back.

It was too armored to cut.

I raised my shield as it turned and swiped its talons at me.

~ * ~

Acolyte Sophia

I know I should keep my eyes closed as I peeked around the tree. But I couldn't help myself. The basilisk wasn't focused on me. I gasped as Angela's hard, overhand swing bounced off the basilisk's thick back. The knight raised her shield as the monster swiped at her with its sharp talons.

I caught a glimpse of golden eye and ducked back around the tree. The elf shouted something in her musical language. A bow twanged again, and the basilisk crowed. I peeked out again, my stomach twisting into knots, my heart screaming to not look.

"Please, no golden eyes, Saphique," I prayed beneath my breath.

The basilisk was rushing at the naked elf. She had her eyes closed. She was tall and graceful, her body covered in green, brown, and black paints. She dived into the brush and seemed to vanish, blending in with the vegetation. Angela, shield held high, charged after the basilisk and scored another glancing blow.

"I need to do something," I whispered as I struggled to remember my training in priestly magic over the terror thudding through my veins.

Priestly magic differed from the arcane arts wielded by the Mages of Thosi, Priestess Michelle had droned. *Mages channel the energy found in the natural world to violate its laws and create powerful effects. Priests draw their power directly from the god or, in our case, goddess they serve. This power manifests in different ways. For us, it manifests in our breast milk and our pussy juices.*

Once you've learned Saphique's mysteries and become a full priestess, you will be able to lactate at will. Now what can we do with our magic? We can heal the sick. We can make potions that break curses and exorcise the dead. We can enchant weapons and armor to defend their bearers. Priestly magic isn't flashy like the Mages. We protect, enhance, and heal.

I could enchant her blade for a few minutes.

I unfastened my belt, dropping the satchel and my enchanted dagger. My robes fell open, exposing my small breasts. I pinched my right nipple. Saphique had given me magic, but I hadn't tried to use it. I concentrated on my breasts filling with milk as I played with my nipple.

"Please, Saphique," I prayed. It wasn't necessary but helped me concentrate on milk filling my tits. "Grant my breasts your sweet milk."

A heat gathered in my breasts. They felt full. My nipples ached. I needed to be emptied. I pulled my nipple and sweet milk squirted onto my fingers. I milked my tit again, letting my creamy drink coat my hands.

I struggled to remember the words of the spell as I darted into the fight.

Chapter Twenty-Five: Lesbian Magic

Knight-Errant Angela

"Angela!"

I turned and gaped as Sophia darted down the path. Her robe was open, her small breasts jiggling. They beaded with white drops of milk. She held her hands out before me, more milk staining her palms. She had her eyes squeezed shut, the only sensible thing she had done.

"In Pater's name, what are you doing?" I demanded.

"Enchanting your blade."

The basilisk crowed as it charged after the elf.

"What? How can you have magic? You're an acolyte? Aren't only priestesses allowed to cast spells?"

"I'm a special exemption," Sophia gasped. "Can I open my eyes?"

"Yeah, you're covered by my shield."

Sophia opened her green eyes. Then she rubbed her milk-covered hands on my sword, staining the metal with smears of white. "Saphique, the Virgin Goddess that loves all women, bless this weapon so it may protect its bearer. Let this sword shine bright, a beacon to defend all women."

I gasped as my sword was engulfed in a pink, pure light. After a few heartbeats, the light dimmed, but left pink flames dancing up and down the blade. The sword hummed in my hand. Power brimmed in it. Hope bloomed inside me. I could defeat the basilisk.

"Good luck," Sophia said and kissed me.

It was brief, and then she fled back to safety. The warmth of her lips lingered and my heart beat faster. "Focus," I muttered and turned, throwing a glance over my shield. The elf had scrambled up a tree. The basilisk's beak tore at the tree while its fore-talons scraped and ripped, throwing chunks of bark to the ground.

I advanced, raising my shield. I peeked around the edge, my sword held up, readied for the thrust.

I stepped on a twig. It snapped loud.

The basilisk turned. I squeezed my eyes shut. The elf shouted from above me. I pictured the battlefield, imagining when I should thrust at the charging basilisk. I pivoted on my left foot as my right leg stepped forward and my right arm thrust at the beast.

My arm shook as the monster impacted the blade. I stumbled back as its weight slid up my sword and into the hilt. The basilisk let out a gurgling groan. Its claws tore at the ground and its tail thrashed. The weight of the collapsing monster ripped my sword from my grip.

I kept my eyes closed. "Is it dead?"

"Yes," the elf said.

~ * ~

Xerathalasia

I dropped from the tree. The basilisk's cum dripped out of my pussy and ran down my thighs. I shuddered, my emotions mixed between the rapture of the monster's cock and the revulsion I had for submitting to its bestial lusts.

I turned my attention to the pair of humans. The knight

164

yanked her sword from the dead basilisk's gullet and wiped her blade clean with a rag she produced from a pouch. She sheathed her sword and faced me. The other woman rushed forward, her robes still open. Her breasts were small, but a mother's milk dribbled down her mounds and across her fair stomach.

"Who are you?" I asked, speaking their harsh tongue. It hurt my jaw. There was no music to it.

"I am Knight-Errant Angela of the Knights Deute, and this is Acolyte Sophia of the Temple of the Pure."

"We did it!" Sophia gasped and hugged Angela from behind. The young lady was excitable, her light-brown hair bouncing across her face.

"You have trespassed on our forest."

Angela stiffened and pushed the acolyte off of her. Sophia gasped as she stumbled back. "Angela!"

"We are searching for the Lesbius Oracle," the knight said. "We are not here to harm your people or your woods. We are on a Quest."

My ears twitched. I bit my lip and then I remembered poor, poisoned Relythionaia. "We can discuss this later. I have wounded hunters."

"Wounded!" Sophia gasped. "I can help."

She was a priestess. "Okay."

The young woman rushed back and picked up her belt. She closed her robes as I fetched my bow and a few arrows that lay scattered about the road. She rushed back, leading a pair of horses. Angela took the reins of a particularly fearsome brute that snorted at me.

"I am not your enemy, friend horse," I said in elvish. The horse snorted and his eyes relaxed.

Angela frowned as I reached out my hand. "He's trained to bite."

"He will not harm me," I smiled and stroked his snout. Then in elvish, "What sort of mistress owns you?"

The horse neighed, the rich sounds proclaiming the

wondrousness of Angela and how proud he was to serve her. The white mare added her whinny and nuzzled affectionately at Sophia's neck. The young woman giggled as the horse nibbled on her ear.

"Stop that, Purity," grinned Sophia. "My ear is not an apple."

It wasn't a crime for a human to transgress our lands, but we did not encourage it either. Usually, we turned them back. If they resisted, or harmed our woods, then we feathered them with arrows and left their corpses on the boundary as a warning. But a knight on a Quest to see the Oracle.

A knight who saved my life.

I led them down the trail at a jog. Sophia gasped and whined at the pace, but Angela had far more stamina. In a few minutes, we reached the unconscious and feverish form of Relythionaia and the petrified statue of Xiloniasa. I shuddered, bending over the young elf and stroking her stone hair.

"I'm sorry," Angela said, putting her hand on my shoulder. "What about the red-haired elf?"

"What?" I asked.

"We were following a red-haired elf when we found you. She must have run past you. Is there a village nearby?"

"No elf passed me when the basilisk was...attacking me." My cheeks reddened. I needed to clean my pussy. "Besides, I have never met an elf with hair that color."

"We did see her," Angela said, her eyebrows furrowing.

Sophia knelt beside me. "Poor thing," she whispered. The acolyte pulled out a small, glass ampoule and threw it down hard.

"What are you doing?" I gasped in horror as the glass bottle smashed on Xiloniasa, splashing her with a milky liquid.

"Holy milk banishes curses," Sophia answered. "Look."

My eyes widened. Everywhere the milk touched her had washed away the stone, revealing Xiloniasa's painted flesh. The living flesh spread across the stone like a stain soaking into a rag. The magic worked faster and faster, banishing the petrification. I trembled for joy as Xiloniasa gasped and sat up.

"What?" the young elf asked as she looked around the clearing.

166

"Xerathalasia. What happened? I saw golden eyes and..."

I hugged Xiloniasa, tears burning down my cheeks. "You were petrified, but the acolyte saved you."

I made my choice. We slew the basilisk. The hunt was finished. I would let my huntresses return to Khalesithan while I would guide the knight and the acolyte north to the Lesbius Oracle.

Chapter Twenty-Six: Healing Milk

Acolyte Sophia

I smiled as the elves embraced. They were both so beautiful and graceful. I had heard elves were hermaphroditic, but neither had a cock. And their breasts were beautiful. They seemed a little perkier than a human's breasts, their nipples upswept and hard.

I moved to the unconscious elf and stripped naked, letting my robe and cloak fall to the ground. My breasts were still lactating, and my warm milk had tricked down to my shaved pussy. Angela leaned against a tree, her eyes hot on my flesh.

I flushed. If she didn't love me, then why did I always feel her eyes watching my body, admiring my beauty? My pussy grew wetter as I knelt next to the wounded elf, her coil of braided, green hair stretched out beside her. A bloody wound stained her thigh, and she whimpered and shuddered on the ground.

"I'll heal you," I whispered, stroking her face.

The elf let out a breathy groan and her ears twitched.

I took a deep breath and shoved two fingers from my right hand deep into my wet pussy. I had practiced this spell since I was a novice, though this was the first time I had ever cast it. "Saphique, bless the font of my womanhood with your loving power."

I gasped as the Goddess's power flooded through my body. My breasts quivered as excitement engulfed my pussy. The pleasure rippled through my body. I threw back my head and moaned as my fingers were bathed by my climax.

"Sweet Saphique," I gasped before I sucked in a deep breath. My pussy continued to tingle as I drew out my fingers. A powerful desire filled me. I needed to be touched and pleasured. I needed to explode with passion.

I fought down my lusts and brought my fingers to my nipples. As I anointed each of my hard nipples with my blessed pussy juices, I prayed, "Saphique, transform my virgin milk with your love. Let my milk heal the sick and infirme."

The milk in my breasts seemed to boil, shooting waves of heat back down to my tingling pussy. I bit my lip as my head swam with passion. The spell had transformed my milk into a healing draught. I could bottle my milk as a potion or allow the wounded elf to suckle from my breast.

I chose to nurse her.

I picked up her head and cradled her to my breasts. I rubbed my hard nipple on her lips. Her nostrils flared as she inhaled the scent of my breast milk mixed with my tart pussy. The elf opened her mouth and latched onto my nipple.

"That's it," I groaned as she nursed.

My milk flowed into her. My nipple burned with pleasure. My pussy clenched. It was like my nipple was connected directly to my pussy. I squeezed my thighs together and massaged my aching clit as I stroked the elf's face.

The wound in her leg glowed pink as the healing magic went to work. The elf suckled harder. I shuddered and moaned as the pleasure increased in me. The elf moved and moaned about my nipple. Her violet eyes opened.

"That's it," I purred. "Keep drinking and be healed."

My hand stroked up her cheek to her long ear. The elf shuddered and suckled harder. She mewled about my nipple. Her thighs shifted and the scent of bluebells filled my nose. It took me a moment to realize it was her arousal.

Elves smelled wonderful.

I stroked her ear again, and she shuddered, pressing her thighs together. "Mmm, you like it when I do this?"

I loved the way she moaned and shuddered as I stroked her ear. I leaned over and nibbled on the end. She bucked in my arms, suckling hard and draining my right nipple. Without missing a moment, she kissed over to my left.

"Oh, yes!" I gasped as the elf pushed me down as she suckled.

I spread my legs as the elf lay atop me. I humped, rubbing my hard clit and pussy against her smooth stomach. I played with her ears as my clit burned with rapture. Over and over, the pleasure sparked through me.

"That's it! Drink your fill," I moaned. "Let the Goddess Saphique's love fill your body."

The elf moaned. Her hips shifted. I humped harder. My pussy clenched as I smeared my hot flesh against her smooth stomach. My fingers stroked her ears faster and faster as the pleasure built in my core. Every time my clit slid across her flesh, I shuddered and came closer to coming.

"Oh, you're a sexy, naughty elf," I moaned. "Keep suckling. Oh, yes! That's it! Wow, yes!"

The elf lifted her face from my nipple and moaned in her beautiful language. It was pure desire. Her body trembled atop me as she orgasmed. I stroked her ears as I stared into her beautiful face, delighted I could give this female elf pleasure.

My pussy contracted. The pleasure boiled through me. I shuddered. My pussy creamed her stomach, smearing my juices up and down her flesh. I moaned in delight as I convulsed. The elf slid up my body, her breasts pressing against mine as her sweet lips kissed me.

I savored the creamy taste of my milk as we writhed together in passion. Her fingers were exciting as they caressed my flesh. I gasped for breath when she broke the kiss. I humped again, rubbing my pussy on her hot thigh and another shudder raced through my body.

"Thank you," the elf whispered in my ear.

"I'm glad I could heal you," I gasped.

The elf smiled and kissed down my body. My head tossed back and forth. The other two elves and Angela watched us. Angela's cheeks were red and her hand had disappeared beneath her chainmail loincloth. She shuddered as she rubbed hard at her flesh. The two elves rubbed each other's pussies, their violet eyes dancing as they watched us.

"Relythionaia will make you cum hard," the elf we rescued from the basilisk grinned.

"I will. Thank you," the elf moaned, her green braid draped across my stomach.

I gasped as the elf nuzzled her face into my flesh. "Turn around. Let me taste you, too! You smell like bluebells!"

The elf gracefully spun. Her height made her have to contort her body so we could both devour each other's pussies. She had such grace. I stroked her smooth ass as my tongue slid through the folds of her pussy. She tasted like a flower's perfume. I drank her juices. I had never tasted a pussy like hers. I missed the saltier taste of human pussy, but elf cunt definitely had its charm.

There were subtle differences. The elf's pussy had an extra layer of folds for me to nuzzle and play with. Her clit was fat, one of the largest I had ever seen. I licked and nuzzled it as the elf's tongue slid through my folds.

"Yes!" I moaned as the elf's tongue contorted and writhed, moving in ways no human tongue could replicate. "Saphique, yes!"

The elf worshiped my pussy. She swirled through all my folds while her deft fingers rubbed at my clit. My thighs spasmed as sweet waves of pleasure washed through me. I concentrated on her clit as my fingers worked deep into her hole. I curled them, wondering if she had that special spot in the depths of her pussy.

The elf moaned and gasped in her delightful language as I stroked through her pussy. She spasmed when I touched the special spot every woman had in their depths. I smiled and stroked the bundle of nerves that would make her erupt. I tongued her clit while she gasped into my pussy.

Relythionaia squirmed and spasmed on my face. Her flowery juices squirted into my lips as she screamed her pleasure. Her pussy spasmed about my fingers as her intense orgasm burst through her. I drank down her squirting juices, proud of my work.

"Now make me cum, elf slut," I purred, humping my hips as I licked and nuzzled at her pussy, allowing Relythionaia to focus on pleasing me.

Her fingers pushed into my depths, rapidly fucking in and out. I squirmed and gasped into her delicious pussy. Her tongue swirled around my clit. Then she nipped it with her teeth and suckled on my bud.

"Oh, yes!" I groaned. My pussy contracted. I let my orgasm trigger my pussy to squirt, forcing out the powerful convulsions that shot out blasts of my juices into the elf's hungry lips as I collapsed and shuddered on the ground. "Sweet Saphique!"

The elf turned around, her face dripping with my tart passion. "Mmm, you have such a cute clitoris, human."

"I'm Sophia," I smiled and pulled her down for a kiss.

~ * ~

Knight-Errant Angela

I shuddered on my fingers as Sophia and the elf shared their kiss, both their faces sticky with their excitement. The two elves beside me were already licking their fingers clean of the other's juices, satisfied smiles on their faces.

The elf I rescued from the basilisk turned to me. "I am Xerathalasia."

I nodded. Her name rolled off her lips. "Well, Xerazalsi," I said, stumbling over her name.

"You can simply call me Xera," she smiled. "I have dealt with humans before. Our words do not come easily to your lips."

172

"No," I laughed. "Well met, Xera."

"I will send my hunters home and lead you to the Lesbius Oracle. It is to the north."

"Good thing we found you. I really would love to thank the red-haired elf that led us to you. I doubt we would ever have located the Oracle without help."

"Yes, it was fortunate for the both of us," Xera nodded. "The Oracle is in a dark and dangerous part of the woods. My people rarely venture there. But I will guide you safely."

"Thank you."

Chapter Twenty-Seven: Elvish Guide

Acolyte Sophia – Western Deorc Forest, The Federation of Deoraciynae

The two other elf hunters appeared silently out of the woods. Like Xera, they were gorgeous, tall and lithe, their bodies painted in greens and browns to let them blend into the woods. Their keen eyes flickered at Angela and me, their ears twitching in obvious curiosity at the sight of two humans in their woods.

I was still naked. It was wonderful to not have to wear the robe. As an acolyte of the Temple of Pure, I had spent many years wearing next to nothing in the warm seclusion of our temple. While traveling with Angela on her Quest, I had to wear more modest robes and a cape to keep any man from seeing my naked, virgin flesh.

But these elves were women. I still had Relythionaia's delicious, flowery pussy juices on my lips. My body still tingled from our love-making. Her pussy had tasted so delicious, more like a flower's nectar than the salty musk I was used to.

Xera, speaking in elvish, addressed her four huntresses. They all glanced repeatedly at Angela and me. I shifted, letting them drink in the sight of my body. I was an acolyte of Saphique, sworn to love all women and spurn the touch of men. Elves were hermaphroditic, but none appeared to have a cock, so I let them look. I toyed with my belly-piercing, a silver stud adorned with a ruby, as I smiled at the elves.

Angela watched me. The knight was always watching me. She didn't love me. She spurned my crush as something girlish and beneath her, and yet her blue eyes always seemed to find me. Her gaze made my heart beat with hope. I squashed that hope.

She had made her feelings clear. She loved Kevin. A man.

So I smiled at the elves. They were beautiful. Especially Xiloniasa. She had an innocence about her. She seemed the youngest though it was hard to tell. Elves didn't age like humans, or so the stories claimed. Xiloniasa looked eighteen, but she could be a hundred. It was a shame all the elves were leaving save Xera. I could have some fun.

When I made love to Relythionaia, my heartache for Angela was buried by lust.

But at least Xera was coming with us. She promised to guide us to the Lesbius Oracle, located somewhere to the north in the forest. Without her, Angela and I would have kept heading east and never would have found it.

The elf hunters broke apart. "My huntresses will look for the red-haired elf and make sure she is fine."

Angela nodded. "She probably saw the basilisk and just kept running."

"Most likely," Xera frowned. "I had not heard hair dying was practiced by the western elves."

If all the elves had green hair, I wasn't surprised that a few wanted to dye theirs to stand out. I was sure she was fine, but it was lucky we came across her. We would have missed Xera and her hunters.

Xiloniasa strolled to me, moving with such grace. She stopped before me. "Thank you," she said in a musical accent, the words rolling off her lips.

"You're welcome," I smiled. "I'm glad I could save you."

Xiloniasa nodded, though I saw something in her violet eyes. She didn't understand my tongue. "Thank you," she repeated. Xera must have told her these words.

I put my arms around her neck. It was hard. Elves were tall. The shortest elf had the height of a man. She leaned down, her ears twitching above her green hair. I planted a hot kiss on her lips. Our breasts rubbed together as my tongue filled her mouth. Her arms wrapped around me, holding me tight as we communicated without words.

I was a little breathless when I broke the kiss, and my pussy was on fire. I wanted to do more, but Xiloniasa broke away, joining the other elf hunters. Angela's eyes were still on me. I looked at her and she jumped, turning to face the departing elves.

The pain in my heart returned. Why did I have to fall in love with a woman who wouldn't love me back? Tears burned in my green eyes. I turned to my discarded clothing. As I bent down to pick up my robe, I wiped at my eyes surreptitiously.

~ * ~

Knight-Errant Angela

My eyes drifted back to Sophia as she bent over to pick up her clothes. Whenever my thoughts wandered, my eyes found her. She was beautiful, in a spoiled brat kind of way. Her ass was curvy, and her shaved pussy glinted wet between her thighs.

Memories of our shared passion flushed through me. My pussy itched, and my hard nipples pressed on my armor. My chainmail loincloth clinked as my hips shifted and my thighs pressed together. Sophia was beautiful.

I looked away as she stood up to pull on her white robe. Xera watched me. The elve's purple eyes were studious, her long, pointed ears twitching. I frowned at her. She stood naked– the elves didn't seem to believe in clothing– with only a belt around her waist from

176

which to hang her quiver and a pouch. She smiled at me as she bent her bow and removed the string, tucking it into her pocket. A bow strung for too long ruined the string.

"Where are your supplies?" I asked.

Xera laughed. "This is our woods. It provides food. We do not have to carry supplies like you humans." She glanced at our horses and their saddlebags.

I nodded my head. "So how far is the oracle?"

"With you humans, probably an eight day walk. I doubt you can move as fast through the woods as me."

"Dangers?"

"Yes. We will have to slip by the giganraneae that surround the Oracle."

I shuddered. They were a race of giant spiders. Intelligent and dangerous. They built traps with webs and hunted humanoids to implant their eggs in. The monsters were birthed by the God Las. His uncontrollable lusts had compelled the god to fuck anything, including a werespider who birthed the first giganraneae.

"Lovely," I groaned. "And why in Pater's cock haven't you and your hunters exterminated the monsters?"

"The Oracle likes them," the elf answered. "The giganraneae know to stay in her valley. If they leave, they will be killed. If we enter, we may be taken...and used."

I shuddered, understanding her meaning.

"Only the most daring of us would ever seek the Oracle." Xera leaned closer. "She likes her privacy."

I nodded my head. That made sense. "She doesn't want to waste her powers on inconsequential requests."

"Most likely." Xera scanned. "Your...companion is ready."

My cheeks flushed. The way she said companion was almost a caress. "That's right. My companion. Nothing more."

The elf smiled.

Sophia walked over, dressed again, leading her white mare. Purity nuzzled at her neck. "Shall we keep trudging through this..." Sophia glanced at Xera, "...*amazing* forest?"

"Yes. We have a long trip ahead of us."

Chapter Twenty-Eight: The Elf's Cock

Xcrathalasia

It was on the third day of traveling with the humans when I came into heat.

The humans were as slow as I feared. They had to lead their horses and walk. Sophia was the worse. Her constant bickering made my teeth hurt. But her sweet caresses as we lay in her blankets helped to make up for it. Each night, she sought me out, kissing and loving me all while Angela watched.

The human knight denied her affections for Sophia, yet her eyes always seemed to dwell on the petite girl. I knew the feeling. I was the same with my wife. The first time I had laid eyes on Atharilesia had sent a powerful heat through me. She had been young, her green hair braided and flashing behind her as she danced around the linden tree on midsummer's eve.

She had entranced me. All night, I couldn't look away. When I finally worked up the courage to speak to her, she had been overcome with excitement that a hunter paid her attention. Neither of us had been in heat that night, so we only made love as women in a bower of sweet moss. It took us three years before one of us was in heat when I wasn't out on a hunt. Atharilesia took my cherry, and we became wedded that wonderful night.

When I woke up this morning, I recognized the signs of my impending heat. My clit throbbed. The transformation had begun. The nub ached. I wanted to stroke my burgeoning cock. Already, it was two inches long, thrusting pink before me. My pussy was wet. I groaned as I stood up, fighting the urge to masturbate. We had to get walking.

"Oh, wow, someone's excited," Sophia giggled when she saw my clit. "That's bigger than it was last night. I could just suckle on your clit."

"I am going into heat," I answered. "My cock is sprouting."

Sophia's eyes widened, and she covered her naked body with her blankets. The girl had never been modest. "Oh, no. A cock?" She bit her lip.

I frowned.

Angela, buckling on her armor, said, "She is sworn to Saphique, the virgin goddess. She must remain pure."

"But she has no hymen." I knew this first hand. I had fingered her several times, her pussy clenching down on my digits as she came.

"Pure of a man's touch," Sophia answered. "No cock has ever entered my flesh, and I mean to keep it that way."

"Oh," I said, swallowing. I had hoped to fuck her. I couldn't impregnate a human, only another hermaphrodite. It wouldn't be cheating for me to fuck a human's pussy. I had been looking forward to it. I don't remember the last time I had fucked a pussy with my cock. The night I impregnated my wife had been a wild celebration. I had been so drunk, I didn't even remember much of that night. For elves, it was adultery to have any form of sex that could cause a pregnancy. I had fucked plenty of elvish asses and mouths, but a pussy was something special.

Sometimes I hated my hunter's duty taking me away from my wife so often.

"Can you look away?" Sophia asked. "So I can dress."

"Oh, yes," I said, my cheeks burning. "My apologies."

"It's okay," Sophia sighed. "I'm not sure how my vows work with hermaphrodites. I wasn't the best acolyte at paying attention to theology. I would just hate to offend my goddess."

I turned my back. My clit throbbed harder. I glanced down. She was still swelling. It was slight, but I could see her growing a little larger. Angela, for once, was staring at me, her eyes locked on my clit, her eyes twinkling.

My pussy clenched; Angela certainly didn't have problems with cocks.

I smiled at her. "Does it excite you?" I asked, stroking my growing clit. "Are you turned on by the idea of a woman with a cock?"

Angela shifted her hips. Her nipples were hard. She didn't answer, instead grabbing her half-breastplate and covering her breasts. They were large, round mounds, and her armor cupped them into a delightful mound of cleavage. A necklace studded with red gems dangled between her lush breasts.

My cock grew longer. I couldn't wait until tonight.

Sophia blushed every time she glanced at my growing cock. It began to swing between my thighs by midmorning, dappled by the sunlight streaking through the canopy of leaves. Angela's eyes smoldered every time I caught her glancing.

The need to cum grew inside me. The first day of heat was always the worst. It was almost agony– sweet, wonderful, all-consuming agony– as my clit slowly sprouted. It throbbed with every beat of my heart. The pink nub faded into the more olive-green tinge of elf-flesh except at the tip. That remained pink. It flared like a mushroom and a slit formed.

Dewy precum beaded at the tip. My cock was full-grown as noon approached. It grew hard and thrust like a spear before me. It throbbed and ached. I wanted to stroke it. I gripped my bow and concentrated on leading them through the woods, following the game trails.

My skin was alive. The breeze that stirred the trees' leaves caressed my hard nipples and swirled between my thighs. My pussy lips shivered as the wind blew across my wet folds. The soil beneath my bare feet felt like silk.

I needed to cum so badly.

But I was a huntress. I could resist.

"Can we stop for lunch?" Sophia asked as she leaned against a tree. "My poor feet are worn into leather."

She wore shoes. How could her feet be hurt?

"Yes," Angela nodded.

I looked around and spotted a delicious pine cone hanging from a tree. It was dry, full of seeds. I snagged and nibbled on it, concentrating on the spicy flavor of the cone instead of my throbbing cock.

~ * ~

Knight-Errant Angela

I kept glancing at Xera's rather impressive cock jutting from her body. It was so...hot. She was a beautiful woman, round breasts, firm ass, sleek thighs, and then she had this amazing dick. It was so depraved and wild. I had never seen the like in my life.

My body burned to touch her shaft.

I focused on chewing on my trail rations, working the dried meat with my teeth. Xera leaned against a tree, taking the last crunching bites of her pine cone. I didn't understand how she could eat that. Bark, leaves, pine cones, and fern fronds made up her diet, seasoned with berries and bitter acorns. She could forage for food, but Sophia and I could not.

But we had enough provisions for a fortnight. Long enough to reach the Lesbius Oracle and cross through the forest back to civilization. I hoped the Oracle would have the answers. I would complete this Quest. Kevin would realize what a fool he was to doubt me.

Anger and hurt stabbed my heart whenever I thought of my

boyfriend. I tried to ignore the pain as my eyes drifted down to stare at Xera's hard cock. It was like Kevin's. The elf's hand stroked it. Sophia gasped, blushing and turning away so she didn't watch the elf masturbate.

My mouth watered as I finished my jerky. That cock was amazing. My pussy itched. "Do you need help?" I found myself asking.

"What?" Xera asked, her voice liquid and throaty.

"With your cock." I swallowed. "I could help you out."

"Would you? I'm sorry. It's hard on the first day to concentrate on anything but it."

"Yeah, looks hard," I smiled.

The elf frowned, not realizing the bad joke I made. I moved to her, my armor clinking. I pushed my red hair off my shoulders before I fell to my knees on the dirt. Precum dripped from the tip. Last night, this had been a little clit.

"Amazing," I whispered as I seized the elf's cock with my bare hand. It was warm and throbbed. It felt just like a human's cock. I stroked it. A drop of precum beaded the tip. I had to taste it.

"Yes," Xera sighed as I licked the tip. I gathered up the drop of precum. It wasn't salty or bitter like a human's, but sweet, like a flower's nectar. Sophia had mentioned how different Elf pussy tasted.

I lifted her cock with my hands so I could lick at the folds of her pussy. My tongue swiped through her nectar– she tasted like a marigold's sweet scent– and slid up to her shaft. Her precum was a little saltier than her pussy, but still far more sweet than a human's. She moaned as I wrapped my lips about the tip and sucked.

"Wonderful!" groaned Xera. Her fingers ran through my hair. They were long and slim, brushing my scalp. I shivered as I sucked, my pussy growing wet.

As I bobbed my mouth and stroked her shaft with my left hand, my right drifted down my body. I rubbed my bare stomach and brushed the top of my chainmail loincloth. I dipped beneath the metal to rub at my hot pussy lips.

I sighed around Xera's cock as I stroked my pussy lips. My mouth and tongue swirled about the crown of her cock. The elf moaned, her hips thrusting her cock deeper into my mouth. Her breasts rose above me, painted green and brown like the rest of her body.

She was so exotic and lovely.

I fingered my pussy. Two digits plunged in and out as I rubbed the heel of my hand on my clit. The pleasure was hot, trembling through me. I moaned and groaned, adding spice to my blowjob. My left hand moved between Xera's thighs to rub at her hot flesh.

"You wonderful human!" groaned Xera. "Oh, that's just lovely. Suck my cock and finger my pussy. Oh, yes! Oh, wow!"

My pussy clenched down on my fingers. My flesh was so hot. My fingers were bathed in my juices. Xera's hips thrust forward, sliding her cock deep into my mouth, brushing the back of my throat. I relaxed, suppressing my gag reflex and deep-throating her cock. I shoved my fingers deeper into my pussy.

This was so wild. I was sucking a woman's cock. Sure she was an elf, but she was still beautiful and sexy. I pictured sucking Sophia's cock, the wonderful acolyte staring down at me with love burning in her green eyes as I pleasured her.

My pussy convulsed. My orgasm shot through me.

My moans were muffled by Xera's thick shaft. I shuddered as I sucked. Her cock slammed harder and harder down my throat. It hurt. I savored the pain, driving away my impossible fantasy of Sophia. I concentrated on pleasing Xera's cock as my pleasure rippled through my body.

Xera's words exploded from her mouth. They were elvish, incomprehensible to my ears. They sounded like a bird singing. The syllables rolled from one word to the next, full of her passion. She drew her cock back so the tip was just inside my lips.

My pussy still spasmed about my fingers when her sweet cum flooded my mouth. I shuddered again, grinding my hand on my clit. A small orgasm flooded more pleasure through me as I swallowed the sweetest cum in the world. It was almost like drinking honey. I swirled it through my mouth, letting it linger before I swallowed it.

"Thank you," panted Xera. "That was what I needed."

Her cock softened in my lips. It didn't shrink back into a little clit, but it wasn't painfully hard and jutting out before her. Xera helped me stand and then she kissed me. No guy had ever kissed me after I blew them. Not without me washing my mouth clean.

It was hot. Xera drank her cum. I couldn't wait for tonight.

~ * ~

Acolyte Sophia

I swore myself to purity.

Xera's cock didn't differ from a strap-on. It wouldn't give me any additional pleasure. I needed to stop thinking about her.

My pussy was on fire after our midday lunch. I tried not to watch Angela blow Xera's cock. But it was so hard. Xera's moans were so wonderful. She was a woman receiving pleasure. But she had a cock.

A cock I wanted to sample.

I was so confused.

I need to be pure. I swore myself to Saphique. No cock would touch me. And a hermaphrodite's cock was still a cock, even if she had big tits. I rubbed my thighs together as I walked, caressing my clit. I silently orgasmed, stifling my moans. It was the third time since lunch, and I was still left frustrated.

My eyes glanced at the elf's dick. It was hardening again.

I shot my eyes forward.

Twilight darkened the forest. We would have to stop soon. I knew what would happen tonight. It was so obvious. Angela walked near the elf, her hips shaking, an excited smile on her lips. She was eager to be fucked.

I would be sleeping alone tonight.

184

I had enjoyed Xera in my bed the last three nights. It helped to take my mind off beautiful Angela. I kept hoping Angela would join us. A threesome might be a nice way for her to relax and maybe an intimacy could form between us. I could show her my love and she would forget about Kevin.

I knew it was foolish, but hope was all I had.

The shadows deepened as the sun sank to our left. My feet were sore. Despite the discomfort, I realized I was growing stronger. My muscles were toned and some of the softness had vanished from my curves, but I hated walking. I had a horse. I wanted to ride Purity.

But the branches were too thick. It was pointless to ride.

Soon it was hard to see the trail we walked upon. My stomach rumbled. I was ready for another tough, bland meal of dried meat impregnated with fruit and vegetables. It wasn't filling, but it did provide energy.

"Here is a good spot," Xera purred, her hand stroking her cock.

Angela smiled. "Mmm, yes it is."

My pussy clenched. I would have to listen to them make love. I wanted to join them. I wanted to feel Xera's cock in me. I patted the pouch at my waist. My magical dildo was in there. I would need her tonight to avoid sinning and breaking my sacred vows to Saphique.

~ * ~

Xerathalasia

Angela stripped naked as I lay on her blanket. Sophia was nearby, lying on her back, her blankets over her naked body. She had produced a dildo from her pouch and it was obvious the young woman was using it.

I wished she would join us, but I respected her vows.

Angela's skimpy armor came off quickly. The young woman was ready. In the gloom of twilight, I could see the glisten of her wet pussy. My eyes were far better than the humans'. I only stopped for their sake. They couldn't stumble blind through the forest.

I admired Angela's naked form. She was muscular and strong, but still had womanly curves. She was like an elf hunter, moving with the grace of a trained warrior. Her breasts were round and bountiful, her skin pale. Lust burned in her blue eyes as she stared at my throbbing cock.

"Damn, that looks great," Angela purred.

Sophia sighed beside us. Her eyes flicking over at my dick before she squeezed them shut.

Angela sank down, her hand grasping my cock. I groaned as she stroked it before she dipped down to play with my pussy. I groaned, my flesh clenching on her invading fingers. She pulled them out, covered in my juices, and rubbed them onto my cock. Did she need lube for her pussy? Sophia always produced copious nectar.

"Should I lick you first?" I asked. "Ready you for my cock."

"Oh, I'm ready," Angela smiled. "I'm just feeling naughty." She licked my pussy, tasting my juices. "Damn, that's amazing."

I touched her breasts, giving her pillowy mounds a squeeze. My fingers brushed her nipples, and she moaned. I grinned, pinching and rubbing her nubs. My ears twitched as I gave her pleasure. Her thighs pressed together and the salty, tangy musk of her human excitement brushed my nose. Human pussies had a much earthier flavor than elves.

My mouth watered. "Are you sure you don't want me to lick you?"

"God, no. I'm too fucking horny. I've thought about this cock all day." She stroked up to the top of my shaft. "Pater's cock, I need to fuck you."

I moaned as she slid up my body, her hand still stroking me. Our breasts rubbed together as her lips met mine. I moaned into the kiss, my tongue swirling about her mouth. Her hand stroked me, sending shudders through my body. My own hands found her firm ass, squeezing her butt-cheeks and pulling her towards me.

I broke the kiss. My cock ached. I needed to experience pussy. I couldn't knock her up. She wasn't one of the five hermaphroditic races. It was safe. I wouldn't be cheating on my wife. "Mount me! I need to be in you! Please, Angela."

"Oh, yes!" the human moaned in agreement.

Her thighs straddled me. Angela lifted her body, her hips swaying as she grasped my cock. I throbbed in anticipation as she guided me to her hot hole. I moaned as she swabbed the tip of my dick through her hot folds.

"I'm going to love this," groaned Angela.

"Oh, my," Sophia gasped. "Oh, wow!"

Her eyes were fixed on us. Angela glanced over, a smile crossing her lips before she ripped her eyes away and stared into my violet eyes. I gripped her hips. The tip of my cock was in her hot pussy. I groaned.

"Please! Fuck me!"

Angela slammed her hips down. I was engulfed in hot, tight, silky pussy. My back arched. My breasts heaved. I almost came. I bit my lips, fighting off the urge as Angela slid back up my shaft. Her pussy clung to my cock, massaging the tip.

I was lost to the pleasure.

"Thank you, Matar!" I moaned in elvish as Angela worked her hips.

My hands found Angela's breasts as she rode me. I loved how supple they felt. My fingers sank into her flesh every time her pussy slammed down on my cock. My dick throbbed, shooting pleasure through my body. I rejoiced to be buried in hot pussy again.

"Yes, yes, yes!" Angela moaned. "Pater's cock! I fucking love it! Damn, Xera! Damn! Elf cock is amazing!"

Sophia gasped and moaned nearby, squirming beneath her blankets. Her blanket slipped down and exposed her small breasts. Her hands worked furiously beneath her coverings, fucking herself hard with the dildo.

The pressure grew in my pussy. I wanted this to last as long as possible, but Angela was so hot and tight. The human leaned over me as she rode me, her beautiful face framed by her red hair. Her blue eyes burned with lust.

Angela moaned, "Damn, damn! I'm gonna explode on your cock! Slata's cunt!"

The human slammed her cunt down on my shaft. Her pussy convulsed. She bucked atop me as she came. Her cunt slid up and down my shaft, massaging me, teasing me. I couldn't hold out any longer.

My hands tightened on her tits.

The pleasure reached its limits.

My cock erupted into her hot pussy's depths.

I screamed my bliss as rapture pulsed out of me over and over.

Angela crashed down on me, squirming as we came together.

Chapter Twenty-Nine: The Knight's Sacrifice

Acolyte Sophia

I was so glad when Xera woke up and her cock was gone. The last three nights had been torture. I had abused my poor pussy with my dildo. I had no choice. I had to fight against my urges to join them and experience that wonderful cock.

Xera and Angela were like rabbits. They fucked three times a night in every position. I had to use my dildo each time. The only plus side, I was so exhausted from masturbating, I slept through the night on the uncomfortable ground instead of waking up every fifteen minutes to roll over and doze.

But this morning Xera woke up and her cock was gone. Only a clit remained.

"Thank Saphique," I muttered as we headed north.

Angela looked faintly disappointed.

I wished I inspired lust in her like Xera did.

The woods seemed to grow into thicker fir trees and the land grew hillier. On our seventh day, we were climbing over rises or winding around hillocks. The pace seemed to crawl. Between the hills were deep valleys. These parts of the woods were dark. Less sunlight penetrated into the valleys, and the trees seemed to press down on us.

I hated how oppressive it was.

On the eighth day, we crested a hill and paused at the valley spread out before us. I shuddered. It was so much darker than the rest of the woods. Thick webs clung to the tops of the trees about the valley like sticky snot blown on a handkerchief.

"Is that the..." I shuddered, my voice trailing off.

"The Lesbius Oracle is in a cave at the center. See the small rise."

Angela nodded. I couldn't take my eyes off the webs. They were spanning from tree to tree. They were enormous. "How big are these giganraneae again?"

"The size of your horses," Xera answered. "Leave the mounts here. They will only be an impediment down there."

I swallowed and my body trembled. "Do we really have to do this?"

Angela took my hand and gave me a comforting squeeze. "This was your idea. It's the only chance we have. I'll be right beside you."

Her hand strengthened me. "Okay."

Xera led. We followed. Angela had her sword drawn. Xera had restrung her bow for the first time since the basilisk. I pulled out my enchanted dagger. It glowed softly when danger was nearby. A faint, pink hue suffused the blade.

I trembled.

We crept down the slope into the valley. I had thought other parts of the forest were dark. It was midday and yet it felt like evening. The trees were covered in webbing. It stretched in thick, dirty-white strings forming intricate patterns. Torn, old cobwebs dangled from branches. I shuddered every time a sticky strand brushed my face, resisting the urge to yell as I ripped the strands away.

Xera paused, pointing at the ground ahead. It looked normal, and then I noticed the delicate, almost invisible, spider silk rising up around it. "Trap," she whispered. "Step where I do."

My body trembled as we followed the elf's footsteps, creeping

190

through the spiders' domains. The woods were quiet. Too quiet. There were no birds singing or animals rustling. This place was death. The animals of the forest avoided it.

I gripped my dagger. The pink glow grew brighter. I nudged Angela. She saw my dagger, her face tight. She nodded her head and kept walking, her eyes scanning the trees. Suddenly, Xera drew an arrow from her quiver and knocked it. She crouched and lifted her gaze.

Something skittered through the trees. My throat constricted. I caught sight of a black body moving on spindly legs creeping along webbing strung between the tree branches. I held my breath. I wanted to run. But Angela was nearby. I wouldn't flee like I had with the panthopus.

The giganraneae crept by. Either it didn't see us or it didn't care. Maybe it couldn't see. Maybe it would only know we were here if we brushed one of their webs. That's how spiders worked, right? They waited for the fly to land in their web. They weren't hunters, but ambushers.

After what felt like an eternity, Xera relaxed and we kept walking through the forest. I had never been more relieved than when we reached the center hill and found the dirt hole that lead down into the earth. To the Lesbius Oracle.

I shivered. I knew we would find hope down there.

~ * ~

Knight-Errant Angela

I was glad to leave the gloomy, web infested vale behind and enter the oracle's cave. Sophia and Xera followed me. My stomach knotted as we entered the dark of the cave. An earthy smell filled my nose. Roots dangled down from the ceiling, forming a curtain we had to push through.

The farther we moved from the entrance, the darker the tunnel grew. A light glowed in the distance at the tunnel's end. The light was a beacon, guiding us. The roots made me shudder. They were like the giganraneae's webs, but not sticky. Still, I flinched as they brushed my face.

"Slata's well-used cunt!" Sophia gasped, her voice echoing back and forth down the cave.

I glanced at her. "What?"

"I stubbed my toe on a stupid root!" she moaned.

"It's not much farther," I told her. "Let's keep walking."

Xera moved with grace. The elf's eyesight was keener, and I doubted she tripped on every root growing across the dirt floor. The light's brightness swelled. It spilled golden around a bend in the cave, washing against the darkness.

The roots thinned as we neared. We moved deeper beneath the hill and more earth was above us. The light grew bright enough for me to see the ground again, able to step without tripping and falling on my face. It was a relief. My heart beat faster as I reached the edge of the golden light.

A soft voice hummed. The Oracle.

Please, Pater, Slata, Saphique, Gewin, and all other gods. Please let her have the answers that will allow me and Sophia to defeat Dominari.

I didn't want to die. I didn't want to lead Sophia to her death.

I reached the corner and rounded it. The golden light flooded from a room covered in silken pillows. Colorful curtains hung on the walls, hiding the earthen cave. More had been strung across the ceiling, sheets of silk that rustled and whispered as an unfelt breeze stirred them. Sitting in the center was a young woman. The Lesbius Oracle. Her skin was dusky like a Hazian, and all she wore was silky, black hair that fell around her shoulders and small breasts. Her eyes opened. They were golden and so very ancient.

She had to help me. Oracles were the daughters of Cnawen, the God of Knowledge, and Rithi, the Goddess of Art. They were demigoddesses, able to peer into the future and pass on what they beheld for a price.

"Welcome, Angela," the Oracle purred, her voice musical. "Have your companions strip your garb and approach."

I nodded, trembling. "Yes, noble Oracle."

Her golden eyes watched as Sophia and Xera helped me strip naked. They removed my armor, pulling it off piece by piece. Sophia's green eyes were wide, full of love and concern. Her crush persisted. I knew the feeling. I had the same girlish love for Lady Delilah, but I had long ago learned that such feelings weren't love.

I loved Kevin. Despite how angry his words had made me. My love only made my anger worse. He should have been my most passionate supporter. Instead, he tried to have me renounce everything that I had strived so hard to achieve. I was a Knight Deute. How dare he try to make me shirk my duty just because I faced almost certain death.

How could he not understand who I was?

How could he love me and fail so miserably to know me? I grit my teeth. I would show him. I would kill the dragon Dominari. I would return and become a full-fledged member of the Knights Deute. He better be ready to give the biggest apology in the world.

I wasn't sure I would take him back. His lack of faith in me cut to my heart. I did love, but could I be with a man that didn't believe in me? I wasn't so sure. Why did love have to be so complicated? Why couldn't I have just stopped loving Kevin after those words?

"You'll find the answers," Sophia said and gave me a hug, her robes soft against my naked body, the pendant Lady Delilah gave me rubbed between my breasts.

I put my arms around her and held her. "Thank you, "I whispered. I'm...I'm sorry I can't love you."

My body grew flushed. She was so wonderful to hold.

"It's...okay," Sophia sighed. She broke the hug, tears glistening in her eyes.

I glanced at Xera. The naked elf gave me a nod. "You will find your answers."

"Thanks." I would miss the elf. She was an interesting travel companion, and her cock definitely added spice to our journey.

I stepped into the room. The oracle rose before me. I gasped at her grace. She made the elves seem clumsy as she walked around me, her golden eyes sliding up and down my body as she studied me. Her every movement made my pussy grow wetter and wetter. Sudden heat burned through me. Juices trickled down my thighs.

The Lesbius Oracle was breathtakingly gorgeous.

"Welcome, seeker," she purred when she finished her circle. Her hands reached out, her soft fingers caressed my cheek. I blushed and shifted. Her touch sent fire rippling through my body. My knees weakened, and I fell to the pillows.

Her hands ran through my red hair. She pulled me to her pussy. A triangle of black pubic hair pointed at her hard, pink clit. Her heavenly musk filled my nose. It was unlike any pussy I had scented – divine and pure. Untouched by men.

Just like Sophia's.

She moaned as my tongue licked through her folds. My nipples ached and my body shivered. Her taste was delicious. The silky, hot folds of her pussy caressed my lips as I nuzzled into her sex. My nose filled with her divine scent. My mind grew foggy. My fears melted away.

The Lesbius Oracle would give me the answers I sought.

I tongued harder at her folds. I wanted to pleasure this demigoddess. My fingers gripped the cheeks of her ass. They were perky and firm. Just perfect. I squeezed and kneaded them as my tongue slipped through the folds of her pussy.

"Yes! Imbibe my passion," purred the oracle. "Open yourself up to my touch."

Her fingers stroked my hair. My body hummed with electricity. Her touch seemed to reach so deep. I groaned into her hot flesh. My hips undulated. Pleasure built within me. My tongue wiggled and swirled. My lips kissed and nuzzled. I drank down her juices. They warmed my insides, sending fuzzy delight shooting to my pussy and nipples.

"Oh, yes!" groaned the Oracle. "Show me your passion. Deliver pleasure unto me."

My fingers worked between the cheeks of her ass. The demigoddess gasped as I teased her sphincter. I sucked and nibbled on her clit as my finger sank to the first knuckle into her hot, tight ass. Her flesh clenched about my finger. The Oracle groaned and hot juices poured into my mouth.

I came.

Delight burst through me. No erogenous part of my body had been touched, and yet the bliss of drinking her ambrosia had given me pleasure. My pussy spasmed. My juices squirted down my thighs. I shoved my finger deeper into her ass as I moaned into her sweet pussy. I shuddered, holding onto the Oracle to keep from falling onto my back.

I forced my mouth to keep licking as the pleasure burned through my body. I tongued her clit. I fingered her ass. I nibbled and licked. The Oracle's moans grew louder. Her hips undulated. Her ass clenched on my finger.

"That's it! Deliver me to rapture, Angela."

Her words spurred me to flick my tongue frantically against her clit. A second finger pushed into her tight asshole. I worked them in and out. Another orgasm shuddered through me. My vision fuzzed. I never wanted to stop drinking her bliss.

The Oracle came.

Her juices flooded my mouth. I drowned in them. No woman had ever gushed so much. They poured down my neck to my breasts. I was anointed in her divine juices. The flood washed over my nipples, caressing them. Electricity shot to my pussy. The flood continued down my stomach to my crotch.

The world exploded in pleasure when her juices touched my pussy. I gasped and heaved. My mind burned. I fell back onto the silken pillows and stared up at the sheets of silk hanging upon the ceiling. They rippled and undulated just like I did.

"Pater's huge cock!" I gasped.

The Oracle knelt between my thighs, spreading my legs apart. She licked at my pussy. Her tongue's touch sent another orgasm shooting through me. She curled her tongue through my folds, tasting me everywhere while drinking down my juices.

"You have such passion to share," the Oracle smiled. "You brim with ecstasy, Angela. Ask your question."

"Can you tell me how to defeat the dragon?" I panted. "How do I kill Dominari?"

"Give unto me your love for Kevin," the Oracle purred and took a second lick through my pussy.

"What?" I gasped as my body bucked and pleasure raced through me.

"You must deliver unto me your love for the man known as Kevin," she repeated. "That is my price and your sacrifice."

I squeezed my eyes shut as her tongue circled my clit. It was so hard to think as the pleasure shot through my body. I loved Kevin. I couldn't give up my feelings for him. Right?

My anger crashed into my love. Kevin hadn't believed in me. He thought I would die. Why should I love a man like that?

Why does love have to be so hard? My heart had pained me since I left Shesax. Kevin's words had weighed at me. I could be free of the burden. I could be free of my love for him. Why should I waste my affections on a man who didn't believe in me? I had my chance. I could choose not to love him any longer.

"You have it!" I gasped as another orgasm burst through my body. "You may have my love for Kevin."

A woman gasped– Sophia.

"Yes!" moaned the Oracle between licks. "It is so sweet."

The pain in my heart faded. My anger towards Kevin diminished. Why had I obsessed so much over a man's words? He wasn't anything important. Had we ever even spoken before he said those words? He was never my lover. Just a man. No one I should care about at all. There was nothing special about him. I smiled, my heart suddenly lighter.

Why had I wasted any time on the man? What a fool I was.

The Oracle licked up my body. Her tongue left heat burning across my skin. Her silky hair caressed my body. She reached my breasts. Her tongue flicked around my nipples, gathering up her pussy juices that had anointed my entire body. Her hands pushed my thighs apart. She settled between them, her hips undulating, her clit rubbing on mine.

"Sweet Sapphire!" I gasped as the Oracle of Lesbius tribbed me. Her golden eyes stared into mine.

"Your future lies open. A path I do see," she purred, her hips undulating harder. Our breasts were pressed together, our hard nipples brushing.

My body writhed. Pleasure burned through me. My pussy rubbed against her hot cunt. The Oracle's tongue licked and nuzzled at my ear. Her rhythm picked up, her excitement growing. She moaned into my ear.

The cave spun about me. The pleasure hammered into my mind. Her every touch was ecstasy. My own hips bucked, grinding my pussy into hers. I wanted to make her cum. I wanted to please this amazing demigoddess. To worship her with my body.

I held her supple form, my hands roaming her back. I groaned and gasped every time her clit nudged mine and sparked off another orgasm through my body. The air was heady with the divine scent of her passion. Her skin was silk, caressing my body. I held her tight, savoring every inch of our flesh pressed together.

"Yes! Deliver your passion unto me. Give unto me such sweet pleasure. Use your body, Angela. Consume me with rapture and the future shall be known!"

"Yes, yes, yes!" I gasped, humping faster. My hands found her ass again. I pulled her tight against me.

"So good!" she moaned. "That is it. That is the rapture I crave." Her hips ground harder, rubbing our clits over and over into each other.

Her head threw back. Her body trembled. The Lesbius Oracle came.

"Daughter of Lilies, beset by betrayals
Duty compels your darkness
A sword is needed. A sword reforged.
To embrace your destiny, the shattered blade must be whole,

Seek out the five holy shards scattered and lost
Companions shall aid you, Daughter of Lilies
All Betrayed
The Virgin Whore touched by no man,
The Quiet Stalker who moves unseen
The Grieving Mage who commands the elements
The Raging Warrior who mourns lost love
The Seducing Bard who shall lose his heart
The Silent Thief who steals more than gold
The Nameless Shaman who shall find her heart
The Flaming Woman who changes your destiny
All Betrayed.
Wield the Hero's Blade, Daughter of Lilies
In the Dragon's lair,
Truth shall slay Betrayal's Lies."

The Oracle's words seared into my mind. I shuddered and came one final time.

~ * ~

King Edward IV Secaren – Shesax, Kingdom of Secare

"Are you still watching the knight?" my pregnant wife asked as she lounged naked upon our bed. Beside her, the slumbering Lady Danielle lay on her belly, my wife's fingers caressing her curvy ass. We had shared the young noblewoman tonight, but the moment my passions had been spent, I had to check on Angela.

"She is at the oracle," I growled. "She is receiving a prophecy."

The words echoed in my mind as I held the twin of the amulet around Angela's neck. I could see and hear what she did. Lady Delilah's device worked as advertised. With it, I had kept progress on Angela's journey. The revelation she sought her own prophecy disturbed me.

"What does the Oracle say?" my wife asked.

198

I chilled. "She's told to seek the Hero's Blade." The words of the Oracle of Sekar echoed in my mind: *You shall die, Mighty King, upon the Hero's Blade.* "The blasted Lesbius Oracle has told her she needs it to kill the dragon. Illth's bloody pox!" My heart beat faster. "Lady Delilah's plan was to lead Angela to her death, not to arm her with the High King's sword."

My wife stood awkwardly, stroking her pregnant belly. My son grew in there. He would be the next king of Secare. No woman would unseat him, let alone the whore-descendant of the High King. Lavinia wrapped her arms around my neck.

"You cannot let her have the sword," she whispered. "You must be strong. Be the king."

"I should have just had her killed and damn the consequences of offending the Knights Deute!"

"But now she is away. Out in the wilderness. Vulnerable." Her lips were hot. A stir shot down to my cock. Her naked breasts rubbed against my shoulder. She was a gorgeous woman, blonde and buxom, as beautiful as any Zeutchian Princess. "I hear there is a warlock in Shesax."

I froze. "A rogue mage of Thosi?"

"Defeated by a warlock... What a sad end to a promising knight's career."

Part Two

~~~

Magic's Clash

Chapter Thirty: The Magery

Journeyman Mage Faoril – Esh-Esh, The Magery of Thosi

"Why are you jerking him off?" Saoria asked as she lounged on her bed in her red robes of a Journeyman Mage, her long, dark-brown hair spilling across one shoulder and the swelling rise of her large tits.

I always felt so inadequate around her. My breasts were nice, round, and dwarfed by the lush pair my friend had. Her curvy body exuded sex. She sometimes seemed more fit to be a Priestess of Slata, letting men and women worship in her embrace, than a Mage of Thosi. But she was skilled, almost as much as I was thanks to my years of tutelage since our time as young apprentices.

"We need to practice," I said, stroking the simulacrum's dick faster. I held a large beaker at the tip of his cock. "And I'm out of cum."

"I don't want to practice," pouted my friend.

We were in our cell in the mid-level of the Collegiate Tower, the headquarters of the Council of Magery and the heart of the College of Esh-Esh. Only here was the arcane arts of magic taught. Students from the known world came to Esh-Esh hoping to have the talent to be even an Apprentice Mage and learn to harness the powers of the elements.

The simulacrum moaned. He grew nearer to cumming. He was an artificial man, created through magic, his pale, muscular body completely hairless. His dick throbbed, and then his cock erupted, filling the beaker with squirt after squirt of cum. He produced far more cum than a normal human, easily ten times as much, and almost overflowed the beaker.

Cum was necessary to a female mage. It was the power source of our magic. For a priest, priestess, or paladin, their magic was powered by the god or goddess they served. For witches, they merely had an innate ability to control the natural spirits of the world. But for a mage, we needed a powerful source of energy, and nothing was more primal than sexual fluids. I could ingest the cum straight from the source, fucking or sucking the simulacrum's, or any other male's, dick. But it was easier to gather the cum and save it for when you needed it. The energy didn't last long in your body. Male mages had to use female juices, and the female simulacrums were engineered to squirt copious fluids when they orgasmed.

"There, that should be more than enough for us to practice with," I said, holding up the beaker swirling with the pearly jizz.

"I don't want to practice, Faoril," groaned Saoria. "I practice all day with Master Soviar. He had me shaping wood until my mind hurt."

There were five elements in the natural world that mages could manipulate: Air, Earth, Fire, Water, and Life. Wood was easy to affect with Life magic. But the more intelligent the organism, the harder they were to change.

"We need to be ready for the test."

"It's in nineteen days," Saoria objected. "That's almost three weeks. We can take one break."

"That's nineteen days to perfect our magic," I pointed out. The test to be a Master Mage was held once a year and only three Journeymen Mages would pass. This year, the Magery Council invited seven Journeymen to test. Over half of us would fail. "If you want to make it, you need to practice." I downed half the beaker, ingesting the thick, salty cum. It filled my stomach, an energy that seethed inside me.

I burned it and sent out a wind. It wrapped around Saoria and lifted her off the bed.

"You bitch!" Saoria gasped as I spun her about, her brown hair whipping around her body and the bottom of her red robe slipping up her sleek thighs. I laughed and then brought her to me and set her down, pushing the beaker into her hands.

"Fine," she muttered, tipping back the beaker and emptying the rest of the cum into her mouth.

The simulacrum moved to a corner of the room, a pleasant, vapid smile on his handsome face. He stood perfectly still, his hairless body sculpted, his cock rigid. It was nearly impossible to make a male simulacrum have a limp dick. When I made Master Mage, I would own my own simulacrum. Only a Master Mage could own one, the rest belonged to the Magery Council and were lent to students.

"Ready?" I asked Saoria.

She nodded.

The stone floor beneath my feet became liquid and rolled over me. I gasped as her magic pulled me down into its gloppy mire. "Clever," I praised as I sent my magic into the stone to fight Saoria's spell while simultaneously precipitating water out of the air and splashing her in the face.

Saoria spluttered, and I pulled my feet out of the liquid stone, conjuring air to lift me. My magic burned through the cum inside me as I controlled the elements. The water I splashed on Saoria was gathered by her magic into a ball undulating before her.

It shot at me, hardening to ice. I used fire, the ice vaporizing into a cloud of steam that rolled past my face. I dispersed the moisture as her magic went into the wooden frame of my bed. The wood groaned and then the nearest bedpost surged out at me, wrapping around my leg.

"I see practicing with Master Soviar paid off," I smiled. I made a blade of stone erupt from the floor, severing the bed post. I reached down and grasped the wood around my leg, shaping it into a spear and using wind to hurl it at Saoria's guts.

We were Journeyman Mages. We had practiced dueling before. It could be dangerous, but it also honed our skills. We were destroying our cell, but we would receive further practice putting everything back together again.

Saoria heaved her mattress before her, the spear thudding into the goose down. Feathers exploded out, dancing in the air, driven by her wind. I held up my arms as they fluttered into my face, blinding me for a moment. Fire flashed, consuming the feathers into ash that rained down to the floor.

Saoria rushed at me, flying across the room. I thickened the air before her, catching her. She slowed to a stop, the air as thick as molasses. "Ooh, that's an annoying one," she groaned, twisting her body.

"Yep," I winked.

Fire exploded around me. I squeaked in shock as my red robe burned to ash and fell off my body. The flames hadn't touched me. She had exquisite control with fire. I hovered naked in the air, frowning at her. Why had she done that? I tightened the air around her and–

"Slata's cunt!" I gasped as a thick, tapered piece of wood shoved into my cunt. She had shaped a dildo and used air to work it in and out of me.

I shuddered as the pleasure rippled through my body. The dildo was thick and covered in ridges that tickled the inside of my pussy. My toes curled and soft moans escaped my lips. I concentrated on my air, holding her in place as she fucked my pussy.

"Mmm, how do you like that trick?" Saoria asked, a big smile on her lush lips.

"It's very...naughty!" I panted. "By the gods, you make the best dildos."

Saoria winked at me.

I twisted the air around her. It sliced off her robe, sending the ruined fabric fluttering to the ground in three pieces. The wind kept spinning, caressing her naked body. I focused it on her breasts, tickling her hard nipples as my body spasmed on the dildo.

"Oh, nice!" groaned Saoria.

I turned her in the air and spread her legs. Dark, neatly trimmed hair covered her pussy. The wind blew through her curls, caressing her pussy and clit. Saoria spasmed, fucking the dildo faster and faster inside me. I drifted closer to her. The tart scent of her pussy swirled through the wind.

"You're going to like this. I came up with it last night. I found it most enjoyable," I purred.

"Oh?" Saoria asked, her eyes wide. "What?"

I shaped the wind into a tight vortex and pushed the mini-tornado into her pussy. Her cunt spread open, her pink depths revealed to me. The wind swirled through her hole. She gasped and spasmed, her juices caught by the wind and dancing through the air like drops of rain.

"Oh, yes! That's so wicked! Oh, my god! It's swirling inside me! Slata's hairy cunt! Yes! That's so wonderful, Faoril! Fuck me with the wind!"

I grinned at her, burning through my cum as I made the tornado spin faster inside her. Saoria spasmed, her breasts heaving. She gasped and moaned as her hair whipped around her in the strong winds.

The dildo inside me grew large, spreading my pussy open. I doubled over as I floated in the air. My pussy screamed with pleasure. The ridges caressed the walls of my cunt. I grasped my nipples, pinching them as I enjoyed her pleasure.

"Let's see if I can copy this," Saoria gasped. "It's so good! Damn, I need to fuck you with a tornado."

"Just keep fucking me with the dildo!" I moaned. "Pater's giant cock, this is wonderful! I'm gonna cum so hard!"

"Me, too!" moaned Saoria. "But you need more."

The cheeks of my ass suddenly parted. Whirling wind pressed between them, caressing my sphincter; I shuddered. The air was moist, almost licking at my asshole. I drifted closer to her, hovering over her body. Our lips met in a hot kiss as she slammed the tornado into my asshole.

The air spun inside my bowels. It caressed across the sensitive walls. I shuddered as the pleasure burned to my pussy. I moaned into her sweet kiss. I grasped her heavy breasts, pinching her nipples as we fucked each other with our magic. The dildo and the tornado ignited the nerves in my body.

I came hard, bucking and spasming against her. Saoria's hands grasped my ass, squeezing my cheeks and pulling me against her body. We spun in the air, held up by our magics. The pleasure spasmed through my body, whipping into my mind. A part of me maintained my spells, fucking Saoria's cunt with my tornado, but the rest of me was consumed in pleasure.

"Yes!" I screamed, breaking the kiss, our nipples pressing together as I bucked. "Sweet Slata's cunt, that feels wonderful in my ass! Oh, yes!"

"Mmm, you are so cute when you cum!" Saoria purred and then spun about beneath me. Her ass slid up my stomach and breasts until my face was buried between her cheeks. "Eat my ass and fuck my cunt with your tornado!"

I buried my tongue into her sour ass, sucking and swirling as I intensified the tornado fucking her pussy. My fingers found her clit, stroking her as my tongue probed deep into her asshole. Her body spasmed beneath me.

"Yes, yes! You wonderful mage! Mmm, you know the naughtiest magic."

I made ice cubes out of the air and rubbed them on her nipples. She spasmed in delight. Her moans echoed through our cell. I rubbed harder at her clit with my thumb as I sucked on her ass. I loved the flavor. She had such a delicious ass.

"Faoril!" she gasped. "Oh, yes! Oh, damn! You are amazing!"

Her asshole clenched about my tongue as she came. She spasmed beneath me. I ended the tornado and moved my lips down to her pussy. I drank her tart juices as they flooded out of her spasming cunt, nuzzling into her silky flesh while her pants grew softer and softer.

"Oh, Faoril," she panted as we descended to the floor, our room in shambles. "You are amazing. You're the best in the class."

I nodded my head.

"You're going to pass," she said, her eyes widening, her lip trembling.

"So will you," I smiled at her. I gave her a hug and kissed her lips. "We'll both pass."

She nodded, her eyes distant.

I looked around at the mess. "Well, we should keep practicing and fix this up."

"Yeah," she muttered. "I need to practice more. I have to be as good as you if I'm going to make it."

"You will," I beamed, pulling the dildo out of my cunt. I sent it to my bedpost and shaped it back into the frame like it always belonged there.

Chapter Thirty-One: Plots and Plans

Knight-Errant Angela – The Oracle of Lesbius, Deorc Forest

The Oracle of Lesbius slid off my body, her dusky skin gleaming with sweat and the juices of our love making. She stood with a willowy grace, her hips undulating as she moved back into her bower, leaving me heaving on the colorful pillows. Her words echoed in my mind. A prophecy that held the key to defeating the dragon Dominari.

There was hope. Tears burned in my eyes. I trembled and shook as the emotion mixed with the bliss still rippling through me. I could defeat the dragon, the first knight ever to succeed. I wasn't on a death sentence with Sophia. My breasts heaved as I trembled. My eyes found Sophia where she watched, the acolyte's smile wide, her green eyes brimming with tears, her hands clasped hopefully before her.

She was so beautiful. I had been so distant from her, pushing her away. I couldn't remember why. Was it simply that I wasn't in love with the girl? There was a...hole in my thoughts. I frowned, my excitement dwindling. I had given something up. Something I had cared about, and it left me empty. I had memories of...someone. I felt like I had known the name just moments ago, but it was gone now. It had been someone I had shared my bed and life with. But who was it?

What did I give up for hope?

The Oracle curled into a ball, her golden eyes closed, and her breasts rose and fell with the simple rhythm of sleep. I pushed myself up, shaking my head. I must have been sure the price was worth it. Whoever I had given up couldn't have been that important to me.

"We're going to do it!" Sophia shrieked.

She rushed towards me and threw her arms around my shoulders as I sat up, her impulsive lips raining kisses about my cheeks. They were delicious, caressing my cheeks with hot fire. I held her tight, sharing in her joy.

Then she froze. "Sorry."

Sophia pulled away. Her face twisted with sadness. I sighed, clutched her hand, and smiled at her. "Don't be. It's okay. We should celebrate."

"Yes, the Oracle gave such sage words," nodded Xera.

The elf huntress lounged against the wall, tall and lush, naked save for a simple belt from which hung her quiver of arrows. Her body was painted with greens and browns, a mottled pattern that helped her vanish into the thick brush of the Deorc Forest. Her hair was green and short, a utilitarian cut, and her pointed ears rose out of her green locks. She was taller than me. She was taller than most humans.

"What did the prophecy mean?" Sophia asked, glancing at the slumbering Oracle. The demigoddess– daughter of Cnawen and Rithi, God of Knowledge and Goddess of Art– seemed at peace. "Am I the virgin whore?"

A grin split my lips. The Oracle's prophecy mentioned half-a-dozen companions to join me. "Well, you are pretty whorish, Sophia. With women, anyways."

"And, I believe, that priestesses of Saphique sell their bodies to female worshipers," Xera added, her ears twitching.

"We don't sell our bodies," huffed Sophia. "For a donation,

women worship the Virgin Goddess in the arms of her priestesses and acolytes. It's a very pleasant duty."

I laughed. It felt wonderful. "Yep, a whore untouched by men."

Sophia put her hands on her hips, pushing in the simple robe of white she wore to cling to her lithe curves. She was a petite woman, but had a curvy ass. Her lips fought a smile. With her light-brown hair framing her delicate features, she made quite the Secaran beauty. I was Secaran, too, though you never would know it by my flaming-red hair. There was a Tuathan in my ancestry.

"Does that make me the Quiet Stalker?" Xera pondered, her face tightening. "I had hoped leading you to the Lesbius Oracle would end my involvement."

"Oh, it can't be you," Sophia gasped.

"Do you think I'm not capable of moving unseen?" Xera's violet eyes narrowed.

"Oh, no, I didn't mean that. You have a pregnant wife. You can't risk your life with us on this journey."

Xera bit her lip. "Words of prophecy are not easily ignored. Doing so can lead to disastrous consequences."

"Well, maybe there's another elvish hunter they're talking about," Sophia pointed out. "Like, um, those other ones who were with you."

"Yet I was the one that chose to lead you to the oracle and involve myself in your quest."

I furrowed my eyebrows. What would happen if she didn't come? Would my quest end in ruin if I failed to find all the companions named? "It has to be her decision to come with us, Sophia. But...it can't be coincidence we were led here by an elvish huntress and then received that prophecy."

Xera nodded. "Yes. I have much to consider."

I wanted to say more, to beg her, but she was a strong woman. She would make the decision on her own. I had to hope her honor would outweigh her desire to stay with her pregnant wife. I grimaced; what a terrible knight I must be to want to pull a woman from her family and ask her to risk her life.

"There's more to the prophecy than companions," Xera said finally. "The shattered blade?"

"The High King's blade," I answered, shifting on my feet. The sword that belonged to my ancient ancestor, the High King Peter.

"But that was broke into five pieces...oh," Sophia blushed. "She did mention five shards, didn't she?"

I nodded. "After his death, they were broken up and scattered across the lands. No one wanted the sword claimed again. Legends say the five pieces were hidden and well guarded. And even if they were found, they would have to be reforged. The blade is made of adamantium. No normal smith can work that metal."

Sophia frowned, "I remember being lectured on this subject as a novice." She tapped her chin. "Ooh, why didn't I pay better attention? One of the pieces was hidden in Murathi, wherever that is."

"Far to the north in lands now claimed by the Larg Orcs," Xera answered. "It is a holy place to them, some ruins they worship at."

"Fun," Sophia groaned. "And let's see...another is hidden in a volcano on the Isle of Birds. I think a third piece was hidden in the Mirage Gardens in the Halani Desert."

I stared at Sophia with eager excitement. "And the other two?"

Sophia furrowed her eyebrows. "Umm...the Haunted Forest. In a ruined castle in the depths of that terrible place."

It was my turn to groan. "They really didn't want this sword reforged."

"It was the High King's blade, the symbol of his empire. None of the usurping kings that carved up his empire could have been happy with that symbol around," Sophia answered. "Oh, the last one is in Rartha. In the Great Vault."

"I have heard of the Great Vault," Xera whispered. "The merchant princes of Rartha store their greatest treasures in there. It is impenetrable."

"And we still need to learn the way to forge the sword," I groaned, my hope dying. "Finding the sword seems a task more monumental than killing the dragon. Do you know of the ritual to work adamantium?"

Sophia shook her head. "I don't recall that lecture, but then I spent much of my time seducing timid novices instead of paying attention to such boring stuff. Sorry."

"Perhaps the answers can be found in the Library of Khalesithan. My wife is a librarian there."

"Elves have a library?" Sophia gasped.

Xera gave her a fixed look.

"Sorry. I didn't mean to make it sound like you were a bunch of...um..." Sophia's cheeks burned. "I'm not making this better, am I?"

Xera shook her head.

Sophia walked to the Elf and hugged her. "Sorry. Can you forgive me for being a dumb human?"

Xera laughed. "You are so impish."

"I know," giggled Sophia before she planted a hot kiss on Xera's lips.

I squeezed my thighs together as I watched. Memories of Sophia's kisses heated my body. Sophia became Lady Delilah in my imagination– my first crush. I remembered the kisses Lady Delilah gave me before I left on my Quest. She was such a beauty with flaming-red hair. I could still picture the first time I saw her riding into my parent's estate dressed in the armor of a Knight Deute. She was the reason I joined the Knights Deute.

I shook my head and forced myself to stand. I was drained from the Oracle's embrace. She had fed off my sexual energy to feed her prophecy. The world swam about me for a moment, and I stumbled before I caught my balance.

"Angela?" Sophia asked, giving me a worried look. "Are you okay?"

"Just tired," I said, reaching for my discarded armor. "We still have some daylight left, let's get moving to Khalesithan." What a hard word to say. Khalesithan.

Xera shook her head. "We should rest here for the night. I do not think the Oracle will mind."

"Why? We still have a few hours left?"

"Do you want to get caught in the giganraneae's vale when night falls?" the elf asked.

I shuddered. The Lesbius Oracle was in the heart of a spidery vale. The dark trees were covered in thick cobwebs. The giganraneae were a race of intelligent, spider-like monsters, an offshoot of the werespiders. They couldn't transform into human form, but still require humanoids for reproducing. The race is all female, and they deposit their eggs with an ovipositor into a humanoid's body. When the eggs hatch, the young feast on the host. The giganraneae keep the host paralyzed and cocooned until their daughters hatch.

"No," Sophia shuddered.

I sank back down to the pillows that covered the floor of the oracle's cave. "We can wait until morning."

My exhaustion pulled me down into sleep.

~ * ~

King Edward IV – Shesax, the Kingdom of Secare

"You sure this is a good idea?" I whispered to my pregnant wife.

Lavinia, my queen, fixed me with a determined smile, her hands resting on her pregnant belly. She was a gorgeous woman, her blue eyes sparkling. "You are the king. You are strong. You can control a warlock. Angela has to be stopped. You heard the Lesbius Oracle. There is a way for her to kill the dragon. Be strong."

I nodded my head. Her words heartened me. I was the king. I had to be strong to make sure that my unborn son would follow me onto the throne. The Sekar Oracle's prophecy would be thwarted. It was absurd for a woman to ever rule, and yet I feared Angela. She was a direct female descendant of Peter's youngest daughter Lily. When the High King died, only his daughter Lily survived him. He had no heir, no daughter could inherit rulership, and his grand empire broke apart into the modern countries of Secare, Valya,

Thosi, Zeutch, Haz, Thlin, and Athlos.

"We cannot let her reforge the High King's sword," my wife whispered. "That sword was broken for a reason."

The sword was forged of adamantium by Krab, the God of Crafting himself, as a gift to Peter. With that sword, the young king had conquered most of the known world. He had called his empire the High Kingdom of Hamilten. But the Goddess Slata was jealous of Peter. He was one of the God Pater's bastard offspring, and Slata had always been jealous of her husband's attention to his by-blows. She had cursed Lily to have only daughters and ensured all of Peter's male heirs perished.

"We should have just had her assassinated from the beginning," I cursed. There were good reasons not to. I had heeded Lady Delilah's counsel. If I killed Angela, it might have turned the Knights Deute against me. So instead, I conspired with High Priestess Vivian to taint Angela's Quest. But now she had a way to slay the dragon Dominari, a task no knight in a hundred years had completed.

I couldn't trust she would fail. I had to ensure it. Even if it meant hiring a warlock, a mage declared rogue and hunted by the Magery Council. My skin crawled. This had to be conducted in secret. Lavinia had used her servants to make contact this afternoon. He agreed to meet at midnight.

"Maybe you should leave?" I whispered to my wife.

"No. I must be here. He expects us both. Besides, he will not harm us. He knows we can give him resources once he succeeds."

"Resources for what?"

"For whatever he needs," my wife purred. "To continue whatever research had him banished by the Magery Council and fleeing their order of execution."

"Exactly," a voice purred out of the darkness.

I jumped. The wall of our bedchamber had opened, forming a makeshift door with a neighboring antechamber. A man dressed in crimson robes stepped in. His reddish hands, marking him as Thlinian, peeked out of the wide sleeves of his robe. The hood's cowl deeply shadowed the warlock's face. Only his orange eyes were visible through the shadows.

"Fireeyes?" I asked, then felt like an idiot. Who else would it be? Particularly with eyes that burned in a shadowy face.

"That is the name I now use," the warlock answered, his voice a rasping whisper.

Behind him, a naked woman entered, her body completely hairless, her eyes lifeless like a doll. She stood a step behind the warlock, silent. My eyebrows furrowed as I studied her body. Her juices stained her thighs, and the hot scent of tart pussy wafted through the room. A diamond pendant glinted between her breasts.

"Why did you bring your whore?" I demanded.

"His simulacrum," my wife whispered. "Only a Master Mage possesses one."

"Your wife is well-informed," Fireeyes answered. "Now, shall we discuss my servant or why you wish to hire my services?"

"I need you to kill a knight on her quest," I answered. "She's in the Deorc Forest at the Lesbius Oracle."

Chapter Thirty-Two: Chittering Forest

Xerathalasia

I woke up with Sophia cuddled against me. The colorful sheets hanging from the top of the Oracle's cave billowed and waved in a slight breeze. Sophia's pale face lay on my arm, her face so cute as she slumbered.

Angela still slept by herself. The Oracle's ritual had exhausted the knight, and she had slept undisturbed for hours. Though we were underground, my instincts told me dawn wasn't far off. Time to rise and face the dangers of slipping out of the vale.

The giganraneae were dangerous monsters. My people only tolerated their existence because they protected the Oracle. If someone wanted to seek her advice, they had to brave true dangers. The giganraneae knew not to leave the vale or our hunters would dispatch them. But any who wandered into the valley were theirs to hunt.

"Matar, watch over us as we stalk through the dark vale," I prayed to the hermaphroditic goddess that birthed the elves and our sister races. There were five hermaphroditic races birthed by the goddess impregnating herself with her own cock, each attuned with one of the five elements. Elves were of life, gnomes of earth, sylphs of air, nixies of water, and dragons of fire.

I shook Sophia.

"Hmm," the sleepy human murmured.

"It's morning," I whispered as I slipped my arm out from underneath her. "Time to break our fast and brave the dangers of the vale."

Sophia's face paled. "Ooh, I had forgotten about that. It's so creepy out there."

"Yes," Angela nodded, stretching as sat up and rubbed sleep from her eyes.

The human knight was a gorgeous woman, large breasts thrusting before her. Her body was lean and muscled. She moved with the grace of a trained fighter as she gathered up the pieces of her armor. She buckled on her half-breastplate, leaving her midriff and a generous amount of cleavage bare, followed by her pauldrons protecting her shoulders. A thick sword belt buckled around her waist from which her chainmail loincloth dangled. Thigh-high boots covered by metal greaves were next, followed by her bracers on her forearms. Elves didn't use armor. We relied on our quick reflexes to avoid hits.

Sophia nibbled on her hard trail rations. I didn't carry supplies. I could forage as we walked, eating the bounty of nature. The humans, however, couldn't eat half of what the Deorc Forest offered. They balked at eating tasty pine cones.

"Let's get this over with," Sophia said. "I hope our horses are still fine."

Angela nodded her head, her flaming hair brushing her shiny pauldrons. "They had forage and were hobbled. They should be fine."

The humans were attached to their horses despite being unable to speak to them. Angela's warhorse, Midnight, had a great deal of loyalty to his rider, and Purity, Sophia's mount, just adored the acolyte.

Angela drew her sword as she led us through the narrow tunnel that led back to the surface. Only the Oracle's chamber was covered in colorful sheets to hide the hard dirt walls and ceiling. Roots of trees poked through, forming a curtain of wispy tendrils that tickled my face as I followed the knight. Sophia was at the rear, almost clutching to me in fear.

Gray light filtered through from the entrance. Dawn had arrived, lightening the gloom of the vale. I shuddered when I stepped out of the cave. The woods were dark and dreary, the dark firs cocooned in torn cobwebs. No birds sang sweet songs to the rising sun or animals scampering through the brush. My nose wrinkled; the foul stench of death lingered through the vale.

I gripped my bow in my hand, the bow strung and an arrow knocked, ready to be pulled back and loosed at any threat. My ears twitched as I strained for any sound. Branches rustled as a breeze stirred the canopy.

Even Sophia was armed, gripping a small dagger in her hand. The acolyte's eyes scanned the trees as she shivered in her beige cloak and white robes. I winced with every dried twig that snapped beneath her careless feet or her clock rasping as the fabric caught on every bush she passed.

"Angela," Sophia whined suddenly.

"What?" the knight asked, turning around.

Sophia's dagger glowed a faint pink.

"Why is it glowing?" I asked.

Angela nodded. "Yes. What enchantment is on that dagger."

"It senses danger," Sophia swallowed. She peered up into the trees. "How much farther?"

"Another hour," I answered.

A shadow moved in the tree. I raised my bow, staring at the branch and shivered. Wispy cobwebs fluttered from a swaying branch. My heart beat faster. My eyes swept around the trees. More branches jiggled and swayed, too large to be disturbed that much by the breeze.

"We're surrounded," I whispered. "There's at least six of them."

"Pater's cock," cursed Angela. She raised her sword in a stance.

"Oh, no," Sophia groaned, clutching her glowing dagger with

both hands. "Saphique, please watch over your servants."

A shadow moved. My bow shifted and, I drew back the arrow. I released. The arrow was a blur streaking into the trees. A skittering snarl erupted. Something dark and spindly moved through the boughs.

The trees erupted with movement.

"Here they come!" Angela shouted, her red hair streaming behind her as she charged at the nearest tree. A spindly body climbed down it.

The giganraneae looked like a large, delicate, black spider, long legs ending at human-like hands gripping the trunk. Instead of a chitinous face, the giganraneae appeared to be a comely woman with multi-faceted, black eyes and dark hair falling in a long curtain around their pale, round faces.

The giganraneae hissed as Angela rammed her sword through its armored thorax. Greenish ichor leaked out as the giganraneae chittered in pain, her body convulsing on the tree trunk. Spindly legs went limp, and the monster fell from the tree, ripping clean off Angela's blade.

Other giganraneae descended from the trees, scuttling down tree trunks or lowering themselves on ropes of silk spun from spinnerets. Each chittered and hissed in their foul language.

My hand was a blur. Draw. Knock. Fire. My arrows streaked out, finding targets. There were far more than six. The giganraneae cried out in pain, hands ripping my arrows from chitinous bodies and throwing them to the ground.

"No, no, no!" Sophia shrieked, flailing with her dagger as one giganraneae lunged at her.

Angela appeared, sword slicing a pair of spidery limbs. Sophia scrambled back as Angela roared and swung. The giganraneae was driven back, body rent by cuts that leaked an ichor as dull green as pond scum.

"Keep against a tree!" Angela shouted at Sophia.

"Yeah," the acolyte nodded, backing away from the fight.

"Xera, can you handle your side?" the knight asked as she threw herself at the next giganraneae lunging at her, blocking the monster with her large kite shield.

"I can!" I shouted, firing my tenth arrow, taking a giganraneae between her multi-faceted eyes.

A third of my arrows had already been fired. I drew the eleventh and feathered a giganraneae leaping at me. It fell in a heap on the ground, legs curling as it convulsed. My twelfth arrow glanced off the hide of a charging monster.

"Matar's seed!" I cursed in elvish.

I reached for my thirteenth arrow. The giganraneae slammed into me, throwing me back to the ground. My bow fell from my grip. Spindly hands grasped my shoulders and thighs. The thing chittered in my face.

"Lovely," the giganraneae said in elvish. "What a delightful mother for my children."

The spinnerets squirted silk on my legs, her nimble hands wrapping it about my feet. I ripped my wood dagger from my belt. The giganraneae fingers tightened on my shoulder. I had one shot. The knife would never penetrate her thick carapace. I had to go for the joint.

I lunged.

My long dagger slid through the joint between the abdomen and thorax carapace. The giganraneae stiffened. I was in her guts. I twisted the knife and screamed. My other arm heaved the monster off me as she convulsed on her back, ichor dripping from her gaping wound.

I kicked my feet, still entangled by spider silk. I reached down and began cutting.

~ * ~

Acolyte Sophia

My heart hammered in terror as I pressed my back against the tree.

222

Angela danced about the clearing, her sword flashing like bolts of lightning, reflecting the dim light. She swung in mighty sweeps, cleaving the monstrous spiders while her kite shield fended off those that tried to attack her from the other side.

Xera regained her feet, cobwebs still clinging about her ankles. She reclaimed her bow and fired an arrow at a giganraneae in the treetops. The thing fell with a chittering scream.

"Yes." I screamed in relief, my sweaty hands gripping my glowing dagger. "That's it."

I wish I could help better. There hadn't been time for me to enchant Angela's sword, but she seemed to be doing fine. Her longsword smashed and cut through the carapace of the nasty things.

"On your left!" Xera shouted. An arrow flew across the battlefield.

"Thank you, Saphique," I prayed as Angela and Xera drove back the monsters.

"Aren't you pretty, dearie?" a voice chittered above me.

I gasped.

Above me, a giganraneae clung to the trees. Her spidery eyes glinted as she stared at me. Long legs and spindly fingers reached for me. I swung with my knife. It bounced off the carapace covering the legs. The hands grasped my shoulder.

"Angela!" I shrieked as it hauled me up into the air.

The giganraneae scampered back up into the tree as my legs kicked. I stabbed with the knife again. The blade bounced off again. A third leg batted the dagger from my hand. It tumbled down into the ground.

"Sophia!" Angela shouted, racing to the base of the tree. "Xera! Shoot!"

The giganraneae lifted me up, holding me before her as a shield while she climbed up the tree. Xera raised her bow. My heart thudded and blood screamed through my veins. The branches swept around us. We vanished into the thick canopy. The giganraneae chittered as I struggled in her strong grip.

"None of that, dearie," chittered the giganraneae as her silk began wrapping about my legs.

I screamed in fear as I was spun about like meat turning on the spit above the fire. I struggled harder, writhing my entire body as I screamed in fear.

"Hold on!" Angela shouted from below.

"You struggle a lot, dearie. Why? Don't you want to be the mother of my darling children?"

"No!"

My heart hammered in fear. Tears burned in my eyes. My legs were cocooned. I struggled, but the silk was strong. I kept shaking and writhing, trying to get my arms free and fight back. My fist struck her chitinous stomach.

My knuckles hurt.

"Now, now, stop struggling, dearie."

"No," I screamed. "I'm not going to. Let me go."

I was turned in her hands, her face just before mine. Her lips were red. Something glistened on them. Not saliva, this was oilier. She lowered down and kissed me on the lips. A sharp, acrid flavor filled my mouth. Everything went numb.

I relaxed. A peaceful lassitude fell over me. My body went limp. I didn't need to fight any longer. I was turned again, the silk working up my body. In fact, this was kind of nice. The world turned, and I giggled as it bound my arms. I was snug and warm.

"That's it, dearie. Isn't that nice?"

"Yes," I whispered.

"Hold on, Sophia. Xera's climbing up."

Through the branches below, flashes of Xera's face appeared.

I giggled, "Hi, Xera."

The silk covered my face. I was completely engulfed in the warm, snug blanket. My eyes grew heavy as I was rocked by the movement of the giganraneae. I could just fall asleep and enjoy peaceful lassitude. It was such a lovely delight.

Chapter Thirty-Three: Spidery Passion

Knight-Errant Angela

Xera dropped from the tree. "Sophia's been cocooned and it's taking her east."

"Pater's cock," I swore. "Can you track her?"

My heart hammered in my chest. Sophia was my responsibility. It was my duty to protect her on the Quest. I couldn't let her be impregnated by a bunch of monstrous eggs and killed when they hatched. No one deserved that.

"Of course," Xera nodded. "The giganraneae is moving fast, but she'll stop to breed with Sophia. We'll catch up then."

"Then let's go," I shouted. I couldn't let Sophia get harmed. She was such a wonderful person.

Xera darted off into the brush. I followed, my armor clinking with every step.

~ * ~

Acolyte Sophia

I drowsed in my snug cocoon, rocked by the giganraneae scampering through the treetops. Despite my lassitude, a heat grew between my thighs. A hot itch that I hoped my giganraneae could satisfy. I squirmed, rubbing my face against the sticky silk.

"Growing excited, dearie?" the Giganraneae asked.

"Yes," I moaned. The silk clung to my lips. It tasted bitter. I spat, trying to get it out of my mouth.

"Mmm, we're almost there. And then I'll pleasure you my sweet mate."

"Mate..." I smiled. "And you are a girl giganraneae? I can't...be with men."

"There are only girl giganraneae, dearie."

"Oh, right." I knew that. It was so hard to think.

"You'll enjoy every moment of my touch."

"Good! I'm getting so wet."

"I can smell, dearie." The giganraneae made a smacking sound. "Mmm, yes. It has been so long since I've enjoyed a human."

My stomach lurched as we descended. I squirmed, a little afraid, but the giganraneae held me with four of her eight hands. She pressed me against her abdomen. I would be safe. The giganraneae wouldn't want me harmed. She wanted to love me and mate with me.

There was a part of me that thought that was a bad idea. I wish I could remember why. It was all foggy in my mind.

"Here we are, dearie," chittered the giganraneae.

My silk cocoon was ripped open by her hands. I spilled out on the loam of the forest, a few strands of silk clinging to my robe and hair. I giggled as the giganraneae stood above me, staring down with her beautiful eyes. Her multi-faceted eyes made her seem ethereal. Her lips lowered, and we shared another delicious, numbing kiss.

Her hands ran across my body. It was like I had multiple lovers undressing me. I shuddered in delight as long fingers opened my robe and explored beneath. Hands stroked my thighs, my stomach, and groped my small breasts. I shuddered in delight, pushing my tongue into her mouth as her fingers teased me.

It was delicious.

She pinched and rolled my nipples, shooting pleasure down to my hot pussy. One finger toyed with my bellybutton while a second hand stroked my side. I shuddered, ticklish delight tingling through me. My toes curled as a pair of hands stroked my inner thighs, working up to the hot folds of my pussy.

"Mmm, you are so responsive," chittered the giganraneae. "What is your name, my mate?"

"Sophia," I gasped, my hips undulating as her fingers teased nearer and nearer to my hot pussy. "Yours?"

"Sliyth," she answered.

"Sliyth," I moaned as I reached up, stroking her smooth chitin. It was exciting to caress her hard, slick hide, so much different than skin. "What a lovely name."

"So is Sophia." One set of hands squeezed my breasts as another rubbed at my sides. "As lovely as its owner."

I blushed. "Ooh, you are so nice, Sliyth."

Our lips met for another kiss as her fingers stroked at the folds of my pussy. I shuddered again, my hips undulating in delight. Her long fingers parted my pussy lips then probed into my depths. I shuddered, clenching down on her fingers. I moaned into her lips as the pleasure stirred through my body.

So wonderful. Sliyth was a delightful lover.

She chittered between kisses, her wet lips moving down my neck. I shuddered as her fingers worked deeper into my pussy. They were so long and thin, different than a human's or even an elf's. I moaned, staring up at the spiderwebs stretched between the trees.

"Mmm, you are just delicious," Sliyth purred, her compound eyes staring at me. They were such a deep black. She had no eyelids, so they never blinked, they only glistened as she shifted. The hands stroking my sides seized my arms, pinning them to my side. Her abdomen contorted beneath her and pointed at me; her spinnerets fired silk.

I gasped as it covered my wrist, pinning me to the ground. I moaned, pulling at the webbing. I couldn't move. She tied my other wrist, then pushed my thighs apart, her abdomen moving. The silky bonds were tight on my hands and ankles.

"So pretty." Sliyth smiled.

A pair of her black hands squeezed my small, ivory breasts. My nipples were hard. I gasped as she leaned over and sucked on my nipple. Her teeth were sharp, nipping at my flesh as I squirmed. My pussy clenched down on her invading fingers.

"Yes, yes!" I panted.

My body convulsed. I was pinned down to the ground, my limbs heaving against the silken bonds. I was so helpless. This monster could do anything to me. My pussy contracted on her fingers.

She could do any naughty, delicious thing to me.

My orgasm crashed through my body.

"Slata's cunt!" I screamed as the pleasure burned through me.

My pussy convulsed about her spidery digits. Her mouth sucked harder at my nipple. I stared into multi-faceted eyes. The dark orbs seemed to swallow me up as I bucked against her probing fingers. The pleasure washed through my veins, driving back the fog.

"Oh, no!" I gasped as the pleasure washed through me.

A giganraneae was making love to me. She would stick her ovipositor into me. I squirmed, my orgasm burning harder. I was so helpless. I was in danger. Sliyth was dangerous. Why did that make my pussy convulse again? Another orgasm rippled through me.

I was helpless. She could do anything she wanted to me.

"Gods, yes!" I moaned as her hungry lips nipped my breasts. Blood trickled. Her tongue licked it up. The numbing bliss shot back through my veins. I shuddered again as she moved lower and lower. She nibbled, leaving little bite marks that trickled blood. Her fingers withdrew from my pussy.

Her mouth replaced it.

"Yes, yes, yes!" I gasped as the bliss burned through me.

I heaved my body against her hungry mouth. Her venom made my pussy writhe. Orgasm after orgasm rippled through my body. I screamed out through the woods. I shuddered and writhed as the bliss burned my body. I couldn't stand it. The pleasure was intense. It consumed me. I never wanted it to end.

"You're so amazing!" I screamed.

"You taste delicious," moaned Sliyth. "My daughters will love your flesh. So juicy and rich. You will sustain them."

Her tongue licked again, wiggling into my depths. Her fingers parted my asscheeks. Fingers thrust inside my bowels. I groaned, bucking as another orgasm washed through me. Her fingers worked in and out of my bowels, the burning heat flowing through me, joining the delight in my pussy.

"It's time," she purred, her lips stained with my tart excitement. Sliyth rose on her legs. Something long and black emerged from her abdomen. It was thin and dripping, the tip bulbous, almost like a cock, but it had an opening at the tip that was too wide for a dick.

Her ovipositor.

"Fuck me with it!" I moaned, eager for her appendage. It wasn't a cock. It wouldn't sully me. My pussy burned to feel it.

"You're eager to be implanted," chittered Sliyth. "You are so beautiful. I will always remember you, Sophia."

"Me, too," I moaned as she crawled over me.

Her smooth, chitinous body rubbed on my stomach and breasts. Her mouth found mine as her ovipositor pushed into the wet folds of my pussy. My back arched as the thin shaft filled up my cunt. My toes curled in delight even as my mind screamed a warning.

This was dangerous.

My pussy convulsed as an orgasm filled me. "Yes," I moaned.

The ovipositor moved inside me. Sliyth stayed still, not fucking me. Instead her organ worked in and out of my sheath all on its own. My pussy clung to it as it probed deeper and deeper into me. My body shuddered as small bumps adorning the ovipositor caressed my pussy. My nerves burned with delight. My body thrashed as it pushed deeper and deeper.

"By the gods!" I screamed as it pressed into my womb. Nothing had ever been so deep in me. "So good!"

"Yes!" chittered Sliyth, her body shuddering atop me. Her fingers in my ass probed deep as she convulsed. "So good!"

Something bulged down the ovipositor, moving towards the tip. My pussy stretched around it. I shuddered as Sliyth writhed atop me, chittering in delight. The round object reached the tip and entered my womb.

An egg.

"Yes!" we screamed together.

A second and third egg stretched me out. I groaned and convulsed as the hot pleasure filled me. I strained against the silk binding me to the ground, wanting to break free so I could hold my monstrous lover as we shared this wondrous moment.

Chapter Thirty-Four: Cleansing Ritual

Knight-Errant Angela

"Yes!" Sophia's voice screamed through the woods, caught in the throes of passion.

I raced forward past Xera, my heart hammering. The giganraneae chittered with pleasure. Fear clutched my heart. What was it doing to my Sophia? I clutched my sword in a sweaty grip as I cut through the spiderweb and used my shield to push the sticky strands aside.

"Sophia," I screamed. "Hold on."

I burst through the clearing. Sophia thrashed beneath the spidery body of the giganraneae. The monster lifted her human-like face, compound eyes focusing on me. The giganraneae ripped her long ovipositor from Sophia's pussy and hissed at me.

The giganraneae charged.

I met her attack. The giganraneae leaped at me, chittering in rage. Her ovipositor withdrew into her body as she soared twenty feet at me. I lunged my sword forward. A stop thrust. The monster crashed into me.

"Gewin's big cock!" I gasped as we fell to the ground.

Air whooshed from my lungs. The giganraneae's body pinned

my shield against my chest, crushing me. The thing chittered in pain. Legs thrashed. I heaved. My sword had stuck through her thorax and out her back. She spasmed and shuddered as she died.

"Sophia!"

I didn't care about the dying monster. I was on my feet and rushing to the acolyte. She shuddered on the ground. Her stomach was distended, filled with the monster's eggs. The young woman writhed on the ground, her eyes unfocused.

"Oh, no!" I shouted.

"Angela," smiled Sophia. "Mmm, you look so beautiful."

I drew my knife and cut the thick mass of silk off her wrists. Xera raced around, freeing Sophia's ankles. The acolyte threw her arms around me and kissed me hard. Her lips were acrid and my mouth numbed. My mind fogged with lust.

I fought it.

I seized Sophia's shoulders and pushed her back, staring into her eyes. "Are you okay, Sophia?"

"I'm so fine, Angela," moaned Sophia. "Mmm, Sliyth made me cum over and over."

"Sliyth?"

"The giganraneae," Xera answered. "Sophia. She implanted her eggs in you."

"It was so hot," Sophia shuddered. "I feel so stuffed right now."

"You're going to die," I gasped. "We have to get them out of you."

"Die?" Sophia's green eyes grew focused. She shook her head, shaking off the monster's ecstatic venom. Fear cascaded across her face. "Slata's cunt! Angela!"

Sophia threw her arms around my neck, clinging to me. I held her tight as she trembled, stroking her light-brown hair. I didn't know what to do. "You have divine magic. Do you know of a spell?"

"I don't know," sobbed Sophia. "I'm going to die, Angela. I can't die."

"You need to think."

Sophia tightened her grip on me, sobbing, "I...I... don't

know...there...I can't...think..."

"Calm down," I told her. "I'm here with you. Don't panic."

"Panic?" she screeched. "I have giganraneae eggs in me. Oh, Gods, I'm so dead."

"You're not dead yet." I cupped her face, wiping at the tears trickling down her cheeks. "So long as you breathe we can figure this out."

"You used that potion to heal Xiloniasa from being petrified," Xera said. "Do you have another?"

Sophia shook her head. "No. It wouldn't work. That breaks curses, and this is something else. I'm polluted by..."

"Sophia?" I asked, staring into her eyes. They flicked back and forth like she was thinking. "Do you have an idea?"

"A cleansing ritual," Sophia smiled. "And I'll need your help. Both of you."

"Of course," I grinned. "What do you need?"

"Your pussy juices."

A hot flush shot through me. "Really?"

"I need to be bathed in it," Sophia purred. She licked her lips, her tongue stud flashing silver. "To be covered in feminine juices to purify my body and drive out the pollution."

"Of course," I said, standing up and undoing my sword belt, my chainmail loincloth rattling. I let it drop, exposing my naked pussy to the air.

"Now?" Xera asked.

"She needs to be healed," I said. "We can't let her die."

Sophia licked her lips, her hand stroking up my greaves to my thigh. "Mmm, I have missed your pussy, Angela."

I blushed. "I...I missed your touch." How long had it been since we made love? Almost two weeks?

Her fingers sent a shiver through my body as she moved higher. She brushed my wet, shaved folds. I shuddered. The hot scent of my tangy pussy filled my nose. Sophia had a mischievous grin on her face as she toyed with my pussy.

"You, too, Xera," Sophia moaned, reaching out her left hand to the elf.

"Of course, Sophia," Xera purred, setting down her bow and walking forward. Her large breasts jiggled and her ears twitched. "I always love your gentle touch."

"And I love how delicious you taste," laughed Sophia.

I grinned, the marigold perfume of Xera's excitement mixing with mine. Elves pussies had such flowery scents. Xera pressed against me, her round breast rubbing on my armor. I put an arm around her, shuddering as Sophia stroked my pussy, and kissed the elf.

Xera's lips were so soft. Her tongue played with mine, pressing into my mouth as she moaned. Sophia played with both our pussies, her fingers working in and out, sending shudders of pleasure through my body. I moaned into Xera's sweet kiss as my pussy clenched about Sophia's probing fingers.

"Mmm, two pussies to play with," Sophia purred. "What a delightful treat."

"Oh, yes!" I gasped, breaking the kiss with Xera. "Your fingers know just where to touch."

Sophia winked a green eye at me. "Well, I am an acolyte of Saphique. I've spent many years learning how to pleasure women."

Her thumb brushed my clit. I shuddered, my hips bucking. My armor creaked as I sucked in a breath. My breasts strained against my breastplate. My nipples were hard, rubbing on the cool metal. My stomach tensed as the pleasure built.

"Such delicious pussies to play with," moaned the acolyte.

Xera cried out in musical elvish as Sophia leaned over and tongued her clit. The elf's arm tightened about me as her hips writhed. Our flesh pressed together. Her large breasts shook and jiggled, her nipples hard, beckoning.

I leaned over and engulfed a nipple. The chalky, bitter flavor of her camouflage paint filled my mouth as I suckled on her hard nipple. I moaned as Sophia rubbed harder and harder at my clit, her thumb moving in fast circles.

"Yummy! Now to taste Angela's tangy pie."

Sophia's thumb moved to the side so her tongue could assault my clit. My hips spasmed as her wet, agile tongue and hard tongue stud caressed through my pussy lips up to the tip of my clit. She swirled her tongue around it, grinding her hard stud against my bud. My ass clenched as the pleasure shot through me.

She pushed a third finger into my pussy, then a fourth. I gasped, releasing Xera's nipple as my body shuddered. My pussy stretched around her fingers while my clit burned beneath Sophia's sweet assault. Then the naughty acolyte curled her hand.

She fisted me.

"By the Gods!" I moaned as she reamed my pussy, fucking her fist in and out of my depths.

I was stretched open. My pussy clung to her fist as she pushed it deeper and deeper into me. Nerves burst with pleasure. My body was filled with it. My back arched. Xera's arms tightened, holding me as I swayed.

"Sophia!" I gasped, a powerful orgasm brewing. "Oh, yes!"

"Cum!" she moaned.

I did. My pussy convulsed about her fist. A powerful wave of pleasure shot through me. The muscles in my stomach tightened. Pussy juices squirted out, splashing on her face. Sophia closed her eyes, moving her face around as I drenched her. My tangy aroma filled the air as my creamy juices coated her face, dripping down to her small breasts.

"Pater's wonderful cock!" I gasped. "Oh, wow! Saphique's naughty mouth! So good!"

"That's it!" smiled Sophia. "That's what I need."

~ * ~

Acolyte Sophia

Every breath was full of Angela's tangy scent. Her juices dripped down my face and neck. I loved it. I clenched my pussy as I savored every last delight she gave me. The juices trickled down my body, reaching my nipples.

I ripped my fist out of Angela's pussy. The redheaded knight stumbled back, almost falling as her body trembled from the intensity of her orgasm. I licked my fingers as I turned to Xera. The elf smiled down at me.

"Are you going to make me cum that hard?" she asked.

"Of course," I purred, pushing a third finger from my left hand into her pussy. I could fist a woman with either hand.

My sticky hand wrapped around her waist, squeezing her ass as I leaned in and licked at her clit. Her flowery excitement covered my tongue as I nuzzled into her pussy. I slipped in a fourth finger, her pussy clenching down about my fingers.

"Sophia!" gasped Xera as I curled my hand into a fist, engulfed by her hot flesh.

Her elvish pussy clenched as I worked my fist deep into her depths. Her hands gripped my hair, holding me tight as she undulated into my thrusting fist. Her juices poured out as she moaned in her melodic elvish.

I loved making a woman go wild with pleasure.

I paid attention to the clues of her body. I had made love to her enough times to understand the subtle differences of elvish orgasms. I concentrated on her clit, flicking my tongue stud against it harder than I had on Angela's while my fist plunged deep into her pussy.

My pussy clenched, stuffed full of the Giganraneae eggs. I shuddered, excited and disgusted all at the same time as they pulsed inside me. I pressed on my clit with my thighs, building my own orgasm as I pleasured the elf.

Xera's moans grew higher in pitch. Her breasts heaved as the pleasure built through her. I flicked harder at her clit and fucked my fist faster in and out of her tight depths. Her hips swiveled. Her pussy grew hotter.

That's what I needed.

I uncurled my fingers inside of her, caressing the wall of her tight pussy.

"Matar!" screamed Xera as her orgasm washed over her.

The elf's pussy convulsed. Her flowery juices squirted out. I let them splash on my breasts, anointing me with her feminine delights. The juices ran hot down my body to my aching pussy. I spread my thighs and let them touch my clit.

"Saphique, Goddess of Purity, cleanse my body!" I called out to my Goddess.

Her power filled me. The pussy juices anointing my flesh glowed white. The femininity of Angela and Xera sank into my body. I shuddered. My orgasm burst inside me as the feminine purity swept down to my pussy.

The first egg spread my pussy open as the magic expelled it. My back arched as the pleasure increased. The egg popped out of my cunt. My pussy burned as the second and third egg came out. I fell over onto my hands and knees, wordlessly screaming in bliss as I was cleansed. Each egg sent such pleasure shooting through me.

"Slata's cunt," I panted when the last egg was forced out. My pussy writhed. My body pure. "Thank you, Saphique. Thank you."

"You're cleansed," Angela shouted. She pulled me up and hugged me to her armor. Tears glistened in her eyes. Our lips met in a kiss.

It was such a wonderful kiss. My heart beat fast. I knew it wasn't love. She was just concerned about me, but I let myself enjoy it anyways. I could pretend, for now, that Angela loved me back.

It was a wonderful delusion.

~ * ~

Xerathalasia

The horses neighed in greeting, eager to see their human masters.

It was a relief to be out of the vale. No more Giganraneae molested us on the way out. The forest outside the vale smelled sweetly of resin, leaves, and the musk of animals. Birds sang in the boughs, deer scampered on the trails, and squirrels cavorted up and down the tree trunks.

The fullness of life was about me again.

"There's my sweet Purity," Sophia smiled, petting the white snout of her mare. "I missed you."

Angela unhobbled her large stallion. She took his reins and joined Sophia. The pair stood close. When they walked into the woods, there had been a rift between them. Sophia was hurt and Angela was distant. I smiled as they walked forward, shoulders almost touching.

They worked well together. And they had such a hard, dangerous road before them. Duty compelled them both. Even Sophia had found the strength to walk towards it. That was probably Angela's doing. The knight walked with a straight back. She was graceful and confident, marching towards her destiny.

Could I walk with the same confidence? Could I leave my woods, my wife, my people behind to help a pair of humans? Destiny called to me, and I was afraid I would not have the same strength these two humans had.

My thoughts were heavy as I led them east to my home.

Chapter Thirty-Five: Sophia's Insatiable Appetite

Knight-Errant Angela – Northern Deorc Forest, The Federation of Deoraciynae

"I can't believe you want to go another round," I gasped as Sophia nibbled on my pink nipple.

Sophia flashed me a mischievous grin, her green eyes twinkling in the moonlight drifting through the thick canopy of Deorc Forest. Her tongue licked my nipple, a slow circle that sent fluttering delight shooting down to my aching pussy.

"You've already made me cum twice," I groaned. "And poor Xera's already succumbed to sleep from your insatiable appetite."

"I'm just so horny tonight," Sophia grinned. "There's something about this forest that is exciting at night."

"And you're sure it's not the company?" I grinned.

Since the giganraneae attack, Sophia and I had been close. For the last two nights, the three of us had shared a bed, with Sophia making both Xera and myself cum many times. Sophia seemed so happy now that the strain in our relationship had mended.

It did make travel more pleasant as we crossed the northern end of the Deorc forest, heading for Khalesithan where the elves' great library resided. It was still slow going, the thick forest forcing us to lead Midnight and Purity on foot. I was glad Xera was patient with our slow pace. The elf huntress was at home in the woods, moving through the rough terrain and game trails with ease.

"It could be the company," Sophia admitted, taking another lick of my nipple. "There is this sexy knight I'm in bed with. She has gorgeous tits and the most wonderful shade of hair."

I blushed as she touched the fiery locks spilling down to my large breasts. She nibbled on the tresses' end with a playful smile on her face. Her lithe body pressed against my side, her hot pussy rubbing on my hip as she teased me.

My pussy was on fire. I wanted to sleep, but I also wanted to cum again.

"I can't resist you. You're like a siren."

"I'm a servant of Saphique," Sophia said mysteriously, "and we have our ways to make any woman as horny as a she-bear in heat."

"That's pretty horny," I admitted. Was it? I never really met a she-bear before.

"A strong, supple, sexy she-bear," Sophia nodded. "Mmm, I think I need to fuck you."

"Good," I groaned. "Let me cum so I can go to bed."

"Oh, would you rather sleep?" Sophia asked, grinning like a naughty imp as she rolled away.

I groaned, pressing my thighs together. "No. You made me horny, and now you are going to fix it."

"I made something," Sophia said. "I've been working on it the last few days."

"Oh, and here I thought you were masturbating when you slipped off during lunch."

Sophia found her pouch and pulled out her dildo made of black marble swirled with white and polished to a mirror's finish. My pussy clenched. I missed having a cock in me. The last one I fucked was Xera's elf-dick when she was in heat, and that was a week ago.

"Yes, fuck me with the dildo."

"Oh, I will," Sophia promised and produced a harness made of fine strips of bark braided and tied together to form straps. I had seen harnesses like that.

"You're really going to fuck me?" I grinned.

Sophia nodded as she slipped the dildo through the harness and secured it about her waist. The dildo pressed against her clit, thrusting out like a shiny cock. "I'm gonna fuck you with my big dick."

"Oh, yes!" I grinned, writhing my hips.

Xera continued to sleep beside us, her back to me, her cute ass peeking out from the blanket that half-draped over her.

Sophia pushed my thighs apart, a big grin on her face. "But first, I need to make sure you're wet enough for my cock."

"Oh, I'm wet enough," I panted, my pussy clenching in anticipation.

Sophia pushed my thighs apart, my leg brushing Xera's soft ass, and ran a finger up my pussy's slit. I shuddered as Sophia brought her finger to her lips and licked my tangy juices from her digit. A considering look crossed Sophia's face.

"Nope, not wet enough. I'll have to fix that."

"Good," I panted as she leaned down and stroked my thighs. My toes curled in delight. I groaned as her hand slid higher and higher. "You're such a tease."

Sophia licked her lips, her tongue piercing flashing. "I know."

As she leaned over, her belly piercing dangled and caught the light, the ruby glittering. That ruby meant she had mastered the art of cunnilingus. I knew first hand how true that was. I groaned as her hot breath washed over my pussy.

"Such a pretty, little pussy you have," purred Sophia. "Like a little clam that's just begging to be devoured."

"Oh, yes," I groaned. "Please, Sophia. Slata's cunt, you made me horny."

The naughty acolyte, her light-brown hair spilling about her face as she leaned in, took her first lick. Her hard tongue stud slid through my folds, contrasting with her softer tongue. Pleasure raced down to my curling toes and up to my aching nipples. I leaned back on my elbows and arched my back, my breasts jiggling.

I loved watching Sophia's eyes as she ate me. They always twinkled with such delight. The girl never tired of eating pussy. I think she would be happy spending all day going from woman to woman, eating their pussies and drinking all their juices.

Her tongue flicked faster, the tongue stud slapping my clit. The hard point sent bucking pleasure through my body. I spasmed every time. I moaned and gasped as she licked with a furious need. She wanted to make me cum fast, but not hard. Just enough to get me soaking for her toy.

"You're so good," I groaned. "Pater's cock, that's amazing. Mmm, you have me on fire."

Sophia's eyes twinkled, and she licked harder. Her fingers stroked my labia as she concentrated on my clit, attacking it with her tongue stud. The acolyte was a master at cunnilingus. She played my pussy the way a master minstrel played the lyre. Sweet moans, Sophia's music, escaped my lips, echoing through the dark woods.

"Yes, yes," I gasped, my hips bucking into her mouth. "Oh, Sophia, I'm going to cum."

Sophia already knew it. She was building me right to where she wanted me. Every touch of her tongue and fingers had purpose. What felt like random, fluttering strokes and caresses were the deliberate moves of a cunnilingus master.

My hands grabbed her light-brown hair, pulling her harder into my pussy. Her mouth swallowed my clit and two fingers shoved into my sheath. Those delicious fingers caressed the top of my pussy and ended on this special spot.

My body heaved as my orgasm burst through me.

Sophia drank down my juices as I thrashed on the bed. The quick, hot orgasm shuddered through me. I heaved once, and then it was gone. My pussy ached. I was still horny. She hadn't satiated me, she made me even hotter.

"Fuck me!" I begged. "Ram that dildo inside me."

Sophia licked her lips covered in milky fluids. My pussy juices had been whipped to a froth. The acolyte crawled up my body, her small breasts jiggling and the dildo waving between her thighs. I pulled her across my body, our breasts pressing together as the stone dildo prodded my pussy.

"Are you ready to be fucked?" whispered Sophia in my ear.

"Gods, yes," I groaned. "Please, I need it so bad."

Sophia grinned and kissed me. I thrust my tongue into her lips, savoring my tangy flavor. Her right hand squeezed my breast, sliding up to find my nipple and pinch. My pussy clenched as the electricity shot down from my aching nipple.

That's when she thrust.

I gasped as she slammed the dildo into the depths of my clenching, sopping pussy. The pleasure was intense, erupting pleasure through me. I squirmed beneath her, enjoying the hard shaft filling me up.

It would only be better if it was a real cock. But the dildo was a nice substitute.

Sophia broke the kiss, staring down at me. Why wasn't she fucking me? I moved my hips, trying to give her the hint I needed to be pounded.

"Holy Saphique," chanted Sophia, praying to her Virgin Goddess, "give life to my toy so I may give pleasure to all who love you."

The dildo vibrated inside me. I gasped as I was suddenly filled with humming pleasure. My toes curled and my legs tightened about her hips. I let out a throaty moan of surprised joy at the sudden burst of pleasure.

"Pater's cock," I cursed to the chief god, the Father of all except the hermaphroditic races.

"Slut," giggled Sophia as she drew back and slammed the humming shaft into my pussy.

"Oh, yes!" I panted. "I'm such a slut for a vibrating dick. Oh, damn. Oh, wow. That's...oh, fuck."

She had used the magical dildo on me before, but never while fucking me. It was wild. My hips bucked into her thrusts and our breasts rubbed together. I ran my hands up and down her supple back and clenching ass. I squeezed her butt-cheeks, pulling her in tight as the pleasure raced through my body.

My pussy loved the sensations. Humming bliss poured through my body. Every part of me seemed to tingle in anticipation of the building orgasm. Sophia's hips fucked me faster; she sensed my pleasure the way only a woman trained in a temple of Saphique could.

"That's it, slut," Sophia whispered into my ear. "Love my big, vibrating cock. Savor the pleasure. Let it wash through you."

"Yes, yes!" I panted.

I humped my hips, grinding my clit into her groin every time she buried that magical shaft into my body. The humming seemed to intensify. My pussy spasmed, a small orgasm rolling through my body. I gasped and shuddered, eager for the big one to consume me.

Sophia's tongue licked and nibbled at my ear. It was one more delicious sensation coursing through my body. I hugged Sophia tight, our silky skin pressed together. Everywhere she touched me burned with fire.

I kissed her as my orgasm swelled. My tongue thrust into her mouth, tasting how sweet and delicious she was. My eyes closed, and I concentrated on her magical shaft and her supple body. My pleasure swelled, intensified.

I came.

I bucked and shuddered beneath her. My fingernails dug into her asscheeks. My pussy writhed about that humming shaft. It was so wonderful. She slammed harder into me. Wave after wave of rapture inundated my mind.

I drowned in bliss.

Sophia thrashed atop me as my climax reached its peak. I held onto this moment of perfect bliss, not wanting to let it go. But then it retreated. Sophia slammed into me one last time, trembling as her own orgasm filled her. She collapsed on me. I held her as we both gasped and panted.

"Wonderful," I whispered, a smile on my lips.

"Angela," Sophia said, her voice strained. "I...I...I'm glad things have changed between us."

"Me, too," I smiled.

"I...I care for you. I mean, you know that."

"I'm sorry I called it a silly crush," I smiled. "It's not."

Sophia swallowed. "And...what about...you?"

I held her trembling body. "I do care for you."

"But?"

"But...there's this hole in my heart. I feel like I loved someone, and my memories were cut out of me. Holding you, being with you, even caring for you helps to fill it. But...is it love? I don't know, Sophia. Maybe." But if I loved this...other person, why did I allow the Oracle to take my memories of him or her away from me? Could I even love?

The only person I ever remembered being in love with was my girlish crush on Lady Delilah. Just thinking of the redheaded knight made my heart thud faster.

Maybe I never loved this...missing person. So I couldn't be sure I loved Sophia. I had been terrified when she was taken by the giganraneae and so relieved when we rescued her. It was wonderful holding her in my arms, and yet...she couldn't give me everything I craved.

"Then let's just enjoy our new closeness," Sophia said, hope in her eyes. "And...and...we'll see where it goes. Maybe..."

Her unsaid words burned in my mind: ...*you'll come to love me.*

"Maybe." I kissed her on the lips. "But...I do enjoy a real cock. Your vibrating, magical dildo is amazing, but there's something nice about a cock cumming inside of you."

Sophia's smile slipped. "Well, I mean, I could never be with just one woman. I love you, but...I'm sworn to Saphique. I want to be with other women, but..."

I nodded my head. "It's perfectly natural."

"So, it's okay. I mean, I understand. You want to be with other people. It doesn't mean you don't lo...care for me." Sophia nodded. "I won't be a jealous bitch like last time."

I gave her another kiss. "You are a special woman, Sophia. I'm sorry it took me so long to realize that."

Sophia shrugged. "I was a spoiled, little cunt those first days."

I grinned. "Yeah, you were."

She rolled off me and took off her harness. She licked clean my juices as my eyes closed. I so needed to sleep. Sophia pressed against me, her head pillowing on my arm. She sighed and murmured, "Good night."

I nodded and fell into a contented sleep.

Chapter Thirty-Six: Tangled with the Dryad

Acolyte Sophia

My excitement still buzzed through me a day-and-a-half later. My late-night conversation with Angela had been so wonderful. I think she did love me. But she was still...fragile from giving up her love for her boyfriend. I needed to be patient and supportive with her.

Not the bitch I had been. I couldn't complain over stupid stuff. Besides, it wasn't so bad any longer. I was growing callouses on my feet from all the walking and my legs and ass were quite firm and toned now. I had lost some weight, but my body seemed even sleeker and more beautiful.

We had stopped for our midday break. We were just past the half-way point to Xera's home. Traveling through the woods was slow, but it was pretty. There were always new plants to see, new vistas nature had produced. In the trees overhead, songbirds serenaded, filling the woods with their sweet music.

I walked out into the woods, eager to relieve myself. Angela sat on a stump covered in white mushrooms sprouting in spiraling rings up the side while Xera sat cross-legged on the ground, her body painted in green and brown camouflage. Elves didn't seem to need clothes; the elements seemed not to affect them.

I disappeared deeper into the woods, pushing through long, leafy ferns that tickled my face as I passed through them. They also left small, red seeds on my white robe. I wiped those off before kneeling to relieve myself.

When I finished, I wiped myself with a leaf and headed back to Angela and Xera.

I gasped in shock when the limbs of a reddish oak tree reached out and wrapped around my waist, pulling me to the trunk. The dark-green leaves, studded with clusters of acorns, tickled my face as small branches seized my arms.

"Help!" I screamed as the branches lifted my arms and pinned them over my head. I struggled, but the branches were so strong. "Please! Help!"

What was going on? Why was the tree attacking me?

I gasped when a new branch slipped into my robe, its leaves caressing my breasts.

A tree was molesting me.

~ * ~

Xerathalasia

I nibbled on my tasty pine cone, savoring the sticky-sweet resin trapped in the center. It was fresh. I loved fresh pine cones. I felt so sorry for Sophia and Angela. They had to chew on disgusting, dried meat. It was covered in salt and made my nose wrinkle at the sight.

They couldn't eat leafy ferns, crispy pine cones, or bitter acorns. They were such delicate creatures in some ways. In others, they were strong. Angela could swing that long piece of metal, her sword, with effortless ease and didn't mind lugging around her large, kite-shaped shield.

I smiled as Angela worked her teeth to tear off a piece of her trail ration. She had to chew it for a long time before she swallowed and ripped off another piece. It was a lot of work for a meal. I finished eating my pine cone, so I began nibbling on a frond, the delicious, bitter juices mixing in my mouth as I devoured it.

A scream drifted through the woods. My long, pointed ears twitched, turning to the sound. "Please, help!"

"Sophia!" Angela snarled and drew her sword and hefted up her shield.

I was on my feet, snatching up my unstrung bow and racing after Angela. Something most have come down from the Rehyn Mountains to the north. Another basilisk, or maybe a wyvern. It could even be a gorgon or a hippogriff.

~ * ~

Acolyte Sophia

"Don't be scared," a giggling voice purred as the tree's leaves caressed my nipples.

My robe was open, my naked body exposed by the tree's lusts. I struggled to break free of the branches, but they kept my arms pinned over my head. The tree groaned as new branches seized my ankles, pulling my legs apart.

I was so helpless. It was like being cocooned by the giganraneae. My pussy clenched and juices leaked out. Why was I so excited? I was helpless. I was at the mercy of this tree and its tickling leaves playing with my breasts.

"You have nothing to be afraid of," the nubile girl purred when she walked around the tree. She had reddish-tan skin, matching the bark of the tree, and hair that was the orange-red of autumn leaves. Her deep-green eyes examined my body as the leaves tickled up and down my flesh.

"Who are you?" I demanded.

"Xantha," she answered. "I'm a dryad, and you looked so pretty I had to play with you."

The dryad moved closer as her tree continued to control me. I knew about dryads. They and their oak tree were connected, both birthed from the same acorn. She lived as long as her tree did. Though she looked like a nubile girl just budding into sexuality, she was really hundreds of years old.

I shuddered as the dryad's hand caressed my stomach. Her touch was lithe and delicate. I groaned and shivered, my limbs shaking in the restraint. I squirmed, the bark rough and exciting on my back. This dryad could do whatever she wanted to me.

I...liked the sensation.

Her lips pressed against mine. She tasted bitter, like an acorn. I moaned into her kiss as her budding breasts and hard nipples rubbed on my small tits. The tree branches continued fondling my tits, squeezing them up into mounds and pressing them against her flesh.

"Mmm, you are so beautiful," the Dryad purred as she kissed down my neck. "I'm so glad you walked by."

"Me, too," I groaned as her lips engulfed my nipple.

A new branch reached down between my legs. A broad leaf rubbed against my pussy. My clit throbbed and ached as the pointed tip of the leaf tickled my nub. I moaned in delight. My arms ached, but I didn't care. The discomfort was worth the excitement of being bound and played with.

Angela burst out of the bushes, sword drawn.

"Wait!" I moaned.

Xera appeared a moment later. The tall elf seized Angela's shield arm. "She's in no danger."

"What?" Angela demanded, her red hair spilling about her shining pauldrons. Her armor creaked as she glanced at Xera. "Why?"

"It's a dryad," Xera answered. "She is in no danger."

"I'm not!" I panted. "Xantha is making me feel so good."

Angela sheathed her sword. "Wow, you just have to seduce every girl you come across, even if they're part tree."

"Uh-huh," I groaned.

Xantha looked up from my breast and glanced at my friends.

"Have no fear. Your companion shall remember this day fondly."

"I will," I groaned, clenching my pussy. "This is so hot being tied up, Angela."

"Really?" she asked as she unstrapped her shield and rested the point on the ground. She leaned on it. "Mmm, maybe I should do that to you sometime."

My eyes widened in delight.

"Then Xera and I could get some sleep."

The elf's laugh was musical.

I didn't care; Xantha sucked on my nipple again.

The leaf rubbed harder at my pussy. I bucked and groaned. It pushed inside me, the edges folding and caressing me. I shuddered and closed my eyes, enjoying every moment of the Dryad's embrace. Her mouth was hot, my nipple aching in her mouth.

"Oh, Xantha, oh, yes. This is so hot. Mmm, yes. I love this. Thank you for grabbing me."

"It is my pleasure," purred the dryad. "You feel so good against my bark." She shuddered. "Oh, yes, keep writhing."

To my astonishment, she came. Her body shuddered, and the tree groaned as it swayed, both moaning in pleasure. A few acorns dropped from the branches, thudding into the ground. Xantha hugged me tight, her wet pussy rubbing on my thigh as she shuddered in delight.

"Yes, you are so wonderful. You make us feel amazing," purred Xantha.

"I've never made a tree cum before," I grinned. "It is a girl tree, right?"

"Of course," Xantha smiled. "We are one being. Do I not look feminine enough for you?"

"She does," groaned Angela. She set down her shield and then shoved her hand between Xera's thighs, Xera's hand reached beneath Angela's chainmail loincloth. Both women shuddered as they fingered each other.

I loved having an audience.

"You are so cute," I purred.

Xantha smiled and knelt. "You taste so good. My leaf is absorbing all your juices."

I shuddered and clenched my pussy down on her leaf. It withdrew and Xantha's licking mouth replaced it. I groaned as the wet leaf pushed up between my butt-cheeks and caressed my sphincter. I heaved against the branches as the leaf forced its way into my asshole.

"So good," gasped Xantha before her tongue licked through my pussy. "Your ass tastes as good as your pussy."

"I'm so glad," I panted, straining against the bonds as the pleasure swelled. The tree groaned, fucking my ass faster and faster as Xantha swirled her tongue through my folds. Her nose brushed my clit, sending shudders through me.

My toes curled as her leaf fucked my ass faster and faster. My bowels burned around the ticklish leaf. I had never experienced its like. Xantha's tongue continued to lick through my pussy. She was skilled, almost as good as a priestess of Saphique. The dryad must have slept with hundreds of women, practicing her skills at pleasuring them.

Leaves attacked my nipples again. I moaned, my back arching. Every bit of my body was on fire. My toes curled. The branch around my waist tightened, holding me against the tree. The bark caressed my back and asscheeks as the pleasure swelled through me.

"I'm being fucked by a tree and her Dryad!" I moaned in delight. "Slata's cunt, this is so hot!"

"Yes!" panted Angela, her fingers furiously frigging Xera's pussy. "So hot. Keep writhing. Mmm, yes."

"Uh-huh," Xera moaned, her camouflage-painted breasts heaving as her orgasm neared.

Feminine moans and the groans of the tree filled the glade. I gasped and panted as my ass and pussy were pleasured. Xantha's slim fingers fucked into my depths, matching the rhythm of the leaf fucking in and out of my asshole.

"Saphique, yes!" I gasped as my orgasm burst through me.

"Delicious," panted Xantha.

My body thrashed in my bonds. I bucked and heaved against her moaning mouth. The tree swayed and shuddered behind me, cumming again. More acorns fell and a few leaves drifted down in lazy patterns as the trunk creaked and the branches rustled.

"Wow, that was so hot," I panted when the pleasure faded from my body. I sucked in deep breaths, my head spinning with bliss.

Xantha stood. Her tree lowered me to the ground and let me go. I stumbled into her embrace. We kissed hard while Angela and Xera came on each other's fingers. I thrust my tongue into Xantha's mouth and enjoyed my tart flavor adorning her bitter lips.

"You were a wonderful lover," Xantha purred. "What is your name?"

"Sophia," I smiled.

"I will always remember you, Sophia." She gave me another kiss and then broke the embrace.

Xantha walked to her tree. She hugged it. I gasped as the bark slowly engulfed her. She merged into the tree and vanished, swallowed. The tree swayed one last time, letting out a groaning moan that almost sounded like, "Farewell."

"I'll remember you, too, Xantha," I nodded, my body buzzing. What a wonderful experience.

Chapter Thirty-Seven: Two Elf-Cocks Are Better than One

Knight-Errant Angela – Khalesithan, The Federation of Deoraciynae

Twilight was falling on the tenth night since we left the Lesbius Oracle as we reached the outskirts of Khalesithan.

I was unprepared for the sight of the elvish city. There weren't buildings like I knew them. The massive trees themselves had been hollowed out to form homes. Ladders climbed up to networks of fibrous rope bridges spanning through the canopies. Soft-blues glowed with a steady light from mushrooms growing on the outside of the mighty trunks. Despite the trees being hollowed out, all of them appeared to be alive.

"Wow," I gasped as I craned my neck. There was a graceful beauty about the construction and skill that belied the simple life. The elves were not unsophisticated as I had been told.

Xera smiled. "Yes, it is a lovely sight."

Sophia's eyes were wide as she stared up into the canopy. Elves moved through the trees, naked save for necklaces clattering about their jiggling breasts or shifting about their slim waists. They were all beautiful and moved with the same grace Xera possessed, looking down with curious eyes, their long ears twitching.

Xera's hunters were the first to greet us, appearing suddenly and greeting their leader with excited hugs. I stood with Sophia, unnerved by the other elves watching us. They were...fearful of us. Snatches of musical whispers drifted down from the trees, too soft to understand even if I spoke Elvish.

The other elves began drifting down as they saw the hunters embrace Sophia and me. One of the hunters, Quenyathalee, sported a thick cock that hardened as she hugged me. She was tall and willowy, and her cock throbbed against me.

"Sorry," she apologized.

"Don't be," I grinned, enjoying the feel of a real, hard cock. It didn't matter that the rest of her was female. In fact, that just made it hotter. "I like it."

Quenyathalee nodded. "Do you remember the red-haired elf you saw?"

"Yeah," I added, my eyes still staring down at the cock. When Sophia and I first entered the woods, a red-haired elf had led us to where Xera fought a basilisk. We never would have met Xera without her.

"We could not find any trace of her."

"How weird," I said, not really caring. What a wonderful cock she had. There was something so hot about elves and their dicks.

"You seem more interested in my cock."

"Uh-huh," I groaned, my pussy on fire.

A naughty smile appeared on Quenyathalee's lips. She leaned over and whispered, "You're not a hermaphrodite. I could fuck your pussy and not have to marry you."

I grinned. Elves were weird. They were free to sleep with whoever they wanted, but when they went into heat once a month and sprouted their dicks, they couldn't fuck another elf's pussy without marrying her. And if they were married, then it would be cheating to fuck another elf that way. Mouths and asses were okay, and, if the elf was pregnant, her pussy was free to be used.

I guess it made sure you always knew if it was your child or not.

Human couples could have that problem if the wife was promiscuous, even if her husband was fine with her roaming ways.

"Then why don't we explore that option," I purred, rubbing her hard, delicious girl-cock.

Quenyathalee grinned at me, her hand sliding down to dip beneath my chainmail loincloth and squeeze my naked ass. "I had no idea human women were so beautiful before we met you."

"But you can speak our tongue?" I said in surprise. "Surely I'm not the first human you've met."

"All hunters must learn your...difficult tongue."

I arched an eyebrow. "Your language sounds like birds singing. It has so many vowels. I have trouble saying your name, Quenya..." My tongue convulsed. "Quenyathara."

"You can call me Thali," she suggested.

"Thank you."

Her hand kneaded my ass. "We're going to have fun tonight."

"Are you hogging the human all to yourself, Quenyathalee?" another Elf asked, short and lithe, with smaller breasts than Thali, but a far bigger cock. My pussy clenched at the sight of her.

"I am, Lorianalathia."

The new elf, I couldn't even try to say that name, glanced over at Sophia surrounded by the young elf huntress and two other excited elves. "She has no interest in cocks. But this one does."

"This one is named Angela," I said, grasping her cock with my hand and giving a squeeze. "Why should I choose you over Thali?"

"Yes, I found her first," Thali said, her fingers dipping into my asscheek.

"We could share her," the other elf said. Her hands roaming my body were so possessive.

I let go of her cock. "I'm not a piece of meat. Why don't you go fuck some elf maid's ass?"

"Oh, I'm sorry," the elf said, looking down at my face. "I was just excited. Being in heat, well, it makes you so horny and my wife is away. I have no pussy to fuck. I'm sick of blowjobs and asses. I need a juicy pussy to fuck."

256

"None of your friends are pregnant?" Thali asked. "I thought you library elves loved to be pregnant."

"Only Atharilesia is pregnant, and she's been enjoying Xerathalasia's sister for the last two days."

"Poor you," Thali sighed.

"Please," the elf begged me. She fell to her knees and stroked up my thighs above my greaves and boots. "I'll make you feel so good with my big dick."

I grinned at her. "Only after you've licked my pussy clean of Thali's cum."

"Yes!" she agreed.

The three of us rushed off as drums beat and wooden flutes sang. I climbed a rope ladder with a pair of horny elves looking up my loincloth at my naked, dripping pussy. At the top was a hollowed-out nook containing a bed made of soft down and covered in fibrous, brown blankets that may have been made from tree bark.

"Let's get you naked," purred the new elf.

"Sure, Lori," I answered.

"Lori?" the elf asked, arching an eyebrow, her ears twitching.

"She can't say your full name," Thali laughed as she pulled off my pauldrons. Her hands were silky on my shoulders.

The elves were eager to get me naked. And I was eager to be fucked by real cocks. My armor fell to the floor in metallic bangs. Their hands and lips caressed my naked body. They touched me everywhere. My body quivered in delight.

We fell on the bed in a tangle of limbs. We kissed and touched each other everywhere. I stroked hard dicks and wet pussies. I groaned in delight as fingers penetrated my pussy. I found Lori's cock, stroking it as she shuddered in delight.

My body trembled. My lips sucked on Lori's small breasts, nibbling in delight as my thigh was lifted. I was on my side, Thali behind me. Her breasts pressed on my back as her hard cock thrust into my pussy.

"Oh, yes! So good! I've never experienced pussy before!"

I released the nipple. "I'm your first?"

"Yes!" she moaned. "Mmm, you are so hot and wet. So different than an asshole."

"See, it's the best," Lori moaned. "Mmm, Angela you have such a tangy fragrance. I've never smelled it's like."

"Why don't you get a taste," I suggested as Thali's dick slammed into me.

"Yes!"

As Lori turned over on her side to lick my pussy, I savored a hard cock filling me. I liked Sophia, but she could never give me this one sensation. Her dildo felt so close, but I knew it wasn't a real cock, that I wasn't actually engulfing my partner. This was so intimate.

Lori licked at my clit. I shuddered in delight as her tongue probed around Thali's thrusting shaft. My body quivered and bucked. Lori moved closer to me, her dick bobbing before my lips. I licked down the shaft from the tip to the folds of her rose-scented pussy. Elven pussies always smelled of flowers.

I licked through her folds. Lori moaned in delight, her mouth sucking on my clit. Her cock throbbed between my breasts as I nuzzled and licked at her pussy. My fingers squeezed her asscheeks, pulling her closer and closer so I could enjoy her delicious folds while my body trembled.

"I can't last long! Oh, yes! So good! Pussy is the best!" Thalia panted. Her strokes grew harder.

"Cum in me!" I begged. "Let Lori lick me clean."

Lori moaned her agreement.

Thalia moaned in elvish, her musical passion rolling over me. Her cock thrust into my depths. Hot cum spilled into me. My pussy erupted in bliss. The pleasure rolled through me as I enjoyed the intimate moment of my lover flooding my pussy.

"So good!" I panted as I spasmed.

"Matar's blessed cock!" moaned Thali as the last squirt of her cum filled me. "That was wonderful."

I nodded my head in agreement.

Thali pulled out of me and Lori buried her tongue in my folds, licking out every bit of elf cum. I shuddered and sighed in delight. I grabbed Lori's cock and pulled it to my lips, sucking it in deep. She was thick, and I had to open wide to swallow her. I couldn't wait for her to be buried in my pussy.

I nursed, not sucking hard. I didn't want her to blow prematurely. Her tongue probed through my labia and folds. She moaned as she feasted on elvish creampie. I shuddered, my eyes squeezed shut as I enjoyed every second of her feasting tongue, small orgasms quaking through my body.

"Mmm, done. All clean." Lori looked up, her face shiny. "Time for my prize."

My pussy clenched. I was eager for her big dick. "Yes," I purred, rolling onto my back.

Lori mounted me. Her thick cock pressed into my pussy. My toes curled as her dick stretched me open. She had one of the biggest cocks I had ever taken. I groaned as a pleasant ache rippled through me. She kissed me on the lips as her hips pumped her cock slowly in and out of me.

Thali lay on her back, her cock half-hard, a look of bliss on her face. "That's hot." She stroked her cock. "Mmm, I think I'm getting another wind."

I broke the kiss, licking my lips– they were stained with my tangy pussy juices– and watched Thali's cock grow hard again, standing up straight and beading with precum. I shuddered, my asshole clenching.

Two cocks were better than one.

Lori gasped as I rolled her onto her back. Straddling her, I half rose, working my hips to slide my pussy up and down her shaft. "Mmm, Thali, fuck my ass. I really need to cum."

"What a horny human we have here," laughed Lori, her hands on my asscheeks. She spread me apart for Thali.

Thali grinned. "They are reputed to be hot-blooded creatures, always looking for their next pleasure since their lives are so short."

"Yes, so stop talking and start fucking before I die," I groaned as I rode Lori's thick cock. "Pound me hard."

Thali rose and moved behind me. The elf huntress was eager for another go. Her breasts pressed against my back as she rubbed her cock through the cheeks of my ass. She found my sphincter and thrust forward.

"Pater's cock!" I moaned as I was stuffed full of wonderful cock. "Yes, that is what I needed."

My hips undulated between the two cocks. My ass and pussy clenched and relaxed as the pleasure built inside me. Thali's hands wrapped around my waist to seize both of my heavy tits. She jiggled them as she worked her cock faster and faster in and out of my asshole, driving me up and down Lori's thick shaft.

"By the gods, so good!" I moaned.

"Matar's cock, yes," panted Lori. "I've never done this before. When my wife returns, we have to give this a try."

"Oh, yes!" panted Thali. "So amazing. Maybe I should finally take a wife."

I didn't care. Pleasure roared through my body from both holes. They clashed together, swirling around each other and building through me. My hips writhed faster, eager for every thrust. My back arched and Thali's delicious breasts pressed into my back.

Thali's hands tightened on my tits. "You are so hot, Angela. Thank you, Matar for bringing this amazing woman to our woods."

Lori bucked her hips up, slamming her thick cock into my depths. I shuddered, my pussy clamping down hard. I squeezed Lori's breasts as my body quaked. My orgasm exploded through me. I shuddered between them, bucking on their wonderful cocks.

"Cum in me!" I begged.

Lori moaned in Elvish, bucking her hips up again. And then her hot cum flooded my spasming pussy. I milked the elf's cock as I collapsed on her chest. Thali thrust faster and faster, pounding my ass as I kissed Lori.

"Matar's cock!" Thali cried out as her cum exploded into my ass.

Chapter Thirty-Eight: The Elf's Choice

Xerathalasia

I was eager to see Atharilesia. My wife was pregnant, and we needed to talk. Should I go with Angela and Sophia like the Lesbius Oracle prophesied? It would mean abandoning my duty to my pregnant wife, missing the birth of our first daughter, and giving up my captaincy of the Khalesithan Hunters.

I crossed the swaying bridge to my tree and entered our home. My wife was on her hands and knees, her pregnant belly round beneath her and her breasts swaying as my sister Nyonthilasara pounded her from behind.

"Xerathalasia!" my wife gasped in surprise, clearly trembling in the throes of her orgasm. "You're back."

I nodded, appreciating my wife's beauty as my sister fucked her. It was sweet of my wife to provide my sister with relief when she came in heat. Nyonthilasara had yet to take a wife. My sister writhed and then finished in my wife.

"Welcome back, sister," she said, her lips tight. "You didn't return with your other hunters."

"I had to repay a debt," I answered.

"Yes, you're so sweet that way," Atharilesia purred, rolling onto her side and stroking her heavy belly. She was only a little more than a month from delivering our daughter.

"Well, I'll leave you to catch up with your wife," Nyonthilasara said, padding past me.

I caught her arm. "Thank you for watching her. I find a comfort knowing she has you while I am away so often."

Nyonthilasara smiled, "I do enjoy spending time with your wife. She finds me such a comfort."

My wife nodded. "I'm glad to have her when you're gone."

"When are you going to take a wife?" I asked my sister.

She sighed, her face tightening. My younger sister hated listening to me. She glanced at Atharilesia. "When I find a woman as wonderful as yours. You are very lucky to have her."

I nodded in agreement. If it wasn't for the dandelion wine Atharilesia and I were drunk on, we might not have married. But I took her that night while drunk on wine, the success of my hunt, and Atharilesia herself. After I fucked her and came in her pussy, I had been happy ever since.

"Enjoy your evening," I said to my sister. "Angela, one of the humans, is here. She is eager for elf cock."

Nyonthilasara nodded and walked away.

Atharilesia stood and walked to a basin that gathered water. The tree's roots drew it up from far below and kept it filled with pure water. She dipped a cloth woven of spongy moss and cleaned my sister's cum from the depths of her pregnant pussy.

Once she was clean, I moved to my wife and kissed her. I had to tell her what happened, but I had also missed her. My kiss grew more passionate than I meant it to, my pussy itching in delight. My hand slid down to rub at her pregnant belly before I reached her pussy.

Atharilesia moaned into my kiss as I caressed her juicy pussy. Her tongue flicked through my lips. I had to speak to her, but I also had to enjoy her. I broke the kiss. "I missed you."

She smiled. "Yes. Your sister helped me pass the time in your absence."

"Good." I licked my lips as I played with her pussy. "Mmm, I missed pleasing you."

Her smile broadened and her thighs parted. "I can please you, too, my wife."

"Goddess, I love you."

Her smile was radiant. I kissed her again before I spun about and pressed my face between her thighs. The sweet scent of bluebells filled my nose. I buried my face in my wife's cunt, savoring her flowery nectar. My breasts pressed against her pregnant belly as I devoured her pussy and licked up all my wife's juices.

But more kept flowing. It was a vain task, but I wanted to try to lick her dry.

Atharilesia's arms wrapped around my hips and pulled my pussy to her lips. Her sweet tongue swirled through my depths while the round swell of her pregnant belly pressed against my pillowy tits. I groaned into her pussy, questing my tongue deeper to devour every bit of my wife. I traced every fold of her labia. I hadn't enjoyed an elf's pussy in over two weeks, and I missed all the extra folds and crevasses I could explore.

"Xerathalasia," moaned my wife as I rubbed her clit with a deft finger. "Mmm, yes."

My ears twitched as her own lips found my clit. Her fingers probed into my pussy as she nibbled and sucked. I groaned and shuddered against her. The pleasure built inside me as we licked and devoured each other's pussies.

Our moans filled our small home. Our hips undulated as the pleasure built and built. Outside, drums and flutes played, a serenade to our love making. I had missed my wife, and I only had been on a short hunt— this Quest would prove long.

I might never return from this Quest.

"Atharilesia!" I gasped as her teeth nibbled on my clit. "Matar, yes! You always know how to tease me."

Atharilesia purred, "I'm so close to cumming. Rub my clit harder."

My fingers obeyed. She moaned around my clit. My ass

clenched. I panted into her pussy as the pleasure built inside me. My nipples rubbed on her pregnant belly. Our bed creaked as we both quivered. I devoured her bluebell-scented juices as my ears twitched and quavered.

We came together, gasping and moaning into each other's pussy. I licked my lips, savoring her flavor as the pleasure roared through me. It was so wonderful to be home again. I didn't want to leave. I didn't want to listen to the oracle and abandon my pregnant wife.

I moved up to lay beside her. I stared into her eyes and stroked her face.

"What is it?" Atharilesia asked. "You seem so sad."

"I...I may have to leave again."

"Already? Has another monster broached our woods?"

I swallowed. "I took the humans to the Lesbius Oracle."

"Yes, Quenyathalee mentioned that."

"Well, she gave them a prophecy. Angela has to find companions and..."

"You think you're one of them?"

I nodded my head. "The Oracle named me the Quiet Stalker who moves unseen."

Atharilesia cupped my cheeks, "Then you must go."

"But...our daughter?"

"Will be fine."

I moved my hand down to her belly. "I do not even know I am the one the Oracle spoke of."

"But you believe you are."

"Yes."

My wife's hand covered mine. "An Oracle's prophesy is not easily thwarted. If this is your destiny, you must embrace it."

Tears burned my eyes. "But...I'll miss our daughter's birth. This quest is long. It will take me across the world. I won't be gone for a few weeks, but months. Maybe even a year. And...it's dangerous."

"So is being a huntress." My wife smiled. "You were born to help people. That's why you are always out leading patrols. How can you turn your back on these humans? Especially after they saved your life. And an Oracle has proclaimed you are a part of their Quest."

I looked into her eyes. "You are not mad at me?"

Atharilesia kissed me. "I'm never mad. I understand the sacrifice you make. I will miss you, but I have the library. And soon I'll have our daughter. And your sister will watch over me like she always does."

I rolled onto my back. The decision seemed easier to make. My wife had given me her blessing. She pressed against me. I closed my eyes and nodded. "I will go."

Chapter Thirty-Nine: Magic's Commands

Acolyte Sophia

My eyes were bleary from reading the books contained in the library, a massive structure woven of ten separate trees each grown together to form huge rooms that spiraled high up into the air. It was exhausting just getting the books and coming back to the reading area. The elven librarians, even pregnant Atharilesia, didn't seem to have any problems scampering up the steep stairs.

I had spent the entire day here instead of having fun. Angela seemed to be finding every elf with a cock and spreading her legs while I had to snatch quickies with elven librarians before we went back to work to find what we needed.

I hoped we found it soon. One day of this was more than I wanted.

"Ooh, I think I have something," Lorianalathia smiled, rushing over with a heavy tome. "it talks about working adamantium. It was originally written in Dwarvish, but translated into Human."

She plopped it down before me. I read through it and sighed in relief. "This is exactly what we needed."

Atharilesia smiled. "My wife will be pleased. She is eager to help you on your quest."

I hugged the pregnant elf. "I'm glad you're so understanding. Most pregnant human women wouldn't be so understanding."

"It was an easy decision. You can't fight destiny. It is better to accept it and drift along on a wind like a falling leaf instead of fighting the breeze. It will only tear you apart. Leaves are delicate and the winds can be so fierce."

"Wow. That sounds hard."

"Yes. You have to let go and trust to fate." She stroked her belly, her smile growing.

I would never be a mother. Though Saphique was the goddess of women, her priestesses were never allowed to lie with a man. Saphique only liked women. I would never experience that one facet of womanhood.

I touched her belly and promised, "I'll make sure your mother comes back." I looked up at Atharilesia. "And your wife."

She nodded.

I copied down the information and sprinkled my ink with sand to help it dry quicker. "I need to go tell Angela and Xera!"

I rushed out of the library and went in search. I found them eating berries and drinking dandelion wine on the forest floor while watching elvish women dance. The dancers were...very distracting. But I was too excited to ogle their heaving breasts and...

I shook my head. "Angela. I have it!"

Angela looked up. "What?"

"I know how we can repair the sword."

"How?" Angela asked.

"It's complicated." I pulled a map out of my pouch and spread it out. It was of the lands that used to be the High Kingdom of Hamilten from the Atholosian Islands to the west to the edge of the Shizhuth Empire to the east. The map showed the icy northern coast where the orc tribes of Larg lived all the way down to the Halani desert across the Nimborgoth, the great sea. "But we can do it. First, we need to gather certain ingredients besides just finding the five sword pieces. In the dwarven Mines of Khragorath, we have to procure adamantium."

"The Lost Mines of Khragorath?" Angela groaned. "In the Fallen Kingdom of Modan?"

"Um, yes," I answered with great care. The dwarven Kingdom of Modan had fallen over two hundred years ago. "Those mines."

"It's practically a quest on its own to get the adamantium," Angela sighed. "What else?"

"We need the heart of the Minotaur of Grahata to imbue into the spell and reinvigorate the sword."

"What?" gasped Angela. "The same Minotaur that prowls the labyrinth and none have killed?"

"You can do it," I grinned. "It has to be easier than killing Dominari."

"It better," Angela muttered. "And why do we need it?"

"Oh, he's the son of Gewin so battle pumps in his veins."

Angela groaned, "What other impossible task do we have to do?"

"Oh, none, we just have to find a mage to cast the Ritual of Reclamation. It's powerful magic, so we need a Master Mage. From my understanding, very few meet the criteria."

"That explains why we need the Grieving Mage who commands the elements," Xera said, quoting the prophecy.

"I thought so, too," I nodded. "Once we have all five pieces of the sword, the Minotaur's heart, and the adamantium ore, we take it to the Altar of Souls where the mage can cast the spell and fix the blade."

Angela looked down at the map and tapped at the far eastern edge of the Princedoms of Zeutch, right where the Desolation of Dominari began. "That Altar of Souls?"

"It's the only place powerful enough to take the forces," I said, squirming. "And it's on the edge of the desolation, not in it. Plus, once we have the sword reforged we won't have to journey far to kill the dragon."

~ * ~

Fireeyes – Western Edge of Deorc Forest, Kingdom of Secare

The forest lay spread out before me. Traveling through it would be too...complicated. The elven huntresses were stealthy. An arrow in the back was not how I wanted to die. I had to detour around the forest to the south. I would lose the trail, but I had the garnet-studded amulet King Edward gave me.

My simulacrum stood beside me, her body naked, her head bowed. I had no need of her pussy juices at this moment, but her tart scent filled my nose. She was always ready to provide the energy I needed to work my spells.

I cast my spell, reaching out to the very distant Rehyn Mountains. I needed servants who could fly across the forest, find Angela, and kill her. A smile crossed my lips. With her death, I would secure King Edward as my patron. My work would continue.

What did it matter how many women I vivisected to further the progress of magic? Those closed-minded fools of the Magery Council didn't have the vision to get their hands bloody. Growth and progress only came through pain and suffering. That was how humans had spread across the entire world, dominating anything in their path.

Civilization stood on the backs of countless millions sacrificed for progress. It was a necessary sacrifice. Just like my subjects, though unwilling, served our species through their suffering and death. Each played a valuable role in making us greater.

It was near midnight when the piercing screech of the wyverns neared. The flying lizards were the perfect monsters to track down and kill Angela. They landed about me, standing on their hind legs and the knuckles of their leathery wings. Poisoned tails swung about and snapped, dragon-like snouts hissed at me.

I poured my magic, bursting with the element of life, into them and made them my familiars. "Hunt. Kill."

My commands burned into their brains, they took to the air, flying northeast across the Deorc Forest.

Chapter Forty: Wicked Conjurings

Journeyman Mage Faoril – Esh-Esh, The Magery of Thosi

I strolled through the docks of Esh-Esh, the cool breeze blowing in off Lake Esh. The blue waters sparkled as the wind rippled waves across the surface. The smaller boats of fishermen with their triangular, ribbed sails bobbed in the waves churned by the larger merchant boats that sailed up the Roytin River from the Free City of Raratha. Only one ship anchored at the docks was different. The Crystal Ship of the Magery Council.

My eyes went from the amethyst ship out to the lake. I tried to see the Island, but it was too far from shore to be visible, lost in the center of the large lake. I tried not to tremble. The test would be held out on the Island.

I turned away. My business was with the merchants, not on trying to see the Island. I needed chalk, and not just any chalk, but the black chalk found only in the Azi Wasteland. There would be at least one merchant that sold the rare rock. Black chalk was only useful to the Mages of Thosi.

The test to become a Master Mage was only a week away. Last night, in a pathetic attempt to sleep, it occurred to me that if I had a potent source of cum to power my magic during the test, my spells would be all the more powerful. For a female mage, cum powered our magic. It was such a vital energy. But not all cum was made equal. Some was far more potent and others were better suited for one element of magic.

I wanted to make sure I passed. Seven of us were taking the test and only three of us would become Master Mages. Failure would mean a year waiting again if I was even allowed to retake it. Often, a single failure was enough for the Council to deny you permission to retake the test in favor of the next class of journeyman mages.

That wouldn't happen to me. I would achieve the rank of master mage. I had the skills. I just had to prove them.

My red robes marked me for a Journeyman Mage. The crowd parted for me. Even a journeyman was worthy of respect in the Magery of Thosi. In a country ruled by the council, even junior members were worth currying favor to cultivate business. Merchants called to me, boasting of the exotic items they possessed, the perfect ingredients for various rituals and spells.

I ignored their words and examined their wares. Stall after stall was a disappointment. Surely someone had black chalk. I moved out from the docks, working through the aisle of stalls. The reek of garbage and rotting fish assaulted my nose. I missed the austerity of the Collegiate Tower.

The Tower rose like an ivory pillar reaching for the sky over the city of Esh-Esh. At its tip, the Beacon burned golden, sending protective spells across the city. At night, the beacon burned brighter than the full moon, painting even the roughest neighborhood of Esh-Esh in golden hues. It was a symbol of knowledge and progress for the world. Here, differences of race, gender, and nationalities were set aside. All were welcome to be enlightened by true knowledge and set free of the shackles of the past.

Thanks to my studies, the very powers of creation, the five elemental forces, were at my fingertips. The cum I swallowed from my simulacrum this morning blazed like a fire in my stomach, available to be used to manipulate the world around me. I could conjure flames, summon winds, precipitate water, move earth, and even enhance life. To me, the world was malleable and infinitely reshapeable so long as I had the energy and the understanding.

Magic, unlike the divine powers of priests and paladins or witchcraft that cajoled or bound natural spirits, required the mage to provide the power. I didn't have a god gifting me a part of his or her divine essence or a primal spirit to manipulate the world around me, I had to provide the energy myself. And that was dangerous. If I used my own reserves, I would grow quickly fatigued.

That was why I carried vials of cum with me, each magically preserved to stay fresh. For male mages, they had to use female juices. But the results were the same— we had a vital power source we could burn instead of our own. And, thanks to our training, I doubt I could even use my life force after my conditioning.

Apprentice Mages were trained harshly to ignore their own life force.

I stopped before a stall and sighed in relief. Finally, a chalk merchant. I stepped up, my eyes scanning. A greasy-haired Athlosian man stood on the other side. I wrinkled my nose at the sour scent and tried not to stare at the tangled mess of silver hair caked with grime on his head.

"Mistress mage," he bowed, his teeth crooked and yellow. "What can I interest you in this fine day?"

"Black chalk," I said. "Do you have any?"

"I do indeed, Mistress, the finest black chalk from the Azian quarries."

He turned around and pulled a felt lined tray covered in various chunks of black chalk. They were rough cut, not the precisely shaped sticks used in classrooms. I picked one up, squeezing it in my hand. The chalk didn't crumble. My thumb ran across the black surface; I smiled at the dark smear left behind on my skin. I brought it to my mouth and tasted it.

My mouth grew dry as I licked the chalky dust. I spat to the side. "Very pure."

"Of course. I wouldn't bring any cheap chalk to Esh-Esh." He rubbed his pale-red hands together. "A gold torch for one."

"A gold torch?" I asked, arching my eyebrow. A torch was the largest coin. I could buy a week at the finest inn with the most extravagant meals for that amount. "This is only worth five silver waves."

"You try to cheat me," he gasped. "Five silver waves? Would you like to bleed me dry?"

Five silver waves was half the cost of a gold torch, and I thought the price more than fair for a piece of black chalk. I folded my arms. "Fine. Six silver waves."

"Nine. I have seven children to feed back in Athlos. You wouldn't make beggars of my children by impoverishing their father."

I licked my lips. Could I afford to part with nine silver waves? I wouldn't have much left of my stipend. "Eight," I answered. "No more. If you don't like it, I can find another merchant. And then your children wouldn't get any money."

"So cruel," he groaned. "Eight. For my poor children."

I smiled. I highly doubted there was a woman in the world that would touch this man if he hadn't paid her first. I reached into my robes and pulled out a purse stitched with arcane symbols. Not too many pickpockets would risk stealing from a mage, but if one did, they would regret it. I opened it and pulled out a golden flame, the coin glinting in the sunlight.

I took my chalk, wrapped in cloth, and my change, then hurried back to the Collegiate Tower. I was eager to cast my summoning and gather the cum I needed. The farther I made it from the docks, the nicer Esh-Esh grew. The revolting smells of the docks gave way to the scents of fresh bed, spices, and flowers as the streets grew more respectable. I passed through fountained squares, the water enchanted into exciting colors or intoxicating scents.

I strolled into the Collegiate Tower and climbed the stairs that spiraled up the center, passing young students in their blue robes and the occasional master in his black. On the twenty-ninth floor, I found an empty summoning room. It was a plain room made of the same white granite as the rest of the tower. The floor was bare, and the door was very sturdy.

Before I closed the door, my friend and roommate Saoria entered. "What are you up to?" she asked, her blue eyes glinting. "Showing off before the test?"

"Getting the most potent cum I can," I answered. "Are you staying? I'm about to seal the room."

"Oh, I'll stay," she smiled.

Like me, she was a journeyman mage about to take the test. A silver ring glinted on her eyebrow as I conjured a yellow orb and hung it on the ceiling to shed light. Her heavy breasts rose beneath her robes– she was far more endowed than me. We were both Thosians, though her brown hair was darker and longer than mine. I preferred to keep mine short. Saoria had the sort of body that men, and more than a few women, found irresistible.

Even I enjoyed playing with her charms.

With earth magic, I sealed the door. The granite stone that formed the walls flowed like water and covered up the door. No summonings were allowed to happen in the Collegiate Tower without this precaution. It kept anyone from blundering in at an inopportune moment as well as trapping anything in here in case the summoning was botched.

For a mage of my skill, it was more of a formality. I was no apprentice about to summon her first spirit or elemental. I had done this a hundred times. From my pocket, I produced the black chalk and unwrapped it.

"What are you summoning?" gasped Saoria.

"Lemures," I answered.

Saoria's eyebrows furrowed. "Oh, you are really trying to overachieve if you plan on using their cum in the test."

A lemure, an angry spirit of a dead mortal, had potent, supernatural cum. It was easily four times the potency of a human's. Few other types of cum were more powerful, and those usually involved strong monsters you would have to expend more energy on subduing then you would receive from their cum.

"I plan on passing," I told her as I inscribed the summoning

274

circle.

The circle had to be nearly perfect. I drew a large circle across the smooth floor. Saoria leaned against the wall, her arms folded beneath her breasts as she watched. She would let me know if I made any mistakes– I wouldn't. After I had drawn the circle, I formed the five-pointed star in the area circumscribed by the black, the tip pointing south. In each triangular arm of the star, I wrote the arcane name for the five elements.

"Are you sure you can handle them?" Saoria asked.

"Yes," I said, waving a dismissive hand at her. "Lemures aren't that bad. You just need to be firm with them. And once I manipulate their cocks, well, they'll be much less angry."

A grin crossed Saoria's face. "Well, you may have a point there. Even the spirit of a dead man likes cumming."

I finished the circle and stepped back. I wrapped up the black chalk and slipped it into my pocket. From another, I pulled out three glass vials with leather stoppers and set them carefully on the ground. I wanted more than enough for the test. I produced a vial full of simulacrum seed and swallowed the salty cum. It was still warm, preserved by the enchantments on the vial. I swirled it through my mouth before swallowing, a hot flush shooting through me.

Every time I swallowed cum it excited me. You had to be a cumslut to be a female mage.

Power churned inside me. I sent the energy out into the magic circle. A black light glowed from it, sucking in shadows instead of producing them. It was anti-light. The room chilled as the circle reached into the Astral Realm.

My heart thudded in my chest. A wrong move here could cause me to summon a far more dangerous spirit, like a banshee or a nightshade. There were dangerous things that prowled through the Astral Realm, the domain of the dead, spirits, and the Gods.

I chanted in the arcane tongue, the strange words rolling off my lips with ease. Unlike manipulating the elements, summoning required words to reach out into the Astral Realm and beckon the entities I desired. The room shook. The unlight grew brighter. My shadow seemed to fall towards the inverse glow. The Realm pulled at me. I stood firm, fighting against being drawn into the circle.

Saoria shivered as a mournful wail echoed through the room. Mist swirled in the circle, black as midnight. Eyes appeared, glowing red. I chanted louder, directing my words at the eyes. Power lashed out of me and into the circle. The unlight burned dark. My shadow tugged at the soles of my feet as it did. I fought against the pull.

The arcane words chained the eyes and pulled them into our world. The mist grew dense, swirling and forming into three bodies. They were gangly, long arms ending in sharp claws that seemed far more solid than the rest of their foggy bodies. They hissed and chittered, slamming at the edge of the circle.

My chants died down. The unlight vanished. The connection with the Astral Realm severed. Three lemures swirled in the circle, bound by its perimeter. They howled their fury, slamming into the boundary circumscribed by my careful preparation.

"How are you getting the cum?" Saoria asked.

"By letting them enjoy my body," I smiled as I slipped off my robe and carefully folded it on the floor. I stood naked before the circle, my pink nipples hard atop my round breasts. My spicy excitement filled my nose. I had been looking forward to this all day.

"That's kinky," laughed Saoria. "No fear of them tearing you apart instead of fucking you?"

"Not with a little life magic," I answered, pouring the energy into my flesh. My pussy throbbed harder. My juices flooded down my thighs as the life magic affected my lubrication's production. My spicy musk grew stronger.

"Mmm, I love that scent," Saoria purred.

"Once they're ready to cum, will you hand me the vials?" I asked.

Saoria glanced where I set down the three vials. She nodded and walked around the circle and picked them up. "I will." Her blue eyes studied the vials. "You enchanted them yourself?"

"I want to make sure my cum maintains its potency," I said, my heart thudding faster. The lemures swirled around the circle, their cocks already swelling hard. My spell worked.

"Always so smart," Saoria laughed.

I stepped into the circle, my pussy on fire. The spirits hissed and swarmed at me. Their ethereal hands seized my body. I shivered at their electric touch. My hand reached out, passing through a lemure's incorporeal body until I found his cock. That suddenly became real and solid in my hand. I squeezed and stroked it.

The spirit cooed in delight, his red eyes widening.

"Yes, you've missed that, haven't you," I grinned. "None of you've had pussy in a while, huh? You give me what I want, and you'll have my delicious snatch."

"...what do you want...?" hissed the lemure, his voice a rasping caress.

"Your cum. Fuck my holes, but do not cum in me," I smiled, stroking his cock.

A lemure passed through my body. I shuddered as electricity engulfed my flesh. My body tingled and my pussy convulsed. His hands seized my breasts, squeezing and kneading them. "...want to fuck you..."

"Uh-huh," I groaned, shifting my hips.

The third lemure pushed his hand through the front of my stomach, phasing through my flesh and into my pussy. I groaned as his spectral flesh sent tingling pleasure rippling through my pussy as his fingers worked inside me.

"...such delicious flesh...we fuck...give you cum..."

"Agreed," I groaned as my toes curled.

My flesh erupted in blissful tingles every time their incorporeal bodies passed through me. I shuddered and fell to my knees as the three lemures swarmed around me. Their hands and lips tasted my skin while their bodies phased through me. I let out delightful moans as I savored the sensations of their incorporeal flesh. My pussy clenched and ached, eager to be filled by a spirit's cock.

"...delicious..." a lemure hissed as his body phased through my pussy and ass.

I spasmed and moaned in delight. A spectral tongue licked at my pussy and a hungry mouth latched onto my nipple. Fingers sank into the flesh of my breasts, swirling through my tits and shooting more wonderful bliss through me.

"Enjoy my body," I gasped. "Let go of your anger for awhile and remember the pleasures of the flesh."

"...so tasty...so warm..."

Fingers parted my asscheeks. The third lemure licked at my sphincter. All three of their mouths pleasured me. My juices dripped down my thighs as my clit was caressed by one of the specters numbing mouths. Their every touch was ecstasy.

My pussy convulsed as I came.

"Sweet Pater's cock!" I screamed, my voice echoing through the sealed chamber as the pleasure roared through my body.

"...yes...yes...so alive..." chittered a lemure as he drank down my juices.

I tossed my head and arched my back. The pleasure rushed to my mind, mixed with the buzzing excitement of their incorporeal bodies passing through me as they writhed and floated about me. My orgasm kept rolling through me. Their every touch prolonged it.

"...must fuck..."

"...yes...must know her sweet flesh..."

"...such sweet flesh..."

"Fuck me!" I begged, barely caring about collecting cum. I wanted to feel their cocks ream me. I waned my living flesh joined with their spiritual essence. "Take me hard! Please!"

"..slut..."

"Oh, yes! Such a slut! I love being fucked! I love cum!" No woman could survive as a mage if she didn't love cum. It was the best substance in the world. It never failed to excite me while collecting it.

A spectral cock rubbed at the entrance of my pussy, sparking electricity through my labia. I groaned, pushing back. The shaft pressed into my folds, thick and corporeal but buzzing with spiritual energy.

My pussy spasmed about the shaft as another orgasm screamed through me. "Oh, fuck! Gods, yes! Fuck my cunt!"

"...hot...tight...wet...life..." hissed the lemure as he pounded his cock through me.

My pussy spasmed about his shaft. Pleasure rippled through me. I moaned and shuddered. It was so intense. His cock lit up my pussy's nerves. He shoved deep into my cunt. My hips pushed back, meeting his passionate thrusts.

"...must fuck..." another moaned as it licked my ass.

"Oh, yes! Use my ass! You can stick your cock wherever you like!"

The lemure moved. His cock phased through my thigh sending a ripple of ecstasy up to my pussy. I shuddered as another small cum burst in my depths. Bliss assaulted my mind. The cock slid up to my ass and became corporeal right before plunging into my tight sphincter.

I was stuffed full of spiritual cocks. The lemures hissed and moaned as they fucked me. Both their shafts reamed me. The pleasure swelled through me. I squeezed my eyes shut and just enjoyed their hard thrusts.

"...suck cock..." the last lemure hissed.

"Gods, yes," I gasped, licking my lip. "Slam that delicious cock down my throat."

The lemure's misty body spun before me, bringing his hard cock to my lips. I opened wide and swallowed his dick. The spirit's body contorted, and he latched his mouth onto my aching nipples. I groaned around his thrusting dick as he sucked on my nipple.

Pleasure filled me. My body writhed as these three spirits ravaged my body. They fucked me with an eager intensity. My ass and pussy clenched down on two of the cocks as the third slammed down my throat.

I loved it. Servicing three cocks was always so exciting, and no mortal cock's touch could send tingling electricity shooting through my body. My toes curled as I rocked my body. I moaned and bucked, eager to make my spirit lovers cum.

"...so good to fuck whore..."

"...yes...hot...wet...so good..."

"...sweet flesh..."

"...fuck harder...good..."

It was good. Another orgasm burst inside me. I had lost count of the number. The pleasure assaulted my body. I sucked on the cock in my mouth, savoring the strange, misty taste of a spectral entity thrusting deep into my mouth.

"...cum...must cum..."

The lemure fucking my pussy sped up his thrusts. He hammered them in far faster than any human male could. My cunt was assaulted by the thrusts, my flesh savoring every inch of his cock reaming my hole.

"...yes...pleasure...cum..."

I lifted my hand, reaching out to Saoria. My friend, her robe undone and one hand playing with her pussy, laughed and seized one of the vials with fingers sticky with her juices. She stepped forward and reached across the circle's boundaries to place it in my hand.

"...hot...cum..." moaned the lemure in my cunt. He ripped his dick out of my spasming pussy and floated around, pressing his dick against the vial. "...yes..."

Misty cum squirted out of his cock into my vial. He hissed with each blast, depositing more and more of the incorporeal seed into the specially prepared glass. With a final moan, the lemure floated away, his red eyes closed, looking satiated.

Saoria took back the vial and stoppered it. "There. All ready for the test."

I moaned in delight, my ass clenching on the cock reaming it. I shuddered as another orgasm rippled through me. The lemure fucking my ass hissed in delight as he neared his orgasm. He ripped his cock out of my ass as Saoria handed me the next vial.

I was exhausted when the final lemure ripped his cock from my mouth and positioned his cock at the glass vial. I licked my lips, eager to taste lemure cum when I drank the jizz during the test. His dick erupted and the spirit filled the vial with milky, misty sperm.

"...yes...good...fuck..." the lemure lazily hissed as he drifted away, joining the other pair.

I took the leather stopper from Saoria and capped it. "Mmm, that was fun."

Saoria nodded her head. "Yeah, it looked like it."

I climbed out of the circle, my legs weak. I had enough energy remaining in my body to channel it into the circle and send the lemures back to the Astral Realm. They swirled apart into black mist and then were swallowed into unlight.

"I think I'll miss them," I sighed as I pulled on my robe.

"Oh?" Saoria asked.

"I was cumming the entire time."

Saoria laughed as I unsealed the chamber.

Chapter Forty-One: Out of the Woods

Xerathalasia – Eastern Deorc Forest, The Federation of Deoraciynae

I paused at the edge of the forest, staring out at the human farmlands of the Magery of Thosi. My stomach clenched. Already, Sophia and Angela had mounted their horses, both glad to be out of the woods and stop walking.

My mouth was dry. I had never left the woods. They were my home. It was the wild of nature. But that ended. From here on out I would be traveling through the human's lands, witnessing nature sculpted and shaped by tools, not through communicating with the trees and shrubs. Elves asked nature to change and transform herself; humans violated her.

"Xera?" Sophia asked, looking over her shoulder. The human priestess wore a white robe and beige cloak, her light-brown hair swirling about her shoulders. "What's wrong?"

"Nothing," I said.

When we left Khalesithan yesterday morning, I knew I would have to leave the forest. I just wish I knew it would be so hard. I looked over my shoulder at the dense woods wishing I could see all the way back to the towering tree where my pregnant wife sat waiting for me to return.

I had to return. I would see my daughter.

There was no room for doubts. I had set myself on this course, and I had to follow where the trail led me. My hand gripped my unstrung bow. The arrows in my quiver rattled as I stepped through the brush onto the grassy field. In the distance a house stood, made of sod, smoke rising from its chimney. Sad animals moved in dirty pens and startled humans watched us from fields sprouting with green shoots.

"It'll be okay," Sophia smiled. "I'm a little scared, too. I've never been out of Secare. But the Magery is supposed to be a safe place."

"Very civilized," Angela nodded. "I see a road ahead. That should lead us to the highway and on to the city of Norv."

I sighed and nodded. My long legs took me up beside their horses. That was nice. Ever since I met the humans three weeks ago, I had to move so slowly through the woods. Now that they were mounted and out of the rough terrain, I could stretch my legs and really walk.

We reached the road. It was a man-made trail far wider than any I had seen in the woods. This one was made of packed dirt with a pair of strange, narrow ruts running parallel down it. I had never seen such tracks. The ground was hard beneath my feet. I missed the soft loam of the forest, but I was a huntress— I would not complain.

As night fell, we reached a village. Smoke was thick in the air. I wrinkled my nose as it drifted in a pall from the village. The buildings were made of more stone ripped from the earth and cut crudely into blocks. Everyone stared at me. Like Sophia and Angela, the humans of Thosi went clothed. They were fair-skinned and brown-haired.

"Why are they staring at me?" I whispered.

"You're naked," Sophia grinned at me. "And very lovely. No one goes around naked outside in human lands."

I flushed. I had never been self-conscious of being naked. Elves did not wear clothes, only jewelry and belts to hang tools and pouches from. Clothes were unnecessary. We were in tune with nature, weathering the cold winters and hot summers with equal ease.

The streets of the village were made of cold mud that squished beneath my feet. The stench grew more and more foul. I wrinkled my nose as Sophia and Angela led us to a larger building. Music came from inside, my ears twitching in rhythm to a pounding drum and reedy pipe.

"What is this place?" I asked.

"Inn," Angela answered as she climbed off her warhorse, her metal armor clinking. "We'll stay the night here."

"Ah, so the Inn people are allowing us to stay in their home?"

Angela smiled and Sophia giggled. "No, Xera. We'll rent a room. Inns are places that provide lodging for travelers."

"Rent? That means...to pay?"

"It's not like your world," Angela shrugged. "Things cost money out here. Nothing's free."

I found that very sad. I could walk to any village or city in the forest and find a welcome bed and wonderful food. No one had to buy anything. Everything we needed was found in the surrounding woods. It was so strange how the humans seemed to put a specific value on everything.

I drew more attention when we stepped into what Angela called the common room. Men drinking fermented, sour beverages glanced at me with hungry eyes. A hot flush rippled through my body. Human males had cocks. Cocks I could fuck without risk of pregnancies. But they were so...ugly. Sophia and Angela, with their strange skin and hair color, had seemed like exotic beauties even with their round ears, but these men...I shuddered. They were big and hairy. There were no soft curves, no swelling breasts.

"How do you lie with these men, Angela?" I asked, grimacing as one leered at me.

"Oh, it's not hard," Angela purred, smiling at the same man that leered at me. "Mmm, he's got a strong jaw."

"You should see what I can do with it," he laughed, licking his lips. His chin was covered in a dark shadow of stubble. "I'll lick your pussy until you scream."

"Maybe," Angela laughed as she sat down at a table.

"Don't worry," Sophia whispered to me. "I don't get it either."

I smiled at the priestess as we sat down. "I thought I would like human men, but where are their breasts?"

Sophia giggled. "Only women have breasts," she purred, then nodded to a buxom woman in a low-cut dress moving through the crowd carrying three large tankards of the foamy drink. Her breasts jiggled and bounced, on the verge of spilling out entirely. "Now that is a delicious sight."

"Uh-huh," I agreed.

The woman set the drinks down at a table, laughed as the men squeezed her ass and fondled her breasts before she scooped up metallic coins and slipped them into a pocket of her skirt. She flounced away and swayed over to us.

"Ooh, travelers," she purred, her eyes falling on my naked body. "An elf?"

My cheeks warmed as she stared at my naked body. Her eyes were appreciative. She touched my shoulder. Her skin was as pale as mine, but lacked the greenish tone that infused an elf. Her eyes flicked down to my crotch.

"No cock? I thought you elves all had cocks."

"Not always," I answered.

A wicked smile crossed her lips. "Ooh, do I have to coax her out. I'm very good at that."

My pussy grew wet, and I squirmed. "Well, it doesn't work that way."

"Oh, what a shame. I would love to boast that I fucked an elf's cock." Then she leaned in to my ear. "But, maybe we can fib a bit, so long as I fuck you."

I shuddered as her hot breath washed over my sensitive ear. It twitched and I moaned, "They'll never hear the truth from me."

Sophia winked at me as the woman straightened. "I'm Vioria, so what can I get you excitin' women?"

"Beer," Angela said, licking her lips, "and your finest dinner."

"We got no fine dinner here," laughed Vioria, "but we have a hearty stew and bread that's not too hard."

"Perfect," sighed Angela. "Oh, and if you can bring some fresh vegetables for Xera."

Vioria's eyes flicked to me. "Xera?"

I nodded. "I don't eat meat."

"But she does eat pussy," Sophia giggled.

"Good," winked Vioria. "I'll be right back."

"You're going to have fun tonight," Sophia grinned. "I'm not surprised, you are so sexy with those pointed ears. Right, Angela?"

"Huh?" Angela said, drawing her eyes away from the man.

Sophia arched an eyebrow. "I know it's been forever since you've seen a man, but you don't have to drool over them at the table."

"But he's so yummy," Angela purred, her eyes glancing back at the man. "Look at how rough those hands are. Mmm, that's a man that knows how to treat a woman."

Sophia shook her head. "Fine. You have your fun tonight. Get it out of your system."

Angela smiled then leaned over and gave Sophia a quick kiss on the cheek. "I'm glad you understand."

Sophia nodded and patted Angela's thigh. "Please, just bathe afterward."

"Ooh, will you join me?" Angela asked.

"I'm not washing a man's cum off you," Sophia shuddered. "I have sworn sacred oaths."

"Will you wash me after I'm done with Vioria?" I asked.

"Oh, I might join you and the maid," Sophia winked. "I don't see any other women here."

"You can join me?" laughed a burly guy at the next table, a thick tangle of hair growing from his face. That was called a beard, I think.

"I'm a priestess of Saphique," Sophia smiled sweetly. "I'm sure you know what that means."

"That you know how to fuck," laughed the man.

"That's Slata, not Saphique," Sophia said. "Saphique has cursed me. Any cock that enters my body shrivels up tinier than a worm."

The man's face fell. "What?"

"My goddess is very jealous," Sophia purred. "But I'm sure the price is something you're willing to pay to fuck me."

The man turned away and Sophia gave a wicked giggle.

Chapter Forty-Two: Extra Sauce

Xerathalasla

It wasn't long before Vioria returned with a platter, setting steaming bowls before Angela and Sophia, for me a plate covered in raw vegetables. One, orange and skinny, glistened with a strange juice. Last, Vioria sat flagons of the foamy, fermented drink before us. She leaned down and whispered, "I put a special sauce on your carrot. A little taste of tonight."

My pussy clenched as I stared at the long, orange vegetable. "Thank you."

I grabbed the carrot first. I had never seen one. Her pussy juices were spicy and delicious. I bit into the carrot and experienced the hard texture, pleasant flavor, and her spicy sauce. I savored the carrot, enjoying her marinade and licked my fingers clean of all her sauce.

"Delicious," I smiled.

"I bet," Sophia grinned before spooning up a bite of her stew. There were carrots in there, mixed with stringy, brown meat.

I didn't understand how humans could eat flesh.

Angela didn't comment on my specially prepared carrot. She was too busy staring at the guy while drinking deeply of her flagon. I picked up mine. It had a sour flavor, like yeast. I brought it to my lips and drank it. A warm buzz flowed through me. It was terrible and bitter. I grimaced and set it down.

"I know, it took me a little getting used to," Sophia nodded. "I prefer wine. It's similar to the blackberry drink your people made."

Not long after, Angela slipped off with the stud, her chainmail loin swinging about her shapely ass as they hurried upstairs. Sophia shook her head and stood up with a yawn. "Good thing I have my toy. You have fun with Vioria."

I nodded my head, looking around for the maid.

She came around from my other side and plopped into my lap. Her arm slipped around my shoulders. "So, do elves always go around naked, or were you just hoping to get laid by a sexy maid tonight?"

"Naked," I answered.

"Ooh, I really need to come visit your forest."

I grinned. "We normally keep humans out, but your females do have nice advantages."

"Oh?" she leaned in, her breasts pressed against mine. I wished they were naked. "Like what?"

"Our cocks can't get you pregnant. We could fuck you all the time."

Her body shuddered. "Sounds like paradise." She wiggled her hips. "Damn, I was hoping you would sprout."

"Sorry. I'm about ten days off from that."

"And I can't convince you to stay?"

"Sorry, our Quest is too important."

Vioria's eyes widened. "I knew it. She's a knight, right? The one in armor?"

I nodded my head.

"Oh, now I am really wet. Come on. I'm off. Let's go have some fun, elf."

"Xera."

"Oh, so pretty." Then her mouth was on mine. I savored her hot kiss. My nipples hardened against her dress. The men in the common room grew excited. Had they never seen women kiss? I ignored them, savoring her soft lips as our tongues played around in her mouth.

She had such a sweet mouth.

My hand squeezed her breast. Her tit was firm beneath her dress. My fingers moved to the lacings of her bodice. They were held closed by a knot. It seemed like a simple pull and it would come undone and I could enjoy those beauties.

I tugged.

"Oh, you're wicked, Xera," purred Vioria. "But I'm not an elf. I don't show my tits around the common room."

"You should," a man roared.

"Then why don't we go to our room so I can see them and touch them."

"Are all elves as bewitching as you?" she asked as she slid off my lap.

"Maybe," I grinned, licking my lips. "My wife is enchanting."

"Lucky elf to have you," purred Vioria as she helped me stand. Her hand went around my waist to squeeze my naked ass.

We reached the stairs and headed up, leaving the disappointed men behind us. Her hand on my ass was exciting. She squeezed me every few heartbeats and her fingers moved closer and closer to dipping between my soft cheeks. We burst in the door and found Sophia already beneath her covers on the only bed.

"Ooh, you brought her here," smiled Sophia. She sat up and the cover slipped down to show off her naked breasts. "Get her naked, Xera, I want to see her body."

"What a wicked priestess," moaned Vioria as I opened her bodice and slid my hand inside. It was warm and her breasts felt wonderful in my grip. I drew one out and bent down to suckle on her nipple She squealed and groaned, her hands running through my green hair. "I have an elf suckling on my tit."

Warm milk squirted into my mouth. I shuddered in delight, swirling the creamy treat around before swallowing. My pussy clenched as the warm milk filled my mouth. She cooed and giggled as she kept stroking my hair.

"Drink Mommy's milk," she laughed. "Oh, yes. Such a hungry elf."

"You're lactating?" Sophia asked in obvious delight.

"I work as a wet nurse from time to time now that I've weaned my son."

Sophia slipped naked from the bed, her small breasts jiggling. She licked her lips, her pink tongue pierced by a metal stud. Vioria gasped as Sophia latched onto her other nipple and suckled. My cheek rubbed against Sophia's as we nursed.

The milk was so exciting. I drank it down. It warmed my belly. My hips shook and swayed. My hands reached behind her and kneaded Vioria's ass as we suckled. My finger wormed between her butt-cheeks and fingered her tight hole.

"Oh, you naughty elf," she gasped. "You're fingering Mommy's ass. I should spank you for that."

"Ooh, spank her," Sophia laughed. "Or me. You can tie me up and spank me."

Ever since the dryad, Sophia loved to be tied up and molested.

Vioria walked away from us and flounced on the bed. She patted her lap and arched an eyebrow. "Well, naughty elf?"

I grinned and licked my milk-stained lips. It was such a sweet, delicious flavor. I hoped Atharilesia was still lactating when I returned. I wanted to taste my wife's delicious milk. I crossed the room and climbed onto the bed, draping my body across her lap.

"What a gorgeous bum," Vioria purred, her hands rubbing it.

"Oh, yes," Sophia smiled and sat before me, her legs spread, her pussy inches from my face. She pulled my hair, and I didn't fight. My lips nuzzled at her labia. I licked, savoring the exciting taste of her tart passion.

Smack!

I moaned as Vioria's hand spanked my ass. Not hard, but enough to make me squirm. The heat shot right to my pussy. I hadn't been spanked since I was an elf-child. It was exciting. I felt so helpless as she disciplined me. She was so strong, keeping me in line.

Her hand cracked down over and over as I licked and nuzzled at Sophia's pussy.

"Such a bad elf," cooed Vioria. "You fingered Mommy's bum."

Smack!

"Ooh, yes, such a naughty elf," gasped Sophia. "She's licking my pussy."

"How terrible," giggled Vioria. Her hand cracked down again.

My pussy clenched. I squirmed on her lap as my cunt grew hotter and hotter. My juices flooded out, coating my thighs. I moaned and groaned into Sophia's pussy as my tongue licked and nuzzled. I was eager for every drop of her pussy I could drink.

Sophia grabbed my hair and humped her pussy into my face. She gasped and shuddered, her green eyes squeezing shut. My tongue flailed through her folds as her excitement mounted. Her tongue piercing flashed as she licked her lips.

"Oh, yes! So good! Keep spanking her while I cum on her face."

"Oh, yes," Vioria agreed and spanked me again. My ass was on fire. "I think she likes it."

"That naughty, elvish slut!" Sophia gasped. Her hips bucked. Her juices flooded my mouth as she came hard. She swayed and groaned. My lips devoured her passion. They flooded my mouth. I drank them all down, so eager for every last drop. Humans had such exciting flavors to their pussies.

Vioria's fingers probed between my legs and rubbed at the bare lips of my pussy, my snatch dewy with my excitement. She swirled her fingers through my lips, moving down to nudge my clit before she stroked my labia.

"Wow, she is wet," groaned Vioria. Her fingers moved away, and she sucked them clean. "Oh, wow. Elves taste like flowers."

"Uh-huh," groaned Sophia as she fell back on the bed. "Oh, Xera, you gave me such a good cum."

"I need more of her pussy," gasped Vioria. "She tastes so good."

"Lick her," giggled Sophia.

"You took your punishment like a good girl," Vioria moaned. "Now let Mommy kiss your pussy and take away the pain."

292

"Yes," I gasped as she pushed me off her lap. I sprawled across the bed, my legs spread wide open. My pussy clenched, eager to be touched and pleasured.

Vioria leaned over, her light-brown hair falling across my skin, hiding her face. Her fingers spread my pussy open. "She has three labia."

"Elves are fun to play with," giggled Sophia. "So many exciting folds to explore."

Vioria buried her lips into my pussy. I shuddered, my ass burning on the mattress as I squirmed. Her tongue swirled through all my folds, excited to drink all my juices down. She ate me with an eager desire. Her lips and tongue explored me everywhere.

"Yes, yes, eat my pussy," I gasped. "Oh, wow. You're so amazing, Vioria."

"And you taste like marigolds," panted the maid. "This is the best pussy I've ever eaten."

Her fingers shoved into my hole as her tongue swirled up my folds to my clit. Sophia grinned, leaned over, and sucked on the tip of my ear. Her tongue was wet and delicious. Pleasure roared through my body right down to my pussy. I shuddered as the two women licked and sucked my sensitive flesh.

"Matar's cock," I gasped as I humped my hips into Vioria's lips. "Oh, wow. That's so good!"

Her fingers pumped faster and faster in my pussy as her lips sucked on my clit. The pleasure rushed through me. The excitement of my spanking mixed with the bliss radiating from my ear and pussy. They built and built within me. A crescendo of passion swelled.

My toes curled.

"Sweet Matar's love!" I gasped in Elvish as my orgasm burst through me. "Thank you for this wonderful gift of pleasure. Oh, yes!"

My body quivered and quaked. I shuddered on the bed as the pleasure raced through my body. My toes curled, and the ceiling spun above me. Vioria moaned her delight as she drank down all the juices flooding out of my pussy.

"Wow," Vioria grinned, pulling her two fingers out of my pussy. "I think I can say I fucked an elf."

"Uh-huh," I panted, licking my lips. "Let me return the favor."

~ * ~

Knight-Errant Angela – Breven, The Magery of Thosi

I had a smile on my face as we rode out of Breven the next morning. That stud had been amazing. My pussy still ached from his cock. Elf cocks were nice, but they still felt like a woman when they were on top of you. I had missed a muscular, strong man pounding me, my tits crushed by a hard chest.

I wasn't the only one smiling. Sophia and Xera both beamed. I had found them this morning in the tangle of blankets with Vioria, the room reeking of hot pussy. Sophia hadn't wanted to get up, but Xera rose and dragged her out of bed.

It was nice being out of the oppressive forest and back into civilized lands. We rode past farms that almost looked the same as the ones back in Secare. The people were a little fairer in skin and hair, and they grew different crops, but they still felt the same.

Close cousins.

It took two days of riding after Breven to reach our first city, Norv, lying on the banks of the Tingul, the great river that divided the Magery of Thosi from the Princedoms of Zeutch. The Princedoms was a collection of twelve smaller countries closely allied and united under an elected government. Across the river was Nevtoth, a minor Princedom sandwiched between Thosi and the wild orc lands of the northern tundra.

Xera was overwhelmed by the city. She had thought Breven and the other villages we passed were large. Khalesithan was a large city for the elves, but it was tiny compared to Norv. The buildings crowded each other and the streets were narrow. I had no idea how she would react to a large city. Shesax, the capital of Secare, was easily three times as big as Norv.

We stayed the night and headed southwest the next day, following the road to Allenoth, the city famed for its university. There were few places of knowledge as prestigious as the University of Allenoth. Only the Collegiate Tower in Esh-Esh and the Bardic College of Az had more renown. From Allenoth, we would head southwest to Esh-Esh. There, hopefully, we would find the "grieving mage" the prophecy spoke of.

The rain started early on our march. Sophia huddled in her cloak, glaring up at the dark clouds storming overhead. I grit my teeth and ignored the chill settling into my body. Xera didn't mind. She danced in the spring shower as we marched.

"Such a wonderful life," she smiled while spinning about, her dark-green hair spraying drops.

The roads grew mired, and the horses slowed by midday. Huge puddles dominated the road. Xera walked across the mud as easily as she did firm dirt, her feet barely even sinking in. As night fell, the rain finally stopped, the sun appearing to the west and shining on us.

We didn't reach a village or town, so we found a small field to camp in. Sophia stripped naked and draped her clothes by the fire so they would dry. I followed suit, taking off my armor and checking it for any rust.

"I'm bored," Sophia purred as she nibbled on her trail ration. A naughty glint appeared in her eyes. We hadn't made love since we left the forest. She had allowed me to indulge my desire for masculine cocks the last three nights. "Want to play a game?"

My pussy grew hot. "Sure," I answered. "What?"

~ * ~

Acolyte Sophia

"Oh, no," I moaned in mock protest as Angela seized me and carried me down to the ground, her naked breasts rubbing on mine.

"You naughty, little priestess," she purred. "You're my prisoner. I'll do whatever I like to you."

"Won't someone help me?" I gasped as a rope went around my wrist. The other end was tied about a fence post.

Xera watched from the fire with amusement as I pretended to struggle. My pussy was so hot as the second rope bound my left wrist. The rough fibers bit in, then Angela easily pulled my arm out and tied it to the fence.

"Mmm, and now you are completely at my mercy," purred Angela, her hand caressing down my stomach to my aching pussy.

I loved this. Bondage was so exciting. I don't know why the temple never taught it. I would change that when I returned. It was so sexy being helpless. When the giganraneae captured me, I had loved being trapped in the cocoon, and then the dryad and her wonderful tree had shown me such delicious delights.

"No, don't touch me there," I moaned as Angela's fingers played with my pussy. My toes curled. "You wicked woman."

"So wicked," Angela laughed.

Wings flapped. I frowned. Something dived out of the dark sky. "Angela!"

"Protesting won't– "

The winged creature grabbed Angela's shoulders. With a powerful flap of wings, my lover was yanked into the air by a thing that looked like a dragon, with wide, leathery wings and a hissing mouth. A tail waved behind it, sharp and bristling.

"No!" I screamed as the wyvern lifted Angela into the air.

Chapter Forty-Three: Watching Eyes

Fireeyes – Southern Edge of the Deorc Forest, The Kingdom of Valya

Through my campfire, I smiled as my wyverns spotted their prey. They dived and snatched up Angela.

If they succeeded in killing the knight, I wouldn't have to keep riding around the Deorc Forest and enter the Magery. That was a dangerous place for me. The Council had issued a warrant for my arrest and trial. They wanted to execute me for my research.

I smiled as I witnessed what the wyverns saw dancing amid the red-orange tongues of flame. My three wyvern slaves had tracked down Angela and her party. The first wyvern dived at the naked Angela. She was a ravishing creature: red hair, large breasts, flawless skin, tall and sexy. She stood over the bound form of the acolyte, Sophia, herself a nubile beauty begging for me to explore and vivisect.

My cock hardened. I seized the smooth head of my simulacrum – an artificial being created by the Mages of Thosi to provide the sexual juices to power magic– and pulled her mouth over my cock. The wyvern screeched right before he snatched up the naked knight.

Her screams rippled the flames, mixing with the pop and

crackle of my fire. All the wyvern had to do was carry her high up and drop her. Thus would end the threat to King Edward's throne, and I would secure his patronage to continue my research unmolested by the small minds of the Magery Council of Thosi.

My simulacrum's mouth sucked hard as I stroked her hairless, smooth head. "Drop her," I groaned to the wyvern, my balls aching to unload into my servant's mouth. "Drop her and watch her fall. Let her insides be dashed onto the ground and then feast upon her innards."

~ * ~

Knight-Errant Angela – Norv-Allenoth Highway, Magery of Thosi

Sharp claws dug into my shoulders. I ignored the pain as leathery wings flapped and hauled me up into the air. Sophia screamed in shock below as my legs dangled over the ground. The air rushed past my naked body while my stomach lurched. The creature carrying me aloft let out a screech.

A gray-green, lizard-like body was above me. The wings were bat-like and the creature had a broad, long snout. A dragon's snout. I was snatched by a wyvern. The creature screeched as his wings flapped furiously to pull us higher and higher into the air.

My mind racked to remember my training. I had studied fighting most monsters. Wyverns preferred to snatch their prey and fly high before dropping them. When they couldn't drop them, they would sting them with a powerful, paralyzing venom contained in a scorpion-like tail.

The wyvern was clearly going with his preferred method of hunting.

The dark ground fell farther and farther away. My stomach clenched in fear. I sucked deep breaths through my mouth. I fought the urge to struggle. Being dropped was the last thing I wanted.

298

There was only one way out, and it would only work if he was a male wyvern.

I reached up with my right arm, sliding along his leathery belly. The wyvern let out another shriek and his claws tightened. I ignored the blood trickling down my shoulders to my breasts as I slid my hand farther and farther down his body, questing for his cock's sheath. Like many animals, wyverns' dicks were kept inside them until they were aroused.

That was what I had to do. I needed to get this wyvern so horny he would want to fuck me instead of kill me.

My fingers brushed a hole. The wyvern let out a throatier screech as I caressed his cock's sheath. I smiled and circled that. "Mmm, you like that, big boy?"

My fingers stroked the opening, probing inside. It was warm, and I brushed something throbbing in the sheath. I stroked it with the tip of my finger, circling around a spongy mass of flesh. The wyvern hissed as the spongy mass swelled and pushed forward.

His cock emerged, thrusting hard and pink along the side of my cheek. The wyvern let out another hissing screech as his throbbing dick, covering in tiny spines, rubbed on my cheek. I grasped it with my hand, stroking his dick, his spines teasing my palm.

A second cock bobbed next to the first, brushing the back of my hand.

My eyes widened. I explored this strange, yet exciting, development. Two thick cocks for me to play with. My hand followed the first dick back and found they formed a Y with the second, the pair thrusting off a central shaft right after they emerged from the sheath.

"Damn," I groaned. "You are one lucky bastard. I bet the lady wyverns love you."

The wyvern hissed again. My pussy, already on fire from tying up Sophia, clenched. My thighs were sticky with my juices. I reached up with both arms, grasping his dicks and fisting him. The wyvern banked and began to descend as I jerked his dicks.

"That's right. You're just eager to fuck me," I groaned. When I started this quest, I didn't know I would have the chance to fuck monsters. I had heard of a few female knights that had become addicted to monster cocks, preferring them to human's. I hoped that didn't happen to me.

But I could understand how it happened.

I stroked the wyvern's dicks faster. He let out a screech of joy as he circled down to a field below, eager to rut.

~ * ~

Xerathalasia

I dived to the ground as one of the winged monsters tried to snatch me. Angela dwindled into the night sky, thrashing in the grip of one of the monsters. A third landed on the bound Sophia, a scorpion-like tail raised high.

They were wyverns.

My heart hammered, almost drowning out the voice whispering on the wind. I snatched a rock from the ground and threw it at the wyvern. It cracked into the monster's head. The wyvern hissed in pain, leathery skin torn and exposing a dull-white skull. It turned and ambled towards me, walking on the knuckles of its wings and stubby hind legs. The dragon-like maw snapped at me.

I needed a weapon. My bow was unstrung. There was no time to string it and attack the monster. My quiver was nearby. Arrows didn't make the best daggers, but in a pinch they were better than nothing.

I danced back. The third wyvern swooped in the sky, wheeling around for another dive at me. My ears twitched as I struggled to watch both wyverns at once. The one on the ground rushed forward surprisingly fast.

I snatched the arrow from my quiver as the wyvern leaped at me. Wings unfurled and the tail raised up over its head. I crouched, my heart racing as I gripped the arrow right beneath the tip. The tail

300

shot forward at me, a black blur.

I dodged and slammed the arrow into the wyvern's neck. It let out a hissing cry as blood squirted from the wound. The wyvern's wings struck me. I was carried to the ground by the thrashing monster. I heaved its dying body off of me and scrambled for another arrow.

"Xera!" Sophia cried as she struggled to get free of her bindings. "Watch out!"

Wings flapped behind me. I dived, hoping I was dodging the wyvern. Claws scratched along my naked back before I hit the ground and rolled. I came up in a crouch as the wyvern sped past and banked in the air. The monster flew with grace as it circled around. My sharp eyes focused on it.

I needed to time this right.

The wyvern finished its turn and flew straight at me. Wings flapped once, giving it more speed as it rushed towards me. The tail wasn't extended. It would try to grab me and carry me off. I had fought wyverns before. They commonly drifted down from the Rehyn Mountains to hunt in the Deorc Forest.

The wyvern hissed. The voice on the wind spoke louder, more commanding. My ears twitched. I suppressed my curiosity. I couldn't be distracted right now.

"Matar, guide my strike," I prayed as the gray-green monster hurtled towards me.

At the last moment, the creature flared his wings, presenting me with its underbelly. Stubby legs tipped by sharp claws reached for me. I thrust with my arrow, aiming for the creature's heart. The stone tip pierced the wyverns chest as its tail swung down beneath its body.

The tail's stinger pierced my thigh.

Heat burned through the wound. The wyvern crashed into me and we fell to the ground in a heap. The wyvern was atop me, its body spasming as it died. The burning in my legs spread with every beat of my heart.

Everywhere the venom traveled into my body fell numb and

limp. My body prickled and felt fuzzy. I gasped, sucking in a breath as I struggled to move anything. I couldn't. I tried to speak, but my mouth wouldn't move.

I could only breathe. My heart thudded in my chest. Fear gripped me. I couldn't move. There was a dying wyvern crushing my body and I couldn't do anything.

~ * ~

Fireeyes – Southern Edge of the Deorc Forest, The Kingdom of Valya

I growled in frustration, my cock going limp. Two of the wyverns were dead, and the third was gripped in the throes of lust. It landed, dropping Angela. I tried to control it. I shouted commands into the fires, but the primitive instincts of the creature to mate were too strong for my spell to overcome at such distances.

The simulacrum kept sucking at my limp cock. All the excitement had vanished from my body. I seized her neck and threw her off of me. She made not a sound as she landed on her side. Instead, she rolled up onto her knees and waited for my next command.

"Gods damn her," I growled as I stared into the fire.

Chapter Forty-Four: Two Cocks

Knight-Errant Angela – Norv-Allenoth Highway, Magery of Thosi

The wyvern dropped me onto the grass. I fell to my hands and knees. The wyvern landed beside me, hissing in eager pleasure as he ambled around me. I should be fighting him. I was on the ground. There had to be a weapon I could use.

But my pussy was excited. He had two cocks. I just had to find out what that was like.

Leathery wings gripped my waist. Hot breath washed over my pussy. A flicking tongue brushed the lips of my pussy. I groaned at the darting caresses. My hips shook as the wyvern nuzzled into my folds. His tongue brushed everywhere, flicking up and down my skin. It was exciting. I humped back into his licks and nuzzles.

"That's it, eat my pussy," I groaned as my fingers tore at the grass. "Mmm, yes. You're hungry for my human pussy. Is it better than wyvern snatch?"

The wyvern didn't answer. He only kept bathing my pussy with his flicking attacks. They were rapid, the forked tongue caressing a different part of my pussy every time. Sometimes they brushed my dripping labia, other times my clit.

My pussy clenched every time my clit was caressed. My hips shook as my tangy juices dripped down my thighs. His wings tightened on me as his lips pressed against my pussy. The tongue flicked out, pushing deep into my sheath, teasing all the sensitive nerves in my cunt.

"Mmm, yes. You love pussy, huh? Mmm, keep licking me. I love it."

His snout moved higher. He sniffed, drawn to the sour flavor of my asshole. His tongue flicked between my butt-cheeks and caressed my sphincter. I groaned, clenching my bowels as his scaly lips nuzzled at my backdoor.

"You naughty wyvern," I groaned as his tongue wormed into my asshole. Burning bliss shot to my pussy. I quivered beneath him. "Oh, I like that. You can lick my naughty pussy whenever you want. Mmm, yes. Keep probing with that long tongue and make me explode. Oh, wow. You are such a great stud."

The wyvern screeched in agreement as he lubed my ass. Did he want to fuck both my holes? Did female wyverns have two pussies? What lucky creatures if they did. I shuddered and groaned, my body on fire to be double penetrated.

The wyvern let out another screech and then his wings slid up my body. The thin membranes brushed my dangling breasts. My nipples tingled as they were caressed by the leathery wings. I squirmed as I was mounted.

"That's it. Fuck me. It's so much better than eating me."

The wyvern screeched in agreement. His double dick pressed at my hot holes. I shuddered as his wonderful cocks pressed into my body. The small spines tickled my sensitive flesh. My bowels burned with bliss and pleasure churned in my pussy as he filled up my cunt and asshole.

"Wow," I gasped as I writhed beneath him. Both my holes were filled. It was like being double fucked by a pair of studs, but these cocks moved in perfect rhythm. "Damn, fuck me! Oh, yes! Pater's cock, this is so fucking hot!"

The two cocks worked in and out of my holes. The wyvern's

wings tightened about me, squeezing my breasts as he fucked me. The cocks tickled my flesh. The spines drove me wild. Nerves burned in both my holes, the pleasure mixing in the depths of my pussy.

I rocked my hips back into his thrusts. My back undulated beneath him. His leathery body rubbed at my supple skin as he took me hard. The wyvern screeched his pleasure to the night as he rammed his cocks over and over into my holes.

"Damn, you're a two cock stud!"

The pleasure swelled inside of me. My pussy and asshole clenched down on his thrusting cocks. I trembled as my orgasm hurtled towards me. I squeezed my eyes shut, savoring the wild excitement of being fucked by a wyvern.

My pussy convulsed. My asshole clenched. My orgasm burst inside me.

I screamed into the night as the pleasure burned hot through me. Pulse after pulse of bliss rippled from my pussy and asshole. The duel pleasures crashed together and then flowed through the rest of my body. The wyvern screeched as my holes massaged his dicks. He fucked me faster and faster, his spines teasing more orgasms from my body.

They crashed through me one after the other. My body was stimulated by his wonderful dicks. His leathery snout rubbed on my cheek as he took me. His tongue flicked out, brushing my cheek and lips. I turned my head and opened wide, kissing my wyvern lover as my body burned with orgasmic delight.

His head tossed back. He let out another screech. His hips thrust his dicks deep into my body. My holes gripped his spiny cocks. They throbbed in me and then came at the same wonderful moment. My ass and cunt were flooded with hot wyvern cum. It jetted into me, splashing along my insides.

A final orgasm heaved through my body as the wyvern dumped all his cum into both my holes.

~ * ~

305

Acolyte Sophia

"Xera!" I called out, struggling to lift my head.

The elf lay beneath the spasming body of the wyvern. She didn't move. My stomach twisted in fear. I pulled at the ropes binding me to the ground. I had to get free to save her. My wrists burned as I pulled.

"Why did you have to tie these so tight, Angela?" I demanded as I heaved with my arms.

All the excitement of being tied up had vanished. Angela had been carried off and Xera might be dead. This couldn't be happening. We were just having fun one moment and then these stupid monsters had to attack us. What where they even doing this far from the mountains?

"Come on," I groaned, pulling at the rope tied around my right wrist. It was connected to a white-washed fence post. I jerked hard, the fibers biting into my wrist. Fear let me ignore the pain. I had to get free.

The fence post wiggled.

"Are you loose?" I gasped in hope.

I pulled harder at my wrist. The fence post wiggled again. The wood groaned. The fence was old and weathered. The entire fence wobbled as I jerked with my wrist. The pain flared every time. Blood trickled around the rope. That didn't matter.

"Break!" I snapped at the fence as I pulled again. "Come on, just break and let me go. Please, fence, just do me this favor and break."

I jerked again.

The fence leaned over. A wooden slat broke off and tumbled to the ground. It was so weak. Nails groaned as I jerked again, working out of the boards. I kept jerking my arm, waving the fence back and forth.

Soil buckled around the base. The fence half collapsed. I had slack in my right hand.

"Yes!"

306

I pulled the fence as I reached for the rope bound about my left wrist. The muscles in my right arm burned from the strain as I fumbled about the knot. My fingernails bit into the fibers, prying them apart. The rope slipped. The knot came undone.

"Hold on, Xera, I'm coming," I shouted as my left hand was free and I went to work on my right. I undid the knot quickly. My wrist was raw and bleeding.

I ignored the raw pain and stood. I raced across the campsite to Xera. The wyvern had gone completely still, finally dead. I seized its leathery wings and heaved it off of Xera's body. Her greenish skin was pale and a sheen of sweat covered her body. Her breasts rose and fell as she breathed. An angry, swollen wound swelled her thigh.

"Their stingers must be poisonous," I said, "but don't worry, Saphique will heal you."

I shoved a pair of my fingers into my pussy as I gathered my thoughts.

I cast the healing spell. "Saphique, bless the font of my womanhood with your loving power." Pleasure rippled through my pussy as the goddess blessed me. I moaned as the pleasure rushed through my veins and filled me with happy bliss.

I pulled out my fingers, coated in my juices, and rubbed them on my now-hard nipples. Tingles shuddered through me as my nipples glistened pink in the firelight. "Saphique, transform my virgin milk with your love. Let my milk heal the sick and infirm."

The spell finished. Heat filled my breasts. I groaned as my tits ached, suddenly full of breast milk. I leaned down, seized my right breast, and guided the nipple to Xera's lips. The paralyzed elf couldn't suckle.

So I milked my tit.

The creamy, blessed milk squirted into her lips. I squeezed again, my hand sliding up my breast to the nipple as another blast of milk squirted out. I groaned, my pussy getting hotter as my nipple tingled.

The pallor on her skin cleared. Her fingers twitched. The swelling in her thigh vanished. Xera's lips locked about my nipple.

Her eyes met mine, shining with joy as she suckled. She gained control of her body and began moving her limbs and toes. Her hand grasped my breast, holding it in place as she sucked and drank every drop of my milk.

"Thank you," Xera panted as she sat up and licked her lips.

I gave her a hug and kissed her creamy lips. "I'm so glad you're fine. But..."

Xera nodded and stood. "We need to find Angela."

"I'm fine," Angela panted, stumbling out of the night. Piercing wounds adorned her shoulders, blood trickled down to her breasts, and cum smeared her thighs.

I blinked at that. Had she fucked the wyvern?

"I see you killed the other two," Angela smiled. "I finished the third off while he lay...satisfied."

My cheeks burned. She did fuck the wyvern.

"I feared you were dead," Xera said. "But I see you know how to react when carried off by a wyvern."

"Arouse them, fuck them, and then kill them while they luxuriate in their orgasm," Angela smiled. "I do feel a little bad. He was a great fuck."

"But he tried to kill you," I objected, rushing towards her. "And you're hurt. Here, let me fix you up."

I reached Angela. Her arms wrapped around me and she pulled me in for a kiss. I groaned and melted into it. My heart beat so fast. I did love her so much. Her kiss was so sweet. Our naked bodies pressed together as we held each other.

Angela broke the kiss and pulled away from me, looking me up and down. She seized my wrist. "You're hurt."

"I had to break free. You did too good of a job tying me up." A smile crossed my lips. "Normally, that would have been so hot."

"But not when you're being attacked by wyverns," laughed Angela.

"Exactly," I beamed. My body buzzed with joy. I didn't care at all about my wrists right now. Angela was safe and sound. "Now, let's get you healed."

I sat down on the grass and pulled her down to my breast. Angela's fiery hair spilled about my pale stomach as she licked up to my left breast. I groaned as Angela's mouth latched onto my tit. My nipple burst with pleasure as she suckled. The milk rushed out of me into her hungry mouth. It was so intimate and wonderful.

"That's it," I moaned. "Drink down all my milk. Mmm, yes. Heal yourself."

Angela's blue eyes sparkled in the firelight as she suckled. I stroked her hair as the pleasure grew in my pussy. I squirmed beneath her, humping my hips and rubbing my hot cunt against her flat stomach.

"You're so hungry for my milk," I groaned as she suckled harder. Her cheeks hollowed as her mouth filled with my creamy treat.

"Mmm, it's so good," Angela grinned before leaning down and suckling again.

I loved nursing her.

~ * ~

Xerathalasia

My pussy was on fire from suckling at Sophia's tit. The human's milk lingered in my mouth. I loved the sweet, melony flavor. I rubbed at my pussy as I watched Angela suckle from Sophia. Angela lay on Sophia, the knight's gorgeous ass wiggling. Cum leaked out of her pussy and asshole.

The wyvern had taken both her holes at once.

I licked my lips and padded behind her, my ears twitching with excitement. Sophia flashed me a smile. She didn't like cum. So I needed to clean Angela's pussy and ass out for the acolyte. I winked at her, then spread Angela's asscheeks.

"Ooh," Angela groaned as my tongue licked at the salty, sour cum leaking out of her well-fucked asshole. "That's nice, Xera."

"Yes," moaned Sophia. "Clean up all that nasty wyvern cum."

"So nasty," groaned Angela, her hips writhing.

"You suffered so much," Sophia purred. "Having to fuck a wyvern."

"He had two dicks," Angela moaned, shuddering as my tongue probed her asshole. "It was such a great sacrifice."

"I bet," giggled Sophia. "I think you need something to take your mind off of your horrible experience."

"What?" Angela asked with a purr. Her hips shifted as she savored my tonguing. I probed my tongue deep into her asshole, gathering up all the delicious cum I could.

"Eating my pussy."

Sophia slid back until her pussy was right in Angela's face. The redheaded human dived in with a groan and Sophia bucked. Her light-brown hair slid off her shoulders as she spasmed, her small breasts jiggling, her nipples still beading with milk. I grinned and buried my lips back into Angela's ass.

"That's so good, Angela," groaned Sophia. "Wash away your terrible experience with my pussy."

Angela moaned as she ate out Sophia noisily. Angela's wet licks spurred me to move down to her own cum-filled snatch. I spread her thighs apart as my breasts rubbed on the ground. I pressed my mouth into her juicy pussy and tongued her.

Tangy, human pussy and salty, wyvern cum mixed on my tongue. I groaned in delight, swirling my tongue around her hot depths. I searched through her folds as I savored her exciting flavors. Human pussies had such different flavors than elves, and the wyvern cum was so strong, bursting with depraved flavor. I loved it.

"Mmm, yes, eat my pussy, Angela. I love your tongue swirling my cunt."

"It's so tasty," Angela purred. "And...oh, Xera, oh, that's nice. You naughty elf. Keep doing that."

"Sure," I grinned before I went back to swirling my tongue about her clit.

My fingers probed at the folds of her pussy while I nibbled on her clit. Angela's hips rose and fell as she shuddered. Her pussy tightened about my fingers. I latched my lips about her clit and sucked hard, breathing through my nose.

Every breath was full of her tangy passion.

"I'm gonna cream your face, Angela," gasped Sophia, "if you keep doing that."

"Good," moaned Angela. "That's why I'm doing it. Flood me with your treat."

Sophia's body undulated, her belly piercing glinting in the firelight. She grabbed Angela's red hair and humped her face against the knight's hungry mouth. I pumped my fingers faster and faster into Angela's pussy as I nibbled on her clit and watched Sophia's passion.

The redhead spasmed. Her pussy rippled about my fingers and her juices flooded my hungry mouth.

"Did you cum first?" gasped Sophia. "Ooh, yes. Keep moaning into my pussy. You get so passionate when you cum."

Sophia bucked again. Her toes curled as she humped and undulated, rubbing her hot pussy against Angela's tonguing delights. The nubile human heaved as she came. Her mouth opened wide and her eyes squeezed shut as Angela drank down all her passion.

"Thank you, Saphique, for gifting women with lesbian pleasure," moaned Sophia as she sprawled back on the grass.

"Uh-huh," grinned Angela as she sat up, her lips stained with pussy juices.

Mine were equally smeared. "I think it is your turn to gift me with that pleasure."

"Oh, yes, Xera," Sophia grinned as she sat up. "Angela, shall we?"

Angela nodded in delight. My pussy clenched as the pair embraced me.

Chapter Forty-Five: Morning

Journeyman Faoril – Lake Esh, Magery of Thosi

I sat at the bow of the crystal ship as it glided through the fog hovering over Lake Esh. The fog was cool and moist, caressing my face as I searched for the first sign of the Island. It had another name, but over the centuries the mages of the Collegiate Tower had just come to call it the Island.

There the test to achieve the rank of Master Mage was held.

My stomach twisted. Once again, I patted the pockets of my red robe, reassuring myself that the three vials of lemure cum were still there. I did this every few minutes. With their potent cum, I would have no problem completing the tests.

I placed my hand on the smooth railing of the ship. It was made entirely of amethyst, shaped by earth magic and imbued with enchantments. Only the Crystal Ship could pass through the protections that ringed the Island. Our destination was an artificial construct, raised out of the lake bed and shaped into a perfect pentagon. The founder of the Magery Council designed it to contain the magical forces of the test and to keep out any unwanted visitors.

Any who tried to approach would be rebuffed by the protective spells. All who plied Lake Esh knew to keep a wide berth around the Island.

I kept my vigil, hoping for the first glimpse.

"It's all happening so fast."

I squeaked as Saoria's words startled me. My friend sat beside me, her face even paler than usual, her blue eyes wide. Like me, she wore the red robes of a journeyman mage, her arms hugging her body, perhaps from nerves or maybe against the cold mist.

"Yes," I nodded. "I don't feel at all ready."

Saoria laughed. "You spent more time practicing than the rest. You are the most skilled of our class. You'll achieve the rank of Master Mage."

"So will you."

Saoria nodded. "I know. I have it locked."

"Wow, where did all that confidence come from?"

"I've been practicing, too." A smile crossed her pretty face. "You're not the only one that's prepared for today."

"We'll both pass," I grinned and gave her an impulsive hug. We had been roommates and lovers for years. I gave her a kiss on the cheek.

Saoria smiled and then peered out in the fog. "Ooh, there it is."

My heart thudded in my chest. The Island appeared out of the mists.

It was obvious the Island wasn't natural. The surface gleamed smooth and flat, disappearing into the fog. The waves of the lake broke against the smooth sides rising five feet above the surface. Runes were inscribed along the perimeter to anchor the protective enchantments.

The air shimmered before the bow of the ship. The hairs on my arms stood up on end. Energy crackled in the air. The Island's barrier approached. The bow of the Crystal Ship knifed into the field. Yellow crackled, rippling down the ship. It washed over me, numbing my entire body. My breath stopped and my heart froze.

And then I was through, gasping for breath.

"Oh, wow, that was intense," Saoria shuddered, her eyes wide.

"I had heard, but I didn't expect. You know?"

"Yeah," I groaned, clutching my hands to my breasts. I looked back down the ship at the master mages and the other candidates. The master mages all appeared unruffled by the passing. Jolly Chevian even had a big grin on his face, stroking his impressive, curly beard while my fellow candidates all looked pale-faced.

The five master mages were all different, from beautiful and sultry Laorlia, only ten years older than me, to the ancient Lord-Mage Alorian, his back straight despite the deep crags age had left on his wrinkled face. The five masters would be our judges, choosing the complex spells we would have to perform as well as dealing with any situations that might arrive. It was the masters that guided the boat, not by wind– no sails adorned the Crystal Ship– but by current, controlling the lake around us to propel the craft to the Island.

The ship turned as we approached the Island, pushed by the current. The boat slowed and then drifted to the Island. The ship's deck was of an equal height to the Island's smooth surface. The boat settled next to the Island. I gazed at the polished surface and the tiny, Arcane script adorning the perimeter.

The Island was the size of a large market square, and its entire perimeter was carved with the magical text. The sheer effort it took to craft the Island made me feel so small in my robes. I wanted to hunch my shoulders and avoid the notice of the genius that had conceived it.

Lord-Mage Alorian, leader of the Magery Council, stood from his bench on the prow. In a voice scratched by age, said, "Today, each of you shall strive to join our ranks. We cannot allow the weak, the unskilled, and the lazy to achieve the level of Master. You will each have to press the boundaries of the magics you have learned to accomplish the test. You shall each be given five spells to perform. We shall judge you in every aspect. And while only a maximum of three are ever selected, do not believe that three will be chosen. We do not seek the best of mediocrity."

"Now, down to the hold with you," plump, motherly Evolia

314

smiled. "We shall call you one by one for the test. When you are finished, you will return to the boat and speak nothing of the test." Her eyes narrowed, and her kindness melted away, her fleshy face grown hard. "We shall know if you do. And you shall fail the test, even if you are the best of the group." Her smile returned. "Now relax and this will all be over soon."

I nodded, my mouth dry.

"Well?" she asked, arching her eyebrows. "Down to the hold."

The seven of us scrambled to our feet and hurried to the crystal staircase that led down into the hold's depths. My stomach twisted inside as Saoria and I followed the other five down the stairs. My hand patted my pocket, touching the enchanted vials.

With lemures cum, I would imbue with my spells with greater power. The judges would have to be impressed.

~ * ~

Knight-Errant Angela – Allenoth, Magery of Thosi

Something wet and hot settled on my face. A tart musk invaded my nose as I rose from sleep. I groaned and opened my eyes to see a pair of flexing, pale butt-cheeks above me while a hot pussy ground on my lips.

"Sophia," I groaned.

"Good morning," the acolyte giggled. "Someone's being lazy. So I thought you might want some hot pussy for breakfast."

I groaned and licked through her folds. Sophia shuddered and wiggled again. "What happened to Delan and Merk?"

"Were those the names of those two disgusting men that you went to bed with last night?" Sophia asked as she wiggled on me.

"Yes," I grinned. I needed another taste of being double-fucked. Even two nights after the wyvern attacked, I was burning to have a cock in my ass and pussy.

I licked her pussy and frowned. "You taste fruitier than

315

normal."

"I told you," she giggled. "It's your breakfast."

Mixed into her tart pussy juice was a citric tang. I licked again, my tongue probing into her depths and brushed a piece of fruit, an orange, marinating in her pussy. I groaned as I sucked the bit of orange out of her cunt. My tongue wrapped around it, pulling the piece of orange closer to my lips.

"Oh, yes," purred Sophia, "enjoy your breakfast."

The pussy-soaked slice of orange popped into my mouth. I chewed it, savoring the mix of tart and tangy flavor. I shuddered, squeezing my thighs together. My tongue probed back into her pussy, looking for another tasty treat.

Sophia muttered something, but I missed it. Then I gasped as something buzzing touched my clit. The naughty minx was playing with her magical dildo. I spread my thighs, cum leaking out of my pussy as Sophia rubbed my clit. I moaned into her pussy, the pleasure shooting through my body.

"I can't touch your pussy with all that nasty cum in there," Sophia purred, "but my toy can."

I groaned into her pussy. I worked my tongue throughout her folds, searching for more tasty oranges. Sophia's pussy walls rippled as she forced a piece of orange from deeper inside of her wet depths towards my hungry lips. Sophia had complete control over her own pussy. She could even make herself cum without ever touching her snatch.

"Mmm, I bet you're just enjoying your breakfast," giggled Sophia.

I shuddered beneath her as I munched on the orange slice, my body bucking with pleasure. My clit shot bliss through me. I spasmed and writhed on the creaking bed as my orgasm swelled within me, growing closer to bursting. I groaned, my back arching as I loved every moment of the bliss.

A third piece of orange pushed out of the depths of her pussy into my mouth. Sophia shuddered atop me as I licked through her folds. My toes curled as pleasure shot from my clit through my body. I bucked beneath her as it swelled.

"That's it, cum," she giggled. "Let me hear you fill the inn with your passion."

"Yes!" I panted as the pleasure rippled through me. "Oh, yes. Keep doing that. Damn, Sophia!"

My orgasm burst through me. I gasped into her delicious pussy. My tongue probed deep as ripples of bliss flooded my body. My clit throbbed for joy as Sophia kept working her buzzing dildo against it. The bed creaked as I thrashed.

"So good," I groaned. "What a delicious way to wake up."

Sophia giggled and then shuddered herself. "One more piece," she gasped. "Oh, yes, here it is."

Her pussy gushed juices, flooding the final piece into my hungry mouth. I opened wide, filling my mouth with pussy juices before I munched on the orange slice. I shuddered in joy as I swallowed the fruit and juices.

"What a wicked breakfast," I sighed as Sophia slid off of me.

"Yep," she grinned. She held her dildo before her, frowning on the cum staining the tip. "And you need to clean that off."

I caught the dildo as she scampered off. I licked the cum and my tangy juices off the tip while watching her naked ass disappear out of my room. I rose and stretched, then headed to the bath where Sophia already waited. We scrubbed ourselves clean then met up with Xera down in the common room.

The elf was ready to leave Allenoth. It was a larger city than Norv. I could only imagine how she would react when she witnesses Esh-Esh. I heard it was even bigger than Shesax or Ostian, and they were the largest cities of Secare.

I mounted Midnight and Sophia mounted her mare. Then we headed out of the city onto the highway that led southwest to Esh-Esh. In three days, we should arrive at the capital of the Magery and find the Grieving Mage.

Chapter Forty-Six: The Mage's Ordeal

Journeyman Mage Faoril – The Island, Magery of Thosi

"Delyia, you first," Evolia called from above after a few minutes of waiting for the tests to begin.

A slim girl stood, her dark-brown hair twisted in a braid that spilled off her right shoulder and down the front of her red robes. She trembled and her hands were clenched into tight fists.

"The Gods luck be with you," I muttered.

"I'll need it," she sighed. "Thank you, Faoril."

It was an hour before Delyia returned, her robes soaked, the scent of salt lingering about her. How had she been ducked into sea water? I wanted to ask, but I knew the rules. My stomach twisted as she sat down in her wet robes, too lost in thought to use a spell to dry herself.

The waiting was the worst. Sometimes we talked while we waited for the next candidate to return. Other times, we closed our eyes and went over spells and incantations. I pictured the seven different magical circles in my mind: triangle, diamond, five-pointed star, hexagram, seven-pointed star, octagon, and the starburst. I remembered the arcane words that had to be inscribed for each circle and the methods for drawing the various angles with no measuring tools.

Welian went second, and he returned with singed robes but a huge grin on his face. Clearly, he was confident he passed. Ventria had a bloody gash across her face and shook as she sat down. She cried into her hands.

Only three of us would pass. Four would fail, and it was clear Ventria was one of those four.

Saoria came back, her head held high as she dripped with black slime. She sank down, a big smile on her lips. I smiled at her, glad she was happy with the results of her test. She didn't look at me. She kept her head held high.

Efele went, and that only left Jerdean and myself. My stomach twisted. I was hungry and unable to eat all at the same time. My concentration on remembering the various magical theorems failed as my nerves assaulted my mind. I trembled as I waited for my turn. I hoped I was next. Waiting was the worst. I looked at Jerdean, and he rubbed at his goatee, his face almost a shade of puke green.

Efele returned with a limp, grimacing at each step down the stairs. Just what happened in the tests?

"Jerdean," Evolia called.

I was last. I wanted to throw up.

I patted my pockets. The vials were still there.

I rocked on my bench as I waited, trying to control my fears. I tried to picture what magic they had everyone perform if they came back looking so bedraggled. Where they even given the same spells to cast? Each one came back stained or injured in a different way.

"Throwia's pain," I muttered, cursing to the Goddess of Suffering. I wanted my misery to end.

"You'll do fine," Delyia nodded. Her robes were dry now. She had come out of her shock and dried herself a few hours ago.

After what seemed like an eternity, and what was probably only an hour, footsteps stomped across the deck. Jerdean walked down the stairs, his robes covered in frost that slowly melted. Bits of ice clung in his goatee and he shivered as he sat down.

"Faoril."

I flinched when Evolia called my name. I almost couldn't stand. My entire body trembled. I passed Saoria, but my friend said nothing. She just stared at her feet. Delyia squeezed my hand and gave me a comforting smile.

"Gods' luck."

"Thank you," I whispered back.

I climbed the stairs and mounted the deck of the Crystal Ship. Evolia waited with a smile on her lips. "Peace, Child. You will do marvelously. We all have high hopes for your performance today."

"Thank you, Master Mage," I squeaked.

I followed Evolia onto the smooth surface of the Island. The fog had long ago burned off. The sun already sank towards evening. We were surrounded in every direction by the blue waters of Lake Esh. Water splashed against the Island's side in undulating waves, a natural rhythm that seemed to match my racing heart.

The other four masters waited at the center, watching me cross the surface. I could do this. I had lemures cum. I pulled out my first vial, popped the cork, and broke the magical seal that would keep the spiritual cum fresh and potent. I downed the salty mix.

It was cold as it went down my throat. A source of energy ballooned inside me.

It shouldn't have been cold.

Fear washed through me. I had never used spiritual cum. Maybe it was supposed to be cold. The lemures had been the spirits of the dead. Their touch had been cold, so why wouldn't their cum be as well?

Why didn't I brink back-up cum? Just in case.

"Journeyman Mage Faoril Lesibourne," Lord-Mage Alorian said stiffly. "You have been invited to demonstrate your skills at magic."

"Thank you for the invitation," I answered, my stomach roiling. I wanted to throw up.

"For your first spell, you shall summon an eldritch horror. You must master it and keep it contained within your magical circle." From the pocket of his robe, the Lord Mage produced violet chalk and handed it to me.

I almost fainted. They wanted me to summon one of the most dangerous beings that haunted the Astral Realm? I glanced down at the chalk clutched in my hand. It was mined from the Isle of Sornia in the Myrt Sea, the perfect chalk to use to bind an eldritch horror.

I could do this. I wanted to step into the highest reaches of magic. This is what it took. I knelt down and drew my magic circle. I had to inscribe the starburst– the ten-pointed star. Drawing a decagon was challenging. Thirty-six degree arcs separated each point of the star on the circle. On the outside of the circle, I marked where they should be. My back ached as I began to draw the ten-pointed star.

The chalk rasped across the smooth surface, leaving behind lines of violet dust. The star formed as I worked around the circle, each arm thin. I paused to rub at my lower back before I made the arcane markings. In each arm of the star I wrote a single, arcane name. First, I wrote the names of the five elements before I moved onto the celestial bodies: the sun, the moon, and the names of the three wandering stars.

Finished, I stood and powered the circle. The violet chalk glowed as it fed off the magical energy the cum provided. My confidence swelled. I had the energy to contain anything in this circle. I began my spell and ripped open a hole between our reality and the Astral Realm.

The Astral Realm was home to thought. The Oracles peered into the Astral Realm to see the future and the domains of the gods were formed out of the sea of imagination. But in between the gods' realms there dwelled other things: spirits of the dead not at peace and darker, stranger creatures.

My words called to an eldritch horror, a thing birthed out of nightmares.

Purple tentacles pushed through the rift. They wiggled and undulated, the tips ending at thick, bulbous tips that resembled cocks. More and more tentacles pushed through the barrier, ripping it open wider. A flesh body spilled out, large, yellow eyes peering at me, a hungry mouth fixed on me. Lust bled through the magic circle.

My nipples hardened beneath my robes and my pussy flushed with excitement. I seemed to have grabbed an eldritch horror of lust. That explained the tentacles ending in cocks. The horror let out almost a sexy hiss, and a voice echoed in my mind.

...succulent flesh...

...juicy, yummy...

...must fuck you...

...must unite our flesh...

I fought against the intrusion of its monstrous thoughts in my mind. The horror's tentacles crashed into the sides of the circle. Purple light flared, rippling along the edge of the circle. I swallowed, my heart beating as the reserve of energy burned.

It was burning too swiftly. Even a normal human's cum should have lasted longer than this. Why was the lemure's jizz running out so fast? I swallowed and cast a look over my shoulder. The Master Mages had retreated all the way to the five points of the Island, watching me.

The horror crashed into the walls again. The energy sparked. Smoke rose from the magical circle as the chalk burned. I grit my teeth, struggling to hold the monster in place. This couldn't be happening. I shouldn't be running out of energy already.

The last of the cum burned out. My hand shot down to my pocket to seize the next vial.

The horror was swifter. Tentacles lashed about my body. Lust flooded me as I was hauled into the air. The eldritch horror exulted in my mind as the tentacles slid beneath my robes.

...fuck your flesh...

"Yes!" I panted as the lust rippled through my body.

Chapter Forty-Seven: Tentacular Test

Journeyman Mage Faoril – The Island, Magery of Thosi

All thoughts were wiped from my mind as the tentacles of the eldritch horror wrapped about my body. The remnants of my magical circle sputtered and then went silent as the creature I conjured from the Astral Plane heaved himself out of the circle.

The horror lifted me into the air above the Island, the world spinning. I glimpsed a straight, artificial edge meet another, the sharp corner of its pentagram shape. Spells and wards protected the perimeter, the Island forming a five-pointed magical circle. It would contain any thing in case a journeyman mage taking the Master's test made a mistake.

Like the one I just made.

Lust burned through me. I shuddered and spasmed as the tentacles held me. The horror was a writhing mass of purple flesh and yellow eyes. Dozens of long, rubbery tentacles undulated from the mass below, some ending in bulbous tips that resembled cocks.

….yummy flesh...

...fuck...

...enjoy...

"Yes," I gasped as the world spun about me. "Enjoy me. Fuck

me."

The light-blue sky and the dark-blue lake whirled about me. Below, the flat island spun as the eldritch horror's tentacles flailed me about. My red robes swirled about my spasming legs. My short, light-brown bangs spilled across my vision, obscuring the world for a moment before whipped away by its thrashing.

More tentacles undulated towards me. A rubbery appendage pressed down the front of my robes between my breasts. My nipples hardened and ached as the tentacle wrapped around one breast and then the other, leaving tingling slime behind. I spasmed and my pussy clenched. My toes curled as the pleasure grew within me.

Cloth ripped. My robe tore open, exposing my naked breasts and stomach to the sun. The tentacle writhed as it seized my tattered robe and ripped it from my body. Other tentacles caressed me. A pair seized my thighs, pulling them apart while another two squeezed and kneaded my breasts.

"So good," I panted as I writhed. My hips undulated. I needed my pussy to be caressed. I was on fire. I needed to cum so badly. "Take me! Fuck me! Make me cum!"

...yes...

...cum...

...feed me your lusts...

Smaller feelers extended from a pair of tentacles to seize my hard, pink nipples. The tentacles coated my nubs in the aphrodisiac slime. My body shuddered as my nipples were stretched and twisted by the thin, noodle-like tentacles. Pleasure shot down to my wet pussy.

A tentacle-cock shoved into my mouth. I ran my tongue around the bulbous head. It was spongy and soft, throbbing as I sucked. I moaned about the tentacle-dick as it reamed into my mouth. I was being used by the monster, feeding it power.

My pussy spasmed as an orgasm rushed through me.

My juices flooded down my thighs. Pleasure hammered through my body. I thrashed in the tentacles' embrace. I sucked harder on the tentacle-cock fucking my mouth. My breasts jiggled as the tentacles played with my nipples.

...delicious...

The horror's tentacles rubbed at my thighs, sucking at my flesh. The suckers absorbed my juices. Ripples of lighter violet ran down the tentacles caressing my legs, bringing my pussy cream to the horror. The fleshy body shuddered beneath me as it fed off my lusts.

...feed me more...

Small, feeler tentacles caressed my pussy lips. They sucked, drinking my pussy juices. My labia and vulva throbbed beneath their caresses. I shuddered as the small tentacles caressed my clit. My little bud throbbed as a small appendage grasped it and undulated, massaging me.

Pleasure exploded through me. My stomach contorted as another orgasm burst inside of me. The bliss flooded my body. Rapture consumed me. The monster rippled and howled below as it played with my pussy.

A tentacle-cock rubbed between my asscheeks, smearing the tingling slime which covered it against my flesh. My sphincter clenched as it pressed against it. The slime lubed the monster's cock. I groaned about the appendage in my mouth as the tentacle-dick penetrated my asshole.

Hot pleasure roared through me as the tentacle-dick fucked my ass.

So good.

The tentacle-cock in my mouth fucked me faster. It pushed at my the back of my mouth. I was too lost to the lust to fight as it slammed down my throat. I sucked breath through my nose. My tongue caressed the rubbery tentacle. It tasted so good. Nothing was sweeter.

I wanted it to cum in me.

...hot ass...

...succulent cunt...

...must fuck...

The tentacles played with my body as the thickest tentacle-dick probed at my pussy lips. My pussy lips stretched and stretched.

Pleasure and pain ran through my body. I spasmed in climax as the thick tentacle-dick shoved into my cunt. I thrashed as it filled me, the small ridges covering the tentacle stroking the inside of my pussy and shooting bliss through me.

My sheath spasmed about the thrusting tentacle. I was fucked in every hole. I dangled in the air and writhed as orgasm after orgasm crashed through me. My juices squirted out of my cunt around the thick tentacle-cock. The monster flashed violet as it drank my lusts.

...pleasure me...

...make me cum...

...slut...

I was a slut. A slut for these amazing tentacles.

Every part of my body was touched. Tentacles caressed my body, fucked my holes, and played with my nipples and clit. Other tentacle dicks pushed against my body. One erupted, spraying white cum across my stomach.

My skin tingled with delight where the cum ran. Another orgasm burst inside me.

...drink my cum...

The tentacle-cock fucking my mouth swelled. I sucked with eager lust. My tongue caressed the tip. The dick erupted. Salty-sweet cum bathed my mouth. I swallowed it in greedy gulps. Power flared inside me as I drank.

I could use that power. But I couldn't remember how. The pleasure was too much.

Blast after blast of cum flooded my mouth. I drank it down and shuddered as my body climaxed again and again. The cum was thick and creamy. It coated my mouth and throat before warming my belly.

More tentacle-dicks erupted, bathing my body in jizz. I loved it. The tentacle-cock in my mouth withdrew. I sucked in greedy breaths as it erupted and drenched my face with its cum. It ran down my cheeks and the bridge of my nose to my lips. I licked with my tongue, greedy for every drop.

"Fuck me! Take me!" I screamed. "Cum in my pussy. Give me all your cum."

...yes...

...take it, slut...

The tentacle-cock in my asshole erupted. It filled my tight bowels with delicious cum. It ran out around the tentacle and dripped down to my stuffed pussy. The cum left a trail of bliss burning across my nethers.

"Cum in my pussy! Give it all to me!"

...whore...

"Yes! Whore! I love your tentacles!"

The thick, pussy-stretching cock slammed into the depths of my cunt. My snatch spasmed around the ridged tentacle. I spasmed in the monster's embrace. A violet pulse ran up the tentacle. The cock swelled and flooded my pussy with delight.

"Begone back to the Astral Plane, horror," a strong voice boomed below.

There were figures standing around the creature, dressed in black robes. I knew them. They were the–

My eyes snapped open. I was taking the test.

The eldritch horror let out a shrieking wail. Its tentacles undulated. The world spun about me as the tentacles waved. I let out a shriek, struggling to think through the lust. I was supposed to keep the horror contained and then send it back.

"Begone!" the mages shouted together, driving their energy into the horror.

The undulating mass of flesh retreated to the shining rift that led back to the Astral Plane.

The tentacles holding me up were severed by slashing air. I shrieked as I fell only to be caught by a gentle breeze and carried naked to the polished stone of the Island. I shuddered and writhed as another orgasm rippled through my body.

My lover fled back into the rift. The world spun about me.

Darkness crashed down on my well-fucked, exhausted body.

Chapter Forty-Eight: Reflection

Knight Errant Angela – Esh-Esh Highway, Magery of Thosi

"What do you think the grieving mage will be like?" Sophia asked as she rode beside me on her mare, Purity.

"I don't know," I shrugged, my armor clinking.

The farmland of Central Thosi spread around us. Traffic was heavy on the highway. Teamsters driving wagon trains of goods passed back and forth, forcing us off the road each time to let them pass.

"I hope it's a girl," Sophia smiled.

"So you can fuck her?" I asked, giving her a grin.

"Maybe." Sophia's green eyes had a naughty twinkle in them.

"Well, we have three days of travel to find out," I answered. The sun sank to the west. "We should think about finding a place for the night."

"There is a village approaching," Xera said. She walked in front, still naked. Every farmer and farmwife we passed stared at the naked elf, freezing in mid-chore or job. Xera walked tall, her back straight, unconcerned by her blatant nudity.

I wasn't a prude, but I don't think I could appear naked for so many to see.

"What if she's a guy, though?" Sophia asked. She bit her lip.

"Then I'll have a man to enjoy from time to time," I smiled at her. "But I'll still share your bed most nights."

Sophia was fun. She made my heart race. She was exciting to be with. But...I wasn't sure if it was love. I couldn't remember what being in love felt like. I had only been in love once, and, well, I couldn't remember who it was or what I felt. I gave up my love to find the answers to defeat the Dragon Dominari.

Was it a mistake? I must have had a good reason to give up...whomever.

Sophia reminded me of Lady Delilah. I had the same heartache whenever I sighted the beautiful, mature woman– my first crush. I could still remember her riding up to my parent's manor in her armor as a Knight Deute, her flaming hair spilling about the burnished pauldrons covering her shoulders.

I touched the garnet pendant about my neck. It was a farewell gift from Lady Delilah. My cheeks burned.

I glanced at Sophia and felt that same...heat. Was this love? Did I love Sophia and Lady Delilah? Or did I only lust for them? They were both beautiful in different ways. Lady Delilah was gorgeous and remote, like a stunning mountain viewed from afar but always out of reach.

Sophia was far more accessible. She was a beautiful, refreshing lake just begging to be entered and enjoyed.

"Tonight," I smiled at Sophia, "how would you like to be tied up to a bed?"

Sophia smiled and shuddered, a flush suffusing her cheeks. "Just so long as no wyverns attack."

"Definitely," I nodded, shifting my shoulders as I remembered the sharp claws snatching me before I was carried off by the attacking monster. "There will be no monster attack."

"Good," Sophia nodded. Her eyes burned with love. It was a true emotion, not shallow like I once believed.

So why wasn't I sure that I loved her back? It just didn't seem fair to Sophia not to love her.

"And I shall find a delicious barmaid or village girl to warm my bed," Xera added.

Sophia giggled, "Yes, the Thosian girls all seem eager to try out an elf."

~ * ~

Journeyman Mage Faoril – The Island, Magery of Thosi

"What went wrong?" Master Mage Evolia asked as my eyes opened. Her motherly expression was stern instead of comforting.

"Wrong?" I asked, my mind fuzzy. My entire body trembled. Heat burned through me.

"With the summoning?" she persisted.

"Oh, no," I gasped and sat up. My body was covered in streaks of dried cum. Magical energy burned inside my body from the eldritch horror. I had received three doses– orally, anally, and vaginally– of the creature's power.

"My...lemures cum wasn't nearly as effective as it should have been, Master Mage," I answered, hugging my body. Abruptly, I became conscious of the five Master Mages staring at my naked, cum-stained form.

"You had lemures cum?" purred sultry Laorlia.

I nodded.

Breliun, a very handsome man with a smile that had left me giddy as an apprentice mage, dug through the scraps of my torn robe. He pulled out a pair of vials that held lemures cum. He examined the vials. "You improperly prepared the preservation charm."

"What?" I blinked.

"How did you fail such a simple spell?" Lord-Mage Alorian demanded.

"I...I..." How? I was so good. And even the newest apprentice could handle the spell without issue. It was the first thing we were taught. Preserving sexual fluids was vital for a mage, whether it was cum for a woman or pussy juices for a man.

"This is very disappointing," Lord-Mage Alorian continued, his back stiff. "You were promising, but to make such a simple mistake..."

"If we weren't here to rescue you..." A nasty smile crossed Laorlia's lips.

I shuddered. I conjured a lust eldritch. The thing would have fucked me to death, absorbing all my sexual energy in the process. Then it would have sought other women to molest with its tentacles and began again.

"Very disappointing," Alorian repeated.

"I have plenty of energy to complete the test," I whispered, my stomach twisting.

"You failed, child," Evolia said.

"Yes, you bunged the barrel, girl," Chevian said, stroking his beard. I had never seen the grandfatherly man without his broad smile.

My head sank. I tried to fight the tears that threatened to overwhelm me. "I...I apologize for my lapse. I...I do not know how I could have improperly cast the preservation spell."

"This is a serious mistake," Alorian said. "I do not think you will be invited to test again next year."

I wanted to throw up. My dream of being a Master Mage was yanked from me. How had I botched it so thoroughly? I was the best mage of my year. I had no doubts that I would pass. Was I in such a confident rush that I didn't cast the simplest spell right?

Tears came. I shook as Evolia conjured a blanket and draped it over my body.

~ * ~

Fireeyes – Kingdom of Valya/Magery of Thosi Border

Discovering the imprisoned fire elemental was a lucky find. The binding spell was ancient, the runes oddly formed. It predated the founding of the Magery Council and the codification of arcane rituals. The circle was a precursor of the starburst, but had nine points instead of ten and strange markings in the star's arms. I had never seen its like.

I drew the circle in my journal before I broke it.

The fire elemental exploded out in a hungry roar. It crackled in the air. Mirages danced around its flaming body. It resembled a primitive sketch of a slim man, the flames dancing and curling to form limbs and torso, rough, imprecise, capturing the essence of the form but not the details. Where the eyes would be, the flames burned white-hot.

I drank a vial of dragon pussy juices. They were hard to obtain. The dragon herself had been a young thing. I doubt I could have procured a vial from an older specimen. The dragon had howled, transformed into a woman, as I induced orgasm after orgasm to obtain ten vials of her passion.

I only had one on me, the rest safely hidden in my lab. Dragons were hermaphroditic beings of fire. Like all the five races birthed by Matar's self-impregnation, Dragons represented one of the five elements. Dragon dew allowed for greater control over fire than other juices.

I chained the fire elemental to my will. It howled and thrashed against invisible bonds. Its flames sputtered as my magic kept its fires under control. Raging like an inferno, it thrashed as I dragged it to the bonfire my simulacrum had started.

In the fire, an image of my target appeared. Angela was in a rude village inn. The entire building was made of wood with a thatch roof. It would be hard to affect magic over such a distance. I needed a medium.

The fire elemental roared like an inferno consuming a forest as my magic devoured its essence. I concentrated on setting fire to Angela's inn.

Chapter Forty-Nine: Fiery Passion

Acolyte Sophia – Lenath, Magery of Thosi

The door to my room in the village of Lenath's only inn burst open. I sat up in my blankets wearing a shift I bought off the tavern maid Xera was enjoying in the other room. My small breasts pressed against the thin linen as Angela marched in, her armor creaking.

"Oh, no," I gasped, my heart racing. "What do you want?"

"You're pretty flesh," Angela purred, drawing her knife.

My eyes widened. What was the knife for? A hot flush ran through my pussy as Angela marched on me. The blade caught the light from the tallow candle burning on the nightstand beside my bed. I shifted on the hay-stuffed mattress, pulling my thighs together.

"Please, don't hurt me," I moaned, tears burning my eyes.

"So long as you don't fight," Angela purred, "I won't have to."

I leaped from the bed and tried to run past her. She caught the neckline of my shift and threw me back. I squeaked as I landed on the bed. Angela was so strong and sexy. My pussy ached. I squeezed my thighs together as I cowered on the bed.

"That was very bad of you," Angela purred.

She seized my shoulders and pushed me down onto the bed.

Her red hair fell around her face as I struggled beneath her. Angela's breasts rose and fell in her half-breastplate. Her large tits were cupped by the metal and made an impressive cleavage.

"You make me so wet, slut," Angela hissed as her knife touched my cheek. "But if you keep struggling, you'll get hurt."

The blade was cold against my cheek. I tried to keep from trembling. Her knife was sharp. She could hurt me. I had to trust Angela. She slid the knife down my cheek to my neck. Just a little more pressure and she would kill me.

"That's it," she purred. "Don't struggle and you won't get hurt."

"Okay," I whispered.

"Mistress," Angela hissed. "That is how you address me, slut."

"Yes, mistress." My clit throbbed. This was so sexy. My heart raced with fear and lust. I was so helpless before her.

I needed to talk to the High Virgin and have her include bondage in the training of acolytes for the Temple of the Pure. It was such an exciting branch of female sexuality not taught. I was sure there were worshipers out there who would both love to dominate women and be dominated by sexy priestesses of Saphique.

The knife slid lower. She reached the neckline of my shift. The blade slipped inside between my small breasts. The cool flat touched my right breast. It slid up to my hard nipple. I held my breath, too scared to do anything as the edge of the knife caressed my aching nub.

With a quick twist, the knife cut open my shift. I let out a frightened squeak. My heart thudded as my right breast was exposed and, thankfully, unharmed. Relief flooded me and my pussy clenched in desire. Angela smiled as she brought the tip of her knife to my nipple and grazed my nub, a deft stroke that didn't cut me, only let me feel the sharp edge.

Pleasure rippled through my body.

"Mistress," I gasped. "What are you doing?"

"Playing with your delicious body," Angela purred.

Her knife slid down my breast and then cut through the fabric of the shift, revealing my other tit. She let the knife's tip graze up my breast. She almost tickled me with the sharp tip as she circled up my small mound to my pink tip.

I fought the urge to squirm and press my thighs together. My tart excitement filled my nose, mixed with tangy musk.

Angela leaned down and sucked my right nipple into her hungry lips. Her knife pressed against my breast as she licked and sucked. I moaned and bit my lip. I wanted to squirm so badly. My body trembled beneath me, but the knife pressed on my flesh kept me still.

"Such a good slut," Angela smiled as she moved her knife. "I can smell how excited you are. You should be scared, but you're not. Do you know why?"

"No, mistress," I squeaked as her knife cut the shift down to my stomach. To my pussy.

"Because you're a horny, nasty slut that just wants to please me."

Her knife reached the hem of the shift. The cut cloth parted away to expose my shaved pubic mound glistening with my excitement. She pressed the flat of the blade against my pussy lips as her lips captured mine in a kiss. She thrust her tongue deep into my mouth.

The blade was so cool on my hot flesh.

My toes curled. I moaned into her kiss. The excitement in my pussy burned hot as she slid the blade up and down my labia. My pussy clenched. Juices flooded out, coating the blade in my sticky passion.

"You make me so wet," moaned Angela. "Do you know what happens to sluts that make their mistresses wet?"

"No, mistress."

Angela shifted on the bed. Her chainmail loincloth dragged across my body as she straddled me. She pulled the chainmail strip up covering her ass as she backed her pussy up to my lips. She settled down on my face, her chainmail clinking as it settled into place. The links were cold as the front strip draped across my breasts.

"They eat their mistress's pussy," Angela purred, rubbing her hot, tangy flesh on my lips. "They make their mistress cum."

"Yes," I moaned into her succulent cunt.

My tongue flicked out. Angela moaned as my tongue piercing slid through her hot folds. Her tangy juices poured into my mouth as she leaned over and ran her dagger up and down my pussy lips. The cold metal brushed my folds.

I gasped when the tip pressed into my pussy. My flesh contracted about the sharp blade. I moaned into Angela's snatch as the excitement mounted. I fought my hips desire to squirm as Angela delicately probed my pussy with the dagger.

One little slip and she would cut me. I had to be still. I had to trust her. It was so hard not to move. My pussy had never been hotter.

"Such a cute pussy," purred Angela. "And so wet. Do you love my dagger playing through your folds, slut?"

I moaned into her pussy. My tongue dug deeper into her hot hole. I swirled it about, eager to please my mistress. The knife pressed deeper into my cunt. I kept my pussy under control as my hot flesh wrapped around the cold metal.

I sighed in relief when she pulled the blade out, then tongued her pussy harder. It was exciting and scary all at the same time. My juices flooded out of my pussy and my toes curled. My entire body trembled. My orgasm swelled in my core. I was so close to exploding.

"Keep licking my pussy, slut," Angela groaned, shifting her hips and grinding her hot flesh across my lips. "You better make me cum, or you'll pay, slut."

"Yes, mistress," I moaned.

My hand reached around to play with her clit. Angela shuddered as my tongue fucked into her hot depths. My fingers circled her hot nub. I licked and nuzzled as she rubbed something thick and hard against my pussy.

The dagger's handle.

I groaned into her pussy as she shoved the handle into my cunt. The round pommel at the base spread my pussy open and then the rough leather of the handle teased the walls of my sheath. I bucked beneath her and rubbed harder at her clit.

My pussy burned with fire. Angela pumped the makeshift dildo in and out of my cunt. I humped my hips and moaned into her delicious pussy. The pleasure swelled. My entire body trembled as every pump of the dagger's handle in my hot flesh brought me closer and closer to cumming.

"You whorish slut," gasped Angela. "By the gods, you know how to eat pussy. Oh, yes. Slata's cunt, I'm going to cum."

I held off on my orgasm. I wanted to cum with my mistress. The air hummed with energy. I shuddered as my toes curled. A tinge of smoke brushed my nose. I frigged Angela's clit hard. Her body bucked atop me.

"Sophia!" Angela gasped, shoving the dagger's handle deep inside me as she came.

Her tangy juices flooded my mouth. The smell of smoke grew stronger. The air hummed with so much power as I drank down Angela's juices. I bucked beneath her as my orgasm burst through me. The pleasure rushed through my body. I gasped and moaned into Angela's pussy as my cunt convulsed around the rough leather of the dagger's handle.

The door burst open.

"I smell smoke!" Xera shouted.

"What?" Angela moaned as she shuddered atop me.

"Can't you smell the smoke coming from this room?"

"I do," I gasped as the final waves of my pleasure ran through me.

Angela slid off of me. "It's just from the kitchen, Xera."

"No. This smoke is different. They are burning pine wood in the kitchen. This is oak smoking. That's what the inn is made of."

"And you say it's coming from this room?" Angela asked.

I sat up, my cut shift slipping off my shoulders. The air hummed. I cocked my head as I studied the room. Xera's ears twitched and her large breasts rose and fell. She pointed to the corner of the room where smoke curled.

"There's no flames," I gasped. All the hairs rose, my skin goose pimpling. "Where is it coming from? And does anyone else feel that?"

"Yes, there is something in the air," Xera nodded. "I can almost hear a man talking. He sounds...commanding."

"Magic," hissed Angela. "There is no way that floor could catch fire. There is nothing burning over there."

"We need to get out of here," Xera exclaimed. "Oh, no. The voice is growing louder."

"Yes. We need to evacuate the inn," I gasped, hopping off the bed. I snatched up my white robe and pulled it around my body, loosely belting it around my waist.

"Saddlebags," Angela gasped. "We need our supplies. Then, Sophia, head to the barn and get out our horses. Xera and I will help get people out and– "

Flames erupted in the corner, hungry red as they ate at the floor. My heart thudded in fear. I scooped up both our saddlebags and fled out into the hallway shrieking, "Fire!"

~ * ~

Xerathalasia

The burning inn lit up the night. Embers fluttered through the sky like falling stars, burning brightly and briefly. The villagers, most wearing their sleeping gowns, scrambled to put out the inferno before it consumed the surrounding houses.

The inn was lost.

Sophia and Angela stood nearby watching. Both had soot staining their faces and Sophia's white robes were soiled. They held the reins to their horses, soothing the frightened beasts. The voice floating on the air was gone.

338

"Who did this?" Angela asked. "Why would someone try to burn down our inn?"

"You have made an enemy," I answered. Those words I heard on the air were familiar. I felt like I had heard them before. But my thoughts were scattered by the roaring fire.

"But how?" Angela shook her head. "I don't even know any mage. Why would one try to kill me?"

"Maybe you just imagined the words," Sophia whispered. "What if the fire started in the next room?"

"My room?" Xera asked. "There was no fire burning in there. I had just finished pleasuring Feris when I smelled the smoke. It came from your room."

Sophia frowned. "Angela's right. We've had no dealing with a mage. There is no one that would want to stop our quest from succeeding."

~ * ~

King Edward IV – Shesax, the Kingdom of Secare

I stared down at the white, ceramic bowl that sat on the desk of my study. Since Fireeyes had departed, I found myself often staring at it. The bowl was filled with water tinged with crimson. A magic circle inscribed around a triangle was drawn in red at the bottom. Fireeyes had left it behind, but not before pricking his finger and adding a drop of his blood.

"I will communicate when the deed is done," Fireeyes had said nineteen days ago. "The bowl will turn red when she is dead."

Nineteen days since I hired the rogue mage. Nineteen days that Angela lived, a threat to my throne and my unborn son's inheritance. It ate at me. Angela was out there. I should have just killed her before she left Shesax. Why did I listen to Lady Delilah and give Angela this chance?

Of course Angela would discover the means to kill the dragon

Dominari, a monster no knight had slain in five hundred years of questing. A laugh bubbled out of my lips. Not only did she find a way, but it was with her ancestral sword.

"She'll kill me," I shouted. "She'll kill me and found the High King's empire anew if you don't kill her, Fireeyes."

I didn't mean to scream at the bowl. I reached for the crystal glass and downed the rest of the amber brandy. The alcohol burned down my throat as I emptied the snifter in three gulps. I set it back down and looked at the crystal decanter.

"My king," my wife purred behind me.

She waddled to me, cradling her pregnant belly. She was only a month away from term. Her blonde hair fell about her naked shoulders. Her breasts, swollen by her pregnancy into lush orbs, jiggled before her. She leaned down and kissed my cheek.

"Come to bed, my king," she whispered. "Do not lose your mind staring into this bowl. Fireeyes will not fail."

"He claimed to have her dead in a fortnight," I slurred. "Two weeks and more have passed."

"So? He will succeed." She rubbed my shoulders. "Trust my plan. Our son shall rule. No prophecy will deny him. We shall make a grand destiny for him forged by our own hands, not the simpering words of an oracle."

I closed my eyes and nodded.

Chapter Fifty: Grief

Journeyman Mage Faoril – Esh-Esh, Magery of Thosi

I didn't want to wake up. I wanted to stay piled beneath my blankets and slip back into unconsciousness. I didn't want to face reality. I would forever be a journeyman mage. There were thousands like me, all gifted, but none trusted with the deepest magics. No kings or princes would turn to me for counsel. No rich merchants would hire my services. I would never rise to sit on the Magery Council.

All because I botched the simplest spell that even the densest apprentice mastered after a week.

The boat ride back to Esh-Esh had been terrible. I huddled in the hold, wrapped in the blanket Evolia conjured, and wept into my hands. Everyone knew I had failed. I returned earlier than any of the others, naked and trembling. No one spoke to me. Not even my friend Saoria.

She had held her head high, certain she had passed.

Right now, in the highest floor of the tower, the results were handed out. I didn't bother waking up for it. What was the point? I already knew I had failed.

I rolled over on my bed and tried to sink back into oblivion.

It wouldn't come. Only bitter recriminations filled me. I had failed. I had prepared for every eventuality. I memorized all seven of the magical circles, I mastered all five of the elements, and I knew all 144 arcane inscriptions and when to use them to effect. I was ready to conjure horrors, battle elementals, and perform feats of magic so delicate that a single misplaced thought would cause the spell to miscast and backfire in my face.

And I was undone by such simplicity. How had I so profoundly failed as a mage?

I thrashed in my bed. Sleep had escaped me. My stomach gnawed with hunger and my throat scratched with thirst. I didn't deserve food or drink. I was a failure. I should just stay in these quarters until I withered away.

I would never be a master mage.

The sun was bright as it drifted through the window. Very inconsiderate of the sun. My blanket was too thin. I squeezed my eyes shut and shuddered as a sudden sob racked me. I couldn't even wallow in peace.

The door to the room banged open. Saoria entered. I didn't peek from my blankets.

"It is time to get up, Faoril," Saoria said, her voice cold.

"No," I muttered.

"Stop pouting and get out of bed, Journeyman Mage," she snapped.

I scrunched up in a tighter ball. "Just go away, Saoria."

"I will not be spoken to that way."

My blankets were suddenly ripped away. Saoria stood facing me, hands on her hips. She wore the black robes of a Master Mage. So she passed. I huddled into a ball and buried my face in my hands, curling up my knees to hide my naked body.

"This is pathetic," Saoria snapped. "You will get up, get dressed, gather your belongings, and vacate my room."

Shock shot through me. "What?"

"Right now, Journeyman Mage Faoril. These quarters are mine now. I will not share them with a girl so inept she can't even cast a

342

preservation spell."

The Master Mages had told Saoria how I failed? My cheeks burned.

"Saoria," I said, sitting up and staring at her haughty face. "Why are you being so mean?"

"How else should I handle a little slut that is loafing in my room?" A sneer crossed her lips.

I flinched beneath her. "Saoria..." Confusion filled me. Why was she acting like this? "Why are you kicking me out of our room?"

"My room. I am a Master Mage. I do not share a room with a lowly Journeyman."

"But– "

"Get up, get dressed and get out. That is an order from a Master Mage."

My mouth worked. My friend had changed.

"You have taken your training as far as it will go," she continued, "so you have no further need of this room. It is time for you to make your own way in the world and not sponge off the Collegiate Tower."

I swallowed. "But... I don't have any money. I spent my last coins getting ready for the test. Can't I stay here...in your room?"

"No. I will not have you lurking around."

"But...I thought we were friends."

Her laugh hurt. It was cruel. She seized my spare, red robe and threw it at me. Tears burned my eyes. I held the robe between my fingers as the tears fell, blotting the material a dark crimson. My body shook as I fought to control my sobs.

"You are just pathetic," Saoria sneered. "Now get out of my room."

"But...all the times we trained together. The times we...made love and shared things. I...I helped you."

"Yes, you did. And now I don't need your help any longer."

"You...used me?" My voice cracked as I said those words.

"Yes."

That one word haunted me as I pulled on my robe. Saoria's

eyes bored into me as I scurried about her room and gathered my belongings. I gathered up the few books I had bought over the years, stretching my stipend as far as possible. I wrapped the leather-bond tomes in oilcloth before packing them into a satchel. I didn't look back as I left the room and stumbled down the many steps to the ground.

I had lived in the Collegiate Tower for ten years. I enrolled when I was eighteen, eager to become a master mage. I stumbled through the grounds and out into the bustling city of Esh-Esh. In the far distance, the lake gleamed in the late spring sun.

I looked away and headed aimlessly into the city.

~ * ~

Xerathalasia – Lenath, Magery of Thosi

We left Lenath early the next morning. None of us had much sleep. The village bustled for half the night fighting the fire. We had to sleep in a field, catching a few hours before we rose. As the sun climbed higher and higher, I worried over that voice I heard before the fire raged.

"Angela," I said. "What do you know of magic?"

"Not much," the knight answered. "Sophia, you cast magic."

"I pray for miracles," Sophia answered, her eyes baggy. "I..." A yawn split her lips, "...only channel my goddess's power. A mage creates the power in themselves through ingesting cum." She shuddered.

"Or pussy juices, if they're a man," Angela added.

"Just as disgusting," grimaced Sophia. "I would never let a man's rough hands and whiskered cheeks get anywhere near my pussy."

"Oh, rough whiskers rasping on your pussy is quite the treat," laughed Angela.

"Could a mage control a monster?"

344

"I guess," Sophia shrugged. "Why?"

"When we fought the wyverns, I thought I heard a voice on the wind," I replied. "I wasn't sure if it was just distant villagers talking or something more. I was very distracted by fighting them and being wounded. But last night, I heard the same voice." The more I pondered, the more certain I was that they were the same voice.

"I didn't hear anything," Angela answered.

"You're human," Sophia said. "Your ears are not graceful and sensitive like Xera's."

A pleased smile split my lips and my ears twitched.

"Neither are yours," Angela pointed back.

Sophia shrugged. "Well, what does it mean? Who wants to kill us?"

"Angela, not us. The wyvern came first for her."

"Why would anyone want me dead?" Angela frowned. "Who would want to stop me from slaying the dragon?"

"You're descended from the High King," Sophia pointed out.

"So are lots of people. It's been a thousand years."

"It's said only the High King's heir could wield his sword," Sophia added.

"Heir's a broad term. It's another way of saying descendant. Besides, my mother still lives. And my aunt, a pair of cousins, and my grandmother. Wouldn't a few of them inherit before me, and yet the oracle says I could wield the sword."

"Oh." Sophia blinked. "I guess you're right."

Angela let out a laugh. "Does someone think I'll restore the High Kingdom of Hamilton? I'm a woman. I can't rule. Only men, in the footsteps of Holy Pater, can rule. Everyone knows that."

Sophia nodded.

I frowned at that. Why could only men rule? There were no male elves, and our society functioned properly. Rebelling against Pater was how Matar created her own cock to begin with. She broke away from his masculine dominance and founded her own children and way of life.

I held my thoughts and instead asked, "What do we do about

this mage?"

"Well, we get a mage of our own," cheered Sophia. "In two days we'll be in Esh-Esh. Then we'll have a master mage to aid us."

~ * ~

Journeyman Mage Faoril – Esh-Esh, Magery of Thosi

As night crept on, and my stomach grew hungry, I entered an inn's common room. I did not know where in the city I was. I had wandered all day through Esh-Esh, weeping over my lost dreams and friendship. How had I never realized Saoria was only using me?

Because I was stupid. I failed to preserve my cum for the test and failed to notice what a viper Saoria was.

The common room was loud, full of travelers. There were blond and tall Zeutchians mixing with dusky-red Thlinians and brown Hazians. A woman with bright-red hair, a Tuathan from the Lesh-Ke Mountains, perched on the knee of an ebony-skinned Halanian. Her right breast was bare and his dark fingers massaged her pale flesh. Minstrels played on a small stage, a man on a hide-drum and a woman playing a lute and singing a bawdy song.

I found a seat at a table in the corner. A busty barmaid sauntered over, the top laces of her bodice undone and her large breasts almost spilling out as she leaned over and smiled at me. "What can I get you?"

"A meal and a pint of beer," I answered.

I didn't normally drink, but everyone around me were throwing back mugs full of the frothy, brown substance. They were all happy and laughing. Why not join them? I had no money. I had no idea how I would even pay for the meal and drinks.

"Sure, madam mage," she smiled and turned with a sway to her hips.

Not master mage.

I pulled up the hood of my robes, hiding my face. My cheeks

were sticky from tears and my eyes burned. I had no tears left. My head ached and a low growl rumbled from my stomach. Moments later, a frothy tankard plopped on my table, spilling a few drops of the brown liquid.

"Here you are, madam mage. Food'll be up soon."

I nodded and cupped the large, earthenware flagon in my hands, ignoring the handle. I brought it to my lips and sipped at the bitter drink. My nose wrinkled at the smell. I forced myself to take a longer drink. The alcohol helped to wash down the bitter drink. The more and more I drank, the easier it went down.

I emptied the flagon and motioned to the barmaid for a second.

That one went down smooth. My insides churned as the alcohol floated through me. Fresh tears trickled down my cheeks as I went to work on my third. I was such a failure. I stared into the frothy, half-empty tankard.

"I'll never be a master mage. Forever a stupid journeyman. Not fair. I'm good. I'm the best mage of my class. Stupid Saoria got in." I grimaced as I said that name. "She's so stupid. How did she pass without me holding her hand?"

No one answered me.

My meal came, a hearty stew full of meat chunks and soft vegetables. I dug in, washing down the stew with more beer. The common room begun to spin. I bet stupid Saoria messed up some spell and made the world topsy turvy.

"Stupid cunt," I muttered. "She's as empty-headed as Biaute. I should be a master mage."

My eyes grew heavy as I worked on my fourth tankard. I earned a nap. I lay my head on my arms while the full inn clapped to another bawdy song. I pondered the lyrics, wondering why they were singing about a farmer's daughter replanting the carrots in her own fresh-plowed holes?

That seemed so stupid.

She plunged the carrot in so deep
the hole all wet and pink
and freshly plowed and full of seed

planted by the miller's son.

The words faded and blessed unconsciousness embraced me.

The hand shaking me ruined it. "Madam mage. Wake up."

"Huh?" I asked. My head throbbed. I lifted my head. The sleeve of my robe was caked to my chin by drool. I grimaced as it tore free.

"It is time to settle your bill, madam mage," the barmaid said.

My head was still foggy with drink. "I don't have any money."

"Oh, no," the barmaid gasped. "Master Dalria will be most displeased. He does not take kindly to those who cannot pay. And you drank so much. I would have thought a mage could pay her tab."

"Great," I muttered and collapsed my head on the table as the barmaid went to fetch the proprietor. "How can this get any worse?"

Chapter Fifty-One: The Grieving Mage

Journeyman Mage Faoril – Esh-Esh, Magery of Thosi

My head lay on the rough wood of the table watching the retreating barmaid. The world was blurry from my drinks. I couldn't believe this day. How could it keep getting worse? I failed my test, I lost my dream, I was broke, and now I owed an inn money for food and drink.

They would throw me in debtor's prison. I would have to perform menial, manual labor until my debts were paid off. I would wither away in drudgery. I deserved it. Tears beaded my eyes. A sob racked me. I turned and buried my face into the crimson sleeve of my robe.

Red for a journeyman mage. I would never wear the black of a master.

How could I have messed up such a simple spell? Preserving cum was something so simple, the densest apprentice could perform it. I must be the worst mage in the world.

Footsteps thumped closer. I lifted my head from my sleeve. The barmaid returned with a ruddy-faced man, his brown hair balding, though he tried to hide it with a terrible comb-over. In his younger years he was a fit man, but his gut had lost the fight against middle age and expanded before him.

"Good evening, Madam Mage," he bowed politely. "Nishia claims there is some small mix-up with the bill."

"No mix-up," I groaned. "I fear I have no money to pay."

Darkness crossed his face. "Well, that is a small mix-up. I see no reason not to take trade for your meal and drink."

"I have a bit of black chalk," I muttered.

"Chalk?" Master Dalria lifted an eyebrow. I believed that's what the maid claimed his name was. "And what would I be needing with chalk?"

"Well..." I trailed off. My head was still warm from the drink. "I could..." What did I have to my name? A few changes of robes and some arcane trinkets.

"Why, you could use your magic, Madam Mage," he smiled. "If you are a mage."

"I am." It was hard to keep the bitter tone from my words.

"Good, good, perhaps a spell to clean my common room."

I sat up. I could do that if I had any energy to power my spell. Did I bring any cum with me? No. I don't think I did. And I no longer had access to the Collegiate Tower's simulacrum. I would have to rely on regular men to provide what I needed.

"I could, Master Dalria," I said, "but I am all out of cum." My face fell and tears burned in the corners my eyes.

A hungry smile crossed the innkeeper's lips. "So it's true what female mages crave."

I nodded my head, heat crossing my lips.

"Well, you're in luck," he said, patting the crotch of his woolen hose. "Seems I have a cock right here. I can give you the energy you need."

My cheeks flushed again. I was used to receiving my cum from the attractive, if hairless, simulacrum created in the Collegiate Tower. The innkeeper was...less than desirable. But, I had a debt to pay. I slipped off my chair and knelt before him.

"Well, I need to see you naked," he leered. "How else am I supposed to get hard?"

A hot flush ran through me. My hands moved to the ties that kept my red robes closed. It was embarrassing stripping before this man. And somehow, that embarrassment churned in my pussy creating heat. My sex itched and grew wet as my robe fell open. I slipped the cotton cloth off my shoulders and sat naked before him, my breasts round and my nipples hardening. I wasn't as busty as Saoria...

I pushed my former friend out of my mind.

"You were hiding some nice curves beneath those robes." He licked his lips as he pushed down his hose. A cock sprang out, half-hard and swelling before me, a pair of heavy, cum-laden balls dangled beneath it.

I licked my lips. The energy I needed for my magic was in those balls.

Dalria groaned as my right hand seized his cock and my left massaged his balls. I stroked his throbbing shaft while my fingers played with his nuts, moving them beneath my fingers. My mouth salivated. I needed cum. I needed to feel like a mage.

Even if I was a terrible mage.

I leaned froward, squeezing my thighs together as the hot itch grew in my pussy. My lips brushed the crown of his hard cock. Salty precum leaked out, a preview of the true delights to come. My tongue flicked out, caressing the crown of his cock while my hand stroked him faster.

"That's nice, little mage," he groaned. His hand grasped my head and ran his fingers through my short, light-brown hair. "Work that mouth."

His words were somehow demeaning. Another hot flush rippled through me, tingling my nipples and clit. I squeezed my thighs again as I moaned. I opened my lips and kissed and sucked at the tip of his cock.

Dalria groaned as my lips parted around his cock. I slid my mouth down and engulfed the head of his cock. I sucked hard, my tongue flailing against the tip. My hand fisted up and down his shaft, brushing my lips while my other hand massaged those balls. I wanted his cum squirting into my mouth.

Dalria's hand tightened in my hair as he grunted, "Suck my cock, little mage. Work that slutty mouth."

I moaned and bobbed my head, taking more of his cock into my mouth. I sucked as I slid up his shaft, forming a tight seal with my lips. My cheeks hollowed as I worked up and down his dick. My ears filled with the wet, sucking sound of my blowjob.

My pussy clenched. It was such an obscene sound.

"Damn, you know how to suck cock," he grunted. "I heard all you little mages were whores at heart. You have to be to power your magic. Mmm, and you're proving it with that sweet mouth."

My eyes squeezed shut. I let go of his balls and shoved my hand between my thighs. My pussy was on fire. I shuddered as I ran my fingers through my neatly trimmed bush and brushed the lips of my aching pussy.

"Yes, you are a slut," he growled and ripped his cock from my mouth.

"What?" I gasped.

"I know you can take the cum in any hole," he growled and hauled me up by my hair.

Pain flared across my scalp. I felt so dirty. I was his whore. I deserved to be treated this way. I was a failure. Dalria spun me about and pushed me across the table. I gasped as the edge bit into my stomach. My hard nipples rubbed on the rough wood, shooting tingles between my thighs.

"You have a hot, hungry hole right here just begging for cum," Dalria growled as he thrust his cock deep into me.

"Yes," I groaned as the painful pleasure shot through my pussy. "I'm just a slut. I need cum."

I savored the degrading words as I bucked my hips. I wanted him to fuck me and spill his dirty cum in me. I was already filthy. The pleasure roared through me. My back arched and my pussy clenched on his pounding cock. Our flesh slapped together and he grunted every time he buried into my wet depths.

The table rocked beneath me as I worked my hips. I undulated.

I wanted his cum. I needed it. My nipples rasped against the table. The almost painful tingles shot to my pussy. Pleasure churned in my core, growing and swelling through me.

"Fuck me!" I hissed. "Slam that dick in me. Use me! Give it to me! Fuck my filthy cunt."

Dalria laughed. "Such a whore! All you little mages are sluts. I'm going to dump so much cum in you."

His hand cracked down on my ass.

"But why this hole? You have another." His fingers spread my asscheeks apart, his finger dipping into and caressing my sphincter. "You're such a slut. I bet you would love for me to cum in your bowels."

That was what I was now. A slut. "Fuck my ass! I'm so filthy! A slut! A slutty, whorish mage."

A failure.

"Pater's cock," groaned Dalria as he ripped his cock out of my cunt, "and Biaute's divine ass."

Hot pain and roaring pleasure shot through my body as he slammed his cunt-lubed cock into my tight ass. I grunted and panted as he slammed into my depths. My bowels clenched on his dick as he buried into my ass. He fucked me hard.

Over and over he slammed into me. My ass relaxed, the pain fading, leaving only the pleasure. My clit rubbed on the table's edge when he buried into me. All the sensations mixed and churned, brewing a powerful storm inside me.

"Cum in my ass!" I screamed as I thrashed on the table. "Flood my ass! Give it to me!"

"Yes, yes! Fucking slut! You love it up your whorish ass!"

"I do!"

My orgasm exploded inside of me. Juices flooded down my thighs. My bowels clenched down on his thrusting cock. My vision blackened and fuzzy lights danced before me. I gripped the table and screamed out my pleasure.

Dalria slammed his dick into my depths. Hot cum flooded me. My trained body responded. Cum was energy. Life force. I absorbed it. The reserves of power filled me to the brim. I could tap it and control the elements of creation.

The innkeeper smacked my ass before pulling out of me. "Okay, slut, clean my common room."

I worked the magic, sending a combination of air and earth to gather up all the dirt. Wind swept through the room, gathering the dirt in a growing ball in the center. I stood up on wobbly legs and controlled the magic, letting the energy course out of me.

Cleaning took delicate work. I disturbed none of the plates, glasses, utensils, or mugs on the tables as I gathered the dirt. I swept up bits of food left on plates. I added water to the magic, scrubbing the dishes clean. The ball of refuse swelled.

"Where do you want it?" I asked.

The barmaid gasped as she picked up a wooden plate. "It's spotless, Master Dalria."

"Refuse bin in the kitchen," the innkeeper said with wide eyes.

I nodded and stumbled to the kitchen. My ass burned from the hard fucking. I deserved it. I reveled in the degradation of submitting to the innkeeper's lusts. I was a failure. This is what happened to pathetic mages.

I found the bin and dumped the rubbish ball before returning naked to the common room.

The innkeeper had a big smile on his lips. "You seem to be in a bit of trouble, slut."

I flushed and my pussy grew warm at that word. "Yes."

"You work your magic on my inn, and I'll give you room and board." His smile grew, and he grasped my ass like he owned it. "You'll sleep in my bed, and I'll make sure you have all the cum you need. In fact, I know more than a few who would pay good money to fuck a mage."

I would be his whore, his prostitute. I was filthy, a failure. What did I care? Tears burned my eyes as I nodded my head.

~ * ~

Xera gasped in elvish when we topped the rise and looked down at the grand city of Esh-Esh. It was easily as large as Shesax. It was still miles away. We wouldn't reach it before the sun began to set. The gleaming expanse of Lake Esh dwindled into the distance. You couldn't see the far shore. The city of Esh-Esh was built on its eastern shore around a natural harbor.

Rising out of the heart of the city was a tall, white tower. It was higher than any building I had seen. The Collegiate Tower. At the top shown a golden beacon. It was almost a mini sun. Even in daylight. At night, I was told it lit the city.

"I never knew it was so tall," Sophia gasped beside me.

"That's where we'll find the mage?" Xera asked, her long ears twitching. The elf had been impressed by Norv and Allenoth, thinking they were true cities. Both of those could fit in Esh-Esh with room to spare.

"Yes," I answered. "Many master mages reside in the tower."

Sophia let out a squeal, "I can't wait to meet her."

"Or him," I countered. "The grieving mage could be either gender."

Sophia grimaced. "Let's hope it's a her."

I winked at her. "Let's keep going. Sun is setting. We'll find an inn and then head to the collegiate tower in the morning."

"Yes," Xera muttered, shaking her head, her green hair swaying about her naked shoulders. Only her belt from which hung her quiver, a pouch of supplies, and a knife clad her body. "So many people."

I heeled Midnight, my charger, and he trotted down the road. Excitement buzzed inside me. I was happy to reach Esh-Esh. We had no further incidents since the fire two nights ago. If there was a mage trying to kill us, and why would there be, he hadn't made a new attempt.

As strange as it was, I believed Xera. Who was our enemy? And why did he want to stop us?

Fireeyes – Yevix, The Magery of Thosi

The Mermaid's Lover, a riverboat, sailed out of Yevix harbor. My magic billowed its sails, driving it up the Royton River north towards Lake Esh. In a few hours, Angela would be in Esh-Esh. That was a dangerous place. The Magery Council wanted me dead and Esh-Esh was the heart of their power. I could work no magic against Angela so long as she was near the Collegiate Tower. Not without alerting those cowards that censored my research.

I needed to get ahead of her. From my spying thanks to the garnet pendant King Edward had provided, I knew Angela planned to move north after Esh-Esh, heading for the orc tribal lands to retrieve one of the pieces of the High King's sword. That meant Murathi, the holiest place to the orcs.

If I sailed up the Royton and across Lake Esh, I could disembark north of Esh-Esh and wait on the highway to Allenoth. No longer would I have to use intermediates to kill Angela. She would face me in all my glory. I would flay the flesh from her bones.

"Master," my simulacrum whispered, her hairless head bowed. She was naked, her perfectly formed breasts heaving. She handed me a vial full of her pussy juices. Her thighs were wet. She had been masturbating. I would need energy to drive the Mermaid's Lover north and get ahead of Angela.

I drank her tart pussy juices, her sexual energy flooding through me. The sails billowed as my wind strengthened.

I smiled. I was so close to Angela's death and winning King Edward's patronage.

Chapter Fifty-Two: Eager Mages for Elf-Cock

Acolyte Sophia – Esh-Esh, Magery of Thosi

I woke up in bed cuddled up against Xera's back. Angela was on the far side, her red hair spilling across her ivory shoulders and onto Xera's green-tinged skin. Angela was so beautiful, and Xera was always so sexy.

I licked Xera's long, pointed ear peaking out her green hair. The elf shuddered, her ass pressing into my groin. A hot flush ran through my pussy. I pushed my hand around her hip and down her flat stomach, reaching for her hot pussy.

"Wake up, Xera," I cooed in her ear. "I'm going to make you – "

I grabbed something hard jutting from her groin. It throbbed in my hand. I let out a shriek and threw myself back. I hit the edge of the bed and flipped off, landing hard on the wooden floor of the inn.

"What's wrong?" Angela asked, the bed creaking as she moved.

I groaned, my poor butt sore.

"Sophia?" Angela asked, crawling over Xera and peering down at me. Her large breasts dangled before her. Concern filled her blue eyes.

"Xera has a cock!" I shuddered. "And I touched it." I felt so unclean. "I need a bath."

I stood up and bolted from the room. I touched a cock. Even if it belonged to a sexy elf. I was sworn to never be with a man. I was a priestess of Saphique, devoted to the lesbian goddess. My stomach curdled as I burst into the bathing room. A bored maid lounged on a chair.

"Miss," she gasped, jumping to her feet.

"Hot bath now!" I snapped as my hand shuddered. "Hurry."

~ * ~

Xerathalasia

I giggled as Sophia dashed naked from the room, her pretty, pale ass shaking.

Angela joined me in laughter as she knelt over me, her breasts dangling above mine. "That poor thing was frightened of this."

Angela seized my hard cock. I groaned, pleasure racing up the tip. I was in heat. The painful ache filled me. My giggles transformed into moans as Angela playfully stroked my dick up to the tip. She still laughed.

I grabbed her breast and squeezed.

"Ooh, you're feeling frisky this morning," Angela purred as her thumb ran across the tip of my cock.

"And you are looking sexy," I grinned. "Mmm, so sexy."

"You're just saying that because you want to fuck my pussy," Angela grinned.

"So badly," I panted. The first day of being in heat was the worst. My cock always seemed to have a mind of its own. Back in the Deorc Forest, I would have my wife's pussy to fuck or, as was usually the case thanks to my duties as an Elvish Hunter, another elf's ass or mouth. I couldn't fuck another elf's pussy. That would be cheating on my wife.

358

But a human's pussy was fair game. I couldn't impregnate Angela. With no chance of pregnancy it wasn't cheating.

And I loved fucking pussy.

"Mmm, so what will you do for me if I let you fuck my pussy?" Angela purred, her grip tightening.

I fingered her hard nipple. "Why, I'll make you cum so hard with my thick shaft."

"Promise?" asked Angela with an arched eyebrow.

"Yes," I moaned.

Angela turned, straddling my head. Her breasts dragged across my stomach as she leaned down and licked my cock. Her pussy was right above my head. She smelled so tangy. Human pussies had earthier flavors than elvish cunts.

I buried my mouth into her silky flesh and licked.

"Oh, yes," Angela sighed between licks of my cock. Her tongue swirled around the crown, sending a hot shudder through my body.

"Mmm," I purred into her cunt. My tongue licked through her folds. She had less crevasses than an elf's pussy, but she still was fun to explore.

I thrust my tongue deep into her pussy's sheath as her mouth engulfed my cock. She sucked hard, trying to draw the cum out of my ovaries. I bucked beneath her, cooing in delight into her hot pussy. My tongue licked and flailed through her juicy sex.

Her mouth vibrated about my dick. I loved it. The humming moans from her lips shot wonderful pleasure through my body. My pussy clenched as I thrust up into her mouth. I gasped and moaned through her pussy, my tongue licking and sucking harder and harder.

Her pussy undulated and ground on my mouth. I found her clit, attacking it, bringing even louder moans and causing stronger hums around the tip of my cock. My hips thrust up, pressing my dick deeper into her warm mouth.

"So good," I sighed in Elvish.

My hands wrapped around her thighs. I caressed her pussy lips, coating them with her juices, before I went north. I slid them between her butt-cheeks and caressed her sphincter. She groaned, her asscheeks clenching around my fingers as they probed and prodded her backdoor.

I pushed a digit into her tight, warm bowels.

Angela moaned loud and long about my cock. My pussy clenched and the itch at the tip of my dick swelled in Angela's warm mouth. I sucked harder on her click and pumped my slim finger in and out of her asshole. Her hips bucked on my mouth and her juices flooded from her pussy.

I drank them down as she came.

Her mouth sucked so hard as she writhed in pleasure. Her stomach caressed my hard nipples, sending shooting tingles to the tip of my dick. The pressure built and built. My finger stabbed deep into her bowels as the cum exploded from my cock.

My entire body shuddered with every pulse. I loved cumming with my dick. It was so much more intense than my feminine orgasms. My cock spewed blast after blast. The salty cum filled her mouth. Angela swallowed with a hungry, eager need while her pussy smeared on my licking lips.

"Wow," Angela sighed after my cock popped from my lips. "That was good."

"Uh-huh," I panted, my cock still tingling.

"And you're still hard," Angela marveled.

"Sometimes, the first cum isn't enough," I moaned. "I'm in heat. My body has been readying for this day for the last four weeks."

Angela spun about, her lips salty with my cum. She leaned down and kissed me. I savored the salty treat as her pussy brushed my hard cock. Angela's hand grasped my cock and guided me to her dripping pussy.

I groaned as she sank down my shaft.

"Xera," panted Angela as she arched her back. Her breasts jiggled before her, the bottom slopes brushing against mine.

"Ride me," I purred. "Let me see those big, juicy tits bounce."

A smile crossed Angela's face and her blue eyes gleamed. "Ooh, you naughty elf."

Angela rose, her breasts thrusting before her, as she bounced on my cock. Those delicious orbs jiggled before me, slapping into her every time she slammed down my shaft. Her pussy was tight, caressing my dick with hot passion.

I grasped her tits and squeezed.

"That's it," groaned Angela. "Massage my tits. Damn, you are fucking sexy."

"I know," I purred, my fingers finding her nipples. I pinched.

Her pussy clenched on my cock.

Pleasure shuddered through me. The bed creaked as she rode me. I thrust my hips up, bouncing her on my cock. The pleasure swelled in my pussy. Angela rode faster. The knight grinned and her flaming hair swirled around her beautiful face.

"Yes, yes! I love your cock, Xera."

I smiled at her. "And I love human pussy."

"I bet you're going to get a lot today," she giggled. "You'll be walking through the city, your cock thrusting hard before you, and all those Thosian maidens will grow so wet and horny for you."

My cock throbbed in her depths. "Matar, yes. I want to fuck them all. So many pussies for me to enjoy."

Angela laughed. She leaned over me, planting her arms on either side of my head as she rocked her hips and moved her pussy up and down my shaft. Her breasts swayed in my hands as she rode me. She ground her clit into my pubic bone as she shuddered in delight.

"Are you about to cum on my dick, human slut?"

Angela's lips pursed in a smile. "I am, elvish whore."

I squeezed her breasts and giggled. "Then do it. Cum on my cock. Massage my dick. I want to flood you with my cum."

"Yes, yes, yes," moaned Angela. She slammed down on me. Her back arched as she ground her pussy against me. "So good. Mmm, yes. I love it."

Her blue eyes squeezed shut and her mouth opened wide as she came. Her hot cunt writhed about my shaft. Pleasure shuddered through me. My dick throbbed in her depths. The pleasure burst out of me. I gasped as my cum flooded into her depths.

Pulse after pulse of pleasure racked my body. I bucked up into her thrusts and joined her, moaning wordlessly. Our voices merged in an aria of pleasure. Angela shuddered, and then she collapsed on me and let out a big sigh.

"Wow," Angela groaned, her pussy still writhing about my softening cock. "That is a wonderful way to wake up."

"Not for Sophia," I giggled again.

Angela rolled off of me and laughed. "That shriek... Slata's cunt, that was hilarious the way she flew off the bed."

~ * ~

Acolyte Sophia

It was hard to enjoy breakfast while Xera fucked the barmaid on the next table, the maid's pillowy tits jiggling with every thrust. Everyone staying in the inn gathered to watch. Even Angela kept glancing over at the pair.

I could still feel that icky cock burning on my hand.

"Take my cum," Xera moaned, her hips thrusting forward.

"Yes, yes, yes," fawned the maid.

"Only an hour ago, the maid was licking my pussy in the bath," I muttered as I took a last bite of my porridge. Even seasoned with honey, I couldn't eat any more. My appetite was gone.

"It'll just be a few days," Angela smiled, patting my hand. "Then Xera will be back to normal."

"I know." I pushed back my bowl. "Well, we should get going. She's done with her fun."

Angela leaned over and gave me a kiss. "Cheer up. We're going to meet a sexy mage who will join our adventure today."

"What if it's a disgusting man," I pouted.

"You'll see. She'll be sexy and beautiful and we'll make love to

362

her together."

I smiled at Angela. I did love her so much. "Thank you. I do feel better."

"Then let's go." Angela stood up, her armor clinking. "Xera?"

"Huh?" asked the Elf.

"You ready to go?"

"Oh, yes." Xera had a big smile on her face. She pulled her cock out of the maid who shuddered and let out an orgasmic sigh. The elf left behind a pussy dirtied by cum.

What a pity.

"Yes, let's find our grieving mage."

I stood up and smoothed my white robe. Xera was still naked, she was always naked, and I almost envied her. In the temple, I would have worn a wrap of flimsy cloth that bared my left breast, stomach, and pussy. Now I was growing used to being clothed all the time.

Angela settled our bill as I strode outside the inn. Esh-Esh bustled like Shesax, and the Collegiate Tower was almost like the Lone Mountain looming over the town. But it wasn't as tall and didn't dominate half-the sky.

Thosians had a similar coloring to Secarans, pale skin, though their hair tended to be a lighter brown, almost blonde. Probably from marrying with the neighboring Zeutchians. But the city was cosmopolitan, and I spotted ebony-skinned Halanians pressing shoulders with dusky-red-skinned Thlinians. A woman with silver, shimmering hair walked by. She was all the way from the island Kingdom of Athlos. Her skin had a curious, bluish tinge and her neck had a graceful sweep.

I even spotted a tiger-headed Rakshasa from the Queendom of Naith.

Angela and Xera emerged from the inn, the elf still blushed and smiling, and we headed into the crowd. It wasn't hard to find the Collegiate Tower. You only had to walk towards the towering structure and you would reach the manicured park that surrounded the massive, ivory tower.

Up close, the tower made me queasy. It was as wide as the Temple of Pure and rose far above my head. Only magic could have allowed such a massive structure to be built so tall. An awe-inspiring demonstration of the Magery Council's power.

The grounds were well-maintained, the lawns verdant and the shrubbery pruned. Young men and women in blue robes scurried about, directing magic to cut the grass and gather up the clippings, or to sweep up the fallen petals from the peach trees dotting around small reflecting pools.

"The blue robes mean they're apprentices," I said, glancing at a young girl, no younger than eighteen, scurrying by. Like Sophia's priesthood, eighteen was the youngest anyone could enroll at the Collegiate Tower to become a mage. "Mmm, just like the novices in the temple. So cute."

A smile crossed Angela's lips. Lying in our bedrolls, I had told Angela stories of the novices I loved to seduce. It always got me in so much trouble with the priestesses, but it was worth it to seduce such youthful girls just crossing the threshold into womanhood.

"And the red robes?" asked Xera, noticing the young woman in a red robe following us. The woman blushed and looked away.

"Journeyman," I answered. "Most mages reach that level. Only a few are allowed to wear the black of a master mage. Journeymen have the skills to leave the college and practice magic around the world. These here hope to become masters."

I nodded, keeping my eyes peeled for any black robes.

I saw none.

We reached the tower's entrance. A bored, young woman in red robes sat at a desk. "What business do you..." Her words trailed off as she stared at Xera's half-hard cock. I did not get the fascination. It was like a thick worm dangling between her thighs, always twitching and throbbing.

"I am Knight-Errant Angela of the Order of Deute. Accompanying me are Acolyte Sophia of the Temple of the Pure and Huntress Xerathalasia."

Angela made a good attempt at Xera's full name.

364

"Oh, my," the journeyman mage gasped. "I see. You are on a...Quest?"

Angela nodded, "And I am in need of a master mage."

"Very well." The mage, she was maybe a year younger than me, scrawled on a piece of parchment. "Apprentice."

A bluerobed youth strode out, gangly with a pimple-covered face. He ogled the elf until he noticed her cock and blanched. At least we agreed on one thing. He snatched the paper, glanced at it, then rushed away, his robes swishing around his feet.

"You may have a seat. I do not know how long it will take."

I sat down on a hard bench. Xera and Angela preferred to stand. The journeyman mage kept glancing at Xera's cock, her cheeks rosy. Xera's eyes fluttered at the girl and her ears twitched. I grimaced. Would I have to watch her fuck another woman today?

"Madam elf," the journeyman mage said, taking a deep breath, "may I ask a question of a personal nature?"

"You may," purred Xera, her cock hard.

Other red-robed and blue-robed girls gathered, peering out of corridors at the elf. The mage manning the desk bolted upright and raced to the elf, clearly afraid another girl would get to the elf's cock first.

"Madam elf– "

"Call me Xera."

The mage flushed. "Xera, may I collect your cum?"

"For your magic, right?" Xera asked. "That's how it works."

The mage nodded. "Elf cum is particularly good at working life magic."

"Of course you may," Xera purred.

The mage fell to her knees and opened her mouth, sucking on the tip of her cock. I looked at the other female mages gathered, many of them greed burning in their eyes. Did they want to experience an elf's cock or just gather her cum?

I tried to ignore the wet, sucking sound and Xera's moans as we waited for the master mage to summon us.

Chapter Fifty-Three: Sophia's Quest

Knight-Errant Angela

Sophia was clearly growing frustrated with the wait. Noon had already come and passed. The young woman manning the desk only told us a master mage would summon us when he or she was ready to speak with us.

"They are very busy," she said with a serious face, her lips tight.

I remembered those lips wrapped around Xera's cock.

The elf was being blown again. The female mages were using magic to keep her hard, and the elf looked like she was in heaven as she came into another glass vial. The grinning mage, perhaps nineteen and wearing blue robes, capped her vial and scampered off.

Sophia lay stretched out on the bench pretending to sleep. She was not happy with waiting. During our trip through the woods, she had lost a lot of her spoiled pretension. She had learned that being pampered didn't help when a monster was trying to kill you, but some of her privileged upbringing still clung about her.

I could almost hear her teeth grinding.

"Knight-Errant Angela?" a stout boy in blue robes said, his face flushed. "Master Mage Saoria Nioamere will speak with you."

"Thank you, Saphique," muttered Sophia as she stood and

brushed smooth her white robe.

"Xera," I said.

"No," groaned the girl working on the elf's cock as Xera pulled away. "She was so close."

"Sorry," the elf said and followed after us. In a low voice, she whispered, "I am so glad. I never thought I could cum too many times. My dick's sore."

Sophia snorted a laugh.

We walked up the ramp that circled the tower. It was constantly pierced by tunnels as we moved up through the levels. The slope wasn't too steep, but I was wearing armor. I ignored the burning in my legs and kept walking.

"I think I'm going to die," Sophia groaned behind me. She breathed heavily.

"You spend too much time on your horse instead of walking," laughed Xera.

Sweat trickled beneath my armor by the time we reached the right floor, my side aching. The stout boy, only slightly out of breath, led us through tunnels to a room. He rapped smartly and waited.

"Yes?" a magnified, feminine voice spoke through the door.

"A woman," I grinned at Sophia.

"Knight-Errant Angela and her companions, Master Mage," the boy answered.

The door opened by magic, or so I presumed. A woman sat at a desk in a small room, clothed in black robes. Her dark-brown hair spilled down the back. She set her quill down and turned on her stool. Her eyes were blue and flashing, her lips pursed in a smile.

Not our grieving mage.

"I was so curious by your arrival," Master Mage Saoria smiled. "Please, come in and let's speak."

~ * ~

Acolyte Sophia

"That was a waste of time," I muttered as we left Saoria's room. The woman had been pleasant enough, but she had made it clear that no master mage in the tower had any interest in going on a quest.

"We have far too important work to do than aide a knight to kill a dragon," she had laughed. "We serve kings and delve into the mysteries of the universe, not assist in something so mundane."

"Well, she did suggest we could find a journeyman mage to join us," Xera pointed out.

It turned out that an accomplished journeyman could cast the Ritual of Reclamation with the same skill as a master mage. "Those journeyman who have taken the test to be a master and failed still have the skill for this ritual," Saoria had said, her tone dismissive and her smile sickeningly sweet. "You can seek them out in the market. This is a task more suited to their...achievements."

"We'll scour the market," Angela nodded as we walked down the ramp.

I grit my teeth. That sounded dreadful. My feet were already sore. I was the daughter of a duchess. I shouldn't have to wander a marketplace like a common housewife to seek out a desperate mage to accompany us.

"I hope Las jerks off all over this tower," I muttered, invoking the God of Lust's misfortune. He was always spewing his cum everywhere. So many monsters and unusual races were birthed by his falling jizz.

Angela laughed. "At least on pompous Master Mage Saoria."

I nodded my head in agreement.

My mood was even worse when we reached the base of the tower and headed out across the ground. Blue and red robed mages, all female, flocked after us, begging Xera for her cum. The elf ignored them despite her hard cock.

There had to be a better way than searching the marketplace for the mage. Maybe I could use a prayer. I didn't know all the magic I could cast. Saphique had gifted me with magic earlier. Normally, I

368

had to achieve the rank of priestess to work her magic, but the Goddess, in her loving wisdom, knew I would need it for this terrible quest.

My steps faltered. There was a prayer that might work.

"Angela," I said. "You and Xera head to the marketplace. I want to try a different method."

"Oh?" Angela frowned.

"There might be a prayer that could work. Saphique could guide me to the right mage."

"But you're not sure?"

My cheeks burned. "Well, I may not have paid as much attention during that class as I should have. The prayer may not do what I think it does. I might waste the entire afternoon searching for the wrong fox."

Angela's forehead furrowed. "You'll be alone in the city."

I rolled my eyes. "Esh-Esh is perfectly safe."

"In some areas," Angela continued.

"I'll be fine. I have my goddess and my dagger." I drew it out. It wasn't glowing. "See, no danger."

"Fine," Angela sighed. "We'll meet back at the inn at sunset."

I nodded my head. "Good luck."

We parted when we reached the end of the tower's grounds. First, I had to find somewhere private. I wasn't about to expose myself before the men streaming around the Collegiate Tower. I looked around and spotted an alley. I ducked down it and hid behind an empty cart.

I took a deep breath as I unbelted my robe. I pushed a pair of fingers into my pussy. I was wet– my usual condition– and I clenched down on my fingers. I took a deep breath and concentrated on my goddess.

"Saphique, I pray that you find what I seek." My pussy grew warm around my fingers as the spell worked. I pulled my digits out, coated in my cream, and I brought my fingers to my right nipple. My body buzzed as the Goddess touched me. "Guide me with your loving wisdom."

Breast milk squirted out, coating my pussy-stained fingers. I gasped, a shuddering orgasm rippling through me as the prayer completed. My fingers tingled, drawing me away from the tower. I held them out, and they turned me and pointed through the building.

I was tracking something.

I belted up my robe swiftly and left the alley, walking around the building. I pointed my fingers and followed them through the city, my heart racing. Had the spell found the grieving mage? Or was I tracking something else?

Like food. I was hungry.

~ * ~

Journeyman Mage Faoril

The man came in me. My body drank up his cum and the sexual energy contained in his seed. Then I performed a simple spell, gathering up his clothes and bringing them to him. The man chortled, pleased he fucked an actual mage.

I wanted to vanish into the blankets.

A week ago, I thought I would be a master mage by now. Instead, I was a whore. I would cry, but I was out of tears. This is what I deserved. If I couldn't perform a simple spell, how could I expect to be a master mage.

"Damn, what a fuck," the man laughed before heading out.

I dressed. I needed to work the common room. I had to earn my food and board. Dalria expected me to work. My red robes on, I slipped out of the small room and headed downstairs to the boisterous common room. Men drank and other whores perched on their knees while the barmaids scurried through the room.

I scanned around, wondering who would fuck me next. I really didn't care.

"It's you," a woman breathed, stepping before me, her green

370

eyes wide. A silver tongue stud flashed as she spoke, "I found you."

"You must be mistaken," I said.

"No," the woman said. She cupped my face. She wore white robes like she was a priestess. "Look at your eyes. Oh, you poor thing. What has happened to you?"

"Nothing," I muttered. "I need to get back to work."

"Work?" The woman frowned. "What work has a mage in a place like this?"

My heart ached. There was such pity in her green eyes. It stirred something in me. My eyes burned. I turned away. "I'm no mage."

"But...you're dressed like one."

"Hey, don't be bothering my workers," Dalria said, ambling to me.

"Worker?" the priestess asked.

Dalria put his hand on my ass, pulling me close. He squeezed. My cheeks burned and I looked down. Why did this woman have to appear with caring eyes? Why did she have to witness how filthy I was?

"She's my best girl. No one earns better than her."

"She's a prostitute?" asked the priestess.

Dalria squeezed my ass again. So possessive. Did he own me? He sold my body whenever he liked. I guess he did. "Yes. This is the only inn where you can fuck a mage. Then she'll demonstrate her arcane arts. She's skilled."

The tear rolled down my cheek.

It was so much easier when no one really looked at me. The men who bought me only saw my body, they didn't look into my eyes. That was easier. I could let them rut on me and sometimes I enjoyed it. I could forget what I was. What I used to be.

The priestess touched my cheek and brushed the tear. "How much?"

And now she was buying me. Money changed hands. I took the priestess's hand and led her to my room. The moment I was inside, I unbelted my robe and let it drop off my naked body. I stood before her trembling.

She hugged me. "Who hurt you? Who made you grieve?"

Her words were soft. "No one."

"I can see it. You're who we've been looking for."

"What?" I blinked blurry eyes. "What do you mean?"

The priestess cupped my face and turned me to stare into her eyes. "My name is Sophia. What's yours?"

"Faoril," I answered. "Journeyman Mage Faoril Lesibourne."

Her thumbs wiped away my falling tears. "Tell me what happened to you? You don't belong here. You don't deserve to have these men use you."

"I do," I croaked. "I failed. I'm worthless."

Sophia shook her head. "I don't think you are."

Her lips touched mine. They were soft and sweet. None of my clients ever kissed me. Her fingers stroked my cheeks as her gentle kiss warmed my body. I shuddered, more tears flowing. My arms wrapped around her. I clung to her.

I cried out my story.

As I told her about my dreams and ambition and how my simple mistake led me to failing the test, she guided me to the bed. We sank down onto it. She smelled so sweet and clean, not like the men I had been with.

"You poor, poor thing," Sophia whispered. "So you made a mistake."

"It cost me everything," I groaned. "I failed."

"I bet you won't make that mistake again," she smiled.

I froze. "What?"

"Everyone makes mistakes," she laughed. "So did you. So what? I made them all the time in the temple."

"This wasn't a little mistake. I could have died." I squeezed my eyes shut. "They won't let me retake it."

"Unless you do something spectacular," Sophia grinned. "Prove that you are worthy. I spoke with Saoria today."

I flinched at the mention of my former friend.

"Yes, she was a bitch," Sophia nodded, "but she also said you could cast the Ritual of Reclamation."

"Saoria said I could?" I frowned.

"Well, not by name. She did say a mage who failed the test could do it." Sophia smiled. "Help us restore the High King's sword. We need you. The Oracle said we needed the grieving mage. You can cast the ritual, right?"

"The Ritual of Reclamation?" I frowned. "Yes. I can. And the High King's Sword? What are you talking about?"

Sophia grinned, and then she told me all about her quest with the Knight Angela. Something changed in my heart. I could prove myself again. I could journey with them and reforge the High King's sword. It would be a momentous quest culminating in one of the hardest pieces of magic. I would prove I wasn't a failure.

I could retake the test.

"Yes, I can cast it," I said, my back straight. I felt...confident.

I had forgotten what that felt like.

~ * ~

Fireeyes – Northeastern Shore, Lake Esh – The Magery of Thosi

The crew of the Mermaid's Lover rowed the riverboat to a sandy shore. I stood on the prow, gazing at the peaceful countryside of Esh. The sun set behind us, painting the fields with crimson. When Angela's business in Esh-Esh was concluded, she would head north. Beyond the horizon lay the highway that ran between Esh-Esh and Allenoth.

I planned on being on that highway waiting for her.

The sailors on the Mermaid's Lover made not a sound as they pulled the oars below deck. Silence was such a wonderful thing. Before I had dominated the entire crew, their constant, coarse talk and bawdy songs had grated on my nerves. With life magic, I had stolen their minds and given them a new will.

The ship lurched as the prow hit the beach. Wood groaned as the ship came to a shuddering stop. The crew moved automatically.

They still knew how to sail a ship, I just removed all the other pesky knowledge from their minds.

Most men really only needed one part out of twenty of their brains. They wasted too much effort on such mindless drivel as thinking, reflecting, and lusting. Most of the sailors slipped off the ship while a few others attached lines and threw them down to the crew on the beach.

Silently, the sailors heaved the boat onto the beach, pulling it out of the water completely. In the morning, the nearby farmers would pray to the gods, thinking one of them had delivered the treasure of the ship and its cargo to them.

I really didn't care what they did with it.

My simulacrum moved to my side, her head properly bowed. She carried my belongings. Like a hound, she heeled me as I moved to the gangplank the sailors ran out. I descended to the sandy strand, my dominated sailors forming up around me. They carried an assortment of truncheons, sabres, and boarding hooks as weapons.

Not the most well-armed group, but even a mob could take down a monster. Or a knight.

Chapter Fifty-Four: Faoril Reborn

Acolyte Sophia – Esh-Esh, Magery of Thosi

The change in Faoril was amazing to witness. She had been a broken woman when she led me to this bedroom, ready to prostitute her body. To me and others. Her pain had been so raw. It was cruel what happened to her.

And then I gave her hope. Her back straightened, a strong smile crossed her face, and her silver nose ring caught the light. An inquisitive gleam entered her brown eyes. She was a petite, beautiful woman with short, light brown hair framing her delicate cheekbones and pink lips.

A stirring of heat formed between my thighs. She was a beautiful woman.

"When do we– "

I cut off Faoril's question with a kiss. My lips pressed hot against hers. I had hoped the mage we were here to recruit, following the prophecy of the Lesbius Oracle, would be a beautiful woman. I was so glad I was right.

Faoril was only startled for a second before she tilted her head, closed her eyes, and kissed me back. Her tongue was aggressive, pressing against mine and playing with my tongue piercing. I could sense what she needed. She had degraded herself for the last few days, allowing disgusting men to rut in her body with no say in the matter. She had been passive as she satiated their lusts, but now she was returning to who she was, rising out of the fog of her depression.

Faoril was a confident woman who knew power. She was a journeyman mage of the Collegiate Tower and came so close to reaching the highest levels of her order. She needed to be assertive again.

So I became passive. I was trained to read and please a woman, to give her what she needed. The training was to serve as a temple prostitute for the women of Shesax. They would make love to me as part of worship to the Virgin Goddess. But Faoril didn't need worship.

She needed confidence.

I moaned into her kiss and shuddered as her hands went to the ties holding my white robe closed. The ties came undone and my robe opened, exposing my pale flesh. Her hands pressed inside, caressing my belly. I moaned into the kiss as tingles ran through my body.

Faoril's kiss grew more passionate as her hands slid up my body to my small breasts. Her fingers were light and delicate. She was not a stranger to a woman's body. My pussy grew hotter. I pressed my thighs together as I knelt on the bed before her.

I gasped as her fingers pinched my hard nipples. Faoril pressed me back as she kissed me. Her fingers tugged on my nipples as I slipped my legs out from beneath me and stretched back on the bed. Faoril was on top of me.

"You are a wicked little slut," Faoril panted as she looked down on me, holding her body up with both her hands planted on either side of me.

"I just couldn't help myself," I whispered, my breasts rising, a flush coloring my cheeks. "You're so beautiful."

Faoril shifted her weight to lean on her left arm as her right touched my side and stroked up and down, sending ticklish delight through me. She reached up to my arm and pressed my robe off my shoulder. I wiggled to pull my left arm out of the sleeve as she leaned down and kissed at my shoulder.

Her lips were soft, and I moaned as she nibbled down to my breasts. Her hair caressed my tit as she worked up to my nipple. Her lips circled the aching nub before she latched on and sucked hard. I gasped when her teeth nipped me between her hard sucks.

"You're so aggressive," I gasped. "You're going too fast for me."

Faoril giggled. "Don't lie to me, little acolyte. You've been with more women than half of Esh-Esh."

"But it's what you want," I told her, stroking her cheeks. "Ravish me. Be dominant and devour me." Then I added with a trembling catch, "Please, these feeling are all so new to me."

Her lips attacked my nipple, nipping and biting. The pain was pleasurable. I squirmed beneath her, my pussy growing hotter and hotter. I resisted the urge to give myself an orgasm by just rubbing my thighs, but it was hard.

Faoril let out a growl as she kissed and nipped to my other breast. She left small, white teeth marks on my skin. I gasped and moaned with every nip. Her right hand squeezed my breast as she climbed up to the summit where my hard, pink nipple waited.

"Please," I moaned. "Don't. I'm not ready for this."

"Oh, you're ready, slut," moaned Faoril as her fingers squeezed harder on my tit. My nipple stood tall and hard, aching to be nibbled on by her. "You want this. You want me to fuck you until you cum. And then you're going to eat my pussy and give me such pleasure."

"Oh, Goddess," I gasped as she sucked my nipple into her lips.

I stroked her cheeks as I squirmed beneath her. Faoril's cheeks hollowed as she sucked my nipples into the depths of her mouth. Then her teeth bit. Not too hard, but just enough to send a jolt of pain zipping through me and mixing with the pleasure.

I groaned and squeezed my thighs together. My pussy was so wet and on fire. While she sucked, her right hand stroked my stomach, her fingernails scraping lightly against my skin. She neared my bellybutton and discovered the ruby piercing. She played with it as she moaned about my nipple, her eyes growing even hotter.

With a hesitant hand, I reached for the red ties of her robes. The crimson hue marked her as a journeyman mage. My hand tugged and her robe fell loose. I pressed inside and found her own breast. I didn't squeeze hard. It was almost a hesitant squeeze, like I was afraid of what I was doing, but too caught up in the passion Faoril inspired in me to stop.

"Mmm, that's it, little slut," purred Faoril as my fingers squeezed her round tit. She had bigger breasts than me even though I was taller. "Play with my nipple. I can tell how hot you are for me. You just want to please me."

"I...I don't know what's going on," I moaned. "You made me so hot, and my fingers...they just itched to touch you. You're so soft, Faoril. So beautiful."

Her lips returned to my nipple. She sucked hard, her cheeks hollowing. I groaned and squirmed beneath her. The hand playing with my belly piercing moved lower, reaching to my bare pudenda. My thighs parted just enough as she pressed between them and found the wet folds of my pussy. I groaned and squeezed on her breast as her fingers stirred through my lips.

"You are so wet," Faoril purred. "You like it when I play with your body, don't you?"

"Yes," I groaned. "I can't help it. You make me feel so...hot. So sexy. My pussy itches."

Faoril held up her fingers. They glistened with my tart juices. "Look at how wet you are."

"For you. You...make me feel so womanly. So wonderful, Faoril."

Faoril smiled as she smeared her fingers around my nipple and areola. I groaned at her delicate touch. And then her hungry lips swallowed me. Her mouth sucked my nipple into her lips as her fingers returned to my pussy.

She shoved two digits into my depths.

"Faoril," I gasped, my hips bucking into her pumping fingers. I groaned and squirmed on the bed, her brown eyes flashing up at mine.

"That's it, little slut," purred Faoril as she kissed up to me. "You just can't resist my touch. You want me to fuck you."

"I do," I moaned as I stared into her eyes. My fingers found her nipple and rolled it between my digits. "I just want to please you, Faoril."

Her lips smiled, and we kissed again. I tasted my tart juices on her lips as her fingers thrust into my depths. Her thumb rubbed at my clit as she inserted a third finger into my pussy, stretching my tunnel out. I groaned and undulated my hips, moaning into her kiss as the pleasure built inside of me.

"Are you going to cum, little slut?" purred Faoril after breaking our kiss.

I let out a whimper of pleasure.

She slid up my body, her breasts jiggling as they drifted closer to my mouth. Her nipple was pink and hard. I licked my lips as her left hand wrapped about my head and pulled me to her breast. I opened my mouth and sucked her nipple into my lips.

"That's it," she moaned as I sucked and played with her hard nub with my tongue. The bed creaked as she undulated. Her fingers worked faster in and out of my pussy. "Show me how much you love my touch."

I moaned about her nub as the pleasure built inside of me. I sucked harder on her nub, my lips swallowing her areola as my cheeks hollowed. I brushed the hard, round end of my tongue piercing on her nub, bringing a gasp from Faoril.

Her fingers pumped deeper. My toes curled. I moaned again. My hips undulated into her pumping fingers. Faoril's thumb rubbed faster on my clit. Pleasure shot into my core. My pussy clenched down on her digits.

"Little slut," Faoril groaned. "Cum for me. You can't resist me. You have to cum for me."

My body shuddered. My lips popped off her nipple. "Yes, yes! I can't fight it! I'm cumming, Faoril!"

The bed creaked as I thrashed. The pleasure flooded through my body. My pussy convulsed on her fingers. I moaned and bucked as the rapture washed through my mind. My eyes closed shut as I wordlessly moaned my bliss.

"Such a little slut," Faoril growled, her fingers digging deep into my cumming pussy. "Ooh, yes."

"Slata's cunt!" I cursed as my orgasm reached its peak. "Oh, yes. Oh, thank you, Saphique."

Faoril ripped her fingers from my pussy and shoved them into my mouth, fucking me. I sucked on them as the pleasure died, reveling in my tart passion. Faoril's face was twisted with wild passion. She needed this release after all these days.

"Little slut," she moaned and seized my light-brown hair.

I gasped as she pulled me towards her. She stretched back on the bed, her thighs parting. Her red robe slipped further open, revealing her neatly-trimmed bush adorning her wet pussy. Her hands pulled me to her cunt.

I buried my face in and licked.

"That's it, little slut," she moaned as she humped against me. "Make me cum with that worthless mouth."

I licked and sucked through her folds. My tongue piercing caressed every bit of her spicy pussy. Her hips humped as she pulled me tight into her snatch. Her hot flesh pressed around me, almost drowning me in her wonderful pussy.

My hands reached beneath her. I squeezed her ass as my tongue pressed into the depths of her pussy. I fucked my tongue in and out of her hot depths. She gasped and moaned as I swirled through her sheath.

"Yes! Eat me! Devour me! Pater's cock, yes!"

The bed creaked as her hips bucked into my lips. My hands squeezed the cheeks of her ass. She groaned as her pleasure built. I could feel her excitement. She needed to cum hard and fast. My tongue flicked up to her clit, batting it with my hard piercing.

"Oh, gods, yes!" Faoril moaned.

My fingers dipped into the crack of her ass. I found her

sphincter and shoved in two fingers. I sank up to my knuckles in her tight, hot bowels. The bed creaked louder as her body quaked. Her fingers pinched and pulled at her own nipples as my tongue assaulted her clit.

"By the gods! Your mouth! Oh, yes! Pater's cock, I'm going to cum so hard!"

I continued my assault. I didn't let up on flicking her clit. The pleasure built and built inside of her. Faoril's bowels clenched upon my fingers. Her back arched, thrusting her breasts up into the air as the pleasure rippled through her.

"Slut!" she hissed. Her body bucked again, and then her orgasm crashed through her.

Spicy juices flooded my mouth. I drank them all down as she quaked and shuddered on the bed. Her legs shot up in the air around my head and then fell back across my shoulders as she fell limp. Her head lolled, and she sucked in huge breaths.

"By the gods, I needed that," Faoril moaned. "I hope I wasn't too rough on you."

"I like it rough," I winked at her, pulling my fingers from her bowels. I popped them into my mouth and savored her sour flavor. "Do you need a minute to recover?"

"I need a day," Faoril groaned.

I beamed with pride.

Chapter Fifty-Five: Elf-Cock Examined

Knight-Errant Angela

"This was a waste of time," I groused to Xera as we left the market behind. "I really hope Sophia's spell guided her to the mage."

"Yes," Xera smiled, "though staying in the city has been a pleasant surprise."

My eyes glanced down to her half-hard cock swaying between her thighs. The elf didn't wear clothing, and her cock was on full display for all the lust-filled eyes of the Thosian women. They seemed to have a cultural fixation on elves and their cocks.

"You're just surprised how popular your cock is," I laughed. "Good timing on when you came into heat."

"It is not something I can control," Xera pointed out. "It was just coincidence that we arrived at the right time in my cycle."

"Let's head back to the inn. The sun's setting. I don't think we're finding any helpful mages."

There had been plenty of journeyman mages looking for work in the marketplace. But when I mentioned the Ritual of Reclamation and fighting the Dragon Dominari, suddenly they were a lot less desperate. Most claimed they couldn't even cast such a powerful ritual.

"We might need to find a master mage after all," Xera pointed out. "Perhaps if we talked to a different one besides Saoria we would have better luck."

I grit my teeth. We wasted most of the day waiting to talk to Saoria at the Collegiate Tower, and then she brushed us off claiming that no master mage had the time or interest in helping with my Quest. She might have been telling the truth.

Mages seemed like a cowardly bunch.

"Well, let's hurry, we can't deny the serving maids at the inn your cock."

Xera's laugh was a beautiful tinkle. She enjoyed being in human lands with her cock. Back home, she could only fuck her wife's pussy. Here, she had all the pussy she wanted. Elvish marriage practices and what they considered infidelity were so strange. In most human kingdoms, a married couple decided on whether to speak monogamous vows or to have an open marriage.

It was rare for the monogamous vows. Most couples didn't want to be that tied down even if they had no intentions of straying. Luben, God of Marriage, did not take kindly to those who broke his marriage vows and would often send his priests and priestesses to punish the man or woman who did.

I think I hoped to marry...whoever I had loved. I tried not to think about the fuzzy holes in my memory. I gave up my love for...that person...to receive the Lesbius Oracle's prophecy. If I had been looking for marriage, there was no way I would pick monogamy.

There was too much fun to be had.

Though the sun had set by the time we reached our inn, the beacon glowing atop the Collegiate Tower kept the city lit. It was strange. There was no true night in this city and the traffic on the streets didn't seem to dwindle as it grew later and later.

"Unnatural," Xera sighed, shaking her head at the artificial twilight gripping Esh-Esh.

"Everything mages do is unnatural," I answered.

"A true shame your kind does not know how to live in harmony with the natural world."

I chose not to answer. I had traveled through her forest and stayed in an Elvish city– I would take this over nature any day.

We stepped into the inn's common room, and I spotted Sophia waving energetically. A red-robed woman sat with her, sipping a steaming cup of tea. I smiled. Sophia's spell actually worked. Xera and I threaded through the common room, the serving maids all sighing as Xera passed.

"Faoril," Sophia said, motioning to us, "this is Angela and Xera."

The mage stood. "Knight-Errant, I would like to offer my services and skills in your Quest. Sophia has explained the situation, and I believe I am more than capable of casting the Ritual of Reclamation. That is, if you would have me."

I glanced at Sophia and she nodded her head.

"Just Angela," I said, extending my arm. "We shall be companions and the road is long."

"Yes, Sophia has explained the circuitous route you have to take. I do agree with your travel plan. It seems the one with the most efficacy."

"Good," I nodded. What did efficacy mean?

"Let's eat," Sophia smiled. "It was...hungry work recruiting her."

A naughty gleam entered Sophia's green eyes. I glanced at Faoril and color tinged her cheeks. It was clear that Sophia had already seduced the mage. I rolled my eyes as I sat down next to her. I leaned over and kissed her on the lisp before whispering, "How was she?"

"Hurting," Sophia whispered back. "But this is what she needs to overcome her grief."

"Madam Elf, you are in heat," Faoril purred. "My, oh, my. After supper, would you care if I performed an examination on you, purely for scientific research?"

Sophia groaned and rolled her eyes. "Not you, too, Faoril. What is it about elf cocks that gets every Thosian maid wet between the thighs?"

~ * ~

Xerathalasia

"Just sit on the bed," Faoril purred as she loosened the ties on her red robe. It parted, revealing her flat stomach, the inner slopes of her breasts, and her neatly trimmed bush. "And I will begin my examination."

"Of course," I smiled. "I am glad to help."

I removed my belt and set it carefully down, making sure my quiver of arrows did not spill out on the floor. I sat down on the bed, leaning back on my arms, and spread my legs. My cock was half-hard and twitching. I had cum many times today, mostly at the Collegiate Tower where a seemingly endless line of female mages wanted to harvest my seed.

Faoril produced a small journal from one pocket of her robe and a measuring cord from another. It was twice as long as her arm and knotted in precise increments. There were other items in the many pockets of her robes, including some which were made of glass and made the minutest tinkling sounds as she moved.

I doubt a human could even hear the noise.

Faoril wrote with a quill in her journal. She did not first dip it in ink. "Is that a magic pen?"

"Magic?" Faoril asked.

"You did not dip it in ink."

"Oh, no," she answered. "The journal is enchanted with fire magic. When I press with the quill on it, the page is scorched and leaves behind black markings. It's not as clear as ink, but in the field one has to make do. Besides, I do not have to wait for the ink to dry."

"Oh," I nodded.

"Now, let us examine your cock." Faoril moved closer and set her journal on the bed beside me. Then she stroked my dick. "I need you to be fully hard."

The mage leaned down and sucked the tip into her mouth. I groaned and my toes curled as the pleasure radiated down my cock and into my body. My pussy clenched and my nipples ached as I hardened into full girth.

"Mmm, much better," purred the mage. "And I must say, your precum is a little sweeter than a human's."

"Thanks," I said, not sure if that was good or bad.

Faoril wrote it down in her journal. Then she placed the measuring cord against my cock and counted out the knots. "Ten and a half inches. Larger than the average human cock. Would you say you are bigger than the average elf cock?"

"Mmm, average," I answered.

"Interesting," Faoril purred. "So elf cocks are bigger than human's. I better not tell any of the men that, they get so insecure about the size of their cocks."

"So do some elves I know," I smiled.

"And your cock sprouts from your clit?" Faoril asked, her fingers stroking my dick.

"Yes."

"Wow. I wonder where all the mass for the dick comes from. Is it internal, perhaps?"

"It just...forms," I answered. "A gift from Matar."

Faoril nodded as she stared at my cock. "Now I need a sample."

"For your magic? Because elf cum is good for life spells."

"Yes, and to see how much cum you produce." Faoril grinned. "This is important research."

"And the fact you get to play with my cock is a bonus?"

Her hand stroked me again. "Yes."

I groaned as she sucked the tip back into her mouth. I groaned and leaned back, my large breasts rising and falling as the human worked her tongue across the tip. She was talented. I guess being a female mage required you to collect a lot of cum.

One of Faoril's hands stroked the base of my shaft, brushing up to her lips, while the other probed at the delicate folds of my pussy. I groaned as she stroked up and down my folds. Her fingers dipped into my pussy.

"Faoril," I gasped in delight as she fingered me.

"Pleasuring a hermaphrodite is interesting," Faoril purred. Her fingers curled inside my pussy, and I shuddered. She dipped down and licked her tongue across my pussy, moving around her thrusting fingers and back up to my cock. "Mmm, a flowery pussy instead of the more earthy taste of a human cunt."

"I like the taste of a human cunt," I moaned.

"So do I," laughed Faoril. Then she swallowed the tip of my cock again.

Her mouth bobbed in rhythm to her fingers reaming my pussy. I groaned as the pleasure raced down my cock and mixed with the delight her fingers churned in my cunt. My sheath clenched down on her fingers as a shudder of pleasure washed through me.

"Oh, you have a wonderful mouth," I groaned.

Faoril moaned about my cock and sucked more and more into her depths. My pussy clenched as the pressure rose. Her tongue swirled about my crown, and then Faoril worked more and more of her mouth down my cock.

I brushed the back of her throat.

"Can you deep-throat me?" I asked.

Faoril thrust her fingers deep into me as her throat relaxed. I shuddered, my hips bucking up into her mouth as she swallowed more and more of my cock. Her throat was so tight about the tip. She swallowed and massaged my dick.

Then she hummed.

I gasped in delight. The pleasure built faster in me. Her throat teased my cock. She worked her lips all the way to the base before she slid back up the shaft. She sucked and moaned the entire time. My cock was in heaven.

"Faoril," I groaned as my pussy clenched on her fingers. My orgasm built. "So good."

Her fingers curled inside of me as she popped her mouth off

my dick. Her free hand darted into her robes and pulled out a vial. She popped off the cork with a practiced movement and placed it at the head of my cock as her fingers massaged inside my pussy.

"Oh, Faoril," I gasped as she brushed a bundle of nerves.

"You do have the spot," Faoril beamed. "And does it affect your cock?"

"Yes," I moaned as she attacked the bundle of nerves. My pussy clenched and relaxed as she stroked harder and harder. The pleasure shot up to the tip of my cock. Pressure built. My body tensed.

And then bliss erupted out of me.

Faoril beamed as blast after blast of my cum squirted into her vial. The thick, whitish liquid filled half the vial while I shuddered and writhed in bliss. Faoril pulled her fingers from my pussy and sucked them clean as I fell back on the bed, my breasts jiggling, my body buzzing with delight.

"Hermaphrodites are so fascinating," Faoril smiled. She held up the vial and swirled the liquid around before she recorked it. My ears picked up the faintest whisper. It reminded me of the voice I had heard during the wyvern attack and the fire.

There had been magic used against us.

"Now that is fascinating," Faoril said as she stared at the cum. "You produced twice as much as the average man. You come close to rivaling a simulacrum's output."

"What spell is on the vial?" I asked, not caring how much cum I produced.

Faoril cocked her head. "How did you know there was a spell?"

"I heard it. Your voice faintly whispering."

"And you believe that meant magic?" Faoril asked, slipping the vial into her robe. The cloth had slipped back, revealing a hard nipple.

"I heard a man whispering when we were attacked by wyverns far from the Rheyn Mountains, and then when our inn mysteriously caught fire on the road from Allenoth to Esh-Esh."

Faoril frowned. "You think a mage tried to kill you?"

"To kill Angela."

"Why?"

"I do not know. But you might be putting yourself in danger."

Faoril rose. "I'll need more cum."

"From me?" I asked. "I know you can cast that spell to keep me hard."

"No, no, there are plenty of men in the common room. I shall harvest them." A smile crossed Faoril's lips. "It can be fun. I will collect another vial from you before we leave in the morning."

Chapter Fifty-Six: Elf's Keen Nose

Acolyte Sophia

"I can't believe she blew every guy in the inn last night," I grumbled to Angela as we saddled our horses. I stroked Purity's white snout and shook my head. "She loves cock more than you."

Angela flushed. "Sorry. But Xera's not going to be in heat for long. I wanted to enjoy her last night after Faoril finished her examination."

The elf moaned nearby. Faoril was on her knees, collecting the elf's cum in a vial. She had a dozen or more of those vials on her, all full of disgusting cum. Xera shuddered one last time as Faoril capped her vial and slipped it into her robe.

"Well, I am all set," Faoril smiled. She gave Xera a quick kiss. "Thank you for your cum."

Xera had a beaming smile on her face. "It was fun giving it to you."

Angela pulled me against her armor. "Tonight we'll stop in that blue inn and I'll tie you up and borrow the maid's feather duster again. I'll tickle you until you cum."

"Promise," I smiled, my body growing hot.

Angela nodded and gave me a kiss on the lips. I clung to her, my heart beating faster. I didn't want to break the kiss and almost fell over when Angela broke it. I gasped and shuddered. She always made me lose my composure.

"Your horse is saddled, Faoril," Angela said. "Have you rode one before?"

"Not much," Faoril admitted. "I've never left Esh-Esh before."

"You'll be sore by lunch," I giggled as I led Purity past her. I remember how much I ached after my first week of riding. Now it still left me tired, but I was used to the strain. My thighs were a lot firmer and toned then before I left.

Angela had to buy Faoril a mount, a mare with a dun coat named Buttercup. The knight had grimaced at the amount. I had to make a stop at a moneylender and borrow money against my mother's estate. She wouldn't even notice the bill when it arrived in a month or more time at her manor house though her steward would undoubtedly complain.

Despite Angela's dismissive attitude to my mother's rank— she was a duchess— it did have advantages.

Outside the stable, I mounted with ease. Faoril, not so much. Xera had to help her keep her feet from tangling in her robes and then she groaned as she hauled herself up in the saddle. She sat there like a sack of turnips, gripping the reins loosely in her hands.

"Grip the reins tight, Faoril," Angela advised, riding past on her warhorse Midnight. He was a large beast, a stallion trained to fight. "Your horse needs to know you're in charge, or she'll go where she wants."

I nodded my head. "And keep your back straight and your feet planted in the stirrups. You need to lift yourself with every step."

"Why can't I ride sidesaddle?"

I winced, remembering how disastrously that had ended for me. "Trust me, if we are attacked, you do not want to be thrown from your horse because you rode sidesaddle."

"Let's get moving," Angela said, "we're wasting daylight."

"Okay." Faoril gave me a smile. "Thank you."

"Oh, don't worry about the advice. We're in this together now."

"No, for giving me this opportunity." Her smile grew wider. She had a pretty one. "Thank you."

I reached out and patted her hand.

Faoril was in pain by lunch. She was so lucky I could call on my goddess's powers to heal her. She was very grateful. When we reached the blue inn, Faoril stumbled off to bed and promptly fell asleep. Angela was true to her word and tied me up and tickled my nubile body.

~ * ~

Xerathalasia – Allenoth Highway, Magery of Thosi

The scent of unwashed bodies drifted on the wind. I wrinkled my nose, cursing my strong senses. Many of the rural humans were not as clean as they could be, but this group smelled particularly foul. I cast my eyes across the pasture, searching for them.

"Is it time for lunch?" groaned Faoril.

The second day on horseback seemed equally as painful for the young mage. Her face was twisted into a grimace and she sat stiffly on her horse. It was such foolishness, but we would travel even slower if the humans were on foot.

"Not too much longer," Angela sighed.

"Why does anyone ride horses all day?" Faoril groaned for the thirtieth time. It was her favorite complaint. "Why can't we hire a coach?"

"Coaches cannot go where we travel," Angela answered. "There are no roads in the orc lands."

My ears twitched. Footsteps thudded upwind of us.

"Angela," I said, "a group of unwashed men approach from our left."

Angela turned her head, gazing at the small hill rising to the northwest of us. "Is that a man on the rise?"

I frowned. How had I missed the figure? He stood on the

392

hilltop in black robes, his head covered in a cowl. "He is dressed like one of your master mages, Faoril."

"Really?" she asked, peering off in the distance. "You sure? He looks like a black blur to me."

"Very sure."

"I do not know why one would be here." Faoril looked around at the farms we passed. "It is curious."

The footsteps grew louder. Why couldn't I see them. The green wheat sprouting in the fields moved in a ripple like men passed unseen through them. "Faoril, could a mage transform something invisible?"

"Yes," she answered. "It's a simple spell to bend light around an object."

"A group of people?"

"That is more difficult," she answered, then her eyes narrowed. "Why?"

My heart beat faster. I pulled a string from my pouch and bent the bowstave. The wood creaked as I attached the string to one end. Leaving a bow strung for a long time ruined the string. "Angela, do you see the fields rippling? That is not caused by the wind, it does not blow in that direction."

"I see it. What do you think?"

"Unwashed men," I answered as I bent and attached the string to the bottom.

Sophia pulled out her enchanted dagger and gasped. It glowed.

Angela drew her sword with a steely ring. "That must be the mage that's been harassing us."

"A master mage?" Faoril gasped. "Why?"

"Does that matter?" Angela asked as she took a tight reign on Midnight. "Can you disrupt the spell?"

"Right, of course." Faoril took a deep breath, then darted her hand into the pocket of her robe and pulled out one of her vials of cum. She drank it down while Sophia made a retching sound. Faoril straightened in her saddle as she slipped the vial back into her pocket. "It feels fine."

"What?" Sophia asked.

"Nothing," Faoril said as she raised her hand and pointed at the disturbance. The air warped before her palm and then a beam of light shot out. The air crackled as the beam passed me, and I heard the mage's voice whispering even though Faoril did not speak. The lance struck the disturbance.

Light burst. The wheat rippled in a circle. The air warped and bent. A horde of rough-dressed men holding swords, clubs, and a few long hooks appeared. They did not react to their spell failing or the spectacular explosion that burst around them.

They marched on wordlessly.

I knocked and drew back. My arrow soared through the sky as Angela let out a load shout and heeled her mount. Midnight ran forward then vaulted over a fence. The ground shook as the large horse landed and raced through the field. My arrow took the first attacker in the throat and he fell without a shout.

"Something is wrong," I whispered.

Chapter Fifty-Seven: Fireeyes

Knight-Errant Angela

Midnight's hooves thudded beneath me as we charged across the field. The bandits hurtled closer. Midnight galloped with excitement, eager for the fight. He was well trained. I lifted my sword and set my shield. I wished I had a lance.

The men didn't scatter. It took discipline to stand before a charging warhorse. Where had these low men found it to strengthen their spine? Two more died, feathered by Xera. I didn't fear the arrows streaking by me. The elf did not miss her target.

The fireball from Faoril was a different matter.

It exploded on the right side of the men. Green wheat crackled and the five bandits fell to the ground on fire. None screamed in pain and none of their fellows reacted at all. What was wrong with them? I glanced up at the watching mage on the hill.

What did he do to these men?

Midnight struck the first men. There was a loud crunch as the man went flying, his body crushed by the weight of Midnight and his barding. My sword swung, cleaving off the head of another man. Then I chopped a hook that reached for me and cut through a bandit's chest. Midnight trampled another two before we broke through, and I began my turn to charge back into them.

Another fireball crashed into them. I tried not to flinch as more of the bandits collapsed on fire. Over half were dead. Why hadn't they broken? Professional soldiers would have trouble keeping morale against such casualties. They turned to face me, brandishing rusty sabres and crude truncheons.

I charged. Midnight neighed in exhilaration as we hurtled towards the survivors.

~ * ~

Fireeyes

I held back my dismay as I watched the sailors slaughtered. They had been spotted far too soon by the elf. And whoever that journeyman mage was, she had talent. She mixed air and fire to create that lance and disrupt my careful work.

It was difficult cloaking that many men. Not that it mattered. Angela had charged through them without taking a wound. I had never witnessed a knight's charge. Her horse was a weapon, trampling the sailors while her sword hacked and cleaved.

"I need more juices," I hissed.

My simulacrum raced to my side and handed me a vial of her pussy juices. She bowed her head as I drank it down. I closed my eyes as the power filled me. The sailors were almost dead. Angela's companions raced through the field as the knight set her sword to felling the last few.

But just because the sailors were dead did not mean they couldn't fight. I had prepared these men. My research had led to this startling discovery. I sent out my life magic to the men, seizing five of their corpses— the linchpins of the corpse horror.

Energy flowed out from the five, seizing ahold of the other corpses and drawing them together.

396

~ * ~

Journeyman Mage Faoril

Energy hummed in the air. Life magic was unleashed by the master mage on the hilltop. The corpses of the hacked, trampled, and burned bandits drew together. Angela's stallion let out a fearful scream and reared. Angela held on tight, shouting at her mount as he reared again.

The knight's hand slipped from the rein and she crashed into the ground. Midnight charged away from the corpses. My horse suddenly bucked beneath me, letting out a nervous whinny as the corpses dragged along the ground, pulling together.

"What's happening?" Sophia gasped in fear.

"Magic," Xera shouted and fired an arrow at the growing mound of corpses.

The arrow did nothing except impale a man already dead.

Angela scrambled to her feet and backed away, her sword held before her. The corpses swelled, all thirty forming into a figure. Multiple corpses were wrapped together to form the legs, and dozens combined to create the torso. Arms sprouted as the last corpses pulled into the abomination.

"What is that?" Sophia asked, slipping off her mare. Her horse reared and then bolted after Midnight.

I slipped off my horse before I was thrown. I had no illusions of my riding skill.

The ground shook as the abomination stepped towards Angela. The knight swung her sword, cutting into the corpses that made up its leg. Though she cut through the dead men's bones, the abomination did not feel it. The foot kicked and slammed into the knight.

Angela screamed as she flew ten feet through the air, her armor gleaming in the sunlight. Then she crashed to her feet in a metallic crunch. Sophia raced to Angela. The ground shook as the

397

abomination took another step.

How had this thing been created?

"Can you do anything?" Xera asked.

"I'm thinking," I answered. I threw another fireball, drawing heat out of the air. There was a lot of it when you concentrated it all in one place. The flames crackled on my hand and I threw. Fire slammed into the corpses, igniting flesh and burning along the creature.

Life magic animated it. Hurting the corpses flesh wouldn't matter. They were just the medium anchoring the spell. We would have to cut it apart, but I suspected the spell would just pull the dead matter back to the abomination.

Sophia opened her robe and rubbed at a hard nipple. It distracted me from the problem of the thing. Why would she do that? "Saphique, the Virgin Goddess that loves all women," Sophia chanted, calling upon her goddess's power. "bless this weapon so it may protect its bearer. Let this sword shine bright, a beacon to defend all women."

Milk beaded her fingers. Then she smeared her enchanted milk on Angela's sword as the knight struggled to her feet. The blade glowed pink with holy light. It might work. Divinely enchanted swords were often effective against spirits and dark spells.

"If we kill the mage, will that end the spell?" Xera asked.

"Maybe," I answered as I watched Angela race forward with her glowing blade.

I needed to figure out how the mage had assembled this thing before I could disrupt it. Angela dodged a second kick and swung with her blade. Blessed by Saphique, the blade parted through the leg. Energy crackled through the air. It was black and foul, reacting against Angela's blade. Her sword sliced through the leg, a clean cut.

But it didn't topple the corpse abomination. The creature held itself together.

The thing swung its fist. Angela brought up her sword, parrying the blow. She stumbled and fell onto her back. Sophia screamed in fear. The abomination strode forward and raised a foot to crush

398

Angela.

The knight rolled to the side. The foot landed with a loud boom, compacting the soil an inch. Such force. Angela swung again with her sword, slicing through the creature's "ankle", which was the bent torso of a man with coarse, black hair.

The energy reacted when her sword reached the middle of the corpse.

Did the mage form a skeletal framework? I cocked my head as the monster dueled Angela. She dodged and ducked its powerful blows. It was shaped like a man. The mage must have prepared these bandits ahead of time.

How would I have done it?

Sophia ran up and seized the front of my robes. "Do something."

"I am," I hissed in frustration. "Let me think."

"But Angela is losing!"

The ground shook. Angela screamed in pain. The knight landed in a heap.

If I was to make this thing, I would use five anchor points. Four for the limbs and one for the torso. He would have chosen five men ahead of time. Would he have drawn magic circles on them? A five-pointed star for symmetry? Then when the men died, he merely had to send out his magic into the five circles. With thirty men, five already branded, each point of the star would only have to seize five other corpses.

Then how were the five corpses attached to each other. A smile crossed my lips. He used a hexagram on the limb corpse, not a five-pointed star. They would all be attached to the torso by the star's sixth point. For the torso he would need a nine-pointed star.

Those were unstable. No one used a nonagon to make a magical circle. They were not the seven stable geometries of triangle, diamond, five-pointed star, hexagram, seven-pointed star, octagon, and the starburst.

"Angela, I need you to expose the corpse in the center," I shouted.

Xerathalasia

I stalked through the field, moving at an oblique angle from the attack towards the hill. The robed figure watched the corpse abomination fight Angela. My bow was useless against the monstrosity, but the mage was different.

If I killed him, the spell might end. Either way, he was a threat.

I crouched through the wheat, moving with care not to disturb the stalks. It was difficult to slip through the plants, they weren't wild and didn't part before me. Man had cultivated and twisted them from the natural grasses they once had been, and they did not respond to my presence.

But I was an Elvish Hunter. No human could spot me creeping through the brush. And this mage was still only a human despite all his power.

My heart thudded in my chest for Angela. I hoped she was holding her own. Faoril and Sophia were there to aid her. They would protect her. Sophia loved Angela. She would not let the knight die here.

The ground shook beneath my feet. Energy crackled through the air. Angela put on a show. The mage would be focused on it. That made my job easier. I lifted my head enough to sight him through the tops of the wheat stalks. I was on the periphery of his vision and with his cowl, he couldn't see me unless he turned his head.

I smiled and moved closer.

~ * ~

Knight-Errant Angela

My body ached. My head rang. Only Gewin's blessing I received before I left kept me standing.

"How am I supposed to expose its chest?" I demanded at the mage. "It's three times as tall as me."

The wind swirled around my body. I gasped in surprise as the breeze lifted me from the ground and hurtled me towards the monster's chest. My arms and legs flailed as I tried to control myself.

"Pater's cock," I cursed.

The monster swung a fist of corpses at me. I tried to duck. I only twisted myself upside down.

Then I was yanked up in the air. The world spun around me as Faoril used her magic to carry me. "This isn't working," I shouted.

"Stop fighting me," Faoril hissed. "I need to see a nine-pointed magic circle. It should be inscribed on a corpse in the center."

"Next time, give me a warning," I groaned as I flipped right side up, my chainmail loincloth swinging between my thighs.

The monster swung its fist again, and Faoril jerked me out of the way as she slid me closer. I groaned as my stomach tried to rise into my throat. She stopped me before the monster's chest. I drew back my sword and swung.

It wasn't my best swing. My feet weren't on the ground. I didn't have the leverage to transmit my body's weight into the swing. It was such a feeble swing, I was surprised when my sword carved into the flesh of the abomination.

Sophia's blessing worked marvelously.

My sword buried into the corpse. "Now what?"

"Cut," she suggested as the beast raised a hand. "Hopefully some pieces will fall off."

I jerked up my sword. The blade vibrated in my hand as the sword struck the energy animating the abomination. I sawed as it worked through, aware of the hand about to slam down on me. I closed my eyes.

My sword stuck something hard. So far, it had cleaved through bone as easily as it did flesh. So what had I struck? I opened my eyes. The monster shook. My sword vibrated in my hands as I sawed it against the hard point.

"I found something," I shouted.

"The magic circle," Faoril beamed. "I don't need to see it if you can disrupt it."

"Trying."

I strained harder. The abomination shook. Black light burst between the corpses. I was blinded. My heart burned and my entire body was filled with pain. I screamed as I was thrown back. The world spun about me again, my stomach churning.

I braced myself for the impact with the ground. It never came.

Instead, I settled down at Sophia's feet.

"You did it," grinned the Acolyte. She threw her arms around me.

I looked back at the corpse abomination. It had fallen to pieces. "How did I do that?"

~ * ~

Fireeyes

I focused on the mage. She had figured out my creation. Who was she? Why was she only wearing red robes? The test was last week. A journeyman of her skill would have been invited to test. No, she would have been forced to test.

"I need more juices," I snarled.

The simulacrum raced back up the hill, holding another vial. I would have to go down there and kill Angela myself. I tossed back my head and drank the pussy juices. More power flooded my body. The five elements were at my control.

I summoned heat.

"Sir!" called out my simulacrum. She pointed to my right.

I turned. An arrow struck me in the chest.

I stumbled back into my simulacrum's arms. Shock filled me as I stared down at the shaft sprouting from my body. The arrow had

402

penetrated deep into my lungs. I struggled to breathe. Blood poured from my lips. I fixed my gaze on the elf. She had snuck up on me. She drew a second arrow.

It struck me in the neck.

My blood poured out. I was dying.

"I have the amulet, sir," the simulacrum said, pulling it out of her pouch and pressing it to my neck.

I had to gather my magic. It was hard. My vision fuzzed as the world grew dark. My limbs were already cold. I had prepared for this. I had delved into the darkest corners of magic. I had bloodied my hands with research the cowards of the Magery Council were too afraid of.

I had prepared a phylactery.

I poured my magic into the gem as my body died.

~ * ~

Acolyte Sophia

I nursed Angela. Her lips sucked hungrily at my breast milk as her battered body healed. I kept staring at the mound of corpses that had animated and tried to kill us. On the hilltop, Xera stood, a knocked arrow pointed at a kneeling figure.

"I think that's a simulacrum," Faoril said as she gazed at the hill. "She would be his source of pussy juices to power his magic."

"Oh," I answered. "But he's dead?"

"I think so," Faoril smiled. "Xera hit him twice with her arrows and she stands over his corpse."

"Who was he?" I asked.

"Yes," Angela growled. "I need to know."

Angela pushed herself to her feet and stalked to the hill. I followed after, closing up my robes and tying them together. Faoril strode at my side. Her eyes were intense. During the fight, she had been so calm, standing there studying the thing instead of panicking.

I knew I wanted to run, but I couldn't let Angela die.

"You were brave," I said.

"Huh?" asked the mage.

"You stood there so calm. Weren't you scared?"

"No." Faoril frowned. "I was...trying to understand it. The thing was an impressive feat of magic. It was a puzzle I had to solve. I really didn't have the mental energy to spare on being scared."

"It was an abomination," I gasped. "Not something to be admired."

"No, it shouldn't be admired." Faoril shook her head. "Training for the test is all about staying calm while things like that happen. A mage that loses her composure cannot be trusted with truly dangerous magic."

We reached the hill and began climbing. A woman without any hair on her head knelt beside the dead mage. She looked calm, dressed in simple white robes in the same style as Faoril. The woman seemed so alien without hair, her head smooth as an eggshell.

"Simulacrum," Faoril asked, "who was your previous master?"

"Fireeyes," she answered calmly .

Faoril gasped. "Why would he be after you?" The mage looked at Angela. "The Magery Council has ordered his execution for the perversity of his magic."

"Looks like Xera did them a favor," Sophia giggled.

"You do not understand," Faoril gasped, "he was the most dangerous warlock in the world. Who are your enemies, Angela, that they could hire this man?"

Angela shook her head, her eyes wide, and shot me a glance. I didn't know what to say. Who would want to stop us from slaying the dragon?

~ * ~

Lady Delilah – Allenoth Highway, Magery of Thosi

I smiled as I sat on the fence, stroking my red hair, and watched Angela and her group stand over the dead warlock. It had been breathtaking watching her fight the abomination made of corpses. She danced with such grace as she flowed through her forms. She was handling the dark warlock's attacks well. It was wise of her to seek Gewin's priest and receive the God of War's blessing.

I needed to go back to Shesax and rein in King Edward. He was not following my plan. Sending a dark warlock to kill Angela would only let her know she had an enemy. The king was such a foolish, young man. I should spank him the next time I see him.

I watched the descendant of the lilies and heir to the High King fight with grace.

Edward had every right to fear her.

Pride crossed my lips. I had guided Angela, subtly nudging her into the knighthood. I had watched her blossom into a woman. My heart beat wildly in my chest. Her beauty had captivated me since first I saw her.

I knew then Angela was the woman I loved.

I slipped off the fence post. I couldn't remain around here. It would not do for Angela to see me. I touched the pendant around my throat. It was a triune set of amulets, each attuned to the others. The second hung around Angela's neck, and the foolish Edward had given the third to the warlock so the foul man could hunt down Angela.

Yes, I was most displeased with his majesty.

I strode down the road, my fingers clenching. He needed to learn his place.

To be continued...

Glossary

Gods

Pater: Father of the Gods, married to Slata. Through her, the dual-sexed races were born. Through his numerous affairs, he has birthed many gods, demigods, and heroes of renown, including the long dead High King Peter.

Matar: First goddess and former wife of Pater. She created her own cock and impregnated herself, birthing the five hermaphroditic races.

Slata: Mother of the Gods, married to Pater. Mother of many of the gods, demigods, and the dual-sexed races.

Saphique: The Virgin Goddess, patron of maidens and lesbians.

Seljan: The God of Commerce.

Rithi: The Goddess of Art.

Krab: The God of Craftsmen.

Biaute: The Goddess of Beauty.

Dauthaz: The God of Death.

Cernere: The Goddess of Thief.

Cnawen: The God of Knowledge.

Firmare: The Goddess of Farm.

Luben: The God of Love.

Iustia: The Goddess of Justice.

Las: The God of Lust, father of many monsters and the single-sexed races.

Lagu: The Goddess of Law.

Gewin: The God of War.

Illth: The Goddess of Illness.

Throwia: The Goddess of Suffering.

Henta: The Goddess of Hunting.

Vedr: The Goddess of Weather

Miscellaneous

The Altar of Souls: An ancient artifact believed to be used by the God Krab to forge powerful artifacts, including the High King's own sword.

Angels: A race of demigoddess born of Pater and his wife Slata. They serve the two gods as their messengers, wearing chastity belts to protect their virtue. Only at their mother's command can they remove their chastity belt and have sex. They have white wings and beatific visages.

Avian: A dual-sex race of humanoids with delicate bones capable of transforming into birds. They live in the islands of the Nimborgoth, especially The Isle of the Birds. They have cultivated the art of shamanism.

Basilisk: A monstrous race created by the Biomancer Vebrin that are lizard-like but with the beak and comb of a rooster. Their yellow eyes cause petrification and their bites are venomous.

Barguest: A race of monsters that superficially resembled dogs. They have no fur but midnight-black skin, razor sharp teeth, longer snouts, and yellow eyes. They can change into a human appearance, but they still have the black skin. Created by a fairy queen that cursed a human forming the first barguest.

Biomancer: A mage who is well versed in life magic. A line of research outlawed by the Magery Council. Biomancer Vebrin is the most famous, responsible for creating many monsters.

Biomancer Vebrin: The most infamous warlock in the world. He died centuries before High King Peter. Through his magic, based out of his labs at Drakin Castle in the Haunted Forest, he created many of the monsters which plague the world. He died under mysterious circumstances.

Centaur: Once a single-sex, all-male race of half-man/half-horse humanoids. They were able to successfully breed with human females to the point that their children are either male centaurs or female humans.

Changeling: A single-sexed, all male race that can only reproduce with married duel-sexed females. They can assume any shape and have the unique ability to take the form of the man any woman loves, including certain memories and mannerism to make the impersonation flawlessly. They seduce women in the form of their husbands and it isn't until the son that resulted from the union hits puberty and turns into his changeling form that this is ever discovered. In their natural form, they superficially resemble elves but with midnight-black skin and white hair.

Coautl: Intelligent, feathered serpent monsters that dwell in the jungle. They can discharge lightning to stun their prey. They were thought to be created by avian shamans.

Dominari: The last living dragon. Five hundred years ago she attacked Eastern Zeutch, destroyed three cities, and created the Desolation, a huge swath of land before the Despeir Mountains left barren by her attack.

Dragon: A hermaphroditic race birthed by Matar and associated by fire. Because this race had few members, the concentration of their Goddess Mother's powers allowed them to shapechange into beasts of incredible size capable of breathing fire and flying. They can control when they have their cocks. Dominari is believed to be the last dragon living and the most dangerous of her race. The rest were exterminated by heroes, knights, and High King Peter.

Dryad: A single-sex race bonded with their tree. Usually friendly to passersby.

Dwarves: A dual-sex race of humanoids that live underground. They have seven males born for every female. Their women have incredible sex drives, while their men have hardly any. A female dwarf will have up to seven husbands to satisfy her desires and is kept secluded to keep them from frolicking with other races.

Efreet: A demigod race born of Seljan and Vedr. They can only reproduce with jinn, often keeping them as sex slave. They have innate fire magic.

Elves: A hermaphroditic race of humanoids birthed by Matar, associated with the element of life. They are tall and graceful and only have their cocks three days a month when the go into heat.

Elemental: Animated forces of nature created by a shaman.

The Empire of Shizhuth: A large empire to the east separated from the western nations by the Despeir Mountains. This land is ruled over by the nagas. Shizhuthian humans are characteirzed by dusky skin and dark hair.

Erinyes: Three demigoddesses birthed of Las and Slata. They represent their mother's anger at being tricked by Las into having sex and punish their mother's enemies. They cannot be killed, but if their quarry makes them cum, they will abandon their mission to kill them.

Faerie: A race of demigods birthed of Las and Cernere. They have great command over spirits, using them to create powerful magical effects. They created their own world, another dimension, that they live in. They have butterfly-like wings and colorful hair.

The Fallen Kingdom of Modan: A mighty dwarven nation underneath the Lesh-Ke Mountains that collapsed 200 years ago.

The Federation of Deoraciynae: The nation of elves living in the Deorc Forest. Deoraciynaen Elves are characterized by green-tinted skin and green hair.

The Federation of Larg: A loose group of orc tribes living in the tundras north of Secare and Zeutch. Largian orcs are characterized by swarthy skin and woolly, black hair.

Ghoul: A human twisted into a murderous, cannibal killer through life magic. Perfected by the Warlocks of Chevsa.

Giganraneae: A single-sex, all female race of intelligent spiders that breed by implanting eggs in women's wombs.

Gnome: A hermaphroditic race of humanoids birthed by Matar and associated with the element of earth. They stand half the height of humans and live underground. They have their cocks for all but three days of a month when they are fertile.

Gorgon: A monstrous race birthed in the Biomancer Verthan's labs. They appear as beautiful women that can transform into serpents. When a man cums within them, he is turned to stone.

Halfling: A race of dual-sex humanoids that stand half the height of a human characterized by bronze skin and metallic hair. They are fame sailors and Nimborgoth. They have seven females born for every male, and their horny males keep harems of wives, capable of satisfying all of them.

High King Peter: The demigod son of Pater and a human woman. Gifted a powerful sword capable of slaying a dragon by his divine father, High King Peter conquered most of the western world and founded an empire. With the aid of his two wives, Queen Aria and Queen Rose, he ruled for decades. But the Goddess Slata, jealous of all her husband's bastards, cursed him, ensuring all his sons died. Only his daughter, Lily, survived but she and her descendants would only have daughters so none of his blood could ever rule again. After his death, his sword was shattered into five pieces and hidden throughout the world.

The High Kingdom of Hamilten: Founded a thousand years ago by Peter, the demigod son of the God Pater. He united the western kingdoms around the Nimborgoth into a unified which sadly did not survive his death thanks to the Goddess Slata's meddling.

Human: A dual-sexed race that dominates much of the world.

Imps: An all-male, single-sex race of red, gnarled humanoids that are almost always masturbating. They reproduce by ejaculating into lava and thus breed like vermin around volcanoes.

Jinn: An all-female race of demigoddesses born from Seljan and Vedr. They can only reproduce with efreet, and enjoy being dominated, often ending up in the harems of efreet as sex slaves. They have innate illusory powers and can be chained into extra-dimensional spaces contained in lamps or bottles.

Karabasan: A male spirit that possesses women and slowly turns them into a man.

The Kingdom of Althos: An island kingdom birthed out of the collapse of the High Kingdom of Hamilten. Althosians are characterized by pale skin with a reddish hue and gold to silver hair.

The Kingdom of Haz: One of the countries birthed out of the collapse of the High Kingdom of Hamilten. Hazians are characterized by light-brown skin and dark hair.

The Kingdom of Secare: One of the countries birthed out of the High Kingdom of Hamilten. Secarens are characterized by pale skin and brown to black hair.

The Kingdom of Thlin: One of the countries birthed out of the collapse of the High Kingdom of Hamilten. A kingdom marked by many islands and a strong tradition of fishing. Thlinians are characterized by reddish skin and light-blond hair.

The Kingdom of Valya: One of the countries birthed out of the collapse of the High Kingdom of Hamilten. Valyans are characterized by bluish skin with red to black hair.

Kobold: An offshoot of the Goblin race who live above ground, common in the Lesh-Ke Mountains.

Lamia: A single-sex, all female race of petite humans with cat-like features including triangular ears, slitted eyes, and a swishing tail. They are playful and prefer going around naked. Many are enslaved by the nagas of the Empire of Shizhuth.

Lemure: A type of spirit that look shadowy and gangly.

The League of Seven: An economic alliance between the seven great city-states of the Nimborgoth consisting of the three human cities (Grahata, Hargone, and Raratha), the three halfling cities (Anolucia, Baraconia, and Thaville), and the nixie city (Orcona)

Mage: A practitioner of magic trained to control the five elements. They use a medium, typically sexual fluids, to power their magic. The term mage has become associated specifically with the practitioners trained and associated with the Magery Council of Thosi.

The Magery of Thosi: One of the countries birthed out of the collapse of the High Kingdom of Hamilten. Unlike the others, it is ruled by the Magery Council of the Collegiate Tower instead of a hereditary monarchy. Thosian humans have pale skin and light-brown to dark-brown hair.

Mermaid: A race of single-sex females birthed when Las's cum splattered the seas. They form triune marriages with local fisthermen and their fisherwives. Found in most costal regions.

The Minotaur: A demigod born of Gewin and Cernere. A brutal warrior and ugly monster Imprisoned in the Labyrinth by his mother.

The Mirage Gardens: A mythical place of riches ruled by a cruel efreet. It's location is never in the same place, always moving around the Hargone Desert.

Naga: A single-sex, all-female race that possess the lower bodies of a serpent. They mate with humans to produce daughters. The nagas of Shizhuth have founded a dark empire. They are capable of shadowmancing and teaching it to their human favorites.

Nixie: A hermaphroditic race born from Matar and embodying the element of water. They are always hermaphroditic with blue skin and blue to seagreen hair.

Ooze: An asexual blob that are jelly-like and ooze around. They ingest sexual fluids of other creatures to aide their reproduction, which is accomplished by splitting in half. They are harmless scavengers. Some varieties can mimic people but behave oddly.

Oracle: A collection of demigoddesses daughters born of Cnawen and Rithi, each appearing as a young maiden. They are capable of giving prophecy to those they have sex with. The most famous are the Oracle Sekar, the Oracle of the Sands, the Oracle of Whispers, and the Oracle of Lesbius.

Orc: A dual-sexed race that stand taller and are stronger than humans with a brutish appearance.

Paladin: A warrior dedicated to a god and gifted prayers of a martial nature.

Panthopuss: One of the Biomancer Vebrin's creations

The Princedoms of Zeutch: One of the countries birthed out of the collapse of the High Kingdom of Hamilten. An alliance of smaller princedoms that elect an emperor to rule over their country under the advisement of the individual princes. Zeutchian humans are characterized by pale skin and blonde hair.

The Queendom of Naith: A country ruled over by the bloodthirsty rakshasas. Naithian humans are characterized by dark-brown skin with brown to black hair.

Rakshasa: A single-sex, all-female race of shapeshifters capable of changing their heads into tigers. They are a cruel race and solitary save for those who founded the Queendom of Naith.

Rothin Forest: A large forest that dominates the heart of the Kingdom of Althos. Home to the largest colony of unicorns.

Shaman: A practitioner of magic that manipulates the five elements through fetishes and totems.

Siren: A single-sex, all-female race that lures duel-sex males into the ocean with their bewitching song, mating with them and drowning them at the same time.

Soulborn Witch: A type of witch born to the Tuathan.

Triad: A unique practice of the Tuathan. Any witch born is believed destined to protect the Lesh-Ke Mountains by marrying a Paladin of Gewin along with her soul-sister, another Tuathan girl born at the exact moment as the witch to a different mother. The two girls are considered "bonded," destined to aide and love each other.

The Tuathan: A race of humans who traditionally dwell in the Lesh-Ke Mountains, typified by fair skin and red hair of varying shades. Rare women born to their tribe are witches.

Unicorn: A single-sexed race birthed by the God Las's indiscriminate masturbation. Unicorns are females capable of shifting between human and their unicorn form. As unicorns, they are hermaphroditic, sprouting cocks. They cannot abide most sentient races except young, virgin girls, attracted to their purity. Most live in the Rothin Forest

Warg: An engineered creature crated by kobold shamans, merging a kobold warrior with a wolf, creating a dangerous and intelligent monster.

Warlock: A term applied to a mage, often one performing evil or not affiliated with the Magery Council.

Warlocks of Chevsa: A cabal of mages who occupied the island of Chevsa in Noliana Bay. Famed for the creation of Ghuls.

Werewolf: A single-sex, all female race of shapeshifters who can turn into wolfish beasts. They capture men for breeding purposes, using them until the men die of exhaustion. Many packs prowl the Haunted Forest.

Witch: A natural-born practitioner of magic who can control the spirits that inhabit the world.

Wyvern: A natural race of flying monsters with bat-like wings and two cocks.

About the Author

Reed James is a thirty year-old guy living in Tacoma, WA. "I love to write, I find it freeing to immerse myself in a world and tell its stories and then share them with others." He's been writing naughty stories since high school, furiously polishing his craft, and finally feels ready to share his fantasies with the world.

"I love writing about women who want to be a little (or a lot) naughty, people expressing their love for each other as physically and kinkily as possible, and women loving other women. Whether it's a virgin experiencing her/his first time or a long-term couple exploring the bounds of their relationships, it will be a hot, erotic story!"

You can find Reed on the internet at the following places:

Twitter: https://twitter.com/NLPublications
Facebook: https://www.facebook.com/reed.james.9231
Blog: http://blog.naughtyladiespublications.com/wp
Newsletter: http://eepurl.com/4nlN5

Printed in Great Britain
by Amazon